A gunshot ripped through the train door, missing Jake by no more than a finger's width. Close on its heels came a second. Then a third. By then Jake was falling, throwing himself to the hard metal grating of the platform floor. As he fell, more shots cut the door over his back.

"I reckon there's someone in there," Cody said from the door of the car behind.

"Seems so," Jake said. "How many you figure?"

"Five, six." Cody shrugged. "Maybe more."

"So how do we get in?"

"I'm not the one to ask," Cody said. "Scouting's my business, not gunfighting. I thought pitching lead was more your line of work."

It was true as far as it went, though Jake rarely had to depend on his proficiency with firearms. His talent generally took care of the problem, and for the moment his talent was out of reach. He edged carefully away from the door . . .

By Mark Sumner
Published by Ballantine Books:

DEVIL'S TOWER
DEVIL'S ENGINE

DEVIL'S ENGINE

Mark Sumner

A Del Rey® Book
BALLANTINE BOOKS • NEW YORK

A Del Rey ® Book
Published by Ballantine Books

http://www.randomhouse.com

Library of Congress Catalog Card Number: 96-97114

ISBN 0-345-40210-3

Manufactured in the United States of America

First Edition: February 1997

10   9   8   7   6   5   4   3   2   1

We do not ride on the railroad; it rides upon us.
—HENRY DAVID THOREAU, *Walden*, 1854

☆ **PART I** ☆

All Aboard

☆ **1** ☆

The storm rolled in from the west and the wagon ran before it.

Muley Owens twisted around on the plank seat and bent down to look under the flapping yellow sails. Between the dusty top of the altered stagecoach and the foot of the sails, he could see little but boiling gray clouds and hard white ground spotted with twisted, salt-loving scrub. Most folks looking over that empty plain would have said it was lifeless. There wasn't cover to hide a half-starved jackrabbit. Muley knew better.

Somewhere back there was a Ute chief name of Chalk Pete and two dozen heartily pissed warriors. They were close. After two days of chasing, they were far closer than Muley would have preferred.

Muley had no indisposition toward Indians in general. Fact was, he might have starved more than once without the help of some friendlies. It was only this particular group he didn't want to meet. If these Indians caught up to the wagon, Muley didn't expect to last as long as spit on a hot skillet.

A ripple went through the sails, and a rope slapped hard against the mainmast. Muley hauled fast at a winch, working to keep the square of canvas taut, but the slack in the cloth could not be defeated. The jib sail deflated like an empty bladder, falling slack against the mainsail. The grind of the iron-rimmed wheels over the alkali sands dropped from a whine to a groan.

Muley clenched his teeth. "Wind's dying," he said.

When there was no immediate answer, he reached around

3

behind him and thumped a fist against the wagon's wooden roof. "The wind's dying!" he said with more force.

"You're not telling me nothing I don't already know," called a voice from inside the coach. A panel at the front of the cabin slid open and the pale, round face of the Rainmaker peered out. "How far back you figure?"

Muley pushed his hat away from his face and squinted at the horizon. "Can't say."

"And if you had to guess?"

"If I had to guess, I'd guess we've got no better than an hour on them," Muley said.

The Rainmaker moaned. "I'm getting tired," he said. "I need a rest."

Muley spat over the side of the wagon. "You go ahead and lay down. I'll wake you in time for the scalping."

The Rainmaker leaned back, disappearing into the shadowed interior of the coach. "What do you suggest?" he asked, his voice hollow and muffled.

"I already did my suggesting back at Salina," Muley said. "Soon as we knew them Utes were coming, I suggested we should have bought horses and got rid of this contraption."

"A horse would have played out by now," the Rainmaker replied.

"You best tell that to those red boys. Their horses cross the flats all the time."

"You don't even know how to sit a horse."

"Neither do you," Muley said.

The Rainmaker brought his flour-white face back to the opening. "Exactly," he said. "And that's why we don't have horses."

Muley's jaw tightened. "Maybe we ought have learned," he said, but he didn't say it any too loud. The Rainmaker had gone and turned the words around on him again. It was irritating the way the man always seemed to win every argument. As he did nearly every day, Muley wished he was back at sea. Whales could smash up a boat, but at least they didn't talk while they were doing it.

He could take some satisfaction in the thought that this

whole mess was the Rainmaker's fault. Muley had been working for the albino for near on two years, and they had done right well drifting the wagon between towns in Nebraska Territory or bloody Kansas. But the Rainmaker had not been happy. There were hotter, drier places farther west, and he'd been sure the people there would pull out their gold teeth to pay for what the Rainmaker could do.

Muley had argued against the idea. He was already half a continent removed from the ocean he knew and the harbor where he'd been raised. He was not inclined to go farther. But his arguments had not prevailed over the slicker tongue of the Rainmaker. So they turned the wagon west along trails that were half overgrown, and moved up into the high arid plains of Dakota and Wyoming. It had been a disaster from the start.

The end of the war and the start of the wild talents had brought rugged times to the West. What with scribblers and signers dredging up conjurations left and right, and sheriffs hard pressed to hold on to their towns, a lot of folks drifted back toward the more civilized areas. Half the towns Muley and the Rainmaker set out for had been empty when they got there. When they found a town still kicking, just as like the people that lived in it would have nothing to do with scrip from the East. In some places they couldn't even trade coins.

Worse yet, it had been a wet spring, and the grass was almost as heavy along the Belle Fourche as along the Missouri. The Rainmaker's services were held in little value by people who had already baled more hay than they could feed in two years. The albino was forced to do his tricks for little more than room and board.

Six months on the high plains had left the pair close enough to broke that they had to sell the Rainmaker's fancy traps just to get by. Muley's arguments against the West began to gain some ground, and it looked like they would soon be heading back to places where the grass grew thicker. Then word had come that someone was looking for them—someone who could pay in gold.

That someone had turned out to be the Mormons. The place called Deseret Country was a darn sight off, but they'd taken the wagon through canyons, across deserts, and around mountains to reach their new customers. It had been the break the Rainmaker was looking for.

The Mormons' towns were doing better than any others Muley had seen. There were some towns elsewhere that looked on talent as a curse—especially such uncontrollable talents as the Rainmaker's—but the saints accepted talents as a blessing from God. They welcomed the people that had them. They were generous with their pay, too. Best of all, the whole Deseret Country had been suffering a drought for three seasons.

By the time Muley and the Rainmaker had come to Salina, the boot at the back of the coach was half full of old jewelry, silver dollars, and more than a little gold. The Rainmaker was in a fine temper. The storm he'd called up over that little town was one of his best, a gullywasher and toad strangler to top all Muley had seen. They left Salina with fat drops still falling and wallets stuffed with loot. Not until they were a mile out of town had they heard about the Indians.

A rider from Salina came out to warn them. It seemed the Rainmaker's talents had come as something of a surprise to a local band of Utes. Without a nudge, no rain would have been expected in the area for weeks, so Chalk Pete had felt safe in making his camp alongside a little stone-bottomed crick. More than a dozen of his tribe had drowned when that crick turned to a river in the space of five minutes. It had not taken the chief long to determine the source of this misfortune.

Muley had never even seen the Indians, but the Mormons weren't likely to lie about such a thing. Ever since, the Rainmaker had been driving the wagon hard to the east, and Muley wrestled with the idea that this time it wasn't going to be enough.

The wind faded to a gusty breeze. The steady progress of the wagon faltered. The big wheels turned over in fits and starts. The sheets flapped and rippled. No matter how Muley tugged at the lines, he could not coax the wagon above a walking pace.

But the wind did not die completely, and the wagon kept

moving. Despite what he'd told the Rainmaker, Muley held a secret hope that the Utes would give up. Every mile the wagon crossed, every minute they stayed alive, was a chance that they might go on living. Muley was less than a year away from forty. In the eyes of many out on the plains, that made him just a hair away from ancient. But Muley didn't feel old. He had every intention of drawing breath for a good many years to come.

The sun dipped low in the west and bloody light began to spill under the tattered remains of the Rainmaker's storm. The wind was down to a gentle breeze. The sail wagon had started life as a regular six-passenger stagecoach. Though Muley had taken pains to lighten the vehicle as much as possible, it still weighed in at almost a ton, and it took more than a breeze to keep it dancing. At its current speed, Muley could have climbed down from the wagon and outpaced the vehicle without breaking a sweat. Still, they'd been running hard for two full days and a night. By now the flooded coulee and the dead Utes were better than two hundred miles back. Maybe . . .

A line of brown dust appeared on the edge of the horizon.

"Oh, hellfire," Muley said. The Utes were moving off to one side, staying out of the muddy path left behind the Rainmaker. Muley, no longtime westerner, could not get a good count on the ponies just by looking at the dust. But then, he didn't need much of a count. One Indian would be enough to do for them.

The wagon took a jarring bump, lurched to the side, then bumped again. Muley twisted around on the driver's box just in time for the wagon to take a kidney-pounding drop. Inside, the Concord coach was generously padded and the seats were held up by a blanket of springs designed to take the thumps out for the passengers. No such protection was provided for the driver. Only a tight grip on the side boards kept Muley from tumbling off the driver's box. He could see now that the failing light had been hiding a wide scar on the alkali plain. Once, it had held the runoff of some desert cloudburst, but now it was only a dry, stony obstacle. There was a groan from the rigging above as the wheels clattered over a bed of cobbles. With a final jerk the wagon came to a stop.

Muley kicked the heels of his boots against the front of the cabin. "You best get that wind up!" he shouted.

There was no response from inside.

Muley looked back at the distant line of dust once again and pounded the wagon with greater urgency. "This ain't no time to be stopping!" he called. There was still no response.

With his back creaking and his knees popping in protest, he climbed down from the driver's box seat and dropped onto the stony ground. Through the coating of fine dust he could still make out the words THE FAULTLESS RAINMAKER written on the coach's side in letters six inches high. Above the letters a line of dark clouds rose up to the wagon's flat wooden top. Bolts of yellow lightning snaked their way around the letters.

Muley had done the painting on the wagon himself, and he was proud of the work. It had taken him the best part of three days to get the letters and the clouds just the way he wanted them. It was a handsome job, and he was sure it had helped drum up business. The Rainmaker didn't seem to appreciate the beauty of the sign. Like most everything that wasn't spending money, the Rainmaker seemed to barely notice it existed.

Muley grabbed a handle nestled alongside the painted lightning and swung open the door of the wagon. The Rainmaker lay inside, sprawled across the cracked leather of the seat with one arm over his white face. Muley could see the bruised flesh around his employer's eyes and the tracery of broken blood vessels that marked his cheeks. Though he was still shy of twenty-five, the white face and thin white hair made the albino look ancient. The Rainmaker was unconscious.

"Hey," Muley said. "This ain't the best time for taking a nap." He took the Rainmaker by the arm and shook him, gently at first, then with considerable force. "You better not be dead on me," he said. "I can't make this wagon roll without you."

The Rainmaker opened one pale blue eye. "I'm not dead," he said. "I'm just purely done in."

Muley gave the man one last jerk and let him go. "Well, you better get yourself undone," he said, "and you better be quick about it. Them Utes is coming up fast."

The Rainmaker stuck out an arm and got himself into a sitting position. Beads of sweat rolled down his white face and dripped onto the collar of his wilted shirt. "Pushing that storm is like freighting bricks up a steep hill," he said. "It's tough enough to keep it rolling for an hour or two, tougher yet when the wind's wanting to run the other way." The Rainmaker shook his head slowly. "Two days is too long. I've got to rest."

"I'm real sorry to hear that," Muley said. He leaned through the door and took their only rifle down from its rack. "I don't suppose you'll mind if I take the Springfield and run while you're catching your winks?"

The Rainmaker blinked his washed-out eyes. "Are they really that close?"

"A-yup." Muley glanced over his shoulder. "You give them a minute and you can ask them yourself."

With a groan, the Rainmaker climbed out of the wagon. The last traces of the dying breeze stirred the tails of his dark coat as he stepped down onto the cobble-strewn ground. "Where?"

"Out there." Muley pointed at the approaching line of dust. "I ain't no expert, but I figure they're about ten minutes off."

The Rainmaker nodded. He walked slowly around the wagon, taking long steps on his thin lanky legs, his white face turned toward the ground. Muley looked on with relief. The Rainmaker would get the wind whipped up, the sails would snap, and they might yet outrun the Utes.

The albino stopped at the front of the wagon, leaned against one of the tall iron-rimmed wheels and shook his head. "I can't do it."

Muley blinked. "You can't do what?"

"Move the wagon," the Rainmaker said. "Wind's the hardest part of weather for me, and with the wagon down here in this ditch . . ." He shook his head. "It'll be hours before I can raise a strong enough breeze to move us."

Out over the salt, the bottom of the deep red sun touched the horizon. The wall of dust was closer.

A cold knot stirred in Muley's stomach. "Well," he said, we'll just have to walk." He took a hesitant step away from the bloody sunset, squinting back toward the Utes. "It'll be dark soon. Maybe if we get far enough from the wagon we can lose them."

The Rainmaker shook his head again. "I'm no more up to walking across this hardpan than I am to conjuring a wind. This is as far as I go."

"Damnation," Muley growled. He had followed the Rainmaker halfway across the continent, but he was by no means ready to follow him to a scalping.

The sky was already dark, but now it began to stir and a fat drop of rain splashed into the dust at Muley's feet. As it usually did whenever the Rainmaker stayed in one place for long, it was beginning to rain. When the wagon was rolling, they could generally stay ahead of the precipitation, but it was a rare day when they could stop for more than a minute without getting wet. The Rainmaker could make the flow vary from a sprinkle to a downpour, but it took a considerable effort for him to stop it entirely.

That was the main thing that kept them moving across the dry lands. Most any town on the parched prairie was grateful to have a rainfall. None of them were too happy when that rain went on forever.

More drops wet the long dry stones that lined the bottom of the ditch. Muley moved to stand against the wagon, trying to keep as dry as he could. It was pure foolishness to think they could outrun the Utes on foot. Those Indians could have tracked a snake over bare stone; two walking men were not likely to get away in this empty country. Besides, everywhere the Rainmaker went, the clouds and rain would follow. The Utes could track them from half a state away.

Muley looked around to where the Rainmaker sagged against the wagon wheel. He supposed he could always leave the albino behind. After all, it was the Rainmaker that had the

Utes riled. If they had the Rainmaker, then like as not they'd leave him to himself.

Muley looked at the fringe of pale hair that jutted out around the base of the Rainmaker's round hat. He shook his head. No. The albino might still call himself his boss, and he might not be able to make any conversation that didn't turn into an argument, but after two years of traveling together, the truth was they were partners. Maybe even friends. A man who went around leaving his partners wasn't worth spit.

The Rainmaker's drizzle grew stronger. Muley had observed in the past that whenever the Rainmaker was tired or sleeping, the rain would come down harder than when he was up and alert. Drawing the wind might take some push, but the albino's talent for pulling water out of the air took more effort to fight than it did to encourage. Already the stones of the wash were dark with moisture. Drops rolled down into the lowest points and formed the start of puddles.

"Whether we can move the wagon or not," Muley said, "we're going to have to get ourselves on higher ground."

The Rainmaker looked up. "What's that?"

"We need to get out of this ditch. That is, unless you want to end up like . . . end up like . . ." Muley's voice trailed away. He looked up the length of the wash, then tilted his head back to stare into the darkening sky. "Can you make it rain harder?"

"Why?" the Rainmaker asked. "I doubt those Indians will lose the track."

"I'm not talking about losing any track," Muley said. "I'm talking about getting out of here. Can you make it rain harder?"

The albino nodded. "There's always more rain," he said.

"Good. Then you get to working on the rain. I'll work on the wagon."

Muley climbed back to the top of the wagon and loosed the ropes that held up the sails. The heavy canvas square crashed to the top of the wagon, and Muley worked fast to roll it and lash it down. He reefed the jib sail against the boom. Then he climbed down and went around to the back to open the rear boot to inspect their meager collection of tools. There was not much—a twist of baling wire, a six-pound hammer, and some nails. It would have to be enough. He took the hammer around to the side of the wagon, pulled back and let fly. The business end of the heavy tool rang against the hub of the left rear wheel. A linchpin banged loose and splashed into a puddle.

"What are you doing?" the Rainmaker asked.

Muley delivered another blow to the wagon wheel. "I'm taking care of the wagon," he said. "You take care of the rain."

Inside five minutes all the pins were gone and the wagon was barely resting on the wheel. Muley moved around to the other side and knocked that wheel free. Then he did the same to the front. By the time all the wheels were hanging loose, the water in the ditch was ankle deep and moving fast. The sun had set, or was hidden by the gathering clouds, and the only light came from the flickers of lightning overhead.

"More rain!" Muley called. "And come on over to the wagon. I don't want you getting washed halfway to San Francisco."

The Rainmaker nodded and waded through the deepening stream. Muddy water spilt around his skinny ankles. He started to get inside the wagon, but Muley laid a hand on the man's arm.

"You better join me up top," he said. "That wagon will keep out the rain, but I'm none too sure how it'll handle water coming from the other direction."

The Rainmaker climbed up to the driver's box, his elbows and knees pointing out to the sides as he bent his long limbs. As always, Muley was surprised by how tall the man was when they were sitting side by side. The Rainmaker didn't weigh any more than a child. Muley had known women that could have thrown the Rainmaker across the room. But he managed to stretch a good number of inches from his few pounds.

"Can you bring any more rain?" Muley asked.

"I don't think I can," the Rainmaker said. "Not right now, anyway."

Muley frowned. The rain was falling harder, plastering his shirt against his chest and rattling against the brim of his hat.

The water in the ditch was running deeper, but it was still no more than half of what he was looking for. "Well, you stay up here and keep yourself a grip. I'm going to take them wheels off."

"Wheels off?" the Rainmaker said.

Muley didn't reply. He climbed down into the swelling stream, steadied himself, and took a swing at one of the rear wheels. It came loose at the first blow. The back of the wagon tilted crazily and came down in the shallow water with a tremendous splash. Brown water washed over Muley's face and he came close to falling into the knee-deep stream.

"Jesus and all the saints," the Rainmaker called. "What are you doing back there?"

"I told you," Muley said. He moved around to the other side and bashed the other rear wheel loose. "I'm taking off the wheels."

The Rainmaker held tight, but the fast fall of the wagon was enough to leave him dangling from the side. "This coach cost me six hundred dollars to buy and another four hundred dollars to fix," he said as he climbed back on top, "and that was before you wasted twenty on fancy paints. I'll thank you not to smash it up."

"Oh, shut your trap," Muley said. He fished in the muddy water and came up with the loose wheels. With a twist of wire, he bound the wheels to the back of the wagon. Then he went around to the front and started on the wheels there.

"You really expect this thing to float?" the Rainmaker asked. Figuring out what Muley was up to seemed to have calmed him down a bit.

"I don't know," Muley admitted. The rushing water was past his knees now and he had a hard time keeping on his feet as he took off the remaining wheels. "If it doesn't, I don't think you'll get much time to think about your thousand dollars."

The last wheel was stubborn. It took Muley a half-dozen blows of the hammer to work it free. But once it came off, the wagon settled neatly in the water. The brown flow came up the side and lapped at the line of gilt-edged letters. The wagon turned slightly as the water pushed it around.

"Looks like we might move somewhere after all," Muley said. He gathered up the last wheel and headed around to tie it with the others. "You keep the rain coming hard, and we'll take ourselves a real boat trip."

"You have any idea where this water empties?" the Rain-maker asked.

Muley hung the wheel up on the back and bound it with wire. "Does it matter?" he replied.

Something bumped against Muley's leg. He looked down, expecting to see a piece of driftwood or a bit of floating tumbleweed. What he saw was the pale shaft of an arrow jutting out from the meat of his thigh.

Pain followed close on the heels of the sight. Muley shouted a warning and staggered back away from the wagon. Another arrow knocked the hat from his head and dug a bloody groove through his scalp. Muley staggered, took a step back, and fell into the boiling water.

The muddy stream rolled him over and over, pounding his bleeding skull against the stone bottom and filling his ears with thunder. The arrow in his leg was caught underneath him and even over the noise of the water he heard the sharp crack as the shaft snapped in two. He came up, got a quick breath, and fell back into the stream. He struggled to get to his feet, but the stones in the gully were smooth and slick. The water pushed him on and on without pause, giving him no chance to arrange himself.

Somewhere in the back of Muley's mind a thought popped up. Even with his own blood warm against his face and his breath burning in his lungs, the thought was enough to set him laughing. After spending twenty years sailing the blue Atlantic, Muley was about to drown in a desert stream no deeper than his waist.

The water brought him against a wayward boulder. The force of it striking his ribs drove out what little breath Muley still had, but he got his arms around the rock, held on, and pulled his head free of the stream.

At first he could see nothing. It was pitch-black, and the rain came down hard as hammer blows. Then the plain was lit by a blast of blue lightning that twisted down to sear the salty ground. In that flash Muley saw three Utes standing not more than a dozen yards away. He also saw a dark form moving slowly down the center of the gully. After a second the lightning came again. The Utes were gone, but the dark shape was closer.

"Owens!"

Muley fought the current and managed to raise his head above the flow. "Here!" he shouted.

With each burst of light the floating wagon was nearer. "Owens!" the Rainmaker called again. "Here, take my hand."

Muley would have liked to do just that, but he was too afraid to move either of his hands from the stone. He didn't have a choice. A moment later the wagon struck the boulder, giving Muley's fingers a savage blow in the process. He let go with a scream and would have been swept downstream again if it weren't for the Rainmaker. The lanky man bent down from the roof of the wagon and snagged Muley by the collar of his shirt. Between the efforts of the two of them, Muley managed to climb onto the swaying wagon.

"My God," the Rainmaker said. "You're bleeding to death."

Muley raised a throbbing hand to his scalp and felt the warm flow. "I doubt it," he said. "Not from this." He lowered his hand and felt the jagged inch of wood that still jutted out from where the arrow had entered his leg. "We're going to have to do something about this one in my leg, though, soon as we fetch up someplace."

"Let's hope that's none too soon," the Rainmaker said. "We need to put some distance between ourselves and our attackers."

Muley nodded. "We might make it all the way to the White, if we don't sink first."

Now that he was out of the water, Muley felt as cold and weak as he ever had in his life. The rain was washing away the blood from his scalp and leg as fast as it flowed out, and it was carrying away his warmth along with it. He shivered and pulled his arms around his chest. He wished he had his hat back. He wished he could crawl inside the wagon and sleep out of the rain. He wished he had never gotten caught up by the idea of figuring out how to sail a wagon.

There was another flash of lightning. In it Muley saw a small figure standing on the bank of the wash. He could not be sure in the brief flash, but it did not look to him like a Ute warrior.

In fact, he thought it was a girl.

☆ 2 ☆

It was Goldy Cheroot that first found the girl.

As was her habit, Goldy began the process of opening the Kettle Black Saloon long before dawn. The Kettle Black was the only saloon in Medicine Rock, and as such it was a center for talk, drink, food, and pleasures of the bedroom. Though the sheriff's office across the street was important, the Kettle Black was the heart of the town. A town might limp along for months, even years, without the protection of a sheriff. Close the last saloon, and the town would blow away before sunset.

Goldy built up the fire in the stove, larded a black iron skillet, and mixed up some fry bread dough. Then she heated some wide, flat biscuits and browned them in the sizzling grease. Later she would make breakfast for Sienna and for the two new sporting girls, but the first hot bread of the day was always for herself. She ladled heavy molasses over the biscuits, poured a cup of cracked wheat coffee, and went over to a table near the front of the saloon to eat her breakfast.

Goldy looked back across her plate at the portrait that hung behind the bar. An artist had painted it for her going on thirty years before. The girl in the painting had blond hair, deep brown eyes, and smooth pale skin—all things that Goldy no longer enjoyed. But that girl lacked thirty years of knowing. Goldy was not beyond pining over the beauty she'd once known, but when it was all on the table, she considered the trade fair enough.

The hours right before dawn were the only quiet time there was to be had at the Kettle. Once the sun was up, Goldy and Sienna would be kept busy pouring whiskey, cooking pasties, boiling beans, cleaning up, stopping fights, and arranging the order of visitors that wanted to spend a dollar in the upstairs rooms. But Goldy allowed no one—no matter how far in the bottle—to sleep in the bar room. Once she closed down at night, the saloon was empty as a Baptist church on Saturday night. So the early morning brought quiet, and a chance to eat her biscuits in peace.

There had been a time when Goldy's morning was spent planning for the whole of Medicine Rock. But as the town grew, it seemed to need less, or want less, of her time. There was talk now of having an election for mayor. Goldy wasn't about to run. It would only give Bernita Hare and the others in her sewing circle a chance to whisper more lies.

Goldy finished up her meal, took her dishes around the counter, and washed them in the cold gray dishwater left over from the night before. When the old chipped plates were as clean as they were going to get, she dried them on her apron and put them under the counter with the rest. Then she hefted the metal dishpan and took it outside to empty it. That's when she found the girl.

Medicine Rock had been growing slowly for the last five years, but it had taken its biggest spurt in just the last week. Wright City, which was situated some fifty miles north, had fallen victim to a combination of talented bandits and weak sheriffing. There was some hope that the town might attract another sheriff with the talent to hold on, but the more timid citizens were already lighting out for more stable parts. Medicine Rock had gained a half-dozen families.

With all the strangers in town, Goldy might not have paid much note to the girl sitting on the board sidewalk outside the Kettle Black. She only gave the girl a quick glance at first, then concentrated on the dishpan. Children did not come much into bars, and Goldy was having a hard enough time keeping up with who the older folks were. Besides, Goldy's eyes weren't what they had once been. Just seeing the girl at all was something of a victory.

"You're sure the early bird," Goldy said as she pitched the dirty water out into the street.

The girl did not reply.

Goldy straightened up and banged the dishpan against the hitching rail to free the muck at the bottom. "If your pa's sent you down here to bag him a fifth, he's in for a disappointment. He'll have to come for it himself." She turned and took another look at the girl. "I don't sell whiskey to children."

The words were hardly out of her mouth before she realized that something was wrong. Close up, the girl didn't look like a town girl at all. With her coal-black hair and dusky skin, she looked more like she might have gotten loose from one of the nearby Indian tribes—though they were not ones to go letting their young wander off alone.

Even if she was an Indian, that didn't explain how she came to be sitting on the sidewalk outside the Kettle Black without so much as a stitch of clothing.

Goldy walked over to the girl and put a hand on one of her bare shoulders. "How'd you get here?" she asked.

The girl looked up at her with eyes the color of hot coffee. The expression on her face was as flat as a top poker shark holding an inside straight. Between Goldy's years in a Nebraska whorehouse before the war and all the things that had come with the talents, there was not much she hadn't seen. There were fewer things still that unnerved her. But the stare from this expressionless girl rattled Goldy right down to her old bones. Those eyes looked deep and empty as a dry well.

Goldy took a step back from the girl and licked at her chapped lips. "Is there something you want?" she asked.

"We're flying," the girl said. Her voice was mushy as oatmeal—the voice of someone in a dream.

"What?"

"We're flying?" the girl repeated. The way she said it was confusing to Goldy. There was no doubt it was a question, but Goldy didn't have an inkling of the answer.

"You want to come on inside with me," Goldy said. She stretched down a hand. "Come on now, 'fore some scoundrel comes along and sees you."

It was hard to tell if the girl understood any of this, but she did take Goldy's hand. Goldy helped the child to her feet and quickly drew her through the door of the Kettle Black.

"Lords, you must be half froze," Goldy said. "You want some coffee?" She was no more in the habit of feeding coffee to children than she was of giving them whiskey, but this seemed like a time for exceptions. Besides, now that she had the girl inside, she could see that she'd made a mistake. The girl still had the round face and small size of a child, but her breasts and hips marked her as a young woman.

"Coffee," the girl repeated.

"That's right." Goldy went around the bar and poured a cup. She took it back to the girl and handed it over. "You want some sugar for that?"

The girl put the steaming cup to her mouth and drank it down so fast that Goldy was afraid she would boil her innards. As she was drinking, Goldy noticed for the first time that she was not completely naked. Her feet were swallowed up in boots that were clearly many times too large for the person walking in them.

"Where'd you come by those boots?" Goldy asked. "Did someone take your clothes?"

"Boots," the girl sighed. "Boots."

A nasty picture was beginning to form in Goldy's head. If this girl had wandered off from some local tribe, maybe she'd run into some bad men out away from town. Lord knew there were plenty of bad men to go around. One of them might have taken it on himself to rape this girl—who, even if she wasn't a child, was not far from it. Maybe she'd gotten away from this bad man and made off with his footwear.

Goldy grunted to herself. It was quite a tale to draw from a pair of boots, but it came to her with frightening clarity.

"Who's this?" said a voice from the top of the stairs.

Goldy looked up and saw Sienna Truth already dressed and ready for the day. "We got company," Goldy said.

"But who is she?"

"Boots," the naked girl said.

"I guess her name is Boots," Goldy said.

Sienna came slowly down the stairs, her dark eyes locked

on the strange girl. At seventeen, Sienna was not a shirker. She took care of her sick brother and did as much around the Kettle Black as Goldy herself. If Sienna had not known how much Goldy liked her morning privacy, she would have been at her chores before dawn. Sienna had a cool feel about her, a calmness that seemed to belong to an older woman. She was not tall, never would be, but she was commanding nonetheless. As she grew older, her face had developed a peculiar kind of angular beauty that made many of the Kettle Black's customers inquire as to her price. But Sienna did not exchange her favors for money, not even when the offer went above ten dollars. The fact that she drew such offers, and that she refused them, was a great sticking point with the sporting girls.

"I found this one out on the stoop," Goldy said. "Nary an inch of cloth on her."

Sienna nodded. "Any idea who she is?"

"No. She ain't said much to this point." Goldy looked down into the girl's flat eyes. "I'm not sure she can say anything much."

The girl slurped down the last of her coffee and held out the empty cup. "Boots?" she inquired.

"If you're after more coffee," Goldy said, "it's yours." She brought the pot over and filled the girl's cup. As the stranger drained her second coffee, Goldy looked over at Sienna. "I thought you might know something about Boots, here. Looks a might Indian to me."

Sienna shook her head. "No. Not an Indian." She laid her hand against the skin over the girl's ribs. The girl drew her mouth away from the coffee but did not pull free of Sienna's touch.

"She's not like me," Sienna said. "or like any Indian I know. Her skin is as fall grass in the sun. It does not even feel the same as my skin."

"If she's not an Indian," Goldy said, "then what is she?"

Sienna shook her head. "I don't know. Maybe we should ask—"

There was noise from the top of the stairs. Goldy looked

up to see Black Alice and Orpah Hacket, both still in their
nightclothes.

"Is breakfast ready?" Black Alice asked.

It was like Alice to be worried about food before anything
else. Though she was not yet twenty, she was already showing
a plumpness in her arms and neck.

"This a new upstairs girl?" Orpah asked. She eyed the
strange girl with more than a little suspicion.

If Alice's thoughts were always on food, Orpah's were
always turning to her work. Not that she liked her work so
much; she just fretted over the prospect of losing it. Though
she wouldn't let on as much, Goldy knew that Orpah was
somewhere on the top side of thirty-five. It was not such an
advanced age elsewhere, but western years were long years,
and they showed on Orpah's narrow face. She was always
worrying that Goldy was going to find some younger woman
to replace her.

"I don't know who it is, yet," Goldy said. "You two come
on down and drink some coffee. Breakfast will be along
directly."

She turned back to the girl, hoping the two women would
leave things go for the moment. But she knew better. Black
Alice was too concerned about her rumbling stomach to stay
out of the way, and Orpah too worried that the girl might be
competition. In a moment they were both down the steps and
sidling over close.

"How come she's naked?" Alice asked. She leaned in and
stared at the girl's face. "Somebody throw her out?"

Goldy took Alice by the sleeve of the gown and eased her
back from the girl. "We ain't sure yet," she said.

"You going to put her upstairs?" Orpah asked.

Goldy had sympathy with Orpah's worries, but the
woman's constant whining was getting on her nerves. "I don't
know."

"Well, I never heard of no Negro sporting girl," Orpah said.
"At least not 'round here. I don't think anyone in Medicine
Rock would pay for something like that."

"Negro?" Goldy looked at the girl and shook her head. "This girl ain't black."

"She is," Orpah insisted. "She's one of them octoroons. I seen her like, down in New Orleans." She moved over to put her hand in the girl's hair. "You can see it in her face, and in the curl of her hair. She's a Negro."

Goldy pushed Orpah away from the girl. She put her hands on her hips and glared at the two upstairs girls. "Half the town is darker than this girl. I hear you calling her any names, I'll . . . Well, could be I'll use her to replace the both of you. You get over to the table and sit yourselves down. When breakfast is ready, you can eat. Till then, keep your traps closed. Hear?"

The sporting girls sulked, but they moved away. There had been three workers upstairs before Goldy had caught Ellie Ree cleaning out a customer's wallet. Ellie had been the most popular girl at the Kettle Black, but Goldy hadn't hesitated to toss her out. Inside a week, Ellie was forced to make the hazardous trip down to Tempest, where the customers were reputed to be both rough and poor. The example of Ellie's fall was not lost on the others.

"Shouldn't we get her some clothes?" Sienna asked. She reached out a hand and pressed it to the girl's cheek. "I think she is still cold."

Goldy nodded, glad for this sensible statement. "I'll go fetch something."

"No." Sienna shook her head. "She looks to be about the same size as me. I will get one of my dresses."

While the young Indian went to get some clothing, Goldy poured the strange girl another cup of hot coffee. The girl took the cup from Goldy's hand and drank from it as quick as she had the first two, apparently unfazed by the stiff, scalding brew.

"You probably ought not have more than that," Goldy said to the silent girl. "There's not much to it but cracked wheat and peanut shells. You'll have yourself a bellyache if you don't watch out."

The girl tilted her head back, drained the cup, and passed it back to Goldy. The expression on her face changed. Some-where in her dark eyes something changed. There was a spark in them now, a brightness that had not been there before.

"Thank you," the girl said. "You've been kind."

Goldy was so startled she almost dropped the cup. "You can talk American after all."

The girl nodded. "Hell is coming," she said. Her voice was different from any Goldy had heard before—soft and liquid as a dew drop.

"What?" Goldy squinted at the girl's face. "What'd you say?"

"Hell is coming," the girl said. "Be ready."

Orpah got up from her chair and came across the room. "Who is it she says is coming?"

Goldy looked around at the approaching woman. "Hush, Orpah."

That was all she said, and saying it didn't take more than a moment. But when she looked back, the girl was gone.

☆ **3** ☆

William Cody sat in a plush velvet chair at one end of a long, dark room and twisted his hat around in his hands.

It was a well-worn hat, a tall old Kossuth that had served Bill well during the war and in the confusion that came after. In most times, he kept the hat firmly mounted on his head. A good hat was essential to a man who traveled around the West. Blazing sun, cold rain, biting dust, frigid wind, and blowing snow—all of them could be deflected, with varying degrees of success, through the proper use of a good hat.

It was only since Bill had arrived in New York City that the hat sustained real damage. Long hours spent waiting in offices had left him with the habit of working the hat between his fingers, kneading the stiff wool brim and turning the hat round and round, until the whole thing was soft and wrinkled as a baby pig. When he stopped to think about it, he could still his nervous fingers. But every time his mind wandered, his hands went back to working at the hat. If he didn't leave the East soon, he expected the hat brim would wear to a frazzle.

Cities, with their people and their godawful smells, were not unfamiliar to Bill. He'd spent the best part of the last year in St. Louis, and years back the Kansas Pacific had sent him all the way to Chicago. That was before the railroad work petered out. He'd been fascinated with the cities then. They were strange places full of odd people. And the oddest thing of all was that all the city folks seemed to have some all-fired consuming interest in the West.

Bill had a real fondness for the open country. He was born there, fought in the war there, and scouted there. He knew what the West was like. But he found it strange, amazing even, that folks who lived in warm houses and ate at cherry-wood tables would spare any thought at all for those sleeping on the ground. They did, though. There was enough interest that Bill had enjoyed many a fine meal for no price but his stories of riding for the Pony Express, or scouting along the Missouri. Eventually, there had been Mr. Buntline and his slim little books—books that hadn't brought Bill much money, but bought him a hundred free hotel rooms.

But these days the meals were poorer and the rooms far between. Talents were what fascinated people now. Whether it was the protection societies in the East or the sheriffs in the West, talents were what defined how folks lived—or even *if* they lived. When people were being torn up by conjurations in the middle of Broadway, no one turned to the West for adventure. They had more adventure than they wanted already.

The last ten years had been hard on Bill. The confusion and inflation that followed the fizzling of the war and the coming of the talents had spelled the end for the railroads. With the government thrown into chaos, what remained of the U.S. Army milled about on its own ground, showing little interest in rooting out Indians from territories that might never become states. There was no work scouting, and not much hunting. For Bill the result was a fair number of hungry evenings.

He'd been staying at a run-down boardinghouse near the St. Louis docks when a strange woman brought the news that there was a railroad building again and they were looking for scouts. Bill had been interested, but not enough to run all the way to New York City. Then the woman handed him a train ticket for just that destination and walked away. Bill did not understand this stroke of luck, but neither did he question it. He was on the train that night.

Since his arrival in New York he'd sat in what seemed like a dozen offices, each one slightly larger than the last. He'd been put up at a boardinghouse so overrun with people, rats, and fleas that it made him long for his saddle roll. Then there was the smell—and the noise.

If he'd known what the city was like before he came, he might have run out the door back in St. Louis.

Bill leaned back in his chair. This house, with its cool blue walls and dark wood furniture, was by far the best place he'd been to in the city. Of course, he'd been told that this was Tarrytown, not really part of New York City at all. Anywise, Tarrytown smelled better.

A door opened far down the long, narrow room and a man entered. He wore a severe black suit with a collarless shirt and a narrow black tie. To Bill's eye the man looked to be about his own age, but then Bill was a poor judge of these city people—they lacked the brands of wind and sun that marked Western faces.

The man walked the length of the room with a brisk, confident stride. "You are Mr. Cody?" he asked.

Bill hurried to get to his feet. He shoved his mangled hat behind his back with his left hand and put out his right. "Yes," he said. "Howdy. You the one I'm supposed to meet?"

The man took the proffered hand and gave it a momentary grip of surprising force. "I'm Gould," he said. His voice, like his grip, was firm. "Please, have a seat. I know you've had a number of meetings to this point, but I can assure you this is the last."

"That's fine," Bill said. "I'm not much for meetings."

Gould released Bill's hand and settled into a chair below the room's only window. Over the man's shoulder Bill could see steamships moving along the Hudson and coal smoke clinging around the buildings of Nyack on the far bank of the river. Most of what could be seen probably belonged to this man.

Bill knew Jay Gould only by reputation, but reputation was enough to rattle his nerves even more. Gould was the richest man in New York—some said the world—and the head of one of the largest of the protection societies. Back in the West you paid the sheriff to protect you from outsiders with talent. In the city you paid the protection society to guard your home and your business from folks with talent, folks with guns, and from the protection societies themselves—who were well-stocked with both. With things in Washington gone to pot, Jay Gould was far more important to the people of New York City than whoever claimed to be president at the moment.

"Your papers state that you have been a railroad agent in the past," Gould said.

Bill nodded. "That's right. I worked the Kansas Pacific after I left the army. They were running out a line from Topeka and—"

"Yes," Gould said. "I'm aware of the plans that the Kansas Pacific had in mind before its demise. I'm more interested in your role. Just what sort of work did you do for them?"

"Well, hunting, mostly. Providing food for the men." Bill dropped back into his own chair and leaned against the soft cushions. "I did some buying, too. I had pretty well the whole run of provisioning on the work crew."

Gould templed his fingers beneath his chin. "What sort of animals did you hunt?"

Bill felt his confidence draw up a notch. "Buffalo," he said. "I reckon I felled somewhere in the neighborhood of four thousand buffalo. That's why the men took to calling me Buffalo Bill."

There was a gratifying expression of recognition on Gould's hard face. "The same Buffalo Bill that appeared in the dime novels?"

"Yessir," Bill said. He gave the man his best smile. "You give me a reason, and I'll shoot you ten thousand of them beasts."

"Buffalo Bill," Gould said. For a moment there was a shadow of a smile on the man's lips, then he was as cold as before. "My son was quite taken with your exploits when he was young."

"I'd be happy to talk to him."

"No," Gould said quickly. "I'd rather you didn't. My son has always been too easily taken up in stories." Gould made a gesture that took in the room. "When he learned that this house was built on the place that Washington Irving called Sleepy Hollow, he almost drove me mad with talk of the Headless Horseman."

Bill nodded, though in truth he had no idea what Gould was talking about. "Whatever you say, sir."

Gould leaned forward in his chair. "It's a different sort of hunter I'm looking for," he said. "I'm after bigger game."

"There ain't much that's bigger than buffalo," Bill said in confusion.

"Towns are bigger."

"Towns?"

Gould nodded. "I intend to take up the great work—to complete the transcontinental railroad which was begun and abandoned almost two decades ago."

Though Bill had heard rumors to this effect, Gould's statement still caused his heart to jump a beat. The first effort to span the continent with rails had failed along with the government. That someone would try and reach to the Pacific now that California was a country of its own seemed as outlandish as any talent Bill had heard about.

"What have towns got to do with it?" he asked.

"I can't run three thousand miles of track through the wilderness without adequate way stations," Gould said. "If this project is to succeed, we must nail down these tracks with a string of solid towns." He brought his fist down on the arm of the chair. "Towns with strong sheriffs."

At last Bill thought he understood. "And you want me to find those towns."

"Yes. I already have a list of proposed sites. I want you to lead my men there, woo the locals, and convince them that the rail will benefit their town."

Bill almost laughed. "There shouldn't be any problem with that," he said. "I never seen the town that didn't want a railroad."

"You may be surprised," Gould said.

"How's that?"

For many long seconds Gould did not reply. Finally, he rose from his chair and turned to look out the window at the river traffic. "Tell me, Mr. Buffalo Bill, do you have any talents?" Each word he spoke steamed against the cold glass of the window.

"Well, sir, my talents have always been strictly for hunting and scouting," Bill said. "This new kind won't have nothing to do with me."

"Nor me," Gould replied. "Nor me." There was another long pause in the conversation as Gould stared through the foggy glass. He spun around. "I believe you'll do nicely, Mr. Cody. Come with me." With that, Gould began walking away.

Bill jumped up from his chair. "You mean you're going to hire me?"

"I've hired you already," Gould said without stopping. "Hurry along before I fire you."

Bill put his battered hat on his head and followed.

Gould's path took them along a carpeted hallway where a pair of maids dusted gilt-edged mirrors and marble busts. Gould passed the women without a word, then turned to walk through a dining room that could have held most houses. Another turn took them through a library with bookshelves that reached from floor to ceiling. Gould stopped beside a dark mahogany doorway, fished a key from his pocket, and unlocked a heavy iron latch.

"Most of my offices are in the city," Gould said as he heaved open the thick door. The light from the hallway revealed a short landing above a flight of stairs leading down. "But I find it advantageous to keep a few of my employees nearby." He stepped through the doorway and gestured for Bill to follow. "Step inside now, and you'll see something that most of the house staff does not even know is here."

As soon as Bill was through, Gould pulled the door shut. For a moment there was thick darkness, with only a distant yellow glow from the base of the stairs to cut the gloom. Then there was a click.

Instantly the landing was flooded with light so brilliant that Bill threw his hands over his eyes. "What's that?"

"Electric lamps," Gould said calmly. He started down the steps. "Come on."

Bill took his fingers away from his eyes and blinked at the row of glass spheres that followed the slope of the stairs. He had seen electric arc lamps years before in St. Louis, but those lamps had been noisy, smoking affairs that produced glaring sparks of blue light. This light was quiet and steady as the sun.

"I'll be damned," he said softly. More than the huge house, these lights showed just how rich Gould really was.

Bill followed Gould down the stairs and into a broad room lit by dozens of the strange round lights. To his surprise, there were at least twenty people in the room, men and women, gathered around a row of gleaming steel tables. All of them were apparently engaged in some sort of work.

A short man in vest and bowler looked up from the nearest table and quickly came to his feet. "Mr. Gould!" He made a sharp bow, bobbing down and back faster than a hen pecking corn. "Something is wrong, sir?" Bill recognized a German accent in the man's voice.

"Not at all, Kastle," Gould replied. "I've brought someone down to meet you." He turned to Bill. "This is William Cody."

The German repeated his little bow. "Good morning, Mr. Cody."

"Cody is to be our new agent for the rail project," said Gould.

"Is this so?" Kastle asked. He looked Bill over more closely, his gray eyes sweeping from head to toe and back again. It was an inspection Bill did not much care for.

"Mr. Kastle is my head engineer," Gould said.

"He runs a train?" Cody had a hard time picturing the German in coveralls and cap.

"No. An engineer of an entirely different sort." Gould walked over to the table and lifted up a device the size of a plump pocket watch. "I want you to give Cody a demonstration. Show him a little of what we've learned."

"Certainly." Kastle took the object from Gould's hand and walked around the table. He spoke briefly with a short, dark-haired woman at the next table, then both of them went to a cleared area at the side of the room.

Gould moved closer to Bill. "Watch closely," he said. "I think you'll find this interesting."

Kastle nodded. At once the woman raised her hands over her head and began to wave them through the air. Glimmers of color followed her movement, streamers of red and purple that twisted and flowed, forming a mass in the space between the woman and Kastle.

"Her talent is most often called signing," Gould said.

Bill nodded. "Yes. I've seen it before."

Signing was not the most common talent, but it was not that rare, either. Bill had seen it used in many a challenge. But the truth was, he'd never seen it used so skillfully.

In only a few seconds the woman had shaped a conjuration that looked nearly as solid as the people around it. The thing stood at least seven feet tall, with skin the color of an old bruise and a mouth that wrapped around its head from ear to ear. At a sharp gesture from the woman, the conjuration hissed and started toward Kastle.

"Now watch," Gould whispered.

Bill was not so sure he wanted to watch. In his experience, meetings between humans and conjurations tended to be messy, and it was rare that any of the mess came from the conjuration's end of the deal.

The woman continued to wave her hands above her face, urging her terrible creation forward. The thing stretched out arms that were covered in bristles like a porcupine, reaching for Kastle with long curving claws. It opened its too-wide mouth and bared row after row of sharp saw-edged teeth.

Then Kastle held up his small device. There was a click, a whir, then a high-pitched buzz. At once the conjuration screamed like a horse wounded on the battlefield. Ribbons of light spiraled out from the thing's chest and flew to the object in Kastle's hand. Like a sweater unraveling from a single loose thread, the conjuration grew thinner, developed holes, and fell apart. Its scream faded along with it, leaving no sound but the quiet voices of the workers at the tables.

Kastle looked over at Gould. "Was this a sufficient demonstration?"

"I believe our point is made," Gould replied. "Thank you."

Bill stared at the German in surprise. "What kind of talent does he have? I never seen anybody work like that."

"No talent," Gould said.

"How can he have no talent?" Bill shook his head. "It takes talent to fight talent. That's how it is."

Gould flashed his first actual smile. "Not anymore," he said. "Kastle here worked with Thomas Edison on electrical devices, but in the last few years I have persuaded him and these other researchers to turn their attention to the nature of these new talents." Gould went quickly across the room and took the device from Kastle's hand, then came back and held out the metal box to Bill.

"Here," he said. "Hold this."

Bill took the object carefully. It was warm, almost hot. There was an outer casing of what seemed to be brass, cut across by stripes of steel polished mirror bright. Openings in this case revealed glimpses of something moving inside, something made of an odd greenish-blue metal. It thrummed in Bill's hand.

"How does this thing work?" Bill asked.

"The thing we call talent is only another form of energy," Gould said. He took the device from Bill's palm and gave it back to Kastle. "It's like fire, or electricity. With the proper tools, we can control it, or even redirect it."

Bill had been there to see the dead men stir at Shiloh— which some said was the start of it all—but not until almost a year later had he run into a man who had a grip on talent. He remembered how the man laughed at him. He remembered how the man had beaten him near to death. Not even a gun could stop him. Against a man with talent, he'd been as helpless as a buffalo facing the wrong end of his old Sharps Big 50. Until now.

"Will you show me how to run one of those things?" Bill asked.

Gould nodded. "Kastle will be accompanying you on your return to the West. He will instruct you in the use of the dampener, and in other devices we have constructed."

A shadow that Bill hardly knew existed began to lift off his heart. "It'll be good to stop being scared of talented folk."

"Don't worry," Gould said. "Soon we'll have this whole business of talent under control."

Bill looked at the small brass box and smiled.

☆ 4 ☆

Jake Bird was working on a beehive when Gravy Hodges came to fetch him. As soon as he saw who it was, Jake made a point of getting some distance away from the hive. Even in the best of times, Gravy tended to be agitated, and from the sour expression on his narrow face, this wasn't the best of times. Having Gravy too close to a hive of bees didn't seem like such a good idea. It was a wonder the man managed to do carpentry without cutting his own fingers off.

"There's trouble," Gravy said as he drew closer.

Jake waved off a few stray bees that had trailed him from the hive. "What kind of trouble?"

"Some strangers have come in, and they're arguing with Bill Hare." Gravy looked around as if he expected these strangers to be on his tail. "They already took some biscuit tins and some salt pork and they say they ain't going to pay for anything." Gravy's walrus mustache was so long that the curled tips dropped down below his chin. When he talked, the tips would go back and forth across each other, putting Jake in mind of the pincers on a wood ant. As excited as he was now, he looked fit to chew down a forest.

Jake squinted toward the buildings of Medicine Rock and frowned. "Where's Josie? She's supposed to be minding the place."

"Why, she's there, Sheriff, but these boys ain't listening to her."

That was a bad sign. The sight of Josie waving a double-barreled shotgun—a gun near big around as her arm—was generally enough to send those bandits without heavy starch

35

on their way. The only bad men that would be likely to ignore her were ones who had considerable talent on their side.

"How many are there?" Jake asked.

Gravy was close to dancing with impatience, but he managed to answer Jake's questions. "Two. One's a big cuss. The other one's a runt. Looks like he might be some kind of Cherokee."

Jake nodded. Any Indian that wore white clothes was like to be called a Cherokee no matter what his real tribe. "Which one of them's got the talent?"

"Both."

"Damn," Jake said. It had been some little while since he had to face more than one talented man at a time. If either of the two had more than a smidgen of ability, this might turn out to be a close scrap.

"You coming?" Gravy asked. He took a nervous step back toward town.

"Yeah." Jake nodded. "Yeah, I'm coming." He loosed the flap on his holster and followed Gravy toward the cluster of buildings.

Jake was nervous about the fight, but he was also more excited than he wanted to show. In his opinion, being sheriff was not a terribly hard job. Certainly there were times when it was dangerous, but in between those times there was nothing to the job but showing yourself around town and collecting the weekly fee from the merchants.

Even when there was trouble in town, Jake's wife, Josie, was as like to handle it as Jake. Though Jake was the sheriff and Josie only a deputy, the truth was, Josie was better at the day-to-day work. She might not have any talent, but there was something about the way she looked down the length of a shotgun that made folks get cooperative in a hurry.

When there was a real challenge, of course, Jake knew he was the one on the line. But there had not been more than three challenges in the last year. Being a sheriff was work that a lazy man could enjoy.

The trouble for him was that he was not lazy. Leastwise, he was not lazy enough to sit around all day. Knocking about the house and working with the beehives took the edge off his restlessness, but it wasn't enough. He needed to be out. He needed to be doing. But he couldn't leave Medicine Rock, and he certainly couldn't leave Josie.

Before they reached the main street of Medicine Rock, Jake could hear the ruckus caused by the two visitors. Something about the noise gave him a bad feeling, and he started to trot. There was a shout, then a crash of wood. Then another shout—one that sounded like Josie—followed the deep boom of a shotgun.

Jake began to run in earnest.

When he got around to where he could see the front of Hare's Dry Goods, Jake was relieved to see Josie standing in the street with the shotgun tucked up under her arm. As was her habit, she wore men's dungarees and a checked shirt. The attire had been shocking the first time Jake saw it, but now it was just part of Josie. The black vaquero hat she generally wore had come loose and fallen down behind her head, leaving her long dark hair to stream out in the Wyoming breeze. She did not seem to be injured.

Jake hesitated a moment, just looking at his wife. It seemed incredible now that he had lived in the same town as Josie for almost a year before he'd seen her as more than the Mexican cook at his boardinghouse. It was obvious that there was no more beautiful woman to be found anywhere.

Standing next to her was a slightly built man who stood only about the same height as Josie. He was red in the face, sure enough, and he had dark hair, but Jake didn't think he was any kind of Indian. He looked more like a man that had simply spent too many days under a hard sun.

"What's going on here?" Jake asked. "Gravy said there were two men fighting with Hare."

Josie nodded at the man beside her. "This is one of the men," she said. "The other is inside."

She had barely finished speaking before there was another crash from the store. A couple of curved pieces of wood—barrel staves, from the look of them—came flying through the door. There was the sharp odor of vinegar. From inside the store something rumbled like an avalanche. Through the small, dusty glass windows a bulky shape could be seen moving about, but it was hard to make out just what it was.

Jake took a good look at the man beside Josie. He wore a shirt of faded blue, and green wool trousers that had more holes than cloth. His hat was army issue, though the man was too young to have fought in the war. For a bandit, he looked more scared than mean.

"Who are you?" Jake asked.

"Tom," the man said. "I'm sorry about the trouble." His face was so hollowed he looked on the verge of starving. His voice was thin as his face, prickly with the harsh accents of the East.

"You got another name, Tom?"

"Tom Sharp."

Another rumble from the store drew Jake's attention. "I take it that's your friend inside."

Tom nodded. "I don't really know him so well," he said. "We was just traveling together." He looked down at the dusty road. "You know, to get across the open country."

"Sure," Jake said. It was common enough for folks to group up when getting across the empty. But when you partnered with someone, you partnered good and bad. Jake was sure that this Tom knew that as well as he did.

Josie tipped the end of her shotgun toward the store. "Bill Hare is still inside," she said.

"Is he all right?"

"I do not know," Josie said. "When I heard there was a problem, I came over here. This man came out when I called, the other man did not."

"What was all the noise about?"

"The other man is a changer. I tried to talk to him, but he would have none of it."

Jake nodded. Changers could be among the most dangerous of those with talent. In general, they were tough, able to take a lot of punishment without stopping. After that, their power depended on their changed form. Jake had seen changers that could do a variety of shapes. His friend Bred Smith could do anything from a bear to a buffalo to another person. Other changers were stuck with one form. No matter what the shape, all were dangerous.

"I guess that shot I heard was you testing out his hide," he said.

"Yes, but that did not work any better than the talking," Josie replied.

"What did he change into?"

"I do not know."

"How could you not see him?" Jake asked. "You shot at him."

Josie shook her head. "I saw him well enough. But what he has changed into is not an animal I have heard of."

Jake looked back at the small man. "Do you know what he is?"

"I think he's an ape," Tom said.

"An ape?"

Tom nodded. "I saw one in a zoo once, back in the Bronx, and what Cap turned into looks mostly like one."

Jake had only the barest idea of what a zoo was, and no idea at all about the Bronx. "Cap is the man's name?"

"Cap Hardin."

The last name put a shudder through Jake. "He's not related to John Hardin, is he?"

"Not so far as I know," Tom said.

"Good." John Hardin had talent as long as the day and temper shorter than a second. So far, he had plagued towns far to the south of Medicine Rock, and Jake was hoping it would stay that way.

Jake rested his fingers against the butt of his old Colt's revolver. "I guess I ought to get him out of there." He took two steps toward the door, set his feet apart, and did his best to sound like the law.

"Cap Hardin!" Jake shouted. "This is Sheriff Jake Bird. Come out of the store. Now!"

Jake had to give the man credit for listening. Cap Hardin came out promptly. In fact, he came out so fast that Jake felt compelled to take several quick steps back. He would have backed up farther but his heel caught on a loose piece of barrel and he fell hard on his butt in the street.

Whatever Tom Sharp had seen at the zoo in the Bronx, Jake doubted it looked quite like what charged out of Hare's Dry Goods. This thing was so broad across the shoulders that just coming through the door made the door wider by two feet. Its legs were much shorter than its arms, but even the legs were longer than a man's. Both of the arms were the length of Jake's whole body, and bigger around. Its head was as large as a nail keg, with small red eyes and curving fangs big as any bowie knife.

If the ape had come for Jake then, it might have ripped his head off before the sheriff could have raised either gun or talent. But it stopped at the edge of the street, raised its massive arms in the air and gave a shout that rattled what window glass remained in Medicine Rock.

While the monster screamed, a change came over Jake. After years of use, he no longer had to work to call his talent. Now it came on him easy as sunlight falling on the prairie. A hissing, crackling sound filled his ears, while all around him the world grew both clearer and somehow less real. He rose up from the ground as if drawn by strings from above.

The ape lowered its arms, bared its fangs, and charged.

"No," Jake said, but what came out of his mouth was not any word of English, or of any other language. What came out of him was pure power.

The ape's bellow cut off instantly. The creature stopped its charge and fell back, a baffled look on its huge dark face.

Jake made an effort to push his talent away, and for a moment his words came out clear. "Stand down," he said. "Change back, and you won't get hurt."

For almost a second he thought it might work. Then the ape sprang forward again, roaring like an angry she-bear.

An answering screech came from Jake's throat, and with it a bolt of fire took the ape in its chest. For a moment snakes of green power twisted over its hide. The sour smell of burning hair filled the street.

The ape staggered back, then leaped toward Jake again with

a flash of speed. Jake jumped aside as one of the beast's fists came slamming down. The blow would have surely crushed him into the dust if it had caught him square. As it was, it only glanced off his shoulder and sent pain dancing from his head to his feet.

"That's enough," Jake called, his words emerging in a flurry of squeaks and growls. "Get back."

His talent seized the ape and flung it against the board front of the dry goods store. Dust rained down from the lap boards and loose shakes came skittering off the roof. The ape bellowed again, but this time there was a note of surprise and hurt in its voice.

Jake trembled with effort as he pushed his talent down and found his voice. "Do you want more?" he said. "I'll kill you if I have to."

There was a shimmering in the air around the ape. With a flash of light, the huge beast was replaced by the form of a man almost as large and only a little less hairy. The expression on the man's face was not one whit less fierce than the one that the ape had worn. Like most changers, his clothes had been ruined or lost in the change, but if he was bothered by his nakedness, he didn't show it. He got to his feet and stood glaring at Jake.

"Don't think you've bested me yet," Cap Hardin said. His voice was deep, and touched by a burr that Jake took for Scottish.

"I don't care if you're bested," Jake said. "So long as you stop."

Hardin stepped down from the walk. He was as tall a man as Jake had ever seen. Taller even than Bred Smith, and that was saying something. Hardin had long dark hair, a stiff bristling beard, and a tangled mass of hairs on his arms and chest. Jake wondered what Hardin's reaction would be were he to point out how much the man resembled the beast he'd changed into. He decided not to test it.

"What made you think you could tear up Mr. Hare's store?" he asked instead.

Hardin spat on the ground. "It wasn't my fault," he said.

"All we was after is food. I tried to buy what we needed, but that bastard wouldn't take my money."

Jake sighed. The scrip situation was causing more hard feelings all the time. Government bills could no longer be cashed in for gold or silver, and a note from an eastern bank did little good when those banks were weeks away by horse. Many a newcomer to the West had discovered that all their paper wealth was rendered worthless by distance. Fortunately, not all those receiving such unwelcome news had the talent and the anger of Cap Hardin.

"There's not much I can do about that," Jake said. "Not many out this way are interested in trading for paper."

"A man's got to eat," Hardin said.

Josie stepped forward. "You do not get food by threatening and hurting people," she said. "If you had asked for it, we would have helped you."

Hardin sneered. "Sure you would."

Bill Hare appeared at the shattered door of his establishment, blinking through rimless spectacles. Like his namesake, he looked ready to bolt at the first sign of trouble. "You going to hang him?" he asked.

"Bill, go back inside," Jake said.

The shopkeeper frowned. "I want to know if you're going to hang him."

Jake looked from Hare to the man who had busted his store. "No. Not if he'll leave town."

Bill Hare might have been frightened of Cap Hardin, but now he was indignant. "But look at what he's done to my shop!" he said. "Who's going to pay for my door? Who's going to pay for two tins of biscuits and that barrel of pickled pork that he broke?"

"Who do you want to pay for it?"

"Him, of course," Hare said, jerking his thumb at Hardin. "He says he's got money."

Hardin snarled. "If you'd taken my money to start with, there wouldn't be no broken door."

Jake was beginning to wish he had never thought of being

sheriff. "All right, let's get this done. Bill, what do you reckon for the damages?"

"Thirty dollars," Hare said promptly. "Sixty, if I have to take it in scrip."

"Sixty dollars!" Hare cried. "For pork and moldy biscuits!"

The shopkeeper crossed his arms over his narrow chest. "My biscuits weren't moldy," he said.

"Maybe not," Jake said, "but your prices are high." He looked around at Hardin. "What kind of scrip are you carrying?"

The big man pulled himself up even taller. "Bank of the Atlantic," he said. "Best there is."

"Give Mr. Hare twenty of it."

"Damned if I will!"

"You'll give it to him," Jake said, "or you'll spend a month in the root cellar under my office." He looked around and saw Tom Sharp still standing in the street. "You do any of the breaking?"

"No," Tom said. "Soon as that started, I left."

Bill Hare made a snort. "He might not've thrown any barrels, but it was him that threatened me first. Said he was a signer, and he'd knock the whole shop down if I didn't sell him some food."

Jake eyed the small man closely. "You do that?"

Tom blinked. "I guess. Maybe."

"Well then, I want you to pay twenty of your own money."

The small man didn't stop to argue, he only dug into his jeans and pulled out a small wad of notes. He peeled a pair of bills off the roll and brought them over to Jake.

"Don't give them to me," Jake said. "Give them to Mr. Hare."

Cap Hardin's face was still set in a scowl. "I ain't paying. That old man's a robber."

Jake sighed and looked over at Josie. "When you shot him before, did it get a stir?"

Josie nodded. "He jumped and yelled like a stuck javelina."

"Good," Jake said. "Shoot him again. It won't kill him, but it might get him feeling more reasonable."

Josie cocked the big shotgun and raised it to her shoulder.

Hardin threw up his hands. "Hold on there," he said. "I'll pay."

"Good thinking," Jake said.

The naked man glanced down. "I need to go in there and get my clothes before I can pay."

"You do that," Jake said.

Hardin stepped around Bill Hare, who turned with a satisfied smirk on his face. "You don't touch any of my goods while you're in there!" he called through the broken door.

Jake leaned over to Josie. "Truth is, I agree with Hardin," he whispered. "Bill Hare charges more than an ice water dealer in hell."

"That does not make it right to rob him," Josie replied. Josie generally held pretty stiff ideas of what was right and what was wrong.

Hardin emerged from the store a moment later wearing a dirty sheepskin coat and a pair of pants that was worn through at the knees. Though the clothes were trail-worn, they were not torn. Evidently he had taken care to remove his clothing before he made his change. "Here," he said, shoving a bank note into Bill Hare's hand. "Take your damn money."

The shopkeeper snatched the bills without a word and went back into the shade of his store. Cap Hardin stepped closer to Jake and nodded. "I guess we'll be going now, Sheriff," he said. "Come on, Tom."

Tom Sharp shook his head. "If it's all the same to you, Cap, I think I'll stay here a day or two. That is, if they'll let me."

"Why do you want to stay?" Josie asked.

The small man shrugged. "I thought I might find some work. I'm pretty handy with a hammer and saw."

Jake thought for a moment. "I suppose you can stay. You didn't really do anything. But Mr. Hardin, I'll have to insist you leave. Tempest is three, four days southeast of here. Maybe they'll take your scrip down there."

Cap Hardin spat on the ground again. "Don't worry, I don't want to stay here anyhow." With that, he hunched his shoulders and stomped off down the main street.

In a few moments Hardin had passed the last building in town and was on the overgrown road to Tempest. The residents of the town, who had secluded themselves behind doors and shades during the conversation, began to emerge onto the street. Noises of laughter and clinking glasses drifted up from the Kettle Black.

"Thank you for letting me stay," Tom Sharp said.

Jake gave the small man a smile. "I'm not sure I've done you any favors," he said. "We already have more than one good carpenter in town. Besides, far as I know, the only carpentry to be done around here is Bill Hare's door. I doubt he'd hire you to do it."

"Well, maybe I'll find something," Tom said. He lifted his hat and ran his fingers through his dark hair. "It was worth staying just to be shed of Hardin."

Josie stepped over to the man and looked at him with a strange intensity. "Can you really do the signing?" she asked.

Tom nodded. "I'm not so good, but I do have talent."

"Why are you asking?" Jake said.

Instead of replying, Josie pointed down the road. "Come to our house," she said. "I will fix you supper myself."

Tom Sharp smiled. "Thank you, ma'am. I appreciate that."

The two of them turned up the road, leaving Jake to stare after them and scratch his head in wonder.

☆ 5 ☆

"You say Laramie's gone, too?" Muley asked.

The sodbuster nodded. "Yup. Leastways it's mostly gone." He paused to wipe the rain away from his face and scratched himself through a hole in his stained shirt. "What I hear is that they had a sheriff get killed, and then another sheriff run off on them. They never did get another."

Muley only nodded. They had been three days at the sodbuster's house, and already conversation had lost its charms. The sodbuster, a wild-haired man who gave his name as Prester, loved to talk. Ever since Muley and the Rainmaker arrived at this worthless little patch of corn, Prester had been talking. He talked about everything, and when everything ran out, he invented something new. He talked so much that even Muley's ear was worn-out.

Muley had hopes that if he stayed quiet long enough, the old man might give up and hush for a minute. So far, the strategy had not produced the desired results.

"You really think this wagon of yours is going to work?" Prester asked. "Myself, I don't think much of it."

Muley shrugged.

"Looks to me like that pole ain't strong enough. Come right down on your head if you don't watch out."

Muley busied himself tying two lengths of frayed rope together. It was raining, of course, and the rope was damp. Muley's stiff fingers slipped again and again as he tried the old familiar knots. He cursed under his breath.

"Yup," Prester said. "Looks to me like this thing will fall apart the first time a stiff breeze comes down off the hills."

"It ain't going to fall apart," Muley said. He threw down the two ends of rope in frustration. "I'm going to check on the sails."

Muley climbed down from the top of the wagon. He stopped once he was on the ground and made sure the bandage of tobacco and burlap was still in place. The Rainmaker had dug out the arrow point without making too big a hole in Muley's leg. Between the time it had taken to reach this place and the time they spent fixing the wagon, the leg had better than a week to heal, but it hurt like hell just the same.

Muley straightened and limped toward the soggy pile of sod that passed for Prester's house. He was afraid at every step that the sodbuster would follow, ready to keep up his never-ending, ever-bleak chatter. Thankfully, Prester wandered off into his miserable cornfields, still muttering to himself.

The door to the sod house had settled at one corner, giving it a skewed look. Muley had to duck to get inside the dwelling. He stood blinking in the doorway, waiting for his eyes to adjust to the dim light. The air inside the soddy was cool and earthy, like the smell of a plow in spring.

The Rainmaker's voice came out of the shadows. "Is the wagon ready?"

"Ready as it'll get, I suppose." Muley could just make out the pale face of the Rainmaker, floating like a ghost in the darkness. Muley felt his way across the room and settled into one of the house's two chairs. There was a patter of rain against the roof, and a steady drip in one corner. The combination of sounds, smells, and shade worked to make Muley drowsy as soon as he sat down. He leaned back in his chair and folded his hands over his stomach. "Are the sails getting close?" he asked.

"Close as I'm likely to make them," the Rainmaker said. There was no missing the note of disgust in the albino's voice. He did not appreciate being pressed into needlework, but Muley's fingers were not limber enough to handle the stitching.

There were more things than sails that needed mending. The trip along the flooded wash had carried the wagon into a creek bed, and from there the stream had sent them northeast all the way to the edge of Colorado Territory and almost into Wyoming. It had been nearly a day before the water went down and left them resting on a sandbar. The wagon had surprised both Muley and the Rainmaker by staying afloat for the whole trip, but the vehicle hadn't survived the journey unscathed.

One of the wheels that Muley lashed to the rear of the wagon had suffered a blow, leaving it with a dented rim and cracked spokes. Though he'd been careful to tie down the sails, they caught on the branches of a tree being carried along by the same flood. The tip of a branch had slit the sheets neat as a razor. Finally, and worst of all, the mast had been broken. This last was doubly irritating because it had happened not during the storm, but while Muley was using a rope to haul the wagon off the sandbar. He'd been cursing himself ever since.

They had made what repairs they could. Muley beat the biggest dent out of the wheel, though there was nothing that could be done for the busted spokes. A leather belt served to hold the mast together as long as there was not much strain. With the damage, they were able to gentle the wagon only a few miles a day. With Muley's lack of skill at hunting, they had been short on food, bullets, and patience when they came upon Prester's sod house.

The soddy was a remnant of better times in the West—what Muley thought of as high tide for people in these parts. Back before the war, the government had encouraged folks to settle the territories, promising cheap land and room to grow. But the land had been dry and hard, giving such meager crops of corn that not one family in five survived their first two years. And there had been the Indians—and winters harder than any in the East.

By the time the war had come to its stumbling end, it was clear that the tide had turned. The wash of people drew back from the West, leaving their towns like puddles on the prairies, and the isolated houses of the sodbusters scattered like jetsam after a storm.

"We should leave at daybreak," the Rainmaker said.

The words woke Muley out of a drowse. He started forward in his chair, waved his arms wildly, and avoided falling over backward by the barest of margins. It was dark, darker even than it had been a moment before. A dim, bloody glow slipped from the stove in the corner of the room.

"Don't kill yourself," the Rainmaker said. "I'd never manage the wagon on my own."

Except for a ruddy glint cast by his pale eyes, Muley could make out nothing of the Rainmaker. "I thought—" He stopped and cleared the sleep from his throat. "I thought we was leaving today."

A laugh came out of the darkness. "Today's come and gone," Prester said. "You slept most of it sitting in that chair."

Muley stretched his back. "Feels like I just sat down."

"You must have been tired," the sodbuster said. "Anybody as can sleep in a chair is generally tired. But if you're to sleep in a chair, then that that there is a good chair for sleeping. Why, I've slept in it myself more than once. There was—"

"It's a fine chair," Muley said, cutting off Prester's chatter. Prester was right, though, he had been tired, and was tired still. The rain continued its hiss against the roof, as it did every night Muley shared a house with the Rainmaker, and the noise seemed eager to carry him back into sleep.

"What do you hear from the East?" Prester said suddenly. "Have we got a new president?"

"Two of them," the Rainmaker replied. "Though I'll be damned if I recall either one's name."

This bare mention of things political was enough to make Muley groan. Since the war, borders between North and South had gotten blurred, broken, and divided six ways from Sunday. Muley had lost track of which states were going which way. He did not know the names of the presidents, nor did he care. All he knew was he needed more sleep, and this seemed an ideal time to get it.

Stumbling about the room in the darkness, he located his bedroll. He dragged himself off to a corner of the one-room house, careful to find a place free of drips and dampness, pulled off his boots and lay down.

"McClellan was the worst of the bunch," the Rain-maker said.

Prester moved over to the chair Muley had vacated. "Who was the tall one?" he asked. "The one before McClellan?"

The reply was lost to Muley as sleep came up and grabbed him again.

Later, how much later he wasn't sure, Muley woke suddenly and sat up in the darkness. The fading echoes of a nightmare chased around his head for a moment, but it left no pictures behind. There was only the sound of his heart racing in his chest and a sour taste of fear in his mouth.

"Glad to see you up," Prester said. "I was about to wake you myself."

Looking closely, Muley could make out the sodbuster's form in the last violet light of the cooling stove. Prester was still in the chair where he'd been when Muley bedded down. "Is it close to dawn?" Muley asked.

"No," Prester said. "That's hours off. But you was making so much noise, you'd've thought all the devils of hell was on you. I reckoned it'd be a charity to wake you."

Muley ran a hand through his tangled hair. "A-yup, I reckon." He looked up at the silhouette of the wild-haired farmer. "Why ain't you sleeping?"

Prester gave a bit of a chuckle. "Sleep don't visit me much. Not since Genevieve and the boys left."

This was a story that Muley had already heard more than once. A Shoshone had done for one of Prester's sons the first year they were homesteading. Two years later pox had come for his wife and remaining son. Of all Prester's gloomy talk, this was by far the gloomiest. It also seemed to be the tale he liked to recall most often.

"I'm sorry to hear that," Muley said. "You'll have to pardon me for a bit." He got to his feet in the darkness and stumbled out into the night to relieve himself.

He was surprised to find his wounded leg feeling better, and more surprised to find that it was not raining. In fact, the sky was clear as a bell. Prester had not lied about the time. There was no sign of dawn, and with no moon to drown them, stars filled the bowl of sky from one rim to another. Standing near an old fence post, Muley could see at least a dozen pale blue shadows spreading out from the base—shadows cast by stars.

As he stood there in the cold night air, Muley decided he was being too hard on Prester. The man had been alone out here for years, and it was a good bet he didn't get many visitors. Prester had suffered some hard knocks, losing his wife and children. If he wanted to talk while he had the chance, that was only to be expected, Muley realized. He himself would have probably gone plumb crazy under the same circumstances.

He finished his business, buttoned the long line of small buttons at the front of his trousers, and turned to go back into the house. But when he turned around, there was a woman standing behind him. In the darkness she was no more than a shape—a small, gently curved form topped with streaming hair.

For a moment Muley was too startled to talk. The woman was like a ghost in the starlight, like something left over from his nightmare. But seconds went past and she was still there, surrounded by star shadows and solid as the fence post.

"Why, miss, what are you doing out here?" Muley asked when his breath returned.

"It's just how things turned," the woman said. Her voice was odd, almost musical, but it seemed weighed down with melancholy.

Muley felt a flush of embarrassment. "I didn't mean to pry." It struck him that this woman might be Prester's lover. Maybe the old sodbuster had a reason for sticking to this worthless land.

The woman shook her head. "I wish I could stay longer, but I can't," she said. "Things don't run straight for some time yet."

"They don't?" Her speech was confusing. Muley reached up to remove his hat, only to discover he wasn't wearing one. "Now, miss, maybe you ought to come inside and sit by the stove. It's cold out here."

"I wish I could stay," the woman repeated. Clouds of wispy

white trailed her breath in the cold air. She came closer, and the smooth details of her face emerged from the shadows. There was a scent about her, something fresh and clean, something that didn't belong in such a worn-out, dried-up country.

A warmth came over Muley that he had not felt in ages. "I wish you could, too," he said. He squinted at the woman's face. "Seems like . . . Seems like I've seen you before," he said.

"Yes," she said. "And again."

"What?"

"This is only a short turn, Muley, but it does run straight for a long time further out. We'll get there." The woman smiled. "I've crossed myself, you see, I know the straight time is coming."

"Straight time?" Muley asked.

Instead of talking, the woman put her arms around Muley's neck and brought her face close to his. Before Muley had time to so much as take a breath, he found the woman's warm lips pressed against his own.

The unexpected kiss left Muley near as flustered as running from the Indians. When the woman pulled away, he stared into her dark eyes and struggled to get his tongue around words. "You . . . you trying to get me in trouble with Prester?"

The woman stepped back, the shadow of the soddy falling across her face. "I don't care about this Prester," she said in her soft, sad voice. "It's you that I'm joined to, Muley. You're the one that I love."

Muley felt as if the ground had gone bumpy as an October sea. "How can you love me?" he said. "You don't even know me."

"I know you better than anyone alive," she said from the darkness. "You just don't know it yet, Muley."

"How can that be?" Muley asked.

The woman smiled, her white teeth shining from the darkness. "You're like everybody else. Your string runs straight from cradle to grave, and you think that's the only way it can go." She reached up and touched Muley softly on the cheek. "I'll teach you different soon enough."

"I . . . I don't reckon I know what you're talking about," Muley said. He was beginning to suspect that he was still really inside the soddy, snoring under tattered blankets. The star-filled night seemed too clear—too real to be real.

"I wish I could explain everything, love," she said, "but the next turn's coming quick. Listen here. You get yourself and your wagon up to Medicine Rock. That's where you need to be." The woman turned and moved away, her shape disappearing into the inky darkness alongside the soddy.

"Where's this Medicine place?" Muley asked. "Why should we go there?"

There was no answer.

Muley walked up to the house, but there was nothing but shadow. He raised his hands and ran his fingers across the damp, crumbly face of the sod. There was no one.

"Miss?" he whispered softly.

A cold wind came whistling down from the north. With unnatural speed the stars disappeared behind a spreading sheet of clouds. In a moment a cold rain began to fall. Muley squinted into the darkness for another wet uncomfortable minute, then went back inside.

Prester was feeding wood from his meager stock into the oven's mouth, bringing the blaze up enough to fill the room with orange light. "If you're done with sleeping, then come over and warm yourself," he said.

Muley eased over to the fire and held out his hands. His fingers had been very stiff of late, and prone to ache when they were cold. The warm blaze felt good. He looked around at Prester. He was of a mind to ask the old man along. It was a miracle that the broken wagon had led them to this spot. More company might not come along for months or years.

"You know, I appreciate the help you've given us," Muley said.

"It's nothing," the farmer replied. "I'm glad enough of the company." He picked up a charred stick and shoved the stove door closed. He looked at Muley and gave a gap-toothed smile. "Though truth is I've had about enough of company. I expect I'm ready to be by myself again."

"You could come with us," Muley offered.

"Naw," the sodbuster said. "I need to stay here, close to Genevieve and the boys. But I have thought of where you ought to go."

"You did?"

Prester nodded. "Come to me while you were outside." He raised his stick and pointed it toward the door. "You need to go that way."

"North?" Muley shook his head. "We were planning on heading for the pass due east."

"You go north," Prester said. "Then turn east up there. Stay on the old trail, and it'll take you right where you want to go."

"And where's that?"

"A little town called Medicine Rock," the sodbuster said.

☆ **6** ☆

Bill Cody leaned against the cushioned train seat with his hat tilted down over his eyes and his hands folded in his lap. Ever since the train chugged out of Sioux Falls he'd been pretending to sleep. When the mood struck him, he watched Kastle and Cullen from under the brim of his hat. More often he simply sat and thought.

The ruse would only work for a few more minutes. Soon enough they would reach the end of the line and he would have to fess up to being awake. But until then he would at least be spared the effort of conversing with the two foreigners who shared the train car.

"I never knew there was so much nothing," Sean Cullen said from his chair by the window. "This place even makes Jersey look good."

Edward Kastle looked up from a yellow-edged journal. Without his bowler hat the scientist's head was naked as an egg and almost as white. "I expect it will only get worse," he said. "This is the wilderness we are entering."

It had not taken Bill more than a minute to decide he didn't care for either Kastle or Cullen. In their own way they were both bullies. Cullen was nothing but an Irish thug. He had raw red knuckles on hands as big as hams, and a blustering, boasting way of talk that rubbed Bill the wrong way. As for Kastle, he had bowed in front of Gould, but now that they were out of the city, the scientist acted as if he were God's man on earth. He looked at Bill like he was something to be scraped off the bottom of a boot.

Bill understood well enough that wealthy powerful men

like Jay Gould had a use for men like Cullen and Kastle. What he couldn't understand was why Gould would send such men west. It was obvious enough that the men didn't want to be there. They had done nothing but complain for five days, and all that time they had only been riding in a fancy train car with a cook to provide the meals and a soft bed at night. Neither of them seemed to have any skill that would be useful once they were off the train. Bill could not imagine what these two would do out on the range.

The sound of the train changed, growing deeper as the engines slowed. The engineer let loose with a long blow on the whistles, followed by a roar of steam as the boiler was thrown open. The clack of the wheels on the rail grew more distinct. Finally there was a screech of brakes and the train came to a stop.

Through the open windows Bill heard a babble of voices. He opened his eyes, tipped his hat back, turned his head and saw that they had arrived in the midst of chaos.

For Bill it was a familiar chaos. Nearly a thousand men swarmed around the tracks. Some sat at long tables, greedily stuffing themselves with flapjacks. Others carried axes or hammers. Men working in pairs walked slowly with heavy wooden ties stretched out between them. Whole scores of men toted lengths of gleaming new rail that bowed and bounced as they walked along. There were stacks of tools, heaps of lumber, and piles of steel. The men moved around and over these piles like ants at a picnic. There were shouts and the bright ring of hammers. Through the open window Bill smelled the flapjacks, and wood smoke, and sweat.

The whole of it made him smile. Some of the best times he'd ever had came in a place not so different from this, and he had feared never to see its like again.

Bill stood up and looked at the two easterners. "Gentlemen," he said, "seems we've reached the end of the line. You'll find there's nowhere on earth quite like a railroad camp."

Cullen glanced out the window and sneered. "Sure and I'd rather be in Brooklyn," he said.

Bill grinned in response. "This ain't New York, boys. You'd best follow my lead from here on out."

"You forget yourself, Mr. Cody," Kastle said stiffly. "You have been hired to guide us and to negotiate with local authorities, but you are not in charge of this expedition. I am." The German grabbed his satchel from the seat and shoved his way out of the compartment.

Bill laughed. "That little fellow's going to find folks around here ain't as easy to boss as them fellers in Gould's basement."

"I'd listen to Kastle if I was you, boyo," Cullen said. He gave Bill a smile that held not one lick of humor. "Things he keeps in that bag could scare a corpse out of its coffin." He stood up and followed the engineer out of the compartment.

The tough's words gave Bill a moment's pause, but no more than a moment. Now that he was in the land where he felt at home, he was not about to start getting scared of bald scientists from New York City.

Bill followed the easterners to the end of the car, where a pair of porters waited. Just as they had with the cook, the men got a considerable amount of attention from the porters. Though the engine had carried thirty cars all the way from New York, there were no other passenger cars on this train. All the rest of the cars were loaded with more metal and timber, ready to extend the railroad's reach to the west. Already men were working up and down the line to unload the cargo. Within the hour the train would be unloaded, turned, and on its way back to the East.

A tall fat man in a dusty suit came waddling up as Bill got off the train. "Glad to see you fellows made it," the man said. "I'm Woodson. Mr Gould wired me you were coming and told me to have supplies waiting." The fat man's eyes went quickly past the others and settled on Bill. "You'd be Cody?"

"That's right," Bill said. He put out his hand. "Glad to make your acquaintance, Woodson." Despite the man's girth, Woodson had a considerable grip. His face showed the squint and color of a man who had spent plenty of time trying to look beyond the horizon.

Kastle stepped forward. "Look here," he said. "This is my affair, and I'll thank you to address me."

Woodson pursed his lips. "I took this to be Mr. Gould's affair."

"Of course," Kastle said, somewhat taken aback. "But I am his highest ranking representative here."

"I see," Woodson said. He did not seem any too impressed with the German's bluster. "Well, come along, all of you. There are mounts and packhorses waiting." He turned away and spoke over his shoulder. "Mr. Gould indicated you'd be in a hurry to get on your way."

Bill was happy enough at the way Woodson had thrown Kastle from his high horse, but he was disappointed to hear that all the preparations were already made. He'd been looking forward to spending a few days around the camp.

A large rail camp was a city in itself. Though it might be several miles down the line from one day to the next, still the men managed to freight tents, bedrolls, and even wooden shanties along with them. Merchants found their way as well, ready to sell popskull at ten times its cost elsewhere, or peddle a hot pasty to those that had tired of the railroad food. And of course there were the girls of the line. That was the part of the camp Bill had been looking forward to most. The majority of the railroad men weren't married, and those that were had left their wives many miles behind. Sporting girls never did such business as they did around a rail camp.

Half a dozen men tried to talk to Woodson as he showed the way between tents and lumber piles, but the fat man waved them all off. They walked on through the main part of the camp and out past boys laying fresh rail under a bright noon sun.

Bill paused in the middle of a step. There was something wrong with the steel. Instead of the cloud-gray color he was used to, it carried an odd blue-green cast. "What kind of rail is that?" he asked.

Woodson glanced toward the workers and shrugged. "Some kind of new steel," he said. "We been laying it all the way from Topeka. Don't see much difference in the way it takes a hammer, but it must be damn fine rail. From what I hear, they've even had crew tearing up tracks to the east to replace them with this new metal."

Kastle moved up beside Bill and nodded. "This is a superior material," he said. "I helped to develop it myself."

Bill looked around at Kastle. The little engineer had popped his round hat down over his bare scalp. Somehow the hat that had looked at home back in the city looked damned ridiculous on the plains. "You know," Bill said. "I believe I'd have slept a darned sight better all the way out here if I'd've known you were the one that made the rails."

Kastle blinked. "I did not make these particular rails. I created the alloy."

Woodson laughed, and even Cullen gave a snicker. If Kastle understood the sarcasm in Bill's remark, he never showed it.

Another minute's walking brought them to a rail where five horses were hitched. "I gave you two for pack," Woodson said. "But they're all saddle broke. I didn't want you to be short a mount if you had a need."

Bill patted the nearest horse on the neck. "They look like fine animals to me." He turned and extended his hand again to Woodson. "Seems like you've taken good care of us."

"That's a fine compliment coming from you, Cody," the fat man replied. "There's plenty in these parts that have not forgotten you."

"Enough," Kastle said. "Put our things on the horses. We should be under way as soon as possible."

Bill shoved his hands in his pockets. "I know you're in charge, but I'd stay here the night if it were up to me. We've only got a few hours of light left to us as it is. We can sleep on good beds, have a hot breakfast, and be off at first light."

Woodson nodded agreement. "Cody's right. You'll travel better if you're rested."

Kastle shook his head. "I will not have reports going back to Mr. Gould that we have been less than expeditious. We will get under way immediately."

The porters from the train carried over the cases of supplies, most of them Kastle's. Bill supervised the loading of the horses and did his best to keep the burden even. He would have liked to leave some of the heavy bags behind, but Kastle insisted that they were all required.

While they were taking care of the packing, Cullen wandered away into the tent city. The Irishman returned a few minutes later with the first real smile that Bill had seen on his face. Despite the brevity of the man's absence, Bill had to wonder if Cullen had gone to sample the pleasures of one of the camp ladies.

The mares that Woodson had provided were all good mounts. A tall gray was by far the most spirited of the bunch, and Bill was tempted to give that mount to Kastle. But in the end he took the gray for himself and gave the city men a pair of more timid sorrels. Worse come to worse, it never hurt to be mounted on the fastest horse.

Bill held back laughter as Kastle and Cullen struggled into their saddles. Then he took the leads of the two packhorses and, with a final wave to Woodson, led the party out of the rail camp.

It was a beautiful afternoon for traveling. The sky overhead was as pure and blue as a robin's egg. As soon as they were away from the rail camp the grass stretched out like a brown blanket in all directions, with the wind running across the plains in golden waves. Bill could not have asked for better.

To Bill's surprise, Kastle sat his horse rather smartly. He had an erect, rather rigid posture more suited to a parade ground than the prairie, but he obviously had some experience in the saddle. Kastle was of the right age to have been a cavalry man during the war. Bill thought about asking, but did not out of fear that Kastle might launch into stories of his exploits in the Grand Conflict.

Cullen proved to be the one who had troubles. Bill had no doubt the man was tough, but Cullen was not about to outmuscle a thousand-pound horse. By the time the Irishman came to understand this, he was as wrung out as any greenhorn Bill had ever seen.

They covered little more than ten miles of grass before the

orange sun touched the horizon. The railroad camp was close enough that Bill could still hear the clang of hammer on spike. He began to calculate whether he might be able to ride back to camp, spend time with the girls, and still get some rest before morning. He'd just about convinced himself it was possible when Kastle pointed ahead.

"Is that smoke over there?" the scientist asked.

Bill squinted toward the setting sun. Kastle was right, there was smoke rising a few miles ahead. It was only a slender white rope, but Bill was irritated that the easterner had seen it first. "It's smoke right enough," he said. "Probably someone laying camp for the evening."

"What should we be doing now?" Cullen asked.

Bill guided his horse a few steps ahead and stood up in his stirrups. "You two wait here," he said. "I'll trot up there and see what's what."

"No," Kastle said. "We all go." Before Bill could say a word in response, Kastle kicked his horse into a gallop and raced off through the grass.

"Wonderful," Bill said, watching the little man race away. "Maybe I ought to let him go off and get himself killed."

Cullen snorted. "Myself, I'm for it. You kill our boyo Kastle, and I can get myself off this ass grinder."

Bill laughed. "It might be pleasant, but I'm in need of my pay." He nodded toward the shrinking figure of Kastle. "We better get after him before he comes across a band of Blackfeet and gets his hair lifted."

Leading the packhorses put considerable limits on how fast Bill could move. He thought about leaving the animals behind—he could always hobble them and return for them later—but the truth was that Kastle was probably in little danger. There were not so many Indians on this part of the plains, especially this close to the rail camp. In fact, it was far more likely that Kastle was running up on scouts from the camp rather than any sort of hostiles.

Dark came over the plains quick, and stars were already overhead by the time Bill and Cullen approached the source of the smoke. Bill was both surprised and relieved to find Kastle off his mount, waiting for him at the back of a low hill.

"There's only one man," Kastle said in a clipped whisper that probably carried a mile over the grass. "I came up close enough to examine him, but I do not believe the man detected my presence."

Bill sincerely doubted that the engineer had snuck up on anyone camped out this way. "Would you agree to let me at least go take a look at the man?" he asked. "Could be I know him."

Kastle nodded. "Finish quickly and come back."

Bill handed over the leads for the packhorses and eased off toward the fire at a gentle trot. When he cleared the next rise, he saw that the fire had been set on a small knob of weathered limestone. The bare patch of ground provided a clear view in all directions. Even from a half mile out Bill could see that Kastle was right—there was only one figure at the fire. From a quarter mile Bill could see that the figure was Emmet Skaggs.

Skaggs had been a fixture on the prairies for longer than Bill had been alive. He was a hunter, and a good enough hunter to keep himself fed for nearly fifty years. Unlike most folks in the West, Skaggs did not like horses. He got around the tall grass country on his own legs, doing his hunting by sneaking up on deer and antelope so close that he often took them with a knife.

Bill thought for a moment about riding back to Kastle and telling him the situation, but he decided to ride on in and have a chat with Skaggs first. It would be good to talk to the old hunter without the two easterners around.

Whatever skills Skaggs once had, it was obvious he was losing them. Bill was able to approach to within thirty yards before the old man jumped to his feet.

Skaggs pulled out his pistol and pointed it at a spot ten feet to Bill's left. "Stop there, you," he said. "I knows you're there."

"It's Bill Cody," Bill said. "I just come to talk."

"Bill?" Skaggs allowed the barrel of his pistol to drop toward the ground. "You hunting for them railroad boys?"

"Sort of." Bill got down off his mount and led the big gray over near the fire. "What brings you this way, Emmet? Ain't this a bit easterly for you?"

Skaggs shrugged and shoved his pistol back into its holster. "I go where the game goes. There's muleys moving this way, and I aim to take them."

Bill sniffed. "That coffee you've got on?"

"What passes for it." Skaggs moved to the fire and took the pot off the coals. "Sit with me and drink a cup. I want to hear what those rail boys is up to." He poured a tin cup of hot coffee and passed it across the fire to Bill. "Could be they'll be needing to hire some more hunters."

"Could be," Bill agreed. He took the cup and savored a scalding sip. "They've got me hunting whole towns."

"Towns?" Skaggs said. "What do—" Suddenly the old man dropped his coffeepot on the ground and grabbed for his pistol. No sooner had he pulled the heavy revolver from his holster than three shots sounded. But it wasn't Skaggs that did the firing.

Blood sprayed out from the old hunter's back and fell sizzling in the fire. The old man staggered a step, started to turn, and dropped to his knees. He hung there a second, a look of consternation on his weathered face. Then he fell facedown. His pistol clattered away on the rocks.

"Goddamn!" Bill shouted. "What'd you go and do that for?"

Cullen moved out into the firelight. "That old fool drew his pistol," he said. "It was himself or me."

Bill balled his hands into fists. His fingers itched to reach for his own gun, but Cullen still held a dark pistol in his fingers, and there was no doubt he knew how to use it. "That was Emmet Skaggs," Bill said. "He wasn't going to shoot you. I knew the man."

If Cullen was concerned about Skaggs' death, not a lick of remorse showed on his rawboned features. "Sure then he shouldn't have pulled his weapon," he said calmly. "In Brooklyn, a man who draws a gun is asking to be kilt."

"Well, it don't work that way out here," Bill said. He crouched down beside the fallen Skaggs and turned the old man over. All three of Cullen's shots had struck the man in the chest, and together they made a hole big enough to hold Bill's fist. It was impressive shooting.

"You go shooting every man who pulls his gun out here," Bill said, "and you'll have to kill half the men in the West."

"Good." Kastle stepped out of the shadows and moved to Cullen's side. "If he kills half the men out here," he said, "then our job will be half completed."

☆ PART II ☆

All Out for Medicine Rock

☆ 7 ☆

Malcolm Truth was dying.

It was a project that had engaged Malcolm for most of his young life, but lately it had become clear that the project was finally about done. He lay in one of the upstairs rooms at the Kettle Black, the same room where he'd stayed for the last two years. The shades had been drawn in the room. No lamps were lit. Only thin shafts of sunlight entered around the edges of the shades, sparkling on slow moving motes of dust and lending a golden glow to Malcolm's pain-wracked face.

His sister Sienna tended him as best she could. Goldy pitched in what she had learned of folk remedies. Sheriff Jake Bird tried to help with his talents. Old Panny Wadkins, who was ill himself, even suggested cures he had learned from the Dakota. For all that, Malcolm was dying.

It was not as if Malcolm had ever been a healthy child. He was born blind and deaf, with only his sister to connect him to the rest of the world. Most folks thought the boy was feeble-minded besides, but Sienna declared that he was as smart as anyone, it was only his deafness that kept him from making himself clear.

Of course, Sienna also maintained for years that Malcolm had a talent for casting the future. They had grown up in a town run by a renegade preacher who was prone to discarding those citizens who were less than useful. Sienna had attributed her own talent to her brother so as to help protect the boy from the preacher's wrath. Only lately had she owned up to being the one with the gift. Even Goldy, who was a caster herself, could not come close to matching the sharpness of Sienna's talent.

Except for his missing senses, Malcolm had looked normal enough when he was younger. But as he grew from a boy to a man, Malcolm suffered a new affliction. His back began to twist around on him. By the time he was sixteen he was hard pressed to walk. At eighteen he had laid down in the old straw mattress in one of Goldy's upper rooms at the Kettle Black. The same room had served for a number of sporting girls in more prosperous days, but all of them together did not likely spend as much time on that mattress as did Malcolm. For two long years he had lain there.

Sienna kept her brother as clean as she could. She brought him food, water, and changed the sheets on which he lay. But after two years Malcolm had ceased to eat the food or drink the water. His twisted body had withered down to twigs and he lacked the strength to lift his head, but his jaws were clenched shut beyond the ability of anyone to open. Despite the best care Sienna could give, it was clear the boy was bound to die.

Goldy found Sienna sitting in the dark at her brother's bedside. The sharp smell of sage rose from the bowl in Sienna's lap, but it was not strong enough to overcome the odor of sickness that clouded the room. Malcolm's eyes were closed and his whistling breath was the only sound.

"You having any luck, child?" Goldy asked.

Sienna looked up, her dark eyes huge in the shadows. "I've been looking," she said. "Looking ahead."

Goldy was surprised. Sienna's talent went so far beyond her own that Goldy thought there needed to be a new name for it. Goldy's castings, and that of every other she had known, were not much clearer than mud—dreams through dark glass— and what images they brought could often be rendered for good or ill. Sienna was different. What she saw was what happened.

But Sienna did not often talk about her talent, and Goldy could not remember the last time she'd shared what she had cast without prodding. "What do you see?" Goldy asked.

"I've been looking for Malcolm." Sienna turned to stare into the shadowed corner of the room. "I look ahead into the next year, and I do not see him. I look into the heat of next summer, and I do not see him."

As always, Goldy was tempted to ask what else Sienna had seen. She moved to sit on the edge of the bed where she could lay a hand on Sienna's shoulder. "Honey, you know he's awful sick. Maybe it's best."

"I look into this winter, and I do not see him." Sienna paused for a moment. "I look into tomorrow's sunrise, but even there I do not find him."

Even though she had been expecting the boy's death for weeks, the news that Malcolm would not last out the day took Goldy by surprise. She'd taken both Sienna and Malcolm in after the death of their grandfather. She had never felt particularly close to the crippled boy, but felt very close to Sienna. Knowing how much Malcolm's death would hurt his sister brought a tightness to Goldy's chest.

"You sure?" she said softly.

Sienna nodded. "He will see the sun set, but will not be here when it rises."

Goldy tried to think of something she might say to comfort the girl, but before she could speak there was a knock at the door. Black Alice pushed the door open and stuck her head into the room.

"Something's coming," Alice said.

"What's coming and where's it coming to?"

"I don't know what it is," Alice said. "But it's heading here. To Medicine Rock." As she spoke, the sunlight that leaked around the shades was suddenly cut off.

Goldy stood up and moved toward the light of the open door. "I best go see what she's going on about." She turned back to Sienna. "Are you going to be all right?"

"Yes," the girl said. "I will be fine."

Goldy didn't feel good about leaving the girl with her dying brother, but she went downstairs with Alice to see what was going on. Even before she hit the top of the stairs she could tell that more people than Alice were fretting over something. The clink of glasses and mumble of voices in the Kettle Black had vanished. There was only one thing that came to Goldy's mind—a challenge. Only a challenge could provide such a sight as to take men's minds off their drinks.

She hoped it was not a serious tussle. Jake Bird had talents as strong as any Goldy had seen, but he'd already faced down one pair of challengers no more than a few days before. When talents were pressed too often, they tended to falter. Besides, Jake tended to be slow about bringing his talents to bear. It was a worry that came over Goldy often. In a job where killing was the business, Jake Bird was no killer.

Goldy pushed her way through the crowd gathered around the door and stepped out onto the boardwalk. She expected to see Jake standing in the traditional spot by the sheriff's office. Instead the street was full of the citizens of Medicine Rock. It seemed that nearly every person in town was standing in the dust, looking off to the west.

Goldy squinted at the horizon but saw nothing. Then she spotted Panny Wadkins at the edge of the street and walked over to him. "What's got folks stirred, Panny?"

The old prospector turned stiffly. Panny's neck had tightened up over the years, and now he turned his whole shoulder when he wanted to turn his head. It made him look something like an old owl. "It's a funny sort of cloud," he said, his voice little more than a wheeze.

Goldy was about to ask what kind of cloud could be funny enough to draw the attention of a whole town when she glanced up and saw it for herself.

It *was* a funny sort of cloud. It hung up in the sky like a snake, twisting and curling across the western sky. It was dark in the middle, dark enough to block out the afternoon sun, but it thinned quickly toward the edges, letting through a hazy red light. From the eastern end came streamers of gray rain. And the strangest thing about this strange cloud was that it was moving directly toward Medicine Rock.

"It's talent," Goldy said softly. "Has to be. No cloud moves like that on its own."

"I reckon," Panny wheezed. He did his stiff turn and marched back into the Kettle Black. Whatever kind of cloud this was, it wasn't likely to contain either gold or whiskey. Lacking these essentials, it could not long hold Panny's interest.

The cloud was only a mile or so away when Goldy saw something strange enough to match this snake in the sky. But where the cloud was strange because it was unique, this new thing was strange because it was so familiar. When she was very young, long before she had gone to be a sporting girl in Nebraska, Goldy had lived with her family in Hoboken. From the ports there she had watched ships drift off to Europe and spotted the tops of sails coming around the curve of the Earth as those ships came home. It was a sight she remembered clearly. It was not a sight she had ever expected to see in Wyoming Territory.

It was not really the horizon that masked the approaching vehicle, but only a gentle slope. As it topped that slope, Goldy saw that the sails were attached to what looked like a stagecoach.

"I seen people try sails on wagons before," said a man who Goldy didn't know, "but I never seen one that could be steered."

Goldy nodded. There was no doubt that whoever was in the wagon was behind the strange cloud. The rainy point of the cloud followed behind the wagon like a loyal hound, jigging with every turn the wagon took.

No matter how entertaining a talent might be, there was always the chance that the person behind it might have more serious motives. Fear drove most of the people from the street as the wagon closed on the town. Goldy stood her ground. If there were some kind of disaster coming, she wanted to see it herself. Across the road the door to the sheriff's office swung open and Jake Bird stepped out onto the wooden walk.

"What do you think, Sheriff?" Goldy called.

Jake shook his head. "Can't say," he replied. "One thing's sure—anyone that can push around a cloud is someone you don't want to tumble with." He looked up at the empty sky above the town. "I've tried moving them myself, and it's a tough row to hoe."

The door to the office opened again and Josie came out along with the scrawny newcomer, Tom Sharp. Josie's presence made Goldy feel easier. Jake might not be quick to jump the bad ones, but Josie would not hesitate to pull a trigger when it was needed. Goldy wasn't quite sure what to think of Tom Sharp. Now that he had a few meals in him, the boy had a pretty face. Not so much handsome, but pretty. He looked too delicate to last long in the West. Josie seemed anxious to keep the boy in town, that much was clear. Why she would do it was clear as mud.

The wagon slowed its approach. As it did, the cloud behind it spread out and lost its clear edges. By the time the wagon settled to a halt in the middle of town, the cloud had become a gray cap over Medicine Rock. Heavy drops of rain began to splash into the dust of the street.

The man at the top of the wagon looked down and gave a nervous gap-toothed smile. "One of you the sheriff?" he asked. There was a peculiar rise and fall to his voice that made Goldy think again about sails and the ocean. It was a long way to big water, but this was a man who knew the sea.

"That'd be me," Jake said. He moved around to stand in front of the wagon. "Is this to be a challenge?"

"No, sir," the wagon driver said. "That ain't how it is. We came here for a place to bed down and some repairs on the wagon, nothing more than that."

"Can you pay?" Josie called from the walk in front of the sheriff's office. She didn't have her shotgun leveled at the man, but it was ready.

"A-yup, that's one thing we can do," the man said. "Scrip or gold, we can pay how you want."

Goldy smiled at that. She needed more gold to lure the whiskey seller from Ogallala, and no matter where money entered Medicine Rock, it was sure to end up at the Kettle Black.

"What is your name?" Josie asked.

The man reached up and removed his battered hat. "Muley," he said. "Muley Owens."

"Who is with you?"

Muley twisted around on his seat and rapped his knuckles against the top of the wagon. "That would be the Rainmaker," he said. Muley knocked louder. "Come out and show yourself," he called.

The door at the side of the wagon opened slowly. From the shadowed interior emerged a pale, lanky form with a striped black coat and a round black hat. He blinked against the light, raising a blanched hand to shade his eyes. From the brim of his hat wisps of snow-white hair escaped.

Josie drew a sudden breath and raised her gun. "The pale man!?"

Jake moved quickly to her side and pressed down on the barrel of the shotgun. "It's not him," he said. "Don't shoot."

For his part, the lanky stranger was frozen by the sight of the woman with her large gun. He stood beside the wagon in the growing rain, one foot inside, one foot in the road. "I didn't do anything," he said in a wavering voice.

Jake nodded. "You heard of a man named Quantrill?"

The man who the driver had called the Rainmaker shook his head. "No."

"Well, he come through here a few years back. Caused a lot of trouble." Jake gestured at the Rainmaker. "He looked a good deal like you."

Goldy had seen how Quantrill treated Jake, and she had heard the story of what he had done to Josie. Considering what had happened, she was surprised that Josie didn't shoot this Rainmaker right off.

"The pale man," Josie said again. Her voice was low and dreamy.

"It's not him," Jake repeated. He pried the shotgun out of his wife's hands. "You killed him yourself, remember?"

Josie nodded slowly. "I remember."

Goldy stepped out into the street. "You the one that's

making this rain?" she asked the white-haired man. Considering the man's moniker, it was a foolish question, but Goldy wanted to make some move before folks got hurt.

The Rainmaker nodded. "It is my talent," he said. "I can raise a sprinkle or a downpour." He finished climbing out of the wagon and stood up straight. "My talent can bring bumper crops in a desert. With me there is no dry season. With me there—"

"Can you make it stop?" Jake asked. "We're getting soaked."

The albino faltered in his spiel. "No. Stopping it's the one thing I can't do."

"Well then," Goldy said. "Why don't we all go inside the Kettle." She started to turn, then hesitated. "You don't bring rain inside, do you?"

"No, ma'am," the Rainmaker said.

Muley climbed down from the wagon. "What's the Kettle?" he asked.

Goldy waved at the door to the Kettle Black. "My saloon."

"That's what I wanted to hear," Muley said. He gave Goldy another smile, revealing a wide space between his front teeth.

Jake was still standing with Josie. "How about it?" he asked. "You want to go inside?"

Josie nodded quickly. "The pale man is dead," she said. "I remember that now."

With that somber pronouncement, the whole assembly adjourned to the Kettle Black.

Muley Owens' words had been good in regards to their payment. He produced a heavy gold brooch in return for his refreshment. It was worth far more than what he asked in return, but Goldy took it. She had not gotten ahead by refusing what bounty she could find.

"We need to replace the mast," Muley was explaining. "That's the pole what holds up the sails. We've patched her as best we can, but it's weak. If we don't get the whole shooting match replaced, it's likely to snap and leave us stranded a hundred miles from the nearest smithy." He took a long draft of whiskey. "We need hardwood. Oak, or maybe ash."

Jake rubbed his chin. "That's a big piece of timber. I'd say that Gravy can probably find some pine for you, but hardwood ..." He shook his head. "There's not much of that around."

The other customers of the Kettle Black got over their nervousness and gathered around the newcomers. Goldy looked on with approval. There was to be no challenge. Better than that, new money was in town, and it was flowing.

"Goldy."

The voice was soft, but it cut through all the noise of the saloon. Goldy looked up and saw Sienna Truth standing at the top of the stair. Her heart fell. She had forgotten all about the girl and her dying brother.

Goldy left Orpah to tend the bar and went to join Sienna at the top of the stairs. "Is it Malcolm?" she said softly.

Sienna nodded. "Yes, but not what you think."

The Indian girl turned and led the way back to the room where Malcolm had lain for his last years. Sienna had lit a small oil lamp which burned on the bedside table, filling the room with weak yellow light.

Goldy looked at the bed and frowned. "Where is he?" she said.

"I do not know," Sienna said. "I went to wet a cloth so I could cool his face. When I came back, this is what I found."

Goldy walked around the empty bed and looked on the other side. She even kneeled down and looked underneath. But there was nothing to find.

Malcolm Truth, who had lain in bed waiting for his death for two long years, was gone.

☆ 8 ☆

Jake Bird was not sure whether he should be happy or frightened. "How long have you known?" he asked.

"Only a month," Josie said. She snuggled up against her husband, bringing her smooth brown shoulder up against his side. "I was not sure until last week."

"A baby," Jake whispered.

It would be their second child. Their first, a little girl named for Jake's friend Hatty, had been born only a year after they were married. She had seemed a robust infant at birth, but two winters later a fever struck the girl. Though compared to most towns in the west, Medicine Rock was growing and prosperous, it had never attracted a doctor. Night and day Josie and Jake took turns holding little Hatty, walking with her, pushing spoonfuls of warmed honey through her tiny lips.

There was nothing that they could do but love the child and pray. They did both as best they knew how.

It had not been enough.

One morning, Jake awoke to find little Hatty cool in his arms. It was his sharpest memory. Her brown eyes had been closed, framed by dark lashes as soft as goose down. Her small round face was frozen in an expression Jake feared he would never understand.

"Do you think it will be all right?" he asked now. His voice was hoarse.

Josie put an arm around his chest and squeezed. "It will be a good baby," she said.

The first light of the impending dawn pearled the windows, casting gray shadows around the bedroom. It was warm under the felt blankets, but Jake shivered. "What if the baby gets sick?"

"And what if it does not?" Josie asked.

Jake closed his eyes, but the still face of Little Hatty was suddenly so clear that his eyes popped open again. "We need to have a doctor in Medicine Rock," he said.

"I thought you would be happy." For the first time, Josie's voice was tinged with sadness.

Guilt stabbed at Jake. For three years since Little Hatty's death, they had tried to have another child. Now it was here and he was acting like it was a curse. "I am happy," he said. He turned over in the bed and brought his lips to Josie's black hair. "I'm just scared, that's all."

Josie stirred restlessly. "Our baby is not even born, and already you are putting it in a grave."

"No," Jake said. "No, I'm sure it'll be fine." But his fear had not shrunk one bit. He could already see the long nights of waiting, the cool, motionless little hands, the terrible small pine coffin.

He wondered if he might ask Goldy to cast the baby's future. Or maybe Sienna Truth could tell him something.

Thinking of Sienna brought Jake around to thinking about Malcolm. The crippled boy had vanished from his room at the Kettle Black, and no one had any idea where he'd gone. But Jake wasn't thinking on that as much as all the illness Malcolm had suffered in his life. There had never been a doctor to look at the boy. A proper doctor might have kept Malcolm's back from twisting. A doctor might have done something for Malcolm's eyes and ears.

A doctor might have saved Little Hatty.

Jake's thoughts were interrupted by a sharp rap at the front door. He groaned and rolled out of bed. The floorboards were cold underfoot as he hurried into his pants. The rap came again before he could manage the long row of buttons.

"Hold on," Jake said. "I'm coming." He pulled suspenders over his bare shoulders and shuffled through the darkened house to the front door. Waiting on the front porch was Tom Sharp.

Tom bobbed his head in greeting. "Goldy thought I ought to come fetch you."

"Well, if Goldy thought you should get me, she's probably right." Jake leaned out into cold predawn air. "Is there time for me to get dressed?"

"I think so," Tom said. "It's something to do with the strangers."

"Muley and the Rainmaker?" Jake shook his head. "I wasn't expecting anything out of those two."

Tom blinked. "Not them," he said. "The new ones."

"What new ones?"

"Three men. They came into town last night."

Jake looked toward the town buildings. "This place is getting too popular," he said. "All right, tell Goldy I'll be there in a minute."

Tom nodded and ran off down the street. Jake stood in the door frame for a moment, watching the man go. There had been some talk around town. Talk about Tom and Josie, and how they were always together. Jake did not lend any credit to such words. Folks in towns as small as Medicine Rock were always looking for something to jaw about. From what Jake had heard, the women seemed to think Tom handsome. Jake couldn't see it.

"Who was it?"

Jake turned and saw Josie standing in the hallway. She'd wrapped herself in the blanket from the bed. With her long hair streaming down over her bare shoulders, she didn't look much like the tough deputy who ran off roughnecks with a double eight.

"It was Tom Sharp," Jake said. "Seems there's some more visitors in town."

"Bad men?"

"No." Jake stopped and shrugged. "At least I don't think so. If they were doing anything wrong, Goldy would have been in a bigger hurry."

Jake went back into the bedroom to find his clothes. Josie followed close behind.

"I want to talk to you about Tom," she said.

"What about him?" Jake asked. Though he did not believe the gossip, he couldn't help but notice his wife's interest in Tom. The attention she paid the little man was beginning to rankle.

"I am pregnant," Josie said. She came around the room and stood close to Jake. "It does not stop me now, but soon it will. Soon I will not be able to be your deputy."

Jake paused. "I don't guess you can," he said.

"You will need help."

"I handled it by myself when you had Little—" Jake swallowed hard. "I handled it before."

"The town has grown since then," Josie said. "There are new families coming all the time. And strangers. You will need help."

Jake saw where his wife was leading. "You want me to hire Tom Sharp to be my deputy."

Josie nodded. "He has the talent of signing. He will make a good deputy."

Jake went back to getting dressed. "I don't know. He's only been in town a couple of weeks, and I've not seen him work any signing."

"You need someone," Josie said. "Who else would it be? The only others in town that have strong talent are Goldy and Sienna, and their talents will not stand a challenge."

"You don't have a talent," Jake said. He finished buttoning his shirt and fetched his hat from the top of the dresser.

"I have you," Josie replied. She let the blanket fall to the ground and laid a cool hand against Jake's face. "The baby will be all right. Make sure that you are."

Jake folded his arms around her and pulled her in tight. Even through his clothes her skin was wonderfully warm. "I'll be fine," he whispered. Then he let her go and grabbed his gun belt off the back of a chair. "But right now I better go see about these newcomers." He gave his wife a kiss and headed out to do his job.

Five minutes at dawn made all the difference in Medicine Rock. The sky, barely touched by light when Tom came to the door, was streaked with blue and purple, red and orange, when

Jake went outside for the second time. A curtain of gold shimmered all along the horizon in the east. To the south the tall peaks were already shining bright as the rising sun glinted from early snows. In another five minutes the colors would be burned away, but while it lasted, dawn in Medicine Rock was hard to beat.

Off in the west a cluster of dark clouds crowded together in one part of the sky. The Rainmaker was out there, bunking at a ranch that had gone unused for years. From the few conversations they had held, Jake developed something of a fondness for the Rainmaker and his gruff companion. But that fondness did not extend to being rained on night and day. Till their wagon was fixed, the Rainmaker stayed out of town.

There were two horses tied up in front of the Kettle Black. Jake paused for a moment and took a look at them. They were good mounts, but their coats were full of burrs. Their saddles and tack were still on. Jake patted a dark mare on the neck and the horse nickered softly. If Tom was right about these men coming in the night, it didn't say much that they would leave their horses tethered till dawn. In Jake's experience, a man who was cruel to a horse was likely to act the same toward men.

Inside the Kettle Black he found Goldy behind the bar. The sharp smell of what passed for coffee in Medicine Rock had, for the moment, overcome the haze of whiskey that generally filled the room. Two strangers sat at the long wooden bar. Jake noted that while the men might have rode in together, they sat with a couple of empty stools in between them. It didn't make them look any too friendly.

The man toward the back was a pudgy, sour-looking character with a bowler hat and a deep-set frown. Even before he opened his mouth, Jake took him for an easterner. The other visitor was just as obviously a man of the West. He wore a battered rawhide jacket, with a faded red bandanna around his neck. His hair was long, and most of his face was hidden behind a stiff blond beard and a curled mustache.

Goldy Cheroot looked up from her place behind the bar. "Here's our sheriff now," she said, waving a gray rag toward the door. "Come on in, Jake, these fellers were wanting to meet you."

Both men turned around on their stools. "Morning," the bearded man said. "Sorry to be putting you out so early." The easterner said nothing.

Jake studied the two men a moment longer. "Tom said three men," he said at last. "Where's the other?"

"Mr. Cullen has gone to make the acquaintance of Black Alice," Goldy said.

"Has he?" Jake stepped up to the bar and took a cup of coffee from Goldy. The smell was bitter, but the cup was warm against his hand. "I'm surprised he found her awake."

"They got their start last night," Goldy said. "Can't say if either of them's awake now or not."

Jake took a sip of the hot coffee. He ignored the easterner for a moment and spoke to the man with the beard. "Those your mounts outside?"

"Theirs," the man said. "But not mine." He nodded toward the back of the bar. "My gray's in the stable, along with the packhorses."

Jake nodded. It said something that this man had taken time to care for his horse. It also said something that he hadn't done for the others. "And who are you?"

Now it was the easterner who spoke first. "Edward Kastle," he said. There was a German accent in the man's voice. Several Dutch or German families lived in Medicine Rock, and it was a tinge that Jake knew well. The man got up from his stool and moved to stand between Jake and the other stranger. He extended a soft hand and Jake shook it quickly.

"Mr. Kastle," Jake said. "And you?"

The bearded man reached past Kastle to grip Jake's hand with a palm rough as a roofing tile. "I'm Bill Cody."

"I heard of you," Goldy said from the other side of the bar.

"So have I," Jake said. He looked hard into Cody's face. "You used to be a buffalo runner."

"Yes."

"You remember coming through Calio about ten, twelve years ago?" Jake asked.

Cody nodded. "Yes," he said. "I was leading a hunt at the time. We damn near got our scalps lifted by the Yankton. Would have, if we hadn't been helped by the sheriff up there."

"That was my father," Jake said.

"I'll be damned." Cody looked Jake up and down. "I can see the resemblance. Your father's a good man."

"He's dead," Jake replied.

"Oh, hell. I'm sorry to hear that."

Kastle cleared his throat. "Your father did a good turn for Mr. Cody," he said. "Maybe now we can do a good turn for you, yes?"

Jake took another long pull of his coffee. It was bitter, and had not one bean of real coffee to it, but it did help clear away sleep. "What kind of good turn?"

Kastle smiled. It was not the least convincing smile that Jake had seen, but it was close. "We represent the Atlantic Pacific Railway Company," he said. "We're considering Medicine Rock as a potential site for a facility."

"A facility," Jake repeated. "And what would that be?"

"He means they want to put a railroad station here," Cody offered.

"There's no railroad out here," Goldy said. She thumped the coffeepot down on the bar and leaned forward. "There's nothing east or west of Medicine Rock for a hundred miles, and we're not worth the track on our own."

Kastle seemed peeved to be brought up short by a woman bartender. "We are not concerned with what lies within a hundred miles," he said. "Our line is to be transcontinental. It will stretch from New York City in the east to San Francisco in the west."

"I thought they gave up on that idea," Jake said.

"The idea has been revived," Kastle said, "and this time we will see it through to completion." He balled his pale fists and pressed them together in front of his chest. "All that is needed are stable communities with strong sheriffs to act as linchpins to this great enterprise."

The man's words brought such a powerful excitement that

Jake had to fight hard not to show it. "You're going to run this line through Medicine Rock?" he asked.

"That remains to be seen," Kastle said. "The line may run through here, or it may run through Tempest. Medicine Rock would suit our needs best, but we would require certain assurances."

"What is it you want?"

Kastle held up one thick finger. "First, your agreement that you would help protect the rail line and other facilities in your area from attack by vandals and saboteurs."

Jake had only a vague idea of what a saboteur was, but he understood well enough what Kastle wanted. "All right."

Kastle raised another finger. "Second, you must agree to aid in pursuit of any criminal seeking to use the rail line as a means of escape."

That one seemed straightforward enough. "What else?"

A third finger rose. "You must—"

Before Kastle could lay out his third condition, the door at the top of the stairs swung back and banged against the wall. A rawboned man with red cheeks and equally red hair appeared. "Morning to you all," he called.

"Good morning, Mr. Cullen," Goldy called in reply. She smiled, baring her gold tooth.

Cullen came down the steps two at a time. "Ah, but that's a fine girl you've got upstairs."

Jake stood up. "I'm Sheriff Jake Bird," he said.

"Are you now?" Cullen said. He had eyes of a bright, midday blue. "Well then, I'm proud to know you." He stuck out a huge bony hand. "Sean Cullen."

"Mr. Cullen," Jake said as his fingers were enveloped in Cullen's tight grip. "I'm glad to see you're enjoying our town." Though Cullen's demeanor was friendly, there was a rim of ice in those blue eyes. Jake had no doubt about the man's position in the trio. Cody was the old western hand and Kastle the head office man. Cullen was the gunman.

Cullen dropped Jake's hand and went to sit on the other side of Cody. From Cody's expression, it didn't seem that the closeness was any too welcome. The scout got to his feet.

"Excuse me," Cody said. "I think I'll go check on my horse."

"Hold on a minute, if you would, Mr. Cody," Jake said. "Let's finish our talk."

Cody nodded and dropped back into his seat. He didn't so much as look at his partners.

Goldy put a cup in front of Cullen and started to pour coffee, but the Irishman waved her off. "Only some whiskey, darling. That's what keeps me moving." Goldy brought out a bottle and put it in front of him.

"Will you accept our offer, Sheriff?" Kastle asked.

Jake looked around at the railroad man. "What was that third condition?"

"Ah," Kastle said. "Only that you agree to the placement of such railway agents in your town as are needed to protect our property."

"I protect my town," Jake said. "Why look for strong sheriffs if you're going to use your own hands?"

"Additional protection," Kastle said simply.

Jake looked across the bar at Goldy. Through the years, he had learned that Goldy was as good a judge of deals as any in town. "What do you think?" he asked.

Goldy shrugged. "Let's hear what's in the bag for us."

Kastle gave another of his thin smiles. "The primary benefit is the rail line itself. This will ensure a steady link to both coasts with attendant financial opportunities. Among other things, it should assure the ready exchange of scrip from all major institutions."

The scrip problem was a gnawing at the heart of Medicine Rock. If the railroad lifted that cloud, that alone would be worth a good deal of trouble.

"What else?" Jake asked.

"Oh, a telegraph line will accompany the rail," Kastle said. "Very likely a goodly number of new residents will also arrive, encouraged, as always, by the thoughts of western opportunities. It's possible the railway itself may want to establish various businesses here, to help maintain valued stability."

It was too much for Jake to take in. A rail line and a telegraph. For longer than he'd been in town, Medicine Rock had
survived cut off from doings in the East. Now they would be
connected to those grand cities, and the chaos that went with
them. Such a change would be so great that he couldn't begin
to think it through.

"We should do it," Goldy said suddenly.

Jake blinked. "You think so?"

Goldy nodded. "We don't take it, they'll go on to Tempest.
How do you think Medicine Rock will fare if the line runs
through there?"

It was a position Jake had not considered. He was on the
point of nodding when he noticed Bill Cody tipping some of
Cullen's whiskey into his coffee cup. "What about you, Mr.
Cody?"

Cody looked around in surprise. "What?"

"What's your thought on the matter?" Jake said. "Should
we take Mr. Kastle and his railroad up on their offer, or should
we not?"

"I'd say take their offer," Cody said quickly. "It's not my
town, but that's what I'd suggest."

"Thanks," Jake said. Bill Cody's words seemed positive
enough, but there was something in his tone that suggested
other than complete confidence in the company paying his
meals. Jake didn't know Cody, but he knew of him. From the
way the old scout reacted to these railroad men, it was clear
there was something badly off track. That gave Jake something else to think about.

Even with Goldy pushing for the deal, Jake figured he
would say no. If everything that Kastle said was true and he
said no, then Tempest would become the center of the area.
People would leave Medicine Rock in droves, and not a few of
them would blame him for any financial mischances caused
by the change in fortunes. But Kastle might be lying. There
were worse things than losing money. Saying no was the
safest thing for the town.

Then another thought whispered at the back of Jake's mind.

It was not a new thought. It was a thought that had echoed on a thousand cold nights and bitter winter mornings.

"A doctor," Jake said.

"What's that?" Kastle said.

Jake moved to stand near the pudgy easterner. "I want a doctor to come and live in Medicine Rock. A good doctor, mind you, not some used-up surgeon from the war."

Kastle shook his head. "I'm afraid that is not a guarantee I can make, Sheriff Bird," he said. "I am authorized only to offer those specifics I have already mentioned."

"You give me a doctor," Jake said, "and you can run your rail line through Medicine Rock. You give me a doctor, and I'll help you any way I can."

The request seemed to have rattled Kastle. "I'm not authorized to expand the deal in this manner."

"Who is?"

"Only Mr. Gould himself."

"Well, then," Jake said, "let's go talk to him."

"No and hell no," Muley said. He gave the length of wood a kick with the toe of his heavy boot. "Look at the knots in that trunk. First hard wind comes up, we'd have ourselves a mast in three pieces."

Gravy Hodges spat between the twin wings of his mustache. "We got cottonwood and we got cedar. Both of them got knots. If you know a way to make it different, I wish you'd tell me about it 'cause I'm tired of sawing them."

Muley chewed on his lower lip and looked around the lumber barn. There was enough plank and beam here to build a small house, but it was not what he needed. This wood was suited to repairing some of the damage to the wagon, and one of the cedar beams might serve to replace the fractured boom, but there was nothing near the length and toughness needed for a solid mast. Though he didn't particularly like it, Muley was going to have to make some changes to the wagon.

"Maybe your smithy can help us," he said.

"Morgan?" Gravy shook his head. "There's no wood at his shop but what's to be burned for charcoal."

"I ain't after his char wood," Muley said. "I want him to make me a collar and some cleats, then we'll see if we can make a mast in two pieces."

"Can you do that?"

"A-yup, so long as you do it real careful like."

Gravy pushed his hat back from his forehead and scratched at his scalp. "Morgan's gone to the south ranches today. I know 'cause I'm to come help him with some wagon work tomorrow. More regular wagons, not your sort." He looked over his shoulder at where the Rainmaker's unique vehicle rested in the shadows. "Day after sound all right?"

"Suits me," Muley said. "If that's as fast as you can get to it."

"All right," Gravy said. "Now I better go to work." He gave Muley a nod, then walked out of the barn.

Muley sat down on an overturned bucket and leaned back against the rough wood of the wall. The lumber barn had once been a stable, and there was still the faint hint of horse manure in the air. It seemed a solid structure, and the house attached to the far end looked better than many in town. But for reasons Muley did not quite grasp, the house had been abandoned. With all the stalls knocked out, the old stable made a fine if somewhat gloomy place for storage. Muley found it quite agreeable.

Truth was, Muley was in no particular hurry to finish his repairs. The Rainmaker had been put up at the edge of town, but except for the isolation, he was being treated fine as punch. The old stables were dry, quiet, and tight enough to keep out the wind. There was warm food to be had without cooking it yourself, and whiskey enough to drown. It was the closest Muley had come to contentment since he left the sea.

The door at the end of the stables squeaked open. Muley looked up to see a man with a full yellow beard and luxuriant mustache step out of blazing sunlight into the gloom of the barn.

"You needing some boards?" Muley asked.

The man took an unsteady step, blinking in the dim light. "No," he said. "Not really." He blinked a few more times and seemed to find his bearing. "I just came over to get a look at this vehicle of yours."

"The wagon?"

"That woman at the saloon says you blew in on a windstorm," the man said. "I wanted to see this wagon for myself."

"Well, she's right over there," Muley said. "You're welcome to take a look, though with the mast broke, she don't look like much."

The bearded man walked around the stacked lengths of

wood to the side of the wagon. Muley had already taken down the makeshift bracing that had held up the broken mast. Without it, only the three-foot stump of the mast and the rows of cleats along the top made the wagon look any different from a thousand stagecoaches in the West.

The man ran his hand along the flanks of the vehicle. "Looks like you started out with a Concord coach."

Muley stood up and went over to join him. "A-yup. This one left New Hampshire in 1855, and the Rainmaker bought it two years back. Then I got my hands on it. They's hardly a plank left from where I started, but most of the design's still there." He pointed at the broken mast. "Generally, we got a thirty-four-foot mast coming right up there. And the boom, of course. That's missing as well."

The man gave a laugh. "I heard people call old Conastogas 'Prairie Schooners,' but I reckon you've got yourself the real thing."

"Well, she couldn't be rightly called a schooner," Muley said.

"Why not?"

"A schooner's got herself two masts, you see." Muley pointed to the back of the wagon. "I thought about rigging her that way when we was starting out, but there wasn't enough space. No, we're more like a sloop; what they call a Marconi rig. Used to be rigged more like a cutter, but now it's a sloop. Though there's not a thing about this rig that's just like what you'd find on any ship."

"How many sails are there in this Macaroni rig?" the bearded man asked.

"Two. We got the mainsail, which is cut bigger in the luff than what you'd see in the water, and the jib sail, which is huge as hell. More like a balloon jib."

"Balloon," the man repeated.

"A-yup." Muley grinned. He found he was enjoying this discussion quite a bit. The wagon attracted attention in every town they pulled up to, but once the door was open, it was the Rainmaker that took all the talk. It was a rare day when Muley had to field even one question about the wagon itself.

"Take a look in here," Muley said. He reached past the man and opened the door at the side of the wagon. "Here's the base of the mast, you see?"

"It goes all the way to the floor." The man stuck his head inside the wagon and looked around. "Must get in the way."

"It does," Muley agreed. "But if we ended the mast at the roof, it would have blown off right away. And just running it in here ain't enough." He bent and knocked against the floor of the wagon. "There was three benches in here when the factory finished. The center one's gone to make room for the mast. What's left can be flipped up to give more room. And look down here." Muley knelt and pointed under the belly of the coach. "There's metal blocks set aft of the base. Helps give us some ballast and braces the mast."

The man considered this for a moment, running his fingers along the turned up end of his mustache. "Why the bracing on just one side?"

" 'Cause we're always running before the wind, you see," Muley said. "All the force is delivered from one direction. That's why the jib sail's so big, as well. We're always going wing and wing, with the wind right behind us."

"I suppose there's many a sailor that would like to have that luxury."

Muley didn't bother to correct the man on the difference between a sailor and a seaman. "It might be a luxury for them, but it's a necessity out here." Muley kicked his toe lightly against the bottom of the wagon. "One thing you won't find under there is a daggerboard. You can't put a rudder in the ground. I got a stick up front that lets me put a lean on the front wheels. When you go to turn, you work the wheels along with the boom, you see? That way you can make her come around sharp enough to stay out of trees and such."

The bearded man nodded again, but it was clear that his enthusiasm for the talk was wearing thin. "Well, sir, she's quite a work," he said. "I thank you for showing her to me."

Muley was proud enough to pop. He could see this man didn't know a lot about ships, but he seemed to be interested, and that was enough for Muley. Designing a wagon to sail grass, sand, hills, and even over rocky passes had not been a trivial job. "Come and see her when the new mast is on and the sails have been raised," he said. "That'll be a sight worth seeing."

The other fellow stuck out his hand. "If I'm still about, I'll do just that."

Muley pumped the man's hand vigorously. "I hope you can see it. My name's Muley Owens, by the way."

"Bill Cody," the man said.

Muley froze. "Bill Cody?" He looked the bearded man up and down. "You're the one, ain't you?"

Cody's reaction was one of embarrassment. He glanced at the corners of the barn, as if expecting to see others listening in. "What one is that?"

Instead of answering, Muley climbed into the wagon and fished around in the space behind the back bench. He came out with two thin, ragged books in his hands. "These here are about you, ain't they?"

Cody took the books and shifted them from hand to hand. "I've not seen one of these in some time. You read them?"

"I've looked at them, but I've not read them through," Muley admitted. "The Rainmaker, though, he's the one that's near enough read them to death."

"The man that moves the storms?"

"The very one. He's got other books about you besides these two. I think he may have them with him."

"I'm glad they pleased him," Cody said. A faint smile appeared in the gap between beard and mustache. "I'd not want a fellow that could drum up a tempest being mad at me."

Muley hooked his thumbs in the belt loops of his wool pants. "You ought to come out to the ranch, stay to supper with us. I know the Rainmaker'd be damned pleased to meet you."

"Thanks," Cody said. "But I think maybe it's best I don't go."

"Go where?" said a voice from the door.

Muley turned 'round to see a pudgy man with eastern

clothes and a round black hat standing near the entrance to the barn. "Who are you?"

"I am Edward Kastle of the Atlantic Pacific Railway," the heavyset man said. "More importantly, I am Mr. Cody's current supervisor. It is up to me to say where he goes and where he doesn't go."

"He just asked me over for beans," Cody said. "It's not like we're going to Carson City." There was a coldness in his tone that hadn't been there a moment before.

"Really?" The man's gray eyes seemed as distant as the moon. "Quite a friendly gesture."

"And no business of yours," Cody said.

The pudgy man came closer. He was several inches shorter than Cody and looked to have all the strength of a wet newspaper, but he showed no fear of the bigger man. "You are an employee of the railroad, Mr. Cody. Everything you do is my business."

"Seems to me I was employed to guide you to this town," Cody said. He took a step forward, standing so close to Kastle that his beard was within an inch of the shorter man's nose. "Till you need guiding elsewhere, I figure my time is my own."

Kastle stood stock-still for a moment. Then he opened his mouth and hissed like a boiling steam kettle. The sound unnerved Muley so much that he took a quick step away from the two men and nearly tripped over a stack of rough lumber. He half expected Kastle to go into a fit of signing or even chattering, but the smaller man displayed no talent. Instead he raised his hand and jabbed a stiff finger into Cody's chest.

"Don't test me, William Cody," Kastle said in a voice that put Muley in mind of the worst captain he'd sailed with. "You know what I can do."

Cody caught the man's wrist and pushed his hand aside. "I know what you can do," he said. "Just don't expect me to help you with doing it." Cody turned, made a sharp nod to Muley, and stalked out of the barn.

Kastle reached into his striped vest and pulled out what appeared to be an oversized pocket watch. Muley leaned forward, trying to get a good look at the device, but Kastle abruptly shoved it back into his vest.

"Ignorant tramp," Kastle muttered. With that he stomped out the same door Cody had taken.

Muley stood and stared at the open door. From what he'd seen before in the West, a man that was insulted as bad as Cody was likely to air out the person dishing the insults. That Cody had not even delivered a fist in response to such treatment was remarkable behavior. Muley looked down at the books in his hands. He'd read more of the books than he let on to Cody. It seemed to Muley that the Buffalo Bill in the books would never have put up with the kind of behavior the real Bill had sat through. Muley put the books down on a pile of boards and went back to work.

The hard trip down the flooded wash had done considerable damage to the wagon. Three of the boards that made up the bottom of the coach were broken, two of them bad enough that there was no choice but to pull them free and replace them from end to end. It would have to be done well. Those were the boards that took the brunt of the force from the mast and held the metal sole plate in place. Gravy Hodges had loaned Muley a good chest of tools—for a moderate cost. Muley got out the hammer and set to work. It took the best part of the afternoon to replace the two splintered boards and brace the third.

There were other boards that needed to be worked on, notably two along the side of the wagon just below the door. But those boards crossed Muley's painted sign. He was in no mind to start tearing up his sign till he'd made sure there was paint around to fix it when he was done. Besides, he had another day to work while he was waiting on Gravy and the blacksmith to help with the new mast.

Muley put up the tools and shut the door on the lumber barn. The sun was getting low in the west. Given a few more minutes, it would drop behind the gray clouds that marked the Rainmaker's residence. Muley started walking toward the ranch, flipping his collar up to keep out the rain that he was bound to encounter along the way.

He looked back a few times, wondering if he might see Cody coming along behind, but there was no sign of the man. It seemed to Muley that the real Buffalo Bill was a far cry from the hero in the novels.

☆ 10 ☆

"That feels right," Jake said. "Now, try moving the other hand up like you did before."

Tom Sharp nodded. There were beads of sweat on Tom's red skin and his hand shook as he slowly raised it. Instantly, there was a ripple in the air. A blur of green and blue shimmered around Tom's arms. From somewhere a deep rumbling noise sounded, like boulders stirring far inside the earth.

"I got it," Tom said.

"You sure?"

Tom licked his lips and nodded. "Yeah. Do it quick."

Jake raised his revolver, aimed it square at Tom, thumbed back the hammer and fired.

The heavy pistol boomed. Tom Sharp staggered, took a step back, and fell facedown on the ground.

"Oh, God," Jake croaked. The revolver dropped from his fingers and bounced on the hard ground. He dashed across the yard and threw himself down beside the fallen man. "Tom? Can you hear me?" He got his hands under Tom's chest and carefully rolled him over. There was a fearful pallor on the small man's lean features.

Then a shudder shook Tom from head to toe. He opened his eyes, coughed once, and gave a thin smile. "I'm not dead."

Jake almost laughed at the surprise in Tom's voice. "Well I would hope not," he said. "I was aiming at your shoulder. I might be a pretty poor shot, but not from twenty feet."

"But I stopped it, didn't I?" Tom asked.

Jake inspected the front of Tom's worn shirt. There were enough holes in the garment that a new one might not have

95

been noticed. But there was no blood. A slug taken in the shoulder might not be enough to kill, but it was sure to be a bloody affair.

A gleam in the dust a few feet away caught Jake's attention. He reached out and found a cone of lead. It was only slightly marred by its trip down the barrel of the gun. Jake rolled the bullet between his fingers for a moment then held it up where Tom could see.

"You stopped it," Jake said.

Tom smiled. "Told you."

With Jake's help, Tom sat. Jake stood up, reached down and pulled the smaller man to his feet.

"You made it past the hardest test," Jake said. "A sheriff that can take a bullet and not be hurt will earn a lot of respect. One that can't stop a slug by talent is likely to stop it with something else—like his head."

Tom swayed on his feet, sweat rolling down his smooth cheeks. "It didn't really hurt," he said, "but I sure felt something. It was like a wind pressing at me from all sides."

Jake nodded. Though his talent was not the same as Tom's, the feeling that Tom described was familiar. "That's the bullet. When you stop one, it's like you take that spot where it's about to hit and spread it all over."

"Sure feels strange." Tom ran a hand over his undented chest and gave a nervous laugh.

"I can't say it feels good," Jake said, "but it would sure feel worse if you didn't stop it."

"Yeah, I suppose it would at that."

"Come on," Jake said. "Let's go over to the Kettle Black. There's a tradition that new deputies enjoy a drink on the town."

Tom grinned. "That's a tradition I don't mind keeping."

Jake smiled back as he led the way around the sheriff's office, but he was not as happy with Tom's performance as he might have been. True, Tom had used talent to stop a bullet in flight. It was a stunt that amazed Jake the first time he'd seen it, and it still gave him a thrill—even when he was the one doing it. It was also an essential part of a sheriff's bag of tricks. Though even the most talented sheriff could catch an unexpected bullet in the guts, knowing how to fend off flying lead said more clearly than any boast that this was a man not to be trifled with.

The problem with Tom's stopping had been the aftereffects. He'd stopped the slug, but had also been dropped to the ground. Without Jake's help, he might be lying there still. When it came time for a real challenge, Jake doubted that the opponent would stop to lend a hand. More likely he'd slice Tom in two while he was lying in the dirt.

They'd have to try it again later and hope Tom took the shock better with experience.

It was getting along in the afternoon, but already the Kettle Black was doing better business than it generally did at night. There were folks like undertaker Adrian Merk, who spent nine days out of ten against the bar, and those like Panny Wadkins, who were to be found in the saloon ten days out of ten. There were also a good number of newcomers. Goldy was parked behind the bar, filling glasses as fast as she could. Sienna Truth walked around the room taking a rag to tables and picking up the empties. Every now and then the door upstairs would open and a man would stumble down. There was never a long delay before another headed up.

The sight of the full bar was probably pleasing to Goldy, but it was another worry gnawing on Jake. With the abrupt increase in population over the last few months, there were a lot more people in town than jobs for them to do. Medicine Rock lacked any big industry that could employ a large number of men. There was no manufacturing outside of a little furniture making, and all that was aimed at folks in town. Medicine Rock's position along the banks of the North Platte gave room for several large farms, and the hills to the north put out a little brown coal. But there was no gold—as even Panny would likely agree.

There was more land out there. Some of the newcomers could probably be encouraged to try their hand at the plow. But there were others who had never worked a farm and weren't about to start. Some of those might find that Medicine

Rock had grown enough to support another business—a second smithy, maybe, or a new grain mill. Most would not.

Those were the ones who worried Jake. Right now they seemed content to sit in the Kettle Black and drink away the remains of their money. Soon enough they would start to grumble. Then there would be little choice but to move them on to someplace else. It was not a chore Jake was looking forward to.

With all the folks in the saloon, there was not a lot of choice in places to sit. Tom picked out a lopsided table in one corner of the room. There was already one man at the table, but he was facedown next to his whiskey glass. From the way he was snoring, Jake didn't expect the man would protest sharing his table.

Tom hooked his chair, turned it around, and sat with his arms across the back. "That was something," he said. "I can't believe I let you talk me into it."

"It was a test we had to make," Jake said.

"Did the sheriff you worked for make you do it when you were a deputy?"

Jake shook his head. "No. When I was a deputy, I didn't know I had any talents."

"So you were a deputy without talents, like Mrs. Bird?"

"I don't know if you'd say I was like Josie," Jake said. "Sheriff Pridy did most of the fighting. He just had me around to back him up."

"So when did you get tested with a bullet?" Tom asked.

"The first person that fired at me meant to kill me," Jake replied, "and it was only luck he didn't do it."

Goldy came over to the table with a bottle of whiskey in one hand and two glasses in the other. Goldy had seemed an old, tired woman the first time Jake met her. Her hair had already gone the color of dust, and the hard western sun had bleached her brown eyes till they were the pale tan of peanut shells. But though five years had passed since Jake came to Medicine Rock, Goldy seemed no older. In fact, she looked better. She seemed to have reached a comfortable age and stuck there.

Goldy sat one glass in front of Tom and another in front of Jake. "You boys look thirsty," she said.

"Give me the ticket for this one," Jake said. He nodded toward Tom. "Deputy Sharp here stopped a bullet with his signing this morning."

Goldy raised one eyebrow. "So it's Deputy Sharp now, is it?" She thumped the bottle down on the table. "Here. You take this one on me. I'll not have it said I was stingy toward a new lawman."

"Thanks, ma'am," Tom said. He tipped the whiskey bottle and filled his glass with the yellow-tinged liquid.

Jake took the bottle from Tom's hand and looked at it. There was a label promising Kentucky bourbon whiskey, but the label was faded out from long use. Whatever was inside, Jake suspected it had never been near the Bluegrass state. "What'd you make this one out of, Goldy?"

Goldy snorted. "Don't think I had anything to do with this rotgut. Talk to those what sell it to me."

"It's been a long time since I tried to stop anybody from cooking their own corn," Jake said. "Maybe it's time we started encouraging them." He poured a finger of whiskey into his own glass and took a sip. The mixture tasted something like black pepper and lamp oil. He coughed and cast a sour glance at the mislabeled bottle. "I don't believe it would be any worse than this benzine we're getting now."

Goldy looked thoughtful. "I put some considering into it before," she said, "but as long as we were getting it from Ogallala, I didn't want to fiddle with my own mash." She raised a finger and tapped her cheek below her right eye. "I might not see so well, but I'm in no hurry to burn my eyes out with rotten busthead."

"You might ask around," Jake suggested. "One of the folks that came down from Wright City might know something about the subject." He stopped for a moment and looked at the room. "If some of these new folks decide to farm, we might get quite an operation going. We might even end up selling our own whiskey to other towns."

Goldy nodded. "I'll ask," she said, "But don't be getting

your hopes up. You're going to have to move these folks along before the month is out."

Jake winced. "It's worth looking at." Goldy gave him a tight smile and went back to the bar.

"You really going to make these folks leave?" Tom asked.

"Yes," Jake said. "And you'll be helping me do it. We have to get them on their way before winter settles in."

Tom took another swallow of whiskey. "It seems like a sad chore."

"It's just something that has to be done." Jake caught sight of Muley Owens at the bar. He hadn't talked to the man in several days, but he'd heard from Gravy that the sailing wagon was fixed. Soon enough Muley and the Rainmaker would be leaving. Jake reminded himself that he needed to get the Rainmaker down to the south ranches before the sail wagon left town. It was a bit dry down there, and the farmers might be willing to pay for a day or two of rain.

"Maybe when the railroad people come back they can help us out," Tom said.

"Help us out with what?" Jake asked.

"With the extra folks. They talked about having some people of their own in town." Tom shrugged. "Maybe they'll hire some of the newcomers."

It was a point to consider. The three railway agents had ridden off to visit Tempest and the near-abandoned town of Laramie. Though Jake was fairly confident they would choose to come through Medicine Rock, he was still a bit nervous about their trip on two accounts. First off, the railroad represented his only real chance of attracting a doctor to Medicine Rock. The idea that they might yet decide to run their line elsewhere was like a cold finger in his gut. Then there was the other half of the bargain. Jake knew if he wanted his doctor, he was going to have to leave Medicine Rock to argue his case.

". . . your talent?" Tom said.

Jake shook his head. "Sorry, what's that?"

"I was just asking how old you were when you found out about your talent?"

"Near as old as I am now," Jake said. "I didn't know a thing about it till a few years back."

"You've come a long way in a hurry," Tom said. "I've known I could do the signing almost since the war, but I've not done much with it." He held up his hand, opening and closing his fingers in front of his face. "Wish I'd worked on it more."

Jake hadn't asked Tom his age, but he reckoned Tom to be in his middle twenties, like him. Tom had mentioned that he spent most of his life in the great open city of New York, working a job for a boiler factory. On his own ground Tom Sharp was probably a competent man. In Medicine Rock he was a tenderfoot.

"Tell me something about New York City," Jake said.

"Like what?"

Jake sipped at the awful whiskey. "Like something that'll help me stay out of trouble with the local sheriffs if I go there."

Tom's brown eyes opened wide. "You going to New York City?"

"Maybe," Jake said. "I may have to if we want to get a good deal from the railroad."

"That'll be quite a trip," Tom said. He looked down at the floor. "Wish I could go with you."

Jake looked at Tom over the rim of his whiskey glass. "What caused you to leave?"

"I'd rather not talk about that," Tom said quickly. "Anyway, if you go to the city, you ought to know that there aren't any sheriffs. They've got these things they call protection societies. Lots of folks get together and pay for those with talent and guns to watch out for their area."

"I suppose where you've got more people you need something different," Jake said. Just the thought of trying to sheriff for a million people set his mind to reeling. "These protective societies sound like a decent idea."

Tom nodded. "They are, if you've got the money to pay for it. The biggest societies have whole armies of talented folks, and an army's worth of guns besides. If you can't pay . . ." He shrugged. "You can't pay and bad things are likely to happen to you."

It was good information to have, but Jake didn't expect much of it would apply to him. These railroad people were sure to have the best protection anyone could buy. "It's rolling on toward suppertime," he said. "I'm going home to Josie. You think you'll be up to stopping another shot in the morning?"

"I have to do it again?" Tom swallowed hard. "I thought we were over that."

"We've got to get you to the point where it comes natural," Jake said.

Tom drained the rest of his whiskey in one long gulp. "If it gets to where being shot at is natural, I believe I'm leaving town."

Sunset came and passed in Medicine Rock even faster than dawn. By the time Jake left the saloon and got to his own house, the sky was already a deep bruised purple and the first stars were peeking through.

Josie sat at the kitchen table reading a book by the light of a beeswax candle. The burning candle lent a sweet, heavy scent to the house that almost covered the odors of cooked beans and ham.

"Tom must still be alive," Josie said without looking up. "You would have come sooner if you had killed him."

"He lived," Jake said. He pulled out a chair and sat down across from his wife. "But he's not ready to hold the town."

Josie glanced at Jake. "What does this mean?"

"It means I don't think I can go off and leave Tom in charge. He's not ready to hold the town."

"I thought you were the one who said our child must have a doctor," Josie replied.

"Yes," Jake said, "but I can't go get him now. Not with you—" He searched for the right word. "—you know, delicate."

Josie laughed. "I have never been delicate," she said. She closed her book and propped her elbows on the table. "You should go now, before I am too huge to help take care of things."

Jake frowned. Ever since the war, towns had revolved around sheriffs. He had never heard of a sheriff going far out of town—not if he ever expected to come back. "Tom Sharp's not enough to hold this town. Not even if you help him."

Josie smiled. In the candlelight, her brown skin seemed to glow. For a moment it appeared that some of the fire was inside her dark eyes. "You do not have to depend on just Tom, or even me and Tom. There are others here that will fight."

"Who? Goldy and Sienna?" Jake shook his head. "Their talents aren't the fighting kind."

"You do not need talent to fight." Josie got up from her seat and came around the table. She put her arms around Jake's shoulder and lowered her head until her cheek was against his. "The people here trust you," she whispered. "If you promise to come back, they will believe you. If you ask them to help while you are gone, they will help. Because you ask."

"You think so?" Jake asked.

"Yes." Josie took his hand and gently pulled him from his chair. "Now come with me. I want to use the bed for more than sleeping while you are still here."

"But—But you're pregnant," Jake stammered.

Josie laughed. "I am not that pregnant," she said.

☆ 11 ☆

Muley held up one hand to shield his eyes from the rain. He'd enjoyed a week of working in the dry barn, but all it had done was remind him how much he hated to be wet. "The topmast goes right into the lower mast," he called. "Lower her down."

"Here it comes." Gravy Hodges let the rope slip between his hands, and the twenty-foot length of red cedar moved slowly down from the pulley set on the roof of the barn.

Muley positioned the smoothly turned wood carefully and guided it into place. The projection at the base of the topmast slid down into the recess cut at the top of the lower mast. With a solid thunk the two pieces of wood came together. Then Muley clamped a hinged collar around the joint and closed it with a linchpin. He shook the topmast. It didn't sway so much as an inch.

"There you are," Muley declared. "A mast in two pieces."

Gravy came around the wagon and stood looking up into the rain. "It's clean work," he said. "I don't think you could get better in Kansas City."

"Hell, you done most of it," Muley said. Despite the rain, he smiled. This new mast was damn fine work. It was better mast-making than anyone had a right to expect when the nearest ocean was two thousand miles away.

The wide door at the end of the barn swung open and the Rainmaker strolled out carrying an umbrella to guard against his own inclement weather. Though he was the cause of the wet, the Rainmaker had chosen to stay inside while the job was being finished. He tipped the umbrella back and took a quick glance upward. "Is that all?" he asked.

"What?"

"Don't you have another part?" the Rainmaker said. "What you've got here doesn't seem as tall as the old mast."

"It's not," Muley said. "The old one was a thirty-four. This one is just shy of thirty. I took some off the foot of the sails to make up the difference."

"But with shorter sails, won't we go slower?" the Rainmaker asked.

"It may be a hair slower," Muley said around a frown. He had worked hard to find an answer to their problems. He'd sawed and sweated and hammered. Gravy had put in considerable work to lathe the mast down smooth. Now the Rainmaker, who'd done nothing all week but sit in his ranch and eat the food that Muley brought to him, had picked out the one particular about the new mast that wasn't first-rate. It nettled Muley no end.

The Rainmaker walked around the wagon. "I don't like the idea of going slower," he said. "Going slower means I have to keep the wind up longer, or raise it higher. Either way it's more work for me."

"Well, hell, we wouldn't want you doing any work, would we?" Muley wiped the rain away from his face. "You don't want to keep the wind blowing, then buy horses."

It was a sore point with the Rainmaker. The wagon moved on wind, and on wind alone. To hitch horses to it would be to admit that he wasn't up to the task. Of course, Muley didn't much care for the idea of horses, either. The stage was pulled by a team of six before Muley fixed it with sails, but there had been a lot of changes made. Nothing was left on the wagon to hitch horses to. Besides, Muley had no idea of how to drive horses, and when they were running ahead of a strong wind, the poor beasts would be hard pressed just to keep up. No, Muley wasn't really interested in horses. But it was an idea sure to irritate the Rainmaker. That alone made Muley bring it up often.

"Can you add to the mast?" the Rainmaker asked. "Could you put another section above what you've got?"

Muley shook his head. "A topgallant would take us another week to design, and then we'd need to make the sheets bigger to match. Besides, the balance of the whole wagon would be all off. I'd be ciphering numbers from now to the Fourth of July."

"So we're stuck with this."

"A-yup," Muley said. "Though I don't much like the sound of stuck. We've done good work here."

"But we're going to be slower," the Rainmaker said.

"Maybe," Muley said. "Maybe not. I put another strip at the top of the balloon jib to get it some more play in the head. And I changed the way the reef lines cut the sail. And the wheels are smoothed up. Could be we'll turn out faster." He shrugged. "Won't know till we're riding the wind."

"And when, exactly, will that be?"

There was some reason for the irritation in the Rainmaker's voice. The citizens of Medicine Rock, along with the farmers living nearby, had grown solemnly tired of wet weather. They were even more tired of paying the Rainmaker to bring it. No more income was coming from the farmers, but every day they spent in Medicine Rock was costing them room and board. It was the sort of formula that always put ants in the Rainmaker's pants.

"It'll take me the rest of today to rig her and see that everything's working," Muley said. "We can blow out of here tomorrow."

The Rainmaker nodded. "Good. Now if you don't mind, I'll return to the ranch."

"I don't mind," Muley said. "Fact, I'd damn near insist. I'd rather not drown while I'm hanging the sheets."

The Rainmaker turned without another word and trudged off. Mud splashed up around his feet and spattered on the legs of his dark suit.

"Will it stop raining now?" Gravy asked.

"A-yup," Muley said. "Leastwise it will once he's a ways off. When he ain't working to make it bigger, that cloud follows him pretty tight."

"Don't that beat all." Gravy wiped his hands on his pants

leg and glanced up at the sky. "Well, I got a roof to mend. You think you'll be needing anything else?"

"No." Muley shook Gravy's hard callused hand. "Thanks for your help."

With Gravy gone, Muley took the sails out of the wagon and unfolded them on the ground. Doing so got mud on the heavy yellowed cloth, but they'd be clean again as soon as the Rainmaker came around. Muley admired the stitching on the sails. He'd done some of it himself, even though his fingers were stiff, but the Indian girl that worked for Miss Goldy—Sara? Sally? He couldn't rightly remember—had done the bulk of the work. The girl had a fine tight stitch. The strips of cloth that made up the jib sail were fit together so well that not a hint of breeze could escape. Maybe they really would be faster.

It took Muley only an hour to thread the ropes through the pulleys and raise both the main and jib. Then he lowered them, using the new reefing lines to tighten the sails snug against the boom. It was done with at least two hours of daylight to spare.

Muley had known it would be. But if he'd told the Rainmaker the straight truth about the amount of time the rigging would take, the Rainmaker would surely have insisted on leaving Medicine Rock that afternoon. Muley wanted one more night of clean sheets and hot grub before they struck out for God knew where. Besides, he had another errand to run.

He left the sail wagon out back of the lumber barn and went through the narrow space between buildings to the main street of Medicine Rock. A block down he pushed through the swinging doors of the Kettle Black Saloon.

Muley had spent some time in the Kettle Black every day since they rolled into town. The whiskey was bad, though it was better than what could be had from the bootleggers who supplied nonbelievers down in Mormon Deseret. But talk was plentiful. Muley had lent an ear to the old prospector, Panny Wadkins, listening to the man spin the story of thirty years spent in the Black Hills and surrounding region. Merk, the undertaker, had filled Muley in on some of the history of Medicine Rock and of how Sheriff Jake Bird had come to be running things. Muley had talked to Gravy, and a wet-behind-the-ears ranch hand called Dewlick, and a liberal-minded Methodist preacher, and even Sheriff Bird himself.

Overall, Muley figured he knew Medicine Rock as well as any town where they had stayed on their long, winding trip. But there was one more person that Muley felt pressed to talk to before they rolled out of town.

He found himself a place at the bar and waited for Goldy to notice. After a few moments she came down and poured a tumbler full of whiskey without his asking.

Goldy looked him up and down as she shoved the cork back in the whiskey bottle. "You look like you been standing too close to that soggy friend of yours," she said.

"That's the truth." Muley picked up his glass and took a swallow. He looked into Goldy's pale dusty eyes. "I got something I need to speak to you about."

"If you're after one of the girls, you'll just have to wait," Goldy said. "Black Alice has been up there near an hour. She should be down soon."

Muley shook his head. "I'm not after the girls," he said. "I was after you."

Goldy gave a snort that turned heads around half the room. "It's been a coon's age since any man wanted me," she said.

"I don't mean to bed," Muley said. He pitched his voice low and leaned forward on his stool, uncomfortably aware of how many eyes were watching. "I heard you had a talent for casting. You and that Indian girl."

The expression on Goldy's face grew suddenly very solemn. "So that's how it is, is it? You want old Goldy to puzzle out your future, heh?"

"Yes."

"And what have you to pay for this?"

Muley started to say something, but Goldy spoke again, cutting him off.

"I warn you now," she said, "it can cost me dear to do a casting, and I expect a dear payment."

Muley reached into his pocket, produced a small round object, and laid it on the bar. It was a brooch, a cameo of fine porcelain set in a mounting of silver. Around the edges of the mount were glints of bright stones. Blue sapphires. Red rubies. Green emeralds.

"Well," said Goldy. "Well, I'll be damned." She lifted the jeweled pin from the worn surface of the bar and held it up to catch the light. "I don't think I've seen the like in thirty year."

"We were paid in it at Deseret," Muley said. "It bought a rainstorm for a whole town."

Goldy gave him a sharp look. "So this is come from the Rainmaker then, is it?"

Muley nodded reluctantly. "Yes."

"And I'd doubt he knows you have it."

"No. No, he doesn't."

"What do you suppose your Rainmaker would do if he knew you had lifted this from the pot?" Goldy asked.

Muley thought a moment. "He'd not fire me," he said, "because there's no one else that can run his fancy wagon." He ran his hand over his chin. "But he'd not be happy about it, that's for damn sure. He'd wag his tongue from here to hell and back."

Goldy turned the brooch over and over in her hand. For several long seconds she didn't speak. Then she slipped it behind the bar. "Here's what I think, Muley Owens. What I think is that whatever you want to know, you want to know pretty bad. If you didn't, you wouldn't risk peeving the one man you keep company with. Am I right?"

"I suppose," Muley said.

"Suppose?"

"A-yup. I mean . . ." Muley squirmed on his stool. "Yes, it's something I need to know."

"I see." Goldy lifted the whiskey bottle to her mouth, took the cork between her teeth and pulled it free. Then she took a swig of the pale yellow fluid straight from the bottle. She tilted her head back, the wrinkles in her cheeks smoothing as her mouth filled with whiskey. Then she bent sharply forward and sprayed the faceful of whiskey onto the surface of the bar.

Drops spattered against Muley's face and shirt. He jumped up from his stool and started to move away, but Goldy lashed out and caught him by the collar. There was surprising strength in her bony red fingers.

"Be still," she said. "Tell me quick what it is you want to see."

Muley was so flustered he could hardly get it out. "A woman. There was this woman I saw."

"When?"

"Two weeks ago beside a sodbuster's shack out in west Colorado. And before that by a creek in Deseret. Maybe."

"Maybe?"

"I'm not sure it was her by the creek," Muley said. "She looked different."

"Different how?"

"Younger."

Goldy nodded. She spat again, bubbles of saliva mixing with the puddle of whiskey. Then she put the point of her finger into the mess and stirred it around the bar. "You're a hard man to follow," she said. "You move too fast for my eye."

"What do you mean?" Muley asked.

"Quiet," Goldy said.

A ripple of colors moved through the mixture of spit and whiskey. For a moment Muley almost thought he saw an image, but it was lost in a swirl like whale oil spilled on the sea.

"I see a girl," Goldy said.

"She ain't what I would call a girl," Muley said. "She was thirty or more, I reckon."

"It's a girl," Goldy repeated, "and one I know." She looked up at Muley. "It's Boots."

"Who is Boots?"

Whether Goldy heard the question or not, Muley couldn't say. The woman's face had turned as red as blood, and a vein pounded in her temple. "This girl's been hurt," she said. "Are you the one to do it?"

"I don't know what it is you're asking," Muley said. "Aren't these things you're seeing off in the future? How am I supposed to know about them?"

"This here's the future," Goldy said, "but not far into it. Are you the one to hurt her?"

Muley took a half step back. "I ain't never hurt a girl," he said, "and I don't suppose I'm like to start any time soon."

"You better hope to hell not," Goldy said. She pulled a rag from behind the bar and began mopping at the mess of whiskey. "This girl's been hurt bad, and the way she's been hurt . . ." She shook her head. "I better not find out you're the one to do this, Muley Owens."

"I already said I don't go hurting girls," Muley said. "Besides, can't you tell who done it from your casting?"

"Casting don't always show you what it is you want to see," Goldy said. "Most times it only shows you what you should see."

"Who says what you should see?" Muley asked. "But why show you this girl? I'm not going to hurt her. What about the woman I asked about?"

Goldy gave the bar another wipe and turned away. "Didn't see no woman," she said. "Only Boots."

"Who's Boots?"

"She's a girl that come through here a few weeks ago. She was hurt then, and now I see she's to be hurt again." Goldy snatched up the whiskey bottle and brought it to her lips. This time she didn't spit it out. Muley saw Goldy's throat work as she swallowed the fiery liquid. At last she put the almost empty bottle down on the bar. "I know what it is for a man to hurt a woman the way Boots has been hurt. Nobody ought to have it happen twice. Nobody."

Muley wasn't sure what she wanted him to say. "Well, ma'am, it wasn't me that hurt her before, and I won't hurt her."

Goldy gave him another look with her tan eyes. There was a jerky restlessness to those eyes now, a symptom of the whiskey, or maybe of her talent. "I believe you," she said. She turned and walked to the other end of the bar. There, she sat and drank the bottle dry.

Muley watched her for several minutes. He wanted to go down and ask for his brooch back. It seemed to him that the casting had done nothing but make Goldy angry. It sure hadn't answered any of his questions about the woman. What Goldy had done wasn't worth a jeweled brooch.

But Muley was too scared. The old woman was already riled. He wasn't sure just what she might do if he was to press her. She might have a pistol behind the bar. She might have more talents than casting.

Muley drained the last of the whiskey in his glass and left the Kettle Black. He walked down the main street of Medicine Rock, looking up at buildings tinged red by sunset. In the morning, he and the Rainmaker would leave town. The plan now was to swing down by Laramie, then turn east. Muley thought it was likely he would never see Medicine Rock again.

He stopped beside the wagon and looked back at the short row of shops and houses. Muley had not shown a lick of talent in his whole life, but as he looked at the town, a cold certainty settled into his gut. It was a conviction that came as close to casting as he was likely to get.

No matter how things were planned, Medicine Rock wasn't through with him yet. He might leave, but he was coming back.

☆ **12** ☆

"Mr. Cody won't be joining us," Edward Kastle said.

Jake looked at the little man who sat his horse stiffer than boots that had been left in the rain. It was a breezy day. To keep his round hat from flying off, Kastle had been obliged to run a rawhide string over the top of his head and around his chin. Except for that concession to local conditions, Kastle looked crisp enough to have been in an office somewhere far to the east. Behind him, Cullen slouched in his saddle. Jake could tell just by the way the gunman leaned that Cullen was saddle sore and bone weary.

"Did Cody quit?" Jake asked. It had been clear enough when the three were in Medicine Rock that there was bad blood between the old scout and the other two. When a man like Cody was forced to work for a man like Kastle, there was bound to be a rough go, but Jake figured this for something more serious.

"Certainly not," Kastle said. His horse snuffled and made a move toward the trough outside the Kettle Black, but Kastle pulled the animal's head sharply up. "While we were in Tempest, we received word that the western operation was proceeding ahead of schedule. In fact, they are now less than a hundred miles from this point."

Jake looked toward the sunset. "You're building from the west?"

"We are building in both directions," Kastle said. "Our western and eastern operations were expected to meet somewhere near the mountains. However, current progress suggests

that the actual meeting point might not be too far from Medicine Rock."

Jake took a moment to digest the information. He supposed
it made little difference whether the rail line came in from the
east or west. His major concern was that he make his deal for a
doctor before the line was laid through Medicine Rock.
"What's this have to do with Cody?" he asked.

Cullen raised his head. "He's gone to see the Chinamen,
sure enough," he said in his rolling accent.

"Has he?" Jake did not know Cullen well enough to be sure,
but he thought the man was lying.

Kastle cleared his throat. "There are agents of the western
line working in this direction. Mr. Cody has gone to intercept
those agents and make them aware of our own progress."

"I see," Jake said. "And what does this mean for us? When
will you be leaving?"

"Right away," Kastle said. "We will rest our mounts tonight
and be out before dawn."

It was good news for Jake's plans, but that didn't stop him
from feeling a dash of fear. He had hoped for a few more days
before he would have to leave Medicine Rock. "You still open
to my coming with you?"

"Yes," Kastle said. "This location seems most amenable to
the current alignment of our rails. It's important that we secure
your cooperation as quickly and as fully as possible."

His words gave Jake new hope. Maybe this rapid progress
was making Medicine Rock more important. From what
Kastle said, he might have new clout in asking for his doctor.
"All right," Jake said. "I'll be saddled and ready at dawn."

"Excellent," Kastle said. "Until then." He bobbed his head
and sent his horse walking toward the stables. Cullen followed
him, groaning with each step of his horse.

Jake was tempted to go into the Kettle Black. Certainly he
should have a talk with Goldy before he left, but the real temp-
tation was to grab some whiskey to burn the butterflies out of
his stomach. He pushed off that thought and walked quickly
across the street to the sheriff's office.

Tom Sharp was waiting in the front room with a game of

solitaire dealt out on the table. Seeing the game laid out there caused Jake a moment of irritation, but he could not really fault the deputy. Tom hadn't been neglecting his work.

The new deputy of Medicine Rock had been practicing his signing with fair diligence. He could now stop a bullet with only a moment's shudder, and could stop two without losing his feet. However, his progress at the more offensive portions of his talent was dishearteningly small. Still, Tom had been pushing his talent pretty hard. He deserved to sit and rest a bit.

"You look shook," Tom said as Jake came through the door. "There a challenge?"

"No," Jake said. He pulled out a chair from the old round table that filled most of the front room and sat down. "It's the railroad people, they've come back from Tempest."

"They didn't change their minds, did they? Is the rail still coming through here?"

Jake nodded. "The rail's to run through Medicine Rock. That is, it will if they'll listen to my deal when I get to New York."

"So you're really going to go all the way to New York?" Tom asked.

"Most likely. Kastle says only this Jay Gould can make the deal I'm after."

Tom sat the rest of the cards on the table. "I should give you a note for my mother," he said. "I've had no way to post anything since I came west, and she lives right there in New York City."

"If you're going to write a letter, you'd better get busy," Jake said. "I leave first thing tomorrow."

"Tomorrow? Damn, but that's fast." Tom ran both hands through his thick black hair. "I'm not sure I'm ready for you to go."

"I'm not sure, either," Jake said. He wished he could be more confident of Tom, but he still had grave doubts about how the little man might handle any sort of serious challenge. "But I suppose we're going to find out. Josie thinks you're ready."

"I'm glad someone does," Tom said. He smiled, showing a set of clean white teeth against his sunburned skin.

Jake forced a smile in return. "You're doing a lot better than most anyone else I know. There's sure no one else in Medicine Rock that can match the kind of talent you been showing."

"I'm not showing much."

"Come on." Jake pushed his chair back from the table and stood up. "Let's go outside and see what you can stir up. You might surprise us both."

Jake followed Tom through the back room of the sheriff's office and out the rear door. The sun was only a few minutes from setting, and their shadows stretched out long and thin against the whitewashed boards of the office. The patch of weeds and dust back of the office was where Jake had earned his position as deputy, and where Sheriff Pridy had been killed by the blood talent, Quantrill. There was nothing here to mark either event except Jake's memories.

"Try what you were doing this morning," Jake suggested. "Seems to me you were on the right road."

Tom nodded. He held his hands out in front of him and slowly pulled them in toward his chest. Almost at once a cold breeze stirred the sage and sawgrass. As Tom brought his hands together, a dust devil sprang up at his feet. Thin streamers of pale blue twisted away from his hands, wrapping themselves into the tiny whirlwind. In the core of the dust devil something began to take shape. It was small, but there was a glint of teeth, eyes, and claws.

"That's it," Jake said softly. "You got it."

The dust devil began to blow apart, but the thing inside it was solid now. With jackrabbit legs and a face of raw bone, it looked no more like a regular animal than other conjurations Jake had seen. But it sure enough looked mean.

The little beast grunted and turned around in the street. The single curving claw at the end of its stunted forelegs scratched at the dusty ground.

"It's real," Tom said. From the sound of his voice, he seemed very surprised.

"It's real enough," Jake said. "Now, can you control it?"

Tom lowered his right hand just a hair. The devil rabbit jumped like a horse kicked by a spur. It took several steps to the left, then stopped. A trilling hiss came from its toothy mouth.

Tom lowered his left hand. The beast jumped again, reversing its course until it was within inches of where it had started.

"It listens to me," Tom said. He started to laugh. "It's mine!"

"Careful now—" Jake began.

Tom gave a twitch with his right hand. The devil rabbit jumped forward, spun around, then ran straight for Tom. Its claws cut deep furrows in the earth.

Tom screamed and fell over backward with the thing he had raised sitting on his chest. It took Jake only a moment to raise his talents, but in those moments the little creature's wicked curved claws had already sliced up Tom's vest, cut through his shirt, and started on his skin.

"Get!" Jake cried.

The word that came from his mouth was not even as close to human speech as the noises the conjuration had made, but its effect was immediate. With a squeal like a wounded horse, the rabbit thing fell away from Tom and rolled in the weeds. It crawled toward a line of sagebrush. In the failing light, Jake could barely see the little creature, but he could not afford to let it get past. A conjuration left to itself might vanish, but it could also grow stronger.

"Go away," Jake said. In the language of his chattering, it was like the tolling of a bell.

The sound struck the conjured beast like a flail. The forearms vanished in a spray of black. The bony face crumbled. The long hind legs kicked, and were gone. It left nothing behind but the fading echo of its scream.

Jake went over to Tom and helped him sit up. "I think you came off lucky. Looks like you don't have anything worse than a couple of scratches."

Tom ran his fingers across the red marks on his chest. "Guess this means I can't control it."

"Looks that way," Jake said. He stood up and brushed the dust from his jeans. "But that's only for now. The way you've been coming along, you'll have those conjurations dancing on a string before you know it."

Tom frowned. "Maybe. If it's all the same to you, I think I'll skip practicing this part while you're gone. I wouldn't want to call something up when you weren't here to put it down."

Jake stuck out a hand and helped Tom to his feet. "You concentrate on stopping attacks. Anybody gives you trouble, you let Josie fire the eight-gauge at them a few times. That'll get their attention."

"Right," Tom said. "I know I wasn't going to get in the way of that big gun."

"It's not the gun so much as the woman that's holding it," Jake replied. "Josie's put paid to more talented folks than I ever hope to. She'll back your play if she's needed."

"Thanks, that's good to know." Tom traced a finger across one of the fresh red welts on his chest. "You mind if I go clean myself up?"

"Go on ahead. I'll see you again before I go."

Tom headed off for the boardinghouse and Jake turned toward his own house at the north end of town. Once again Tom's performance was cause for concern. Josie might catch some overconfident scribbler or signer, but most folks who would mount a real challenge had the talent to stop a bullet— or even eight-gauge shot. A simple changer like Cap Hardin would be more than able to hold off Tom and Josie. Josie's shot might sting, but a changer would tear off her arms before Josie could load a third round.

Jake was still a hundred feet away from his house when his nose brought him the smell of Josie's spice pot chicken warming on the stove. For Jake, it was the best smell there was, and it promised the best dinner in the world. With everything else that Josie did, it was easy to forget that she'd spent several years working as a cook at a boardinghouse. But Josie hadn't forgotten how to run a kitchen. Her spice pot chicken and a plate of sourdough biscuits made such a meal that Jake could not imagine better.

Inside the house, Jake found his wife ready to put the food on the table. He was surprised to see her wearing a blue dress, and her hair pulled back with a matching ribbon. It was an outfit Jake hadn't seen her wear outside of church in years.

"Did someone come over and tell you?" Jake asked.

Josie looked up from her cooking. "Tell me what?"

Jake started to explain about the railroad men, but decided to back up a step. "What caused you to get dressed up?" he asked.

"We are having company for dinner tonight," Josie said.

"We are?"

"Yes. Goldy is coming, and Sienna, and one other."

"Who?" Jake said, though he was sure the answer was Tom Sharp. Josie had been feeding the skinny Sharp at least one night out of three since she'd picked him to be Jake's new deputy. Jake had told himself a dozen times that Josie was just trying to be polite, but her attention to the deputy was wearing on him. It didn't help any that the women in town were talking about how good-looking Sharp was.

"Boy, your seeing has gone plumb to pot," said a deep voice from the front room.

Jake spun around and saw a familiar tall silhouette in the doorway. "When did you get here?"

"Early enough to eat the last of your pie," Bred Smith said. The tall black man stepped into the light of the kitchen, and the lamplight shone from his wide smile.

Jake went over to Bred and held out his hand. Bred's huge hand swallowed Jake's like a wolf gulping down a rabbit. "I swear, you're starting to put on some weight," Bred said. "This girl of yours better watch all the fine cooking, or you'll not fit through the door."

"It looks to me like you could use some cooking," Jake said.

Over the last five years, Bred had come through Medicine Rock only three times. The last time he stopped had been almost three years before, not long after the death of Little Hatty.

The years since then had aged Bred. Jake knew that the old soldier, trader, and trapper was somewhere on the high side of fifty, but it didn't prepare him for the way white hair had spread across Bred's scalp till it all but pushed out the black. Some of the heavy bulk in Bred's chest and shoulders had gone during those years. His thick buffalo hide coat sat low on his shoulders, too big now for the man who had made it.

"I believe I could use a hot meal, at that," Bred said. He drew back his hand and patted his stomach. "Things are getting sparse out there. I could do with some chicken fixings."

Josie walked between them carrying a bowl of meat in peppery sauce. The smell that came from the food was tempting enough that it drew Jake's head around as she passed.

"I think you'll get what you're after," Jake said.

There was a knock at the front door, and Jake excused himself to let Goldy and Sienna into the house. Goldy did not hold back, but hurried to hug herself against Bred.

"Why, Miss Goldy," Bred said, "I swear you get yourself younger every year."

Even Sienna, who was normally as quiet and still as a person could be, was quick to wrap her arms around Bred. "I've missed you," she said simply.

Bred put his big hands on her shoulders and held her out at arm's length. "You must be busting hearts over three territories," he said.

"She is," Goldy said, "but she don't seem to notice."

Josie steered the whole group to the table and laid out the food. A shortage of proper chairs forced Jake to perch on an empty barrel, but once he got to the food, his poor seat was forgotten. After a bit, as the chicken and biscuits went down, the talk came around to Custer, and Quantrill, and the whole terrible summer that had seen three towns die and Medicine Rock get its second start.

And from that they came to Hatty. It was a name twice dipped in sorrow. Jake and Josie could not help but remember their lost little girl. All of them remembered the woman who had saved Jake, and probably the rest of them as well, when she sacrificed herself to stop the mad thing living under George Custer's skin.

Bred hung his head at the talk of Hatty. Jake suspected that the big man's feelings for Hatty had gone beyond friendship. But Bred was an old black soldier and Hatty a white woman. Such pairs did happen out on the range, but not without a share of trouble.

"Malcolm is gone, too," Sienna said as they sat around the remains of the meal.

Bred nodded. "I know," he said. "I'm sorry to hear it."

"How did you know that?" Jake asked.

There was a pause while Bred chewed and swallowed his last bite of chicken. "Ran into a woman about a week west of here. She said you might need some looking after."

Jake waited, but that seemed to be Bred's last word on the subject.

The meal cheered up again as Josie told about the coming baby. Sienna in particular seemed excited by the news. Jake hoped it might help bring the girl back to life. There was also considerable discussion about the railroad, the prospects for Medicine Rock, and several assertions that it was time Bred gave up wandering and settled in the town.

Finally Goldy began to worry about the management of the Kettle Black. "Orpah knows where every penny of her own money is," she said, "but she don't watch as close when it's mine." Both Goldy and Sienna said their good nights and went off to tend business.

Bred tapped his old cob pipe full of something that might have been tobacco and headed out onto the porch. Jake found him there puffing blue smoke and looking at the stars.

"Fall's being good to us this year," Jake said. "I was expecting some cold by now."

"It's not far off," Bred said. "This time next week, I reckon you'll see some weather."

Jake looked for a good way to jump into his next subject, but he couldn't find anything better than starting right in. "Bred, I need your help."

"Why?" the black man asked. "Looks to me like you got this town on good feet."

"It's this thing with the railroad," Jake said. He leaned against the porch rail and looked at the lights burning in the windows of Medicine Rock. "I need to travel to New York City to talk to the boss of the railroad."

"New York City? Lawd, but that's a walk and then some. What you need to go for?"

"So we can get a doctor in town."

"I see," Bred said.

Jake didn't doubt that Bred did see. Bred was not a fast talker, but his mind was plenty quick. It would not take him a second to reason out why Jake was so set on having a doctor about.

"If you're going all the way to New York," Bred said, "it's going to take you till spring to get back."

"No. Least I hope not," Jake said. "They've got the rail line built within three days' ride now. I figure to ride out, get on this train of theirs, and be in New York before a week has passed."

"The railroad," Bred said. "The last railroad I seen was moving troops across Tennessee." He drew on his pipe and puffed out a cloud of smoke. "I never did get a chance to ride it myself, but it was sure something to see."

"Well, the railroad's going to be right here in Medicine Rock in just a few weeks." Jake looked to the east, imagining the approach of this steel monster. He had seen trains in books but had a hard time moving from those old drawings to a good idea of what the real thing was like.

Bred tapped out his pipe, sending a shower of sparks over the handrail. "You don't need to say any more. I'll be happy to come with you. Shoot, it'll be like old days, won't it?"

Jake was glad the night was dark. At least his friend couldn't see him flush with embarrassment. "I wasn't going to ask you to go with me. I'm riding out of here at first light with some fellows from the railroad."

"What? You think I can't keep up anymore?" Even in the darkness Jake could see Bred straighten himself up. "I may be getting on, but I never seen the horse that could keep ahead of me for a whole day."

"No," Jake said quickly. "I'm sure you can keep up. It's just that I need you to do something more important."

"Like what?"

"Stay here and watch after the town for me." Jake waved his hand toward the cluster of buildings. "There's not many in this whole place that are competent. Josie's competent, but she's got no talent, and a baby coming besides. I have a new deputy, but he can't sign well enough to conjure a dung beetle. You're the only one that has both a talent and the gumption to use it. I need you here to watch out for Josie and the rest of them while I'm gone."

For a moment there was no sound but the wind moving between the buildings, and Jake had a terrible fear that Bred was going to turn him down.

"I'll stay," Bred said.

Jake let out a tight sigh. "Thank you. I appreciate this."

Bred walked the length of the porch, the floor timbers groaning softly under his weight. "I hate to see you off alone," he said. "You tend to stir trouble."

"This time I'm more worried about the town."

"What about your seeing?" Bred asked. "It tell you this is the thing to do?"

Seeing was one of Jake's least predictable talents, but in many ways his best. It was the seeing that had helped him make critical choices in the fight with Custer. More than once the seeing had saved Jake's life, and that of others.

Jake hung his head. "I don't get the seeing anymore."

"Since when?"

"Since the baby passed on," Jake said. Though the wound was three years old, it opened up in Jake and pulled tears from his eyes. "I saw it was going to happen. I saw it was coming, but I saw nothing I could do for it."

The boards groaned again as Bred moved to Jake's side. "Sometimes they's nothing that you can do." His large hand came down on Jake's shoulder and gave a firm squeeze.

"Don't fret yourself. I'll watch over this town while you go get a doctor for your wife and new baby."

The two men stood on the porch for several minutes longer. Overhead the stars seemed to burn brighter as one by one the lamps of the town were put out. Even when there was no light but that from the Kettle Black, they stood there staring into the night.

Jake had no idea what was on Bred's mind. For himself, he only wished he could see this sight again soon. He hadn't been born in Medicine Rock, but decided long before that he didn't want to be anywhere else. This was home.

☆ PART III ☆

Tickets, Please

☆ **13** ☆

Muley was wet, tired, and angry.

He'd wanted to head east straight away. There were more towns in Kansas than there were west, and they hadn't been there for some months. More than one patron of the Kettle Black had said that after the wet spring, the summer east of the Black Hills had turned off drier than usual. It could well be that some of the Kansas towns would be willing to pay for some moisture for crops of winter wheat.

But as usual the Rainmaker had other plans. Tempest was little more than a day's travel, and the Rainmaker was not one to pass up a dollar that close at hand. So they had gone down to see if they might get a day or two's pay from the ranches there. What they got was trouble.

The sheriff in Tempest had smelled a challenge. No matter what Muley said, the man couldn't get past the idea of having someone as talented as the Rainmaker about without fighting him. Only a timely storm had carried them out of town alive, and even then the back of the wagon cracked from a double load of buckshot.

To top it off, now they had run into a real storm. Clouds and cold rain had come off the Laramie Range, along with a smattering of sleet and wet snow. The winds from the natural storm played holy hell with the Rainmaker's efforts, leaving Muley to tack and steer the wagon through winds that changed from moment to moment. He was forced to reef in the balloon jib and go with only the mainsail. And he was wet.

The trail took a turn to the south and headed down a slope. Muley fed a few arms of line into the jib, letting it catch the

north wind and give the wagon a bit more momentum in case
this downslope was followed by a sharp uphill grade. He
didn't want the Rainmaker blaming him for trapping the
wagon in yet another ditch.

Thunder rumbled down the hills to the north. Muley pulled
the brim of his hat down, squinting against a wall of rain that
suddenly crashed over the wagon. The wagon reached the
bottom of the slope and splashed through water halfway to the
axles. Though the stream cut the wagon's speed considerably,
enough momentum remained to carry the craft on up the slope
and into more gales of rain.

"Tempest," Muley snarled into the chill rain. "Let's go to
Tempest, he says. What a damn fine idea."

In the next flash of lightning Muley tried to get an idea of
the land ahead. There was a cluster of small cedars on the left.
Beyond that were rolling hills covered in stiff buffalo grass.
There didn't seem to be anyplace that offered shelter for the
night. The lightning died, and Muley's vision was lost in the
dazzle of afterimage. He risked letting loose a little more sail,
hoping to get on to somewhere more promising.

The left front wheel sank down in a drop Muley hadn't
seen. Whether it was a buffalo path or a prairie dog run, the
jolt was bad enough to send Muley's teeth slamming together
and raise an unsettling snap from somewhere in the wagon's
frame.

The Rainmaker slid open the panel back of Muley's seat.
"What in blue blazes are you doing out there?"

Muley twisted around. "Trying to make up for your damn
mistake," he shouted. "We'd never be in this—"

Lightning flashed again, cutting into Muley's words. In the
blast of light he saw an expression of terror on the Rainmaker's white face.

Muley spun around in time to see an ungodly figure
standing in their path. He grabbed the boom and pushed it
hard to the right, at the same time letting the jib sail fill to its
limits. The sail wagon shuddered, leaned up on two wheels,
and came down with a crash. There was another flash, and the
bloody, horrible figure was right there so close on Muley's left

he could have reached out to touch it. The flash ended, the figure lost in darkness. The sail wagon left the path and went bouncing down a hill, the wet prairie grass whistling along the sides.

They had gone nearly a hundred yards before Muley suddenly reefed both sails, tied down the boom, and jumped from the wagon.

The Rainmaker opened the door of the wagon and peeked out. "Where are you going?" he asked. "Didn't you see that thing?"

"I saw it," Muley called over his shoulder.

"You go back there and it might get you!" the Rainmaker shouted.

"I'm hoping to get him," Muley said.

"What?"

Muley didn't bother to reply. The wet grass was slippery underfoot and he had all he could handle making his way back up the slope in the dark. With each flash of lightning he peered ahead, hoping to see the face he had caught in passing, but he reached the top of the hill without seeing anyone.

"Hey there!" Muley shouted. "Where are you?"

Thunder rumbled again, and as it died Muley thought he heard a groaning off to his left. He stumbled in the dark and fell to his hands and knees. As he started to get up, his hand came down on something warm and damp.

"Cody?" he said.

"Here," said a weak voice. The next blast of light showed a tangle of wet hair and the bright red of blood.

Muley managed to locate the man's shoulders and got a hand under each. Finding the best footing he could manage on the wet ground, he heaved Bill Cody to his feet. The old scout tried to help, but his feeble movements were as much hindrance as aid. Muley slipped and slid down the hill, on the edge of dropping Cody every moment.

There was a light bobbing at the bottom of the hill. The Rainmaker stood beside the wagon holding up an oil lantern and peering fearfully into the dark. "Muley? You there?"

"I'm here," Muley said. "And I could do with a hand."

The Rainmaker came forward with the lamp held above his head. "Who's that with you?"

"Your hero," Muley said. "That fellow from all the books."

"Buffalo Bill Cody? What would he be doing out here?"

Cody raised his head. In the light of the Rainmaker's lamp, Cody's face was streaked with gore. A flap of skin was loose from his scalp. Under it was a crust of dried blood, torn flesh, and a streak of bare skull.

The Rainmaker shrank back. "Good Jesus. What happened to him?"

"Shot," Cody said. His mouth moved a moment longer but no more words came out. His head rolled over against his shoulder and his bright blue eyes closed.

"Is he dead?" the Rainmaker asked.

"Not yet," Muley said. "We need to get him inside."

"Inside with me?"

"A-yup, unless you got some other dry spot handy."

The Rainmaker opened the door and Muley pulled Bill Cody inside the wagon. There were padded benches at the front and back of the small interior. Most days they served as chair and table for the Rainmaker. But they also made do for beds between towns. Muley moved Bill Cody to the front bench, the one that was generally Muley's to sleep on. The Rainmaker came inside and hung the lamp from a hook at the center of the cabin. In its yellow light Muley got his first good look at Cody's wounds.

The scalp wound was the most obvious. From the look of things, the bullet had struck no more than an inch above Cody's left eye and then skidded off his skull. Either the caliber had been low or Cody's skull was of exceptional hardness. Whichever way, he'd been lucky. Muley didn't doubt he had one hell of a headache.

The resulting wound was messy. If Muley could clean the track well enough, he thought he might be able to stitch the loose skin down around the wound. That would leave Cody with only a small scar. If the flap of skin died, things would look considerably worse. A big chunk of blond scalp would have to go, along with an inch or more of forehead. Muley hoped it didn't come to that.

"Get into the sew kit," Muley said to the Rainmaker. "I'm needing my gear."

While the Rainmaker was fumbling at the back of the wagon, Muley started to peel off Cody's jacket. That's when he found the second wound. A bullet had passed clean through the scout's left forearm. From the size of the openings, Muley guessed that this shot, like the one to the head, had come from a small caliber weapon. He hoped the slug had missed the bones. He could stitch up the wounds, but if there was more damage inside, gangrene might well set in. If it did, then Cody was dead.

The Rainmaker came up with the leather sewing kit and brought it over to Muley. Most of the needles inside were meant for repairing tears in the sails. Even the smallest of the heavy, curved needles would be a crude tool for stitching a man's face. But it was what they had. Muley ran a damp rag over the cuts, rubbing hard to bring blood and flush out the poisons, then he threaded the needle with white cotton thread and pulled the edges of the bullet track together.

The Rainmaker watched over Muley's shoulder. "I thought he was some kind of conjuration," he said.

"So did I, at first."

"Where did all that blood come from? His face is covered. I've never seen so much blood."

"Cuts on the head bleed a lot," Muley said. He rubbed his fingers across the top of his own head. "A boom clipped me up on the crown once, and I thought I'd bleed a bucketful before it stopped."

Muley finished his work on Cody's scalp. The tools might be coarse, and Muley's fingers stiff, but his stitchwork was tight. Human skin stretched in a different way than sailcloth. Still, it seemed to Muley that his work was better than most of the doctoring he'd seen. A couple more stitches on each side served to close the wound on Cody's arm. Through the whole thing Cody neither moved nor made a sound. If it hadn't been for the steady drip of blood, Muley might have thought the man dead. When everything else was done, he wiped the blood from Cody's face and arranged him on the bench as best he could.

"He's getting mud all over the bench," the Rainmaker said. "Blood, too."

Muley snorted. "You can take it up with him when he's awake. I'm sure he's sorrier about bleeding than you are about the blood. Feel around back there and get me a chewing plug."

The Rainmaker leaned over the back of the rear bench. "Is this really Buffalo Bill?"

"A-yup. It's him. I told you I talked to him back in Medicine Rock."

"I know. It's just that, well . . . he doesn't seem nearly as tough as the books make him out to be." The Rainmaker came up with a twist of dried tobacco. Muley took it from him and bit off a mouthful.

"I doubt you'd be tough when you'd been shot twice," Muley said around the chaw. "Hell, I doubt you'd be alive." He pulled the tobacco out of his mouth and pressed the moist brown cake against the wound on Cody's forehead. Dark juice ran down Cody's face. It was ugly, but it would help keep the wound from festering.

Muley straightened up as much as he could in the cramped space and leaned against the side of the wagon. Outside, thunder still rumbled and the wind rocked the wagon. Though the sail wagon was meant to run through storms, it was not built for this buffeting from all sides. They needed to find some way to get out of the weather or risk taking more damage.

"You think you can stir up a western breeze?" Muley asked.

The Rainmaker blinked his watery eyes. "Now? Isn't there enough wind out there?"

"I need a steady wind to help me cut across this storm."

"Can't we just stay here?" the Rainmaker asked.

"We might," Muley said, "but whoever did this to Cody is probably still about. Maybe you ought to get out the rifle."

It was a lie. The wounds to Cody were at least a day old. But the threat had the desired effect. The Rainmaker took a quick glance at the wounded man and nodded. "Maybe I can get up something of a wind."

"I thought you might." Muley opened the door and winced at the gust of wet, cold air that spilled into the wagon. "Make it as stiff as you can. I don't fancy sitting out there in the rain all night."

Muley splashed around to the side of the wagon and climbed to his seat. The boom was tugged this way and that as he let out the sails. At first the wagon only rocked in place, unable to pick up the wind it needed to move up the gentle slope ahead. Then the Rainmaker's talent began to work. With a sharp snap, the mainsail filled and the boom came around. Muley quickly raised the balloon jib and the steel-rimmed wheels started to turn. Soon they were going up the slope at a brisk clip, and down the next slope even faster.

With the wind steady at his back, Muley found the storm less vexing. It was still cold, and he was still soaked to the skin, but at least not so much rain blew into his face.

After only a few minutes the heart of the storm passed to the south. Lightning continued to flash, but it was at an ever increasing distance. Even the rain slacked off. Muley thought about calling down and telling the Rainmaker to stop. They could stay here through the night without hurting the wagon. But he decided to keep going. The Rainmaker's fear had brought up the best west wind in days, and Muley didn't want to waste a minute of it.

The breeze blew them clean out from under the clouds and out into a prairie lit up by a quarter moon. There had been some rain here, and the grass looked like silver in the moonlight. Muley let the jib out to its limits. The sails fluttered and ropes creaked.

With the smell of the storm still lingering in his nose, and his eyes held half closed, Muley could convince himself that he was back at sea. The silver backs of the hills became rolling swells. The distant line of mountains on the horizon was the first sight of some exotic island. Muley's lips turned up in a smile. Maybe this island would be the home of the mysterious woman who had kissed him in the night.

The wagon came to the edge of a wide, shallow stream and Muley took it straight across. Water splashed up around the wheels, brilliant in the moonlight. Tired as he was, he felt he could go on forever. He had no talent, but to be at the helm of the wagon on a night like this was a magic all its own.

Abruptly, the sails began to fall slack. Muley pushed the boom back and forth, but there was no more breeze to be had. Evidently, the Rainmaker's fear, or his talent, had run out.

Muley rolled in the sails and tied down the boom. With the wind gone, he felt suddenly exhausted. He climbed slowly down and swung a pin through the front wheel to hold it in place. Then he walked around the wagon and went inside.

He was surprised to find Bill Cody not only awake, but sitting up and drinking some of the Rainmaker's small supply of brandy. "We staying here?" Cody asked.

"A-yup, unless someone's going to make more wind, I reckon we are," Muley replied. Despite what the Rainmaker had said before, it appeared to Muley that Bill Cody was one tough old cuss. To be up and about after such treatment as he had received was extraordinary. "How are you feeling?" Muley asked.

"He woke up just a minute ago," the Rainmaker said. "I thought it would be all right to let the breeze fall."

"Most likely it will," Muley said. He looked around at Cody. "Who was it that shot you?"

"Sean Cullen."

"From the railroad? I thought you were working with them."

"I was," Cody said. He drained down the rest of the brandy and passed the glass back to the Rainmaker. "Thank you," he said. "That was the best medicine I could hope for."

"Why did this Cullen plug you?" Muley asked.

Cody shook his head. "I wasn't too fond of what they'd done, or what they were about to do, so I tried to stop them." He reached up and gingerly touched the stitches on his head. "Kastle didn't take that so well."

"He had the Irishman shoot you?"

"Yep, nearly did me in, too, except for that damn little gun of Cullen's. A fancy rig, but not much kick to it. They must grow thinner heads back in New York."

"But why?" Muley insisted. "What could they do that was worth shooting you over?"

Cody looked down at the floor of the wagon. "I should have left them after what I saw in Dakota. But I didn't. Now I reckon I'm paying for it." He coughed. "I think I better rest a bit," he said weakly. He leaned back against the side and squeezed his eyes shut.

"You go on and rest," the Rainmaker said. From the tone of his voice, the Rainmaker seemed to have recovered his admiration for his dime novel hero.

Cody opened his eyes and looked over at Muley. "I'm putting you out, Mr. Owens." He pushed himself up from the bench. "I'll go on outside."

"Sit yourself," Muley said. He sat down on the floor of the wagon and leaned against the door. "I'll park myself down here."

"Thank you," Cody said. He settled back with a groan. "Damn, but my head hurts."

"We can have you in Rapid City tomorrow," the Rainmaker offered. "We can get a doctor to look after you there."

"Rapid City?" Cody frowned and shook his head. "You won't find any help there."

"Why not?"

"Don't take me to Rapid City," Cody said.

"Then where do we go?" Muley asked.

Bill Cody slumped down and put his hands across his face. "Far away," he said. "Far enough that I don't ever hear about Rapid City again."

"What?" Muley waited for further instructions, but it seemed that Buffalo Bill was asleep.

☆ 14 ☆

"Why 'Hell on Wheels'?" Jake asked.

Sean Cullen glanced down at the sign that marked the edge of the railroad camp. "It's only a bit of sport for the boys," he said.

Jake looked out at the sea of tents, shacks, and people. Sport or not, hell seemed an all too accurate way to describe the rail camp. There were easily twenty times as many people here as there were in Medicine Rock. Maybe more. Even Calio and Laramie, which Jake had reckoned to be large towns at their peak, were not a patch on this crowd. But this wasn't a town. It was a moving, cussing mob—a storm of people.

With them were piles of steel the size of many buildings, and heaps of garbage almost as large. Lines of men carried food from one end of a large tent, while more went out the other side to empty buckets of slop into a stagnant stream. Smoke came from the tents of smiths. Laughter rolled from a huge tent that had to be a kind of moving saloon. The air was full of the stench of hot metal, burning coal, cooking food, sweat, and sewage.

Farther back along the line, where the storm had already gone past, the ground had been stripped clear and stomped flat. Scattered over that ground were broken crates, torn paper, and pure garbage. In the center of the destruction was the blue-green gleam of the rails.

Kastle had ordered Jake and Cullen to wait on the edge of the camp while he went in to make arrangements. This hadn't set well with Cullen, who'd been talking about little but the sporting girls at the camp ever since they left Medicine Rock.

For Jake it was just fine. Even at this distance the railroad camp caused an unpleasant churning in his stomach. He had no desire to spend any more time in this place than was needed.

Off in the distance there was a screech like nothing Jake had heard before. He squinted toward the shadowy rolling hills and saw a streamer of smoke rapidly approaching.

"What's that?"

"Ah," Cullen said. "That there would be the train. Looks like we picked our time well. Sure and we'll be rolling on our way by nightfall."

A few minutes later the train came charging into the camp. It was huge. Jake had imagined the train as something on the order of a big stagecoach, but it was far vaster than that. The steaming black engine was as long as a house, and behind it was a car heaped with enough coal to heat Medicine Rock through the winter. Then another car, equally as big, and another car behind. Car after car followed. Ten of them. Twenty. The line was so long that the rear of the train was lost out of sight over the next hill. Jake had not imagined that people could build anything so immense.

It came to rest with a tremendous crash of steam and a shrill grinding of metal. Almost before it stopped, doors were flung open along the sides of a dozen cars. Ramps were put quickly in place. Men swarmed up into the train like ants after a picnic, carrying away the supplies needed to build the rail line even farther into the West.

Jake stared at the train in horror. Could he really let such a thing come to Medicine Rock? What would it do to the town to have such a beast rolling past or to have this hell of a camp tear through? For the first time Jake thought he had some idea of what he'd really promised. It was not just that Medicine Rock was going to have a railroad. Medicine Rock was going to be a railroad town.

It was an entirely different thing.

A dark mare and a stiff-backed rider appeared among the tents at the edge of the camp. Kastle skirted around a stream of waste and kicked his mount up the hill. Even after all the days he'd spent in the saddle, the engineer's posture on his mount had not changed one whit. He rode his tired, dirty horse with the erectness of a man about to pass the reviewing stand on a parade ground.

"Can we come in from the wilderness?" Cullen called as Kastle drew near.

"Momentarily," Kastle replied. He brought his mare up next to Jake's mount. "I have good news for you, Sheriff."

"What's that?"

"It seems that the extraordinary pace of building should bring about a union of the western and eastern extensions within the next two weeks."

"How is that good news for me?" Jake asked. "I need to speak to your Mr. Gould before the track goes past Medicine Rock."

"I was coming to that," Kastle said. "In anticipation of the impending union, Mr. Gould has left his residence. He is at this moment en route to our regional office in Sioux Falls. We can meet him there two days from now."

The words struck Jake like a cool breeze. "That is good news," he said. They had ridden less than three days to reach the camp east of Medicine Rock. If they were able to meet with Gould as soon as Kastle indicated, Jake thought, he could be back in Medicine Rock before the end of the week.

"Sure and that's wonderful," Cullen said. "Now, can I please go into camp before the train pulls out?"

"Go ahead," Kastle said. "Only be sure that you're on board within the hour. As soon as that train is unloaded, we're going back."

Cullen put his heels to his horse and went into the camp at a gallop. In seconds he was lost from sight.

"Where should I go to wait?" Jake asked.

Kastle looked at him with his cold blue eyes. "You might follow Mr. Cullen's example. There are . . . opportunities here that you might not find in Medicine Rock."

Jake clenched his teeth. "No. I'd not do that to Josie."

"As you wish," Kastle said. "But there is no reason your wife should ever know."

"No," Jake repeated.

"In that case, you may as well wait within the passenger compartment of the train."

Jake looked at the long line of cars. It was clear that the cars came in different forms and sizes, but none of them were familiar. "Where is that?" he asked.

Kastle turned and rode away. "Come along," he said over his shoulder. "I'll show you."

Jake flicked the reins and followed. The closer Jake drew to the train, the more his queasiness increased. He pulled his bandanna up over his nose, hoping to block some of the overwhelming stench, but it did nothing for his surging stomach. By the time they reached the side of the train, Jake was barely able to remain in his saddle.

"Are you all right, Sheriff?" Kastle asked.

"My stomach," Jake gasped. "I think the smell here's bothering it."

"You do appear somewhat bilious," Kastle said. "Perhaps getting you on the train might help."

Jake got shakily down from his mount. The gelding had been his horse for the past two years, and Jake did his best to hold back his illness while he saw to its care. Finally he followed Kastle up the steps onto the train. Almost at once Jake's ailing stomach was joined by a blinding headache. He stumbled, and would have fallen had Kastle not grabbed his arm.

"I believe you should lie down and rest, Sheriff," the engineer said. "We'll be under way soon."

Jake nodded, afraid that if he opened his mouth, more might come out than words. Kastle steered him down the carpeted aisle of the first car, past rows of wooden benches, across an open platform, and into another car. This second car had a narrow hallway along one side instead of the center, and rather than benches, there were a series of doors on Jake's right. Kastle pushed open the second door. Inside, Jake found a room that looked more like something from a fine house than anything he had expected to see on a train. It was a large room, so large that he found it hard to believe it all fit within the train car. There was thick purple carpet on the floor, and walls of dark wood paneling decorated here and there by prints of men on horseback. There was a pair of dark blue wingback chairs in the most distant corners of the room, with an oval table and four armchairs closer at hand. Each of the chairs was accompanied by what looked like a cigar box and a shiny brass spittoon. A single window ran from floor to ceiling at the center of the room. Through it Jake could see men carrying lengths of track alongside the train.

Kastle led Jake to one of the chairs at the table. "Wait here, Sheriff. I'll contact the staff and inform them of your condition. Perhaps one of the cooks might prepare a physic."

Jake managed another weak nod and slumped down in the chair. He couldn't remember ever feeling so ill. He had taken a pistol butt to the forehead without receiving such a headache. A needle-toothed conjuration had bitten a hole in his side without bringing so much pain to his gut. Surely it would take more than odor to cause such an illness. Jake slumped down in the chair and closed his eyes. He wondered just what deadly disease he had come down with. He only hoped he would live long enough to make his meeting with Gould.

The sound of the door latch caused Jake to open his eyes. A man in a clean gray uniform stepped into the room with a crystal tumbler in one hand. "Sheriff Bird?"

"Yes," Jake said. It pleased him that his voice didn't sound so bad.

The uniformed man came closer. "Mr. Kastle said you was feeling dyspeptic."

"I'll be all right."

"Well, sir, I brought a seltzer." The man put the glass down on the table near Jake. "I thought it might help settle your stomach."

"Thank you," Jake said. He lifted the glass and sipped at the contents. The liquid inside was clear, but it made bubbles like a glass of beer. Jake eyed the drink for a moment and decided not to risk drinking more. Adding a glass of bubbles didn't sound like the kind of thing his stomach needed.

The man left and Jake sat quietly in his chair. His head and stomach settled a little, but only a little. He still felt bad enough that death was surely near.

Kastle had said they would be leaving in less than an hour, but it seemed like a day before Jake heard more voices outside the door. Cullen came into the room in a burst of cigar smoke and whiskey fumes. Instantly, whatever progress Jake had made on recovery was lost.

The Irishman fell into the chair next to Jake and slammed his fists down on the hardwood table. "Civilization," he said around a fat cigar, stretching the word out till it might have been six. "I tell you, boyo, you can't but appreciate all the finest things until you've done without them for an age."

"What were you missing in Medicine Rock?" Jake asked. From the way Cullen talked, he seemed to take Jake's town as some cluster of savages.

Cullen pulled out his cigar and smiled, flashing a mouth of large yellow teeth. His cheeks were flushed red with drinking. "Variety," he said. "Your girls were good for where they were, but to have only two . . ." He shook his head. "How any man can live with so little I'll never understand."

Jake pulled himself up in his chair and was about to reply, but before the conversation could go further, Kastle came into the room.

"Are you feeling any better, Sheriff?" Kastle asked.

"A little," Jake said, though it was a lie. The pounding in his head was now so strong that he marveled the rest of them could not hear it.

Kastle took a seat across the table. He sat as rigidly upright in his chair as he sat on the back of a horse. "We'll be moving from this point at any moment," he said. "Because there are no facilities at this location, we'll be forced to back up to the nearest side rail. This will slow our progress somewhat. However, by dawn we should be headed in the right direction. The chief engineer tells me we should be in Sioux Falls by early tomorrow afternoon."

In time with his words came a loud whistle. Seconds later the floor shook and the train began to move. Despite Kastle's statement that their progress would be slow, the scene outside the window was soon sliding past as fast as a racing horse.

Jake rubbed his hand against his throbbing forehead. "I'll be glad to get to Sioux Falls," he said. "I'm anxious to talk to Mr. Gould."

"There'll be no need for that," Kastle said.

"What?"

"Because I am already here," said a new voice.

Jake turned to see a man standing at the open door. He was a man of medium height, medium build, and he wore a suit that was as plain and dark as soot. But there was a composure about the man's face, a certainty, that made it clear he was not a man who took orders from someone else.

"You're Gould?"

The man nodded. He walked over to the table with a swift, easy stride, took the final chair, and reached for the box of cigars. "I'm sorry to come on you as such a surprise," he said. "I have just arrived in the West, and I wanted to get a personal view of the work here. Even the crew boss did not know I was coming today."

"You don't need to apologize to me," Jake said. "All I wanted to do was talk with you. Sooner is better."

Gould opened the box on the table and took out a cigar. He raised it to his nose, sniffed, and favored Jake with a calm smile. Everything about the man seemed settled, almost sleepy. "I'm here," he said. "But before we have our discussion, let me address a few questions to Mr. Kastle."

"What do you need to know, Mr. Gould?" Kastle said promptly. There was a great difference in the engineer. All the bossiness that had been so clear in him from the day he arrived in Medicine Rock was covered up like a snake under a log.

"I only want to clarify our earlier discussion. Sheriff Bird here represents the full defensive capabilities of Medicine Rock?" Gould asked.

"Yes," Kastle said. "There are other talents in his town, but none of them have any direct bearing on our project."

Jake frowned. "What are—"

Gould held up a hand. "One moment, Sheriff." He turned back to Kastle. "And who is left in his place?"

"Tom Sharp, Mr. Gould."

"Sharp?"

"Small man. Signer."

"Ah." Gould nodded. He took a small device from the box and clipped the end from his cigar. "Well then, it appears we have both saved even more time, Sheriff Bird."

Jake shook his head in confusion. "Does that mean you'll agree to send a doctor to Medicine Rock?"

Cullen began to laugh. "You'll be needing a doctor, boyo. You'll be needing him more than anyone back in that horse trough of a town."

Jake pushed his chair away from the table and got to his feet. The room swayed drunkenly around him. "Are you pulling out of our deal?"

"I suppose you could say that," Gould said.

"You'll have to find somewhere else for your railroad, then." Jake staggered to the door of the room. "You'll not have Medicine Rock."

"I'm afraid you miss the point, Sheriff." Gould put his cigar down on the table and fixed Jake with his cold eyes. "We already have it."

"Now?" Cullen asked.

"Certainly," Gould said. "Try not to make a mess. The carpets in here cost me almost five thousand dollars."

Cullen reached into his vest and came out with a small pistol. It was black as night, and squared off in a way that Jake had never encountered, but there was no doubt about its purpose.

In response, Jake reached for his talent. For years the chattering had come almost without his asking. There would be danger, and Jake would feel his talent settle over him like a cool cloth. Through more than two dozen challenges it had been as steady as the sunrise—until now.

Instead of his talent, what came was a wave of pain so bright and hard that Jake screamed.

Cullen laughed. "You having trouble there, Mr. Sheriff?"

He got slowly to his feet and pointed the black pistol toward Jake. "Here," he said. "This'll end your aching."

"No!" Jake cried.

The pistol's report was loud in the room. Jake felt the blow like a mule's kick. He fell back against the door, wobbled for a moment, and slumped to the floor with the sharp smell of gun smoke in his nose.

Blackness swam over Jake, threatening to drag him down. But with it came a chilling wind that drove the pain from his head and stomach. He felt something hot and hard in his hand. Jake opened his fingers, and the bullet fell onto the carpet. It was different from any slug he had seen before, with stripes of copper red and greasy green running through the dull lead.

"What's this?" Cullen said. He walked over to Jake and picked up the bullet. "How did he stop this beauty?"

"Yes, Kastle," Gould said in his cold, calm voice. "I thought you guaranteed the performance of this weapon. Why is the good sheriff not dead?"

"A fluke," Kastle said with a nervous quaver. "A second attempt should end it."

"We'll see," Gould said. "Cullen, test his theory."

Jake raised his hands. "Please," he said. "Don't."

Sean Cullen threw his hands over his face and took a quick step back. "Damn him to cold hell!" he shouted. "He made those noises and it feels like my face is burned right to the bone."

"Shoot him!" Kastle shouted. "Do it quickly."

Cullen turned, aiming the gun with a shaky hand. His face was red and raw as a side of beef.

Jake kicked his heels against the thick carpet and pushed himself up the wall. "Stay back from—"

The pistol sounded again, and again Jake was knocked to the floor. There was a sharp pain in his chest, a pain that grew when he took a breath. But once again the bullet trickled from his hand onto the carpet.

"Stay back from me," he warned.

Cullen's cry was not a shout this time, it was a scream. He pressed his left hand to his face, covering his eyes. Blood began to flow from his nose. "What's that noise he's making!" he cried. There was a sizzling sound, like bacon on a fire.

"It's chattering," Kastle said. "One of the rarer talents."

"It seems we have another fluke," Gould said. He got up from the table and took a step toward Jake. The bland expression on his voice had not changed. "He stopped your special bullets, and now he has manifested his talent in the one place where it should have been impossible." Gould looked around at Kastle. "Tell me, how were these miracles achieved?"

Kastle swallowed hard. "He's stronger than we thought, but he has to be at his limits. Another shot should finish him."

"Let us hope," Gould said.

Jake got to his feet, turned, and fumbled at the door latch. His hands felt stiff, clumsy. He could not puzzle out the strange door. From across the room Sean Cullen sobbed and cursed.

Another shot sounded. It drove the air from Jake's lungs and sent him stumbling away from the door. He saw Cullen, the pistol still in the Irishman's hand, though his face was torn, bleeding and blackened like beef held over a campfire. Another shot. Jake jerked and fell to his knees. The tightness in his chest was greater. Sparks of blackness played at the edge of his vision. Another shot. The air filled with swirls of red.

Jake raised his head and looked square at Cullen. "Stop that," he said.

The sound that came from his mouth was soft, like the movement of a snake over stone. But its effect was tremendous.

Cullen was thrown back against the round table. The heavy table rose up on its side, spilling its load of cigars and spittoons, and toppled. Blue flames licked across Cullen's face and hands. He screamed again, but it quickly faded into a whimper.

Gould ran a match across the wall panel and touched it to the tip of his cigar. "Remarkable," he said. "Kastle?"

"Yes, Mr. Gould?" The engineer's voice was tight as a fiddle string.

"Do we have other measures prepared for such an event?"

"Yes, Mr. Gould. Stand close, sir." Kastle fumbled in his vest and came out with an object like a thick pocket watch. It didn't look anything like a gun, but there was no mistaking the way Kastle pointed the thing toward Jake.

Jake tightened his fist and held it up. "Keep back," he said. Streaks of pure white shot from Jake's fingers, arcing across the room. But not one of the bolts struck home. A foot from Kastle's chest the fire bent to the side. A chair was smashed to kindling. The window at the side of the room was blown from its frame and sent spinning into the night, letting in a roar of passing air. Even the back wall of the room heaved and cracked under the force of Jake's talent. Kastle and Gould were untouched.

"Well," Gould said. The wind that whistled through the shattered window was so loud that he had to shout to be heard. "It seems that at least one of these devices functions as advertised."

"Yes," Kastle said. He reached into his vest and produced an object the size of an apple. "Here," he said. "This should finish what Cullen started."

Kastle ran his fingers across the crown of the small object and a cone of brilliant red light shot out. Jake stepped back, but not before the light had touched his outstretched hand.

Cold. The light was red as a fire, but it was colder than any ice. Jake's arm fell to his side, numb and useless.

"Ah," Gould said. "It appears we have both an effective defense and a formidable weapon. Very good, Kastle. Now end this thing before some two-bit sheriff costs me a fortune."

Kastle walked forward confidently, holding out the object. "He will be dead in only a few seconds," he said. He ran his fingers across the metal apple.

Jake jumped straight toward Kastle, hoping to knock the object away. But he was battered and ill and his leap came a moment too late.

The terrible cold light was already shining. It swept over Jake from head to foot, cold as a January stream, taking his body away.

He was only vaguely aware of falling, bouncing from the

broken table, rolling past Kastle, past Gould, and through the shattered window. He felt nothing. It was unreal, like images from a picture book. For a moment he was flying through space. There was a roar of wind and a jumbled sound of voices.

Then the ground came up and struck him like a charging buffalo. Jake could not feel the pain, but he heard the crisp, wet sound of breaking bone. He tumbled on, and on down slopes he could see but not feel, unable to make the least move to stop himself. He reached the bottom of some nameless gully, splashed in a muddy wallow, and finally came to a stop with his face turned up to the stars. He was broken and as still as a child's discarded doll.

The sound of the train, already far away, grew farther still. The thump of engines and click of wheels grew faint. Then it was gone.

☆ **15** ☆

Sienna Truth was waiting by the closed door of the Kettle Black when Goldy came down the stairs. She stood with her arms crossed and her face to the small window at the side of the door, staring at the dark street outside.

Goldy pursed her lips and looked at her in surprise. "Lands if you ain't up early."

"I'm too worried to sleep," Sienna said. "I had ..." She paused and turned around. It was evident that the girl had been crying. Quite astonishing behavior for Sienna. "I had bad dreams," she finished softly.

That news came as no particular surprise to Goldy. Since Malcolm disappeared, Sienna had suffered troubles almost every night, some of them bad enough to leave her screaming. The girl was generally so composed, it was rattling to see just how much her brother's disappearance had thrown her from her stride. Goldy was so used to Sienna being the one that kept things calm, she barely knew how to comfort her.

"You hungry?" Goldy asked. She came close to Sienna, shivering in the cold breeze that blew in through the loose-fitting window. "Some bacon, maybe?"

"No," Sienna said. "I don't want anything." She wrapped her arms tight around herself and looked down at the floor.

Goldy put her hands on the girl's shoulder and pulled her toward the bar. "You come away from the drafts and eat some bacon and flapjacks. It'll make you feel better."

Sienna moved away from Goldy's touch. She went to a table near the warm stove and sat. She looked up at Goldy for a second, and it seemed she was about to say more, then her gaze turned down to the floor and curtains of hair fell to mask her face.

Goldy felt a touch of irritation mix with her sympathy. It was one thing to mourn someone, but she felt there should be limits on such things. If you went on mourning forever, you'd not get your chores done. Over the week, Sienna had not been near as helpful around the saloon as she was before, often doing no work for a day or more. Nor had she been taking care of herself. Her long black hair had lost its well-brushed sheen. The dress she was wearing was dusty and rumpled. There were lines in her face and neck that showed clear enough how many meals she had missed.

If the girl didn't shake off her doldrums soon, Goldy feared Sienna would have to take to bed herself.

Pine knots snapped inside the stove as Goldy put on the coffee and larded a skillet for hotcakes. "You think we can get those beds changed upstairs?" she asked, hoping to get Sienna's mind on something other than her brother.

Sienna just continued to sit, her pretty face hidden behind her hair.

Goldy sighed. "Child, you need to do something apart from sitting and fretting. It would do you good to think about something besides your brother for a bit."

Sienna looked up, her huge brown eyes brimming with tears. "It wasn't Malcolm I was dreaming about," she said. "It was you."

"Me?" Goldy looked at her in surprise for a moment, then began to laugh. "Girl, if all that's worrying you is that you seen me dead out there somewhere, you can stop fussing. I've known all my life I would come to a bad end."

"It's not just you," Sienna said. "It's Sheriff Jake, and Mr. Bred, and Josie, and Deputy Sharp, and—" She jumped up from her chair and wrung her hands together. "It's all tossed together. I can't sort it."

Goldy stopped laughing and came around the table to Sienna's side. "It's not a dream you had, it was a vision, something from your talent."

Sienna nodded.

"Only you had a vision you can't make head nor tails of, is that it?" Goldy asked.

Sienna nodded more vigorously, tears flying as she moved her head. "It was never like this before," she said. "Always I could see what was coming. I couldn't always tell anyone, but I could see. Now, since Malcolm is gone—" She broke off and drew in a ragged breath.

Goldy wrapped her arms around the girl and hugged her tight. Sienna put her head on Goldy's shoulder and began to cry in earnest. "Hush, now," Goldy said. "It's all right."

"No," Sienna groaned, her voice muffled against Goldy's dress. "I can't see what will happen. Everything is confused."

There was a part of Goldy that almost wanted to start up laughing again. Sienna had said for years that it was Malcolm who had the talent and she only passed on the word. But everyone had figured Sienna only said such things to protect her crippled brother. Even Sienna had finally admitted that the visions were hers. Now it seemed Malcolm really had been a part of the talent.

"You can still see something," Goldy said. "Give it time and you may sort it out."

"But I don't know what's coming," Sienna said between great tearful sobs.

"You're still ahead of most everybody else," Goldy said. "The rest of them, they don't have a sniff of what's coming down the road."

Sienna pushed herself away from Goldy and snuffled back her tears. "How do they stand it?" she asked.

"As best they can," Goldy replied.

Abruptly Sienna turned and ran up the stairs. A moment later, from down the hall, came the sound of a door slamming.

Goldy stared after the girl for a moment, then went back to fixing breakfast. It had never occurred to her that Sienna's talent might allow her to see so much, or that its absence would upset Sienna so greatly. But it seemed to Goldy it was a good thing that Sienna was crying. In her experience, the sooner you cried about something, the sooner you were likely to be over it.

"What an interesting problem," said a voice from the door.

Goldy looked up to see Deputy Tom Sharp leaning against the door frame. "What are you doing here before dawn?" she asked.

The deputy pushed himself away from the door and strolled toward the stove. "I was hungry," he said. "Thought I'd come over and see if I might fetch some breakfast here."

"I don't cook breakfast." Goldy was bothered that she had not heard Tom enter. For that matter, she hadn't heard the front door open. There should have been a bolt in that door, but now it hung wide open.

"Seems to me that you were just talking about hotcakes," Tom said. "That would be breakfast enough for me."

Goldy shook her head. "That's only for me and my girls. I don't cook breakfast for the whole town." She squinted at the short man's dark eyes. "How long you been listening?"

"I always listen." Tom hooked a chair with the toe of his boot and pulled it back from the table. He dropped into it, threw back his arms and stretched his mouth in a yawn.

"Well, I wouldn't say much for your manners," Goldy said.

Tom laughed. "Manners aren't my long suit," he said. "Tell me, you think your girl could really see everything that's coming? I never heard of anyone that had the casting as strong as that."

Goldy picked up her skillet and sat it on the edge of the stove to warm. "What Sienna's got is not what I'd rightly call casting. It's different from what I do."

"That's right," Tom said. "You have a talent yourself, don't you?" He leaned back in his chair and thumped his boots up on the nearest table. "I'd be pleased if you would cast for me sometime. I need a look into the future."

"You don't get your feet off my table, you'll not have much future," Goldy said.

The deputy laughed again, but moved his feet. "You're a feisty old gal, ain't you?"

Goldy gritted her teeth. The longer this conversation went on, the less she liked it. "Why don't you move on about your chores, Deputy. I already said there's no breakfast for you here."

"That's too bad." Tom got to his feet and gave a deep sigh. His pretty face turned down in a frown. "You'd think that folks in a town like this would want to keep on better terms with the law."

"You ain't the law," Goldy said stiffly. She walked past the stove and around the end of the bar. "Don't expect you can boss me around like you're the sheriff."

A thoughtful expression came to Tom's face and he rubbed his fingers across the faint stubble on his chin. "You're thinking that because you're friends with Jake, it doesn't matter how you treat me. That it?"

"I been friends with Sheriff Bird before he was sheriff. But that don't make a difference in how I treat folks that bust in on me before dawn and start making threats." Goldy dropped her hand below the bar and closed her fingers on the grip of a heavy revolver. "I make a rule to be blunt with everyone that threatens me in my own place."

"I've not made any threats," Tom said.

Goldy snorted. "If I was you, I wouldn't start. I've seen some of your signing."

Tom nodded and strolled slowly toward the door. "You're right. It wouldn't do for me to make threats I can't back up." He paused at the door and flashed a quick smile. "I believe we may be talking again soon." With that, he pushed through the swinging shutters and left the Kettle Black.

Goldy kept her hand on the gun for some time. Even when the coffee began to boil and steam she stood there, waiting to see if Tom Sharp was going to make a move. Finally the sun cleared the western horizon and orange light filled the street outside. Goldy took a deep breath and went back to fixing her breakfast.

She did not know what to think about Tom Sharp. His words implied contempt for both her and Jake, but she had seen no action to back up those words. Before Jake left, Tom had been different. He'd seemed younger than his years, like a puppy dancing at the heels of an old cattle dog.

It was evident to Goldy that much of what Tom had said and done amounted to acting. She suspected the Tom Sharp that had come into the bar this morning was much closer to the genuine article than the fellow who'd sipped free whiskey only a few days before. Part of the difference might be the simple fact that Jake was out of town. There were many men who started to feel their oats when they took a position as important as the one Tom had been given, and not a few that soon outgrew their britches. But there was more here than that.

Of everything, it was Tom's new confidence that bothered Goldy most. She had played plenty of poker in her days, and been privileged to watch some of the best players in the West. She knew bluffing, and she knew confidence. Tom Sharp thought he had an ace in his vest.

She would have to talk to Bred, Goldy decided. The old changer was not as spry as he'd once been, but he was still tough as buffalo leather. No sunburnt easterner was going to push Bred around. If it came down to it, she was sure a few swipes from the paws of the great bear would take the starch out of Tom Sharp. Old Bred could turn himself into a bear that would make a grizzly yelp for Mother.

A stumbling at the top of the stairs announced that Black Alice was up and about. "There anything to eat?" she asked.

"Soon will be," Goldy said. "Coffee's ready if you want some."

It was a foolish question. So far as Goldy remembered, there was no food or drink that Black Alice had refused. Goldy took down a pair of cups and poured them full. Some trade goods had come up from Tempest over the last week, and with them a new excuse for coffee. The current brew was made from running water over toasted barley and as much chicory as could be found. Goldy added some burnt potato peels to her grounds. In her opinion it gave it more of the bite of the real thing.

Black Alice took a cup of coffee and held it up against her cheek. Her room was on the northwest corner of the Kettle Black, and it tended to be the coldest in the place. "Where's Sienna?" she asked. "I thought I heard her down here."

"She was here, but she went back upstairs." Goldy looked at the door at the head of the staircase. "Why don't you go up there and fetch her and Orpah? I'm about to have some flap-jacks, and they'll not be worth eating when they're cold."

"Flapjacks?" Alice said. "With sorghum?"

"With sorghum," Goldy agreed. "Or even honey if you want it."

A smile took over Black Alice's face. She was as fond of sweets as Panny Wadkins was of drink. "Sure," she said. "I'll go fetch the others." She threw down the rest of the coffee and started for the stairs with a bounce in her step.

Goldy shook her head and smiled. A lot of people might look on Black Alice as something of a spoiled woman, but she was still nothing but a child on the inside. The best thing for Alice would be for some young buck to take a fancy to her and propose marriage. What life could be earned from a store or ranch around Medicine Rock would be a hard life, but in the long run it would be a lot easier on Alice than another twenty years in the beds at the Kettle Black. A marriageable man would be a good thing for Sienna, too. Maybe now that her brother was gone, Sienna might start to notice just how many men were waiting for her to look their way.

There was a scream from upstairs. It was not the scream of someone who saw a mouse cross the hallway, or even the scream of someone who had cut their hand on some sharp edge. This was a raw, throat-searing scream that went on until it trailed off in a hoarse rattle.

Goldy couldn't move. It was Alice screaming, she knew that well enough. And she also feared she knew what Alice was screaming about. Goldy could see it in her mind clearer than any casting in any pool of whiskey.

Slowly Goldy put down the skillet and got her feet moving. She couldn't even feel her feet as she went up the staircase. Sienna had been so upset. Her brother was gone, probably dead. Her talents were all scrambled. She should have seen it coming, Goldy told herself. She had never thought Sienna would go this far. Goldy wondered how she would get on without the girl.

But when Goldy reached the hallway at the top of the stairs, Sienna was standing there, alive as ever. Black Alice was bent over the smaller girl, her back shaking but no more sound coming from her ruined throat.

"What is it?" Goldy asked in confusion. "What's wrong?"

Sienna looked at her with her dark eyes. "Orpah."

Goldy pushed past the two young women and came to Orpah's room at the end of the hall. Even before she looked inside, she smelled the thick odor. An odor that made her think of the stink after a hog slaughter.

Winter light spilled into the room from a pair of windows, giving the scene a stark, gray solidity. Goldy's eyes went first to the bed, but Orpah was not there. Then Goldy turned her head—and saw what had made Black Alice scream.

Orpah was hanging upside down from the wall. She was naked head to toe, her skin almost white as snow against the dingy paint—except for her face. Her face was bloated, twisted, and red as a blood blister. Only a few inches below the ceiling her feet had been snugged together with a length of barbwire then nailed to the wall. Her arms were run out to the sides, nails run through each palm and into the plaster. Dark sticky blood had run down her legs. More blood dripped from her hands and ran in thin lines down the wall.

But all that blood didn't amount to a drop compared to what had spilt from the great tear in her throat. So little remained of Orpah's throat that Goldy was surprised her head didn't drop right off. There was a pink-white glint of bone and a few shreds of red meat. The floor under her torn body was deep with blood. Blood had pooled on the uneven floorboards and run almost to the door. It seemed to Goldy there was enough blood to fill a washtub.

Below the torn throat, Orpah's green eyes stared out from her swollen face. Her long hair hung down to dip into the pool of gore.

"Who?"

Goldy looked around and saw Sienna standing close behind her. "What's that, child?"

"Who did this to her?"

"I don't know." Goldy stepped into the room, careful to avoid the expanding lake of blood. At first glance she could see nothing that suggested who else might have been in the room. The girls had both been busy the night before, but Goldy didn't remember any customers that stayed the night.

A movement outside the window caught her attention. Goldy crept over to the glass and looked down.

The sheriff's office was right across from the Kettle Black. On the walk in front of the office Tom Sharp stood with his arms folded across his chest. He was looking up. He was looking right into Goldy's eyes.

Sharp's lips began to move. Though he was outside and across the street, his words seemed to echo in the blood-soaked room.

"I don't make threats."

☆ 16 ☆

There was a persistent rumor that said a bite from a changer
would pass their talent on to the one that was bitten. So far as
Bill knew, there was not a lick of truth in the rumor. But if
there had been a changer present, he would have gladly put
out his arm for a bite.

Changers healed fast. Bill had seen a changer take a double
load of buckshot at such short range that it punched a hole
straight through his gut. Two days later the man had ridden
out on horseback and killed the person that attacked him. It
was tough to kill a changer.

Bill wished that he had even a touch of that talent. As it
was, his arm ached like a son of a bitch, and that wasn't a
patch on his head. His head hurt so bad, he lacked the cuss
words to describe it. Every bump of the wagon brought on
whole new countries of pain.

"Would you like some more brandy, Mr. Cody?" the Rainmaker asked.

Bill started to nod, then thought better of it. "Yes," he said.
"I believe I would."

The Rainmaker fumbled to draw out his flask. He held a
small tin cup in one hand and did his best to pour the amber
liquid, but a sudden lurch of the wagon caused him to spill a
stream of liquor across his knee. He held the cup out to Bill
with an embarrassed look on his pale features.

"Just let me know if you want more, Mr. Cody."

"Oh, I will." About a gallon of good bourbon sounded right
to Bill, but this thick, sweet brandy was all that was available
for the moment. At least the Rainmaker did not complain

157

about how he was draining the bottle. His head swum as he took another sip. If he should pass out before consuming the rest, Bill figured that was all the better.

The small panel at the front of the wagon slid open and Bill winced as sunlight stabbed into the dimly lit cabin. "Where's my wind?" Muley called from above.

"It's not your wind," the Rainmaker shouted back. "I've never seen you making it."

"I don't see you making it, either," Muley replied. "This is the third time it's dropped off in the last hour. I guess you don't care much about getting to the camp by sunset."

"I doubt you can even find the camp," the Rainmaker said.

"Not without wind I won't." Muley shut the panel with a snap.

Bill gently rubbed his head. "I wish he wouldn't do that," he said. "Every time he shuts that thing, it feels like I been shot all over again."

The Rainmaker frowned and brushed ineffectively at the stain on his pants leg. "I do apologize, Mr. Cody." Though there was little light in the coach, Bill could see that the albino's white face had gone flush with embarrassment.

"Bill," said Bill. "All my friends call me Bill." He stroked his beard for a moment. "Most of my enemies call me Bill, too. Hell, almost everyone calls me Bill."

The Rainmaker smiled. "Thank you, Mr. ... Bill. I'm honored."

Bill smiled. It had been many years since anyone had been so impressed to meet Buffalo Bill. He would have laughed, but that would have only flustered the man worse. "Tell me, you got a name besides Rainmaker?"

The Rainmaker seemed astonished at such a question. "It's Howard," he said. "Howard Spencer."

"Well, Howard, I'm glad to know you." Bill put out his hand and the Rainmaker shook it. The brandy was beginning to round the edges from Bill's pain. At the same time, the liquor had built up a comfortable warmth in his gut. Sleep began to seem like an idea that ought to be considered. Bill shifted around on the bench, slumping down in the corner.

"No one's called me Howard in fifteen years," the Rainmaker said. "Muley doesn't even know that's my name."

"I can appreciate the problem," Bill said. "Being a notable has its difficulty. Everyone back East, why, they always want to call me Buffalo Bill Cody. They might forget the Cody, and sometimes they forget the Bill, but I'll be damned if they ever forget the Buffalo." He shifted in his chair, cushioning his head with his uninjured arm. "All I ever did to a buffalo was shoot them, but those easterners talk like I was one. Sometimes they even called me Mr. Buffalo."

"You're famous."

"Hardly famous, Howard." Bill started to laugh, but a new wave of pain in his skull stopped that idea quick. "Only reason anybody knows me is because of some dime novels."

The Rainmaker was slow to answer. "It wasn't a writer that named me Rainmaker," he said. "It was my mother."

"Then talent must have come on you young."

"Talent?" The Rainmaker shook his head. "I've seen signers and scribblers conjure up creatures or knock down a bullet in flight. That's talent. What I have isn't talent, it's a curse."

Bill gave a shrug. "I suppose it's not always pleasant."

"Not pleasant?" The Rainmaker shook his head. "My family owns the Spencer gun works. You know it?"

"I've owned one of the carbines myself," Bill said. "Fine gun."

The Rainmaker nodded. "A lot of people own them. My family is not poor." He fished in the pocket of his dark suit and came out with a large locket. "Here, these are my parents."

Bill clenched his teeth against the pain as he moved out of his comfortable position and stretched to take the locket from the Rainmaker's hand. Inside the golden case a tall, severe man and a short, pretty woman stood flanking a boy of about seven. He was a likely looking boy, with a grin at the corner of his lips.

"The child is you, I take it," Bill said.

"Yes." The Rainmaker pulled the locket back and returned it to his vest. "That was before. That was when my father still talked about West Point, and my mother still called me her beautiful child—before the war. The rain came on me barely a week after Shiloh."

Bill nodded. "Shiloh was the start for a lot of folks."

"It wasn't steady at first, but inside a month it was raining all the time. My skin changed, too, like the rain washed the color right out of me." The Rainmaker held out his hand and stared down at his own long white fingers. "My parents were not keen on the idea of a son that looked like a ghost. Neither were they too fond of living under a rain cloud every day and night. First thing they did was send me off to boarding school, but it didn't last. No one there wanted me, either. After that they sent me to a house up in the woods. There it could rain on me and no one else had to get wet." He balled his fingers into a fist. "I was there almost two years and my parents never visited once."

"How old were you?" Bill asked.

"Nine," the Rainmaker said. "I was nine years old when they sent me up the hill. I was eleven when I ran out into the rain and made my own way down. I've been making my own way ever since."

Bill had seen boys of nine that had been left with the responsibilities of men. But those had been western boys, boys that understood hard choices from the day they were born. For an eastern boy, raised to soft sheets and hot food, nine might as well be an infant.

"I'm sorry for what happened to you," Bill said. "For what it's worth, it seems to me you've done well on your own."

"Well enough to keep food on the table," the Rainmaker agreed. "But not as well as I'd like."

Bill settled himself back onto the bench, careful not to knock against his wounded arm. "What would you like, Mr. Spencer?"

The Rainmaker opened his mouth, shut it, and sat in silence for a moment. "You know what I've seen the last fifteen years and more? I've seen rain. Doesn't matter much to me if this wagon is rolling through Dakota, or Deseret, or Ohio, what I see is rain, rain, and more rain. That is, when I don't see snow." He shook his head sharply. "I've collected enough money to build myself a fine house, because that's what I thought I wanted. But no matter where I build that house, it would only be a house in the rain." He stopped for a moment, and when he continued, his voice was very soft, little more than a whisper. "What I want is a dry place, Mr. Cody. And a chance to warm myself in the sun."

"Mr. Spencer, if it's ever in my power to give you those things, you'll have them." Bill gave as good a smile as he could muster. "That's a promise from Buffalo Bill."

The panel at the front of the wagon slid open again. "I see something ahead," Muley called. "You want to come up here and take a look?"

Bill groaned. It seemed he was never going to get his rest. "Coming."

Bill hadn't noticed the slowing of the sail wagon, but when he pushed open the door, he found that they had come to a stop. The sun, shining brightly only a few minutes before, was now masked by the cloud that followed the Rainmaker. The rain itself had not yet caught up with them, but from the cool moist breezes that blew against Bill's face, they were not far off.

Muley waited by the front of the wagon. When Bill drew close, he pointed down the long gentle slope into the valley ahead. "That there looks like your railroad camp."

Bill squinted. Only a few years back he had been able to spot a single antelope crossing the plains more than a mile away. Now he had a hard time spotting a railroad at the same distance. If he squinted hard, he could just make out a series of dark shapes and several columns of smoke rising into the air. "It looks right," he said. "You think we can get down there before dark?"

"A-yup, we could," Muley replied. "Only I'm not so sure we ought to. Right now we're just a cloud rising over the hill. We get any closer, they're going to know there's someone with talent coming at them."

"They'll know that anyway." Bill leaned against the side of the wagon. "There aren't so many Dakota or Cheyenne around as there was before Custer did his dance, but there's enough to cause trouble. A camp like this . . ." Bill shook his head. "These folks have eyes all over. They probably saw us this morning and watched us roll all day. By now everyone down there knows where we are and when we're coming.

Muley folded his arms and looked toward the camp with a scowl. "I'm still not too keen on going down there. If it was that Kastle fellow that shot you, why should we go strolling up to him?"

"It was that mick Cullen that did the shooting, but your point's well taken." Bill stroked his beard. "I don't expect we'll find Cullen or Kastle at the camp. The man I'm looking for is this fellow Woodson."

"You think he can do anything about what you've seen?"

"I don't know," Bill admitted. "I've no doubt that everything Kastle's done, he did for his boss, Gould. But that don't mean the men on the line know what's up. The folks I worked with on the old Kansas were not the sort that would put up with all this killing. I don't think these boys will be any different."

Muley shook his head. "You ain't even told us what it is that these fellers did, or what it was they were planning that got you so perturbed with them."

"You'll hear it all soon enough," Bill said. "God knows, with what I've got to say, I don't want to say it any more than I have to."

At that moment the rain caught up to the wagon. Fat drops began to fall with increasing regularity, dropping through the tall grass with a sigh. Muley climbed back onto his bench while Bill fled to the interior of the cabin. The minor exertion of getting up and down had brought with it an increase in his headache. Bill sat on his bench with his eyes shut tight, fighting back a wave of pain.

It wasn't until he opened his eyes a few minutes later that he saw the Rainmaker in similar distress. The pale man's face was stretched tight as a drum, his teeth bared in a smile of pain. Beads of sweat rolled from his high forehead and flowed around his deep-set eyes.

"What's wrong?" Bill asked. "You feeling poorly?"

The Rainmaker gave a stiff nod. "It only started a few seconds ago, but it's getting worse."

"Maybe a touch of brandy would cut the hurt."

"No, I—" The Rainmaker suddenly gave a little grunt and pitched forward. If Bill had not moved to catch him, the lanky man would have gone sprawling on the floor.

The small panel slid sharply open. "My wind's gone to hell," Muley said. "What's going on?"

"Your friend's not well," Bill called in reply. "I think he's needing a doctor."

"Damn. Hold on then, I'll roll her down the slope. Maybe there'll be a doctor at this rail camp." Muley pushed the panel closed.

For several minutes Bill sat there listening to the wheels bump over the old rutted track as he held up the thin unconscious form of the Rainmaker. His own pain was bad enough that he wanted to lay down, but he didn't trust himself to move without dropping his fellow passenger. Finally he heard voices outside the wagon and knew they had at last reached the camp.

Bill felt a mixture of relief and nerves. He would have to convince the railmen to stop Kastle, but from the way Woodson had acted the first time, he didn't think there would be much trouble with that. At any rate, Bill hoped to find a decent meal and a soft bed for the night. That thought was enough to bring a smile to his face.

All at once there was the sharp crack of a pistol, then the boom of a louder gun.

"Muley!" Bill shouted. He struggled to push the limp form of the Rainmaker away, but before he could free himself, the door of the wagon flew open.

Standing outside with a double-barreled shotgun in his grip was the fat camp chief, Woodson. "Get out," he said. His voice was little better than a snarl.

Bill blinked in surprise. "We need help."

Woodson snorted. "If it's left to me, the only help you'll get is help to the end of a hanging rope. Now get out of there or I'll shoot you where you sit."

Bill struggled to his feet, laying the Rainmaker as carefully as he could across the floor of the wagon. "What is this?" he asked as he climbed down from the wagon and looked up at the perch along the front. "Where's Muley? This man needs a doctor."

"Does he?" Woodson turned his head and spat on the ground. "Does he need one worse than those folks in Rapid City?"

"Rapid City?" Bill held up his hands. "That's part of what I've come to tell you about."

"You'll get your chance to talk," Woodson said. "You can talk to the judge all you want."

"I still don't understand," Bill said. "Why should I need to talk about anything with a judge?"

Woodson swung the shotgun around, bringing the barrel against Bill's head with enough force to send him spinning off his feet. He stumbled back against the wheel of the wagon, bounced, and fell to his knees in the trampled grass.

"You're lucky to be talking to anybody," Woodson told him. "I thought you were a man to be trusted, but God help me I was wrong." A pair of burly workmen, stripped to the waist, came up on either side of the camp boss. "Pick him up, boys, and take him over to my tent," Woodson said. "Be sure you hold his hands still. We don't know yet how he works his talent."

"Talent?" Bill mumbled. His head was full of wool and searing pain.

One of the workmen took Bill's arm in a savage grip and hauled him to his feet. "You mean this here's the fella?" he asked.

"That's right," Woodson said with a nod. "This is the man who killed a whole town."

☆ **17** ☆

Jake dipped his hands under the surface of the stream and cupped the water in his hands. It was a slow, meandering creek, and the water was cloudy, almost stagnant, but he was in no position to be picky. He drank down the bitter water, dipped up more, and drank that, too.

It had been years since Jake had spent any serious time out of Medicine Rock. Except for the damnable year following his father's death, he'd lived the rest of his days in one town or another, seldom spending so much as a night out of doors. Still, it sometimes seemed that those months of shelter were only time spent waiting—waiting for the day when he would find himself again out on the plains, injured, lost, and alone.

Jake slowly raised his head and looked around. It was different country than he found around Medicine Rock. There, the ground was mostly bare and cactus was near as common as the grass. In this place the grass was neck high and so thick that the hills looked woolly. There was water, and no cliffs or canyons in sight. Altogether it was a better sort of place to be lost than the dry, barren badlands where Jake had found himself the last time he was in such a situation.

It wasn't even proper to say he was lost. Up the hill there was the railway line to show the way back toward Medicine Rock. All he had to do to get out of this fix was to get up and start walking. Except he couldn't.

Near as Jake could figure, his right leg was broken in three places. He was only reckoning two of those breaks by knots of pain, but the third was clear enough. Midway between his knee and ankle a jagged bone jutted through the skin like a bloody red finger. Every attempt to move his leg sent the bone darting in and out of his shin. It hurt like hell, but the hurt wasn't even the worst of it. The worst was that it made a sound when it moved—a thick, wet sucking sound. Jake figured it for the most unpleasant sound he'd ever heard.

Besides the leg, Jake thought he had broke a rib or two. He wasn't sure if it had happened in the fall from the train, or if it was the result of Cullen's bullets. Either way, there was a distinct tightness in his chest when he tried to draw more than the shallowest of breaths. And God help him if he should cough.

A falcon called from somewhere close at hand. A breeze rustled the dry grass. Though it was September, it was uncommonly warm, with only a few small clouds to mar the deep blue sky. It was a beautiful day for anybody with two good legs and the strength to move.

Jake pushed himself up on his arms and stared up the long slope. The last time Jake had been in such a fix, Bred Smith came along and took him to Hatty's cabin. Between the two of them, they had kept him alive when by all rights he should have died. But Bred was back in Medicine Rock, and Hatty was dead more than five years. If he was to get out of this predicament, he would have to do it for himself.

The train tracks were about the only thing around. If he could get up there, he might be spotted by folks riding by. Of course, the only folks he knew of who would be riding the train were the folks who wanted him dead. He might make the painful belly-crawl up the hill only to be finished off when he got to the top. Or he could stay where he was and die for certain.

Dying for certain didn't sound especially bad. At least the pain in his leg would go away. Anything that would stop that infernal pain couldn't be all bad.

Except he knew better. Dying now would mean leaving Josie and the new baby behind. Worse yet, it would mean dying where they would never know what had become of him.

Jake gritted his teeth, got his arms underneath him as best he could, and began to move up the hill. Right off, his guts threw back the bitter water he had sipped. He gagged and spat until his stomach seemed to be reaching for his backbone. Then he started crawling again.

The hill could not have been a hundred yards from top to bottom, but climbing it was like scaling Pikes Peak. Every little movement brushed the shattered leg against some new obstacle. Every breath flexed Jake's broken ribs. It took him most of the morning to move twenty feet up the slope, and by the time he had done so, it felt like his chest was full of broken glass and his leg packed with live coals.

He took another look up the hill. It would be a terrible thing to die without seeing Josie again, and a more horrible thing still to leave the new baby without a father. But it was beginning to dawn on Jake that he was not going to have much choice in the matter. He was not going to make it up the slope. In fact, he wasn't sure he could move another foot.

"You're going the wrong way," said a woman's voice.

Jake twisted his head around and saw a slender figure standing between him and the blazing sun. He tried to shade his eyes, but all he could make out was the dark fall of hair and the curves of her shape.

The hairs at the back of Jake's neck bristled, and he felt a cold that had nothing to do with the weather. "Hatty?" he whispered.

"No." The woman came forward. It was not Jake's dead friend, but another woman, one with smooth golden skin and eyes as dark as Josie's. She had a few strands of white in her glossy black hair and thin lines at the corners of her strange eyes. Jake reckoned her age at somewhere above thirty and less than forty.

"We have to hurry," the woman said. "Muley is almost twenty miles from here and I've been walking all night to reach you."

"Muley?" Jake's head was fuzzy enough that he had to search a bit to put a person to the name. "How could Muley know I was here?" Getting out the question took all the breath he had and left him wheezing for air.

"You told him."

Jake shook his head as best he could. "I haven't seen anybody."

"Not yet," the woman said, "but you will. He didn't tell me today, anyway. He told me years ago. Now, we've got to hurry. I don't have much time left."

"Hurry where?" Jake asked. He couldn't figure how anyone could have known he was going to end up lying in a ditch beside the train tracks, but he didn't feel well enough to argue.

"Quiet. I've got to get you down the hill before the string twists again."

Jake had no idea what the woman was talking about. He saw no string, and didn't know why it should matter if it twisted or not. He had a sudden thought that this woman might be crazy, but right on its heels came the thought that he didn't care.

"Who are you?" Jake asked in a hoarse whisper.

"A friend of a friend," the woman answered. She moved around Jake and got her hands under his arms. "I'm not strong enough to lift you, so I'm going to have to drag you. You okay with that?"

"Okay?"

"Is that all right with you?

Jake nodded. "Its better than—" He paused for breath. "—lying here. You taking me to Muley?"

"No, he's busy with other things right now. I'm taking you to see a friend of yours."

"Out here?"

"You'll see," the woman said. "Let's go."

The woman was small but strong. She got Jake turned around with his head facing downhill and pulled him through the thick grass like a horse dragging a sledge. It was not a pleasant way to travel—Jake's bad leg flopped over the ground, and he moaned under his breath. But it beat the tar out of moving on his own.

They reached the bottom of the slope and the woman began to pull Jake along the side of the sluggish, reedy stream. Frogs hopped out of their way as they passed, and darning needle flies slipped away from the stream to skim around Jake's bleeding leg. After a hundred or so sharp bumps the pain in the leg had begun to change. It was no longer so keen as it had been. Instead it became a kind of low, constant throb. At the same time, Jake realized that he'd lost all feeling in his right foot. In a vague way, Jake knew that this was a bad thing, but at the moment just getting away from the pain seemed a prize worth any price.

The grass was thinner once they reached the floor of the valley, and the woman had a hard time pulling. Their progress became slower and they had to stop every few minutes to let the woman rest her arms.

A fog was stealing over Jake. He began to lose track of where he was and what had happened. Several times he thought it was Josie leaning over him, and he tried to tell her how much he loved her and how sorry he was about missing the baby. Then he thought again that it might be Hatty, and he tried to ask her what it was like to be dead. Getting some advanced word of how the land laid seemed like a good idea.

A sharp slap to the face split the fog. "I have to go now," the woman said.

Jake looked around as best he could. He could see no house or sign of people. As far as he could tell, the woman had only succeeded in dragging him to the exact middle of nowhere. "You're going to leave me here?"

"I have to," the woman replied. "I could try to pull you further, but I can feel the string tightening. I've got to run for help while I can."

"What string?" Jake asked.

The woman shook her head. "I haven't got time to explain that now," she said. "Stay here and someone will come."

Jake started to laugh. It hurt his ribs something awful, but he had a hard time fighting off the giggles. "I don't plan on going anywhere."

"Good," the woman said. To Jake's surprise, she bent down and kissed him on the cheek. Then she stood and started walking away.

"Wait," Jake called. He raised up his head and put all the

strength in his voice that he could manage. "What's your name?"

The woman paused, then smiled. She had a hell of a smile. "Boots," she said. Then she turned and trotted away across the grass.

"Boots," Jake whispered. He let his head sink down against the sandy ground. "Thanks, Boots." Then he closed his eyes and slept.

When he opened his eyes again, there was a prairie dog beside him. Jake jerked his head back and tried to move away, but there was something wrong with the way his eyes were working. He moved his head again and pushed himself back on his elbows. It was at that point he understood that instead of a small animal sitting close to his nose, he was looking at a considerably larger animal sitting a good ten feet away. This particular prairie dog looked to be about five feet tall, maybe taller. It stood up on its hind legs and looked down on Jake with black button eyes. And it wore glasses.

"Hello," the prairie dog said. Its voice was high, with something of a buzz, but the word was clear enough. "I guess you're Sheriff Jake Bird."

Jake felt his mouth drop open and didn't do a thing to stop it. "You talk."

The prairie dog made a huffing sound that might have been a laugh. " 'Course I do," it said.

Jake raised one shaking hand to his forehead. Sure enough, he was feverish. "Am I dead, or only crazy?" he asked.

It was hard to read any expression on the prairie dog's rounded snout, but Jake got the idea that the creature was smiling. "No on the first item," it said. "I'm afraid I can't say about the second. Now come on along home so we can get started on that leg."

"I can't move," Jake said.

"You don't need to." All at once a half-dozen more prairie dogs appeared out of the grass. These were smaller than the one that talked, but still considerably larger than the common variety, as big as collie dogs. They clustered around the speaker like chicks after their mother and turned round black eyes toward Jake.

"The boys here will take you home," the largest rodent said.

Jake tried to remember what it was that prairie dogs ate. It was not something that had ever seemed worth investigating before, but now it seemed of particular importance.

"You're taking me to your hole?"

"Don't worry," the prairie dog said. "You'll like it." It removed its glasses and rubbed them against its brown fur. "All right, boys, let's go."

The smaller prairie dogs came over to Jake and sniffed at him. Then a dozen small hands grabbed him by the shirt and pants. Jake stifled a groan of pain as the rodents lifted him from the ground and started walking.

Burdened with Jake, the creatures moved quite slowly, shuffling along on their hind legs like pallbearers at a funeral. It was the strangest travel Jake had ever done, but it was considerably less jarring than being dragged down the hill. The largest prairie dog strolled alongside, sometimes strutting on its hind legs, sometimes dropping to all fours.

One of the smaller prairie dogs gave a whistling bark. The leader made his huffing laugh. "Aaron says you're a very heavy person."

"Aaron says," Jake repeated. It seemed only proper that the creatures should have names.

"Aaron's always the first one to complain."

The trip turned out to be a short one. Within five minutes of the start of the strange journey, they approached a series of low cones on the ground. Jake recognized them well enough as prairie dog holes, only these holes were big enough for prairie horses.

With astounding delicacy the prairie dogs positioned him above the opening. More creatures appeared from below ground and helped lower Jake into the hole. They went down about ten feet, enough that the sky dropped to a blue circle surrounded by dark walls of earth. The tunnel then ran along sideways for a few yards, then down another dozen feet or more. By the time they reached the bottom of the second drop, the light was reduced to a faint gray-blue glow. A few steps down the next passage and even that was gone.

After that it was a matter of turns, twists, slopes that went up and then slopes that went down. All of it happened in pure pitch-darkness, with only the soft step of the shuffling feet on the dirt floor. As the slow passage went on and on, Jake once again began to wonder if he was dead. The pain in his leg gone, he seemed to be floating in perfect blackness, and what was happening seemed too strange to be real. He was moderately convinced that he must have died up by the train tracks. Everything that had happened since then was just part of what happened after. But there was no preacher he'd ever heard who mentioned prairie dogs in either heaven or hell.

Miles of darkness seemed to pass before he saw a growing light ahead. A few moments later Jake was carried into a chamber about the size of the bedroom in his house. Which is just what this room seemed to be. An oil lamp hung from the ceiling, filling the room with warm yellow light. Though the walls were of brown dirt, there was a woven rug on the floor. Pressed up in one corner was a bed with a stack of pillows and a faded blue comforter. There was a table beside the bed, a trio of tattered books, and a single straight-back chair. Against the dark wall was a round-topped trunk almost as big as the bed.

Jake was anticipating being placed in the bed, but the prairie dogs brought him to the center of the room and laid him square on the rug. Their giant leader moved across the room and took a seat in the chair.

"All right, boys, go take care of yourselves for a bit," the spectacled creature said.

The small prairie dogs gave a few whistles, then disappeared into the mouths of four dark passages that opened into the room.

The big prairie dog folded its furry forelimbs across its chest. "You know," it said, "you are in a hell of a mess."

"I know," Jake said. He looked down at his shattered leg where the torn pants leg had peeled back to show the bloody wound on his shin. "You said you were going to do something about my leg?"

"I said *we* were," the prairie dog corrected. It shook its round head. "That leg of yours has gone sour already. I expect I'll end up chewing it off close to the top." The creature opened its mouth and showed white teeth as long as Jake's hand.

"Chew?" Jake looked around at the dark mouths of the tunnels. He was in no shape to try and escape. He wasn't even sure which of the tunnels he'd been carried through.

The prairie dog made his huffing laugh. "It's a joke," it said.

"Thank God," Jake said. He forced a smile in return. "I need my leg."

"Oh, the leg has to come off," the prairie dog said. "It was only the chewing that was a joke."

"But it can't," Jake said. He tried to sit up, but that brought on a new fit of coughing. By the time it subsided, he was too weak to say more.

The form of the giant prairie dog grew murky. There was a grinding, squeaking noise as the creature's fur jumped up and down. Then the fur began to fade. A round-faced man with iron-gray hair and a dark stubble on his face sat in the chair where the prairie dog had been.

"Look, son," the man said. "That leg is poison. I know something about healing, but I don't have the kind of talent that can handle this."

"You're human," Jake wheezed.

"Of course," the man said. "You think prairie dogs can talk?" He shook his head. "I'll tell you all about me later, but we need to take care of that leg right now."

Jake looked down and trembled. "It really has to come off?"

"It does unless you do something about it."

"What can I do?"

The man leaned forward in his chair. "Boots says you have a strong talent. Use that to fix your leg."

"I can't," Jake said. "It doesn't work like that."

"It's my experience that talent does what you set your mind for it to do," the man said. "I know something about this chore. Maybe I can teach you."

Jake felt too tired to raise a finger. He remembered how hard his talent had come to him on the train and wondered if he had the strength even to bring the chattering, much less bend it to a new task. "I don't know."

The man got up from his chair and went over to the chest. "I figure you've got about eight hours to learn," he said as he pulled up the top. He fumbled inside, then let the lid fall closed. When he turned around, he had a well-used wood saw. "After that—" He flexed the blade of the saw between his hands. "—we'll see if I can cut a straight line."

A railway man thumped down a plate of beans. "Here," he said. "And this is more than you deserve."

Muley rocked forward in his chair. "How am I supposed to eat them with my hands tied like this?" The cords that bound him to the hard chair dug into his wrists as he wiggled the chair toward the plate of food.

"Either put your face in them beans or starve. Don't make no difference to me." The guard was a burly southerner with an ill-tended beard. From the way his arms strained the seams of his shirt, Muley figured the man could lay a twenty-foot steel single-handed. He had fists the size of country hams, and he seemed anxious to use them.

"We didn't do anything wrong," Muley said.

The guard sneered and jabbed a thick, dirty finger into Muley's face. "I seen Rapid City. I seen it, you hear? And I talked to one of the folks that saw what happened. Don't you go telling me you ain't done nothing wrong." He shook his head. "Chickamauga weren't so nigh bad as what I seen in that town."

"Whatever happened in Rapid City," Muley said, "what makes you think it was us that did it?"

"You think you gonna fool us, boy?" The southerner spat a wad of tobacco across the tent. "Too bad for you, there was some folks leaving Rapid City the day it happened. They already told us they seen Buffalo Bill Cody and two strangers come into town, then they seen the flash."

"Flash?"

A broad palm smacked against the side of Muley's head.

175

"Hush!" the guard said. "We already had the easterners come through here and tell how Cody run off and leave them to die. Ain't none of you fit to walk on."

Muley sighed. He had been protesting his innocence ever since the railroad men captured them, but no one seemed to listen. Whatever it was that they had seen in Rapid City was too strong for them to get past. The idea that they might be after the wrong folks didn't concern them near as much as the idea that someone had to pay for what had been done.

The burly guard gave Muley a final sharp look and walked out of the tent. As soon as he was gone, Muley pulled his hands free of the ropes and massaged his aching wrists.

Whoever had done the rope work had not considered the difficulty of tying down an old seaman. Muley had spent years working wet stiff rope into snug knots, and he often had to do so in the middle of the night and the center of a storm. Just as often as he had to tie those knots, he had to loosen them. He was good at it. His fingers were not so limber as when he'd been climbing the rigging of a big three-masted schooner, but they were more than adequate for undoing what some ham-fisted rail worker had done.

He got up from his chair, blood tingling through his sleeping legs, and crept over to the flap of the tent. No guard in sight. It was just after dusk outside, and evening fires were being kindled. It was raining, of course, and some of the fires were being built beside hastily erected shelters. For the last two days it had been raining steadily. Muley took it as a good sign that the Rainmaker was still alive and somewhere nearby. Whatever the rail men might have done to him, it hadn't broken the Rainmaker's talent.

Muley considered for a moment waiting for full dark, but on the previous evening the guard had slept at the end of the tent. He would rather risk running around in the shadows instead of trying to slip past the huge southerner.

Muley slipped out of the tent, stepped around to the side, and turned back into the thick of the camp. The rain was cold. He guessed that somewhere in the night it might turn to snow. In the meantime, he missed his hat.

There were several thousand folks in this place they called Hell on Wheels, and Muley had met only a few. He'd thought about it a good bit over the last two days, and figured that if he didn't draw attention to himself, he might walk around the place without drawing any stir. True, his face did show some swelling and dried blood from the beating delivered soon after their capture. But he was willing to bet that in a camp of this sort there was more than one face marred by fisticuffs. He would take his chances.

The question of where the Rainmaker and Cody were being held was one that Muley had not been able to reason out. As usual, the Rainmaker's clouds had flattened out when he stopped moving. Muley couldn't count on that to find them. He'd been pulled apart from the other two at the beginning. The rail boss seemed to think Cody had some hidden talent, and the Rainmaker was clearly enough among those touched by ability. But the rail boss, for some reason, took Muley at his word that he was free of talent. The assumption that he was harmless had probably saved Muley a good deal of beating, but it irked him nonetheless.

The last Muley had seen of the other pair, the rail boss and a goodly crowd of others were taking them off toward the center of the camp. So that was the direction where he started his search now.

Hell on Wheels might have called itself a moving town, but beyond that statement it wasn't like any town Muley had visited before. There was the central line of the tracks and the tight stacks of supplies. But once away from that strip of order, everything else was chaos. Men had pitched their sleeping tents in clusters of all sizes and arranged them at every angle. Mixed in with these were tents and shacks that served as laundries, saloons, and general stores. In the muddy paths between the tents there were puddles that stank of more than rain.

It was apparent there was no restriction on the men as far as drinking or gambling; or if there was, it was ill-enforced. Most every man Muley passed seemed to be involved in a game of chance or a bottle of gin. Often they were chasing both at the same time.

The final gray light of day faded from the clouds, leaving the flickering red light of fires to cast shadows through the rain. Muley wandered back and forth along the twisting rows. Despite the rain, there were a number of men moving around the camp. As he'd expected, no one paid much attention to him. He kept one eye peeled for his muscled guard, but he spent most of his time peeking through tent flaps and open doors for a glimpse of his companions.

After several minutes of searching, Muley began to grow frustrated. His guard would soon be back and find him missing. Once the alarm was raised, he expected to be caught in short order. Maybe the best thing would be to leave the camp before anyone started looking. Then he could catch up on another day and find the Rainmaker and Cody.

Muley was considering this plan when he spotted something that changed his mind. Jutting up from the middle of a group of square army-style tents was the dark line of the sail wagon's mast. Moving as quick as he could without running, he pushed around the workers in his path and skirted the tents until he could clearly see the wagon. It looked fine. The sails were still tied down, as he'd left them, and there was no obvious damage.

From the nearest tent Muley heard a buzz of voices. He went up to the heavy canvas and listened closely, but none of the voices seemed familiar. The next tent was dark and silent. He risked pushing the flap open, and found nothing inside but a stack of crates and some tools.

At the third tent he heard Cody.

Muley stood near the entrance for long minutes, water running down his face and dripping from his nose and chin while he listened to the rise and fall of voices inside. He could not quite make out the words, but there were definitely two voices. One was Cody's, the other wasn't.

Muley crept back to the empty tent and squinted into the shadowed interior. There were several large hammers that might have made good weapons, but they were so heavy that he could barely lift them, much less swing them. He settled on a shovel.

He bounced the tool in his hands. If there was only one other person in the tent with Cody, he might trick them out and give them a quick bash with the shovel—if he was lucky. If there was more than one, he'd get caught for sure.

But before he had chance to do anything about his plan, there was a shout from outside. He went to the tent flap and saw the burly guard standing in front of the next tent, and another man standing with him. After a moment Muley recognized the fat camp boss, Woodson.

"Damnation," Muley said softly. He drew as far back into the supply tent as he could while still managing to see.

". . . gone," the guard was saying. "I weren't out of there longer than a breath. That Yankee must have had a talent for traveling."

"Idiot!" Woodson shouted. "He's got no more talent than you've got brains."

"But—"

Woodson held up his hand. "Hush. Get as many boys as you can find and head them to the south. Run, you fool!"

The guard nodded and sprinted away. Woodson stood for a moment shaking his head, then moved off in the same direction.

As soon as the boss was gone, Muley slipped out of the supply tent and hustled across the short stretch of mud to the tent where Cody was held. Inside he found not only Cody, but the Rainmaker as well.

Both men were bound to chairs, just as he had been. From the looks of things, they'd also received rougher treatment. Cody's eyes were circled in bruises, and a blow to his head had partly undone Muley's careful work with the needle, spilling blood down one cheek. The Rainmaker looked worse still. He sat with his chin down against his thin chest and his eyes closed. Against his white skin the dark bruises looked dark as storm clouds. Blood dripped from his nose, from his lips, and from dozens of places on his face where knuckles had split his skin.

Cody looked up with surprise in his blue eyes. "My God, you're loose."

"A-yup," Muley said. "And I'll have you loose here in a second." He dropped the shovel and moved around to work at the knots holding Cody to his chair.

"I've been talking to Woodson," Cody said. "I think I can convince him we didn't have anything to do with Rapid City. Old Kastle and Cullen filled his ear before we got here, but I think I can turn him."

Muley paused. "You want to stay here and talk to him? Way I figure it, they'll probably hang us or shoot us as soon as they're tired of beating on us. But I'll leave it to you. You want to stay, we stay."

It took Cody no more than a second to make up his mind. "Hell no, get me loose."

The knots around Cody's wrist were snug, but it took Muley little time to have them off. He was just moving over to free the Rainmaker when there was a scream from outside.

"What was that?" Muley said.

Cody shook his head. "Someone hurt. Sounded like a woman."

The scream came again, and this time it was followed by sobbing.

"Sounds like a child to me," Muley said. He went across the tent and picked up the shovel.

Cody started to get up from his chair, wobbled on his feet for a moment, then sat down hard. "What are you going to do?" he asked.

Muley shoved open the tent flap. "I'm going to make sure that child's all right."

"We need to be moving," Cody said. "Old Woodson is smarter than he looks. It won't be long before they get back to look in on us."

The scream came a third time, stretching out longer than before. It was a tearing sound, a noise as hopeless as an animal marching into the slaughterhouse.

"You see if you can get the Rainmaker's ropes loose," Muley said. "I'll be back quick as I can."

Leaving the tent, he followed the sound of crying to a larger tent set off by itself about twenty yards away. This one had a wooden frame and a wooden door set at the front. A small flap of canvas extended from the side of the tent to form something of a porch. In this dry space stood a lean, bearded man with only a fringe of dark hair around an otherwise smooth head. The bald man rose as Muley came near.

"Where you going?" he asked.

Muley nodded toward the tent. "Sounds like someone's needing help in there."

The bald man laughed. "That's just one of those young ones," he said. "They always kick up a fuss the first time or two, but before you know it, they'll settle right down." The man spat a wad of tobacco on the ground. "You wait your turn, and she'll be as fine as you ever had."

Muley nodded. "How much?"

The question brought a smile to the bald man's narrow face. "Only five dollars. I'm telling you that's a bargain. You'd never get—"

The rest of the man's sales talk was cut off when the shovel blade hit against his skull like a mallet on a melon. The man buckled at the knees and fell to the ground in a boneless heap. The wound to his bare pate bled like a bucket with the bottom knocked out. Muley figured that the man would live, but he didn't wait around to be sure. Instead he pulled open the creaking door and went inside the tent

The girl was not as young as he'd expected, probably somewhere in her middle teens, but she was far too young for what was being done to her. Everyone was. Tears poured from her dark eyes in such quantity that Muley could hear the sound of the drops splattering the ground.

The man who stood behind her was a monster. The salesman outside had been balding, but this man was hairless. His face and neck were a mass of red angry flesh and glistening pink scars. Where his nose should have been, there was nothing but a shriveled line of gristle between two dark, ragged openings. The scars ended abruptly at his neck, leaving his bare chest smooth and pale. He looked for all the world like someone had plunged him head first into a pot of boiling water and not pulled him out till he was well on his way to being cooked.

"Get away from the girl," Muley said.

The scarred man looked around. His face parted in an expression that might have been a smile if he still had lips to smile with. "You wait your turn now, boyo. There's enough here for satisfying both of us."

Muley swung the shovel. It cut the air with a deadly whistle, but the scarred man ducked and came up on the other side of the blow. The missed swing carried Muley off balance. Before he could recover, the scarred man had his hands on the other end of the shovel.

"I know you," the scarred man said. "I seen you right enough, back there in Medicine Rock. You're the one what drives that stagecoach with bed sheets atop it."

"They're sails," Muley said. He tried to tug the shovel loose, but the man's grip was tight. The man's bloodshot eyes stared into his face with an expression of such pure meanness that Muley had no trouble making it out. The burned man seemed to know who Muley was, but Muley was sure he recalled seeing no such creature in Medicine Rock.

"Well, boyo," the man said, "you can make your fancy wagon roll. Now we'll see how well you dance."

The scarred man might have been naked and without a weapon, but he moved with confidence. He twisted the shovel around, forcing Muley to step forward or let go. Then he reversed direction and shoved hard the other way.

Muley was flung back. He slipped, lost his footing, but kept his grip on the shovel. As he fell to his knees he gave a tug of his own. He pulled the shovel to the side with as much force as he could muster, then pushed up.

The scarred man was forced to lower his arms. The expression on his boiled mouth turned to a circle of surprise just before the hardwood handle cracked him right between the eyes. His bloodshot eyes rolled crazily around their raw sockets.

Another sharp pull and Muley had the shovel free. He drew

his arms back, took a deep breath, and drove the blade of the shovel into the man's gut.

The shovel did not go too deep, but it went deep enough to draw a well of blood and a satisfying cry of pain. The burned man dropped to his knees and pressed his hands across his wounded stomach. Blood leaked between his fingers and pattered on the floor. "Lord, man," he said in a voice that was not much more than a moan. "Lord, but you've kilt me." With that he toppled on his side and lay bleeding on the floor.

"You ain't dead," Muley said. He raised the shovel over his head and considered for a moment finishing the work. But he didn't. He might have killed the man in a fight, but he couldn't strike a man who was unconscious.

Across the tent the girl sat on the dirt floor and looked up at Muley with wide dark eyes. She had her knees pulled up against her chest and her arms clamped tight around her legs. Even dirty and terrified she was a comely girl, with long, curling, coal dark hair and skin that was as smooth as a peach but colored like hot tea. It was easy to see why she would fetch a price in such a rough place as the rail camp. She opened her mouth and said something, but not in words Muley could understand.

"Where you from, girl?" Muley said. He wondered if she might be a Mexican, or maybe part Indian. "Can you speak American?" The girl nodded quickly but said nothing.

Muley spotted several worn olive blankets heaped on the floor. Evidently they were meant to serve as a bed. He picked one of them up and went toward the girl. She pushed herself back against the side of the tent, her head ducked down like a dog that expected a swat.

"Here," Muley said. "I ain't about to hurt you."

The girl trembled but didn't try to move away as Muley dropped the blanket over her shoulders. She pulled it quickly around her and held it tight.

Muley looked at the scarred, bleeding shape on the floor, then turned back to the girl. "I figure you better get out of here. The folks that run this place ain't likely to be pleased with what I've done. They'll string me up, and they might do the same to you."

"No," the girl said. She held the blanket carefully around herself and started to get up, but as soon as she got past her knees she winced, shook her head, and looked down at her feet.   •

Muley followed the direction of her gaze. The girl's feet were bare, but more than that, they were red and swollen.

"Damnation," Muley said. He bent down for a better look. "What in hell did they do to you, child?" There were stripes on her feet, red raw wounds where someone had brought down a strap or rod across her soles. It was a punishment Muley had seen applied to disobedient sailors. Some of those men had never walked without pain again. "They didn't want you running away, did they?"

"No," the girl said.

Muley thought for a moment, then picked up another of the blankets from the heap. The cloth was old and frayed at the edges, and he had no trouble tearing it into strips. Then he unlaced his own boots and slipped them off his feet.

"Stick your feet over here," he called to the girl. "See if this doesn't help."

The girl hesitated a moment then extended her legs toward Muley. He took her small left foot carefully in his hand and began wrapping strips of the blanket around it. She was shaking so bad that he had trouble getting the strips snug without making them too tight. When he'd swathed her foot in the bandages, Muley tucked it down into his large boot. The shoe was far too big for her tiny feet, but he hoped the boot would keep the bandages from getting wet in the muddy street outside. With one foot finished, he turned his attention to the other. The girl jerked and made a few soft sounds as he worked. Considering the state her feet were in, it was a wonder to Muley that she didn't scream her head off.

When he was finished, he stood and offered the girl his hand. "Come on there. We're getting pressed for time."

The girl took his hand and slowly brought herself to her

feet. At her first step her grip tightened down, but she didn't stop or yell.

Muley led her out of the tent and past the bald man who lay in the mud outside. They went through the cold drizzle to the tent where he'd left Cody and the Rainmaker.

Inside they found the Rainmaker both awake and agitated. "Where in God's name have you been?" he cried when Muley came through the door. His pale eyes swept over the girl. "Are you going to tell me you left us here to go get some whore?"

The blood rose in Muley's face. "She ain't no whore," he said. "Can't you see she's not but a child?"

The Rainmaker was not satisfied. "I've seen many a whore younger than her."

"You damn lazy albino." Muley balled his hands into fists and stomped across the tent with every intention of adding to the Rainmaker's bruises.

Bill Cody stepped between the two men. "Hold up there," he said. "I don't mind you thumping on each other, but can we wait till we're out of this camp?"

"That's just what I was saying," the Rainmaker said testily. "I'm ready to leave."

Muley pressed his lips tight together. He tried to remind himself that the Rainmaker was at his worst when he was scared, but that didn't do much to take the sting out of the man's words. "You'd not be leaving at all if it weren't for me getting you loose," he said.

"And we appreciate it," Cody said quickly. "Now let's get out of here before Woodson and his boys get back."

The four of them went out into the night. What had been a sprinkle only minutes before was now a driving rain. Muley had no doubt that the storm was only a symptom of the Rainmaker's anger. Two men went running past the group as they made their way along the muddy path, but they didn't stop to talk.

"We've been lucky so far," Cody said. "They've been looking for you outside of camp."

"They're over on the south side," Muley said. "I heard Woodson send them that way."

"Then we better head north," Cody replied.

The Rainmaker stopped in his tracks. "North is difficult," he said. "The wind's coming out of the northwest. It's easier to head south."

Cody shrugged. "You do what you want to, but the south side of this camp is going to be full of men with big rifles. Your family's in the business. I'm sure you have a good idea of what a fifty-caliber carbine can do to a man."

"Right," the Rainmaker said. "We go north."

They reached the sail wagon and the Rainmaker jumped inside. Muley climbed up to his post while Cody held open the door so the young girl could come in.

But she only shook her head. "No," she said. Instead she turned and started to climb up with Muley, holding the wagon with one hand and keeping the blanket fast with the other.

"You better go on inside, girl," Muley said. "It's going to be damn cold and wet out here."

The girl sat down on the bench beside him, her bare legs and Muley's oversized boots jutting out from under the blanket. "No," she repeated. "I'm staying with you."

Muley chuckled. "Well, I'm glad to hear you can say something besides no. All right then, hold onto my boots, we're heading out."

As the door on the wagon slammed, the wind suddenly shifted around to the south. Muley loosed the jib and pulled up the mainsail. He had to be careful, letting out only a small amount of sail and laying on the boom to steer the wagon between the tightly spaced tents.

"Where are the horses?" the girl asked.

"No horses," Muley said. "Just us and the wind." He let out another foot of sail and the wheels pulled loose of the mud. With a creak of wood and steel the wagon began to roll through the muddy lane. Muley risked raising the main a foot farther. Then another foot. The Rainmaker's wind was brisk— for a change—and the wagon picked up speed quickly. Muley jerked on the lines that moved the boom and twisted the front wheels of the wagon, steering past more tents and around a stack of rails. As the camp began to thin out he raised the sail till it was almost full, letting more air into the jib as he did so. The wagon bounced over ruts and splashed through puddles. It was moving well now, passing the pace of a running man.

Somewhere behind them came a shout. Muley peered back through the rain and saw a trio of vague shapes moving after them in the darkness. There was a brief flash as someone fired a weapon. The rain made it sound no louder than a pop gun.

"They're after us now," Muley said. "We'll be lucky if they don't get us, too."

"Yes," the girl said, but there was no concern in her voice.

When he looked over, Muley was surprised to see her smiling. Smiling made her look even younger. And prettier.

"What is it?" Muley asked.

The girl shook her head, sending her long wet hair swinging around her face. "It's like we're flying!" she shouted.

And then she was gone.

☆ **19** ☆

There was no town hall in Medicine Rock. Whatever civic pride the town felt had always been satisfied by a solid sheriff's office and good board sidewalks on both sides of the main street. Whenever there was a need for the people of the town to get together, Medicine Rock Methodist was pressed into service.

The new preacher, a lean-faced young man by the name of Hardesty, didn't seem to mind this occasional invasion of his church. Considering that a normal Sunday service would net him not more than a dozen churchgoers, it was the only time he saw his church anything like to full.

Goldy was late arriving at this particular occasion. The truth was, she had not intended to come at all, but at the last minute hadn't been able to stop herself. She'd turned up the Closed sign on the door of the Kettle Black, left Sienna to tend to Black Alice, and marched over to the church with murder on her mind—Orpah's murder.

The crowd acted like every church crowd Goldy had ever seen, filling up the room from back to front. Some of the women near the back, Bernita Hare in particular, whispered under their hands as Goldy passed. She suspected they thought that old whores and bartenders should not be let into a proper church. There had been more such whispering over the last couple of weeks. The fact that Medicine Rock was about to be reconnected to the East seemed to provide a sudden boost of morality to some of the folks in town. Bill Hare had announced his intention to run for mayor. Goldy expected that the skinflint probably expected to make a mint selling off lots to new settlers.

Two rows from the front of the church, Goldy spotted Bred Smith sitting with Josie Bird. To Josie's left sat the Caide brothers, the only other black folks in Medicine Rock. On either side of Bred and the Caides was a gap a good three bottoms wide. If there was anything that would get a person ranked below drunks and whores, it was black skin. Goldy took a seat beside Bred.

Bred favored her with a quick nod. He had the good sense not to smile. "You doing all right, Miss Goldy?"

"I'm still doing," Goldy said. "I guess I should be happy with that." She settled herself on the hard bench. Hopefully, this farce would not go on too long. Her back was not up to the stiff posture demanded by the church pews.

Josie reached past Bred to take Goldy by the arm. "How is Sienna holding up?"

Goldy frowned. "Better than Alice, but not as good as I'd like. The girl was shook by her brother going God knows where, and then her talent got squirrelly, and now this." Goldy shook her head. "But at least she's taking meals and she's not sobbing day and night. That's more than I can say for Alice."

The hum of conversation in the room dropped to a rustling whisper, and Josie leaned back into her own seat as two figures walked up the aisle to the front of the church. One was Reverend Hardesty, his young face already traced by more worry lines than most men twice his age. Mostly he seemed to worry that the tiny congregation of his church would not contribute the funds he needed to keep himself fed and respectably clothed.

Hardesty was not a drinker. He didn't go out of his way to preach against alcohol—to the great disappointment of some of his congregation—but neither did he drop by the Kettle Black. Goldy thought the man looked like he could use a couple of shots of whiskey to cut his worrying. She could have used a shot herself.

Right behind the preacher was Tom Sharp. The deputy wore a crisp, clean blue shirt with a black vest over the top.

His pants were new, with not a single patch on them, and the dark leather of his gun belt made a soft creak with each step. The silver star of his office gleamed from his chest. He was still a very short man, but now he also looked like a formidable man. It was a far cry from Sharp's ragged appearance when he'd entered Medicine Rock.

Hardesty spoke first. "It's a terrible occasion that brings us together, terrible. Many of you were with us earlier today for the funeral of Miss Orpah Hacket."

It was clear that the preacher had a different idea of what made "many" than Goldy. By her count there had not been more than fourteen people there to say good-bye to Orpah, and that was counting the two paid singers. It was also clear enough from his face and voice that the preacher was none too upset. He didn't have the good grace even to pretend to sorrow.

"Some of you may not have approved of the way in which Miss Hacket lived her life—" Hardesty continued.

Some in this case seemed to be a larger number than many.

"—but none, I think, could approve of the way in which she died."

Finally the preacher had hit on something that Goldy could agree with. As Hardesty continued his talk, she let her gaze shift over to Tom Sharp.

The deputy was standing with his hat in his hands and his eyes fixed on the floor. Anyone looking at him might be thinking that he was considering the awful death of poor Orpah. Goldy didn't buy it any more than she bought Hardesty's little spattle of hypocrisy.

For the first few hours after Orpah's death, Goldy had been sure Tom was the culprit. There was the argument they'd had, and the words she'd heard while standing beside Orpah's body. But then Bred had shown up and said Orpah had been dead for near on an hour. Goldy was not sure how someone could tell such a thing, but if Bred said it, she was inclined to believe it. Which meant that Orpah was already dead when Tom had come in the Kettle Black that morning.

For a day Goldy had clung to the memory of the whispered

words. But by the time Orpah's funeral had come, she was no longer so sure about what she'd heard. Tom Sharp had shown no more than a touch of talent. It was easier to believe that he was just ornery than to believe him capable of doing what had been done to Orpah. But if he didn't do it, then who in Medicine Rock had?

Hardesty went on about Orpah for no more than a minute, then turned his talk into a sermon against sin and the kind of end it might bring. He did not mention whoring or drinking in specific, but it was clear enough that these were the sins in question.

Goldy ground her teeth. It was something she almost never did. Her teeth were her pride, the one bit of physical beauty that had not fled from her over the years. Half the people her age strained their food through store-bought porcelain choppers, but Goldy hung on to all of her teeth. Even the one gold tooth that had given Goldy her name was not a sign of her old age, but the result of a rambunctious harness clerk back in Nebraska. For Hardesty to set Goldy grinding her teeth took considerable irritation.

Finally, the preacher finished with a flourish. It seemed to Goldy that he was blaming Orpah for her own death. If it seemed that way to the women in the back pews, it did not stop them from sending Hardesty off the pulpit with solid applause and a chorus of "Amen."

Then it was time for Tom Sharp.

The deputy advanced slowly, scanning the townspeople with a calm look in his eye. He did not stand behind the pulpit, which would have hidden him almost to the neck, but stood off to one side. "We're all upset by what's happened," he began.

Goldy leaned forward, waiting to hear what Sharp intended to do. Then the deputy's face was suddenly split by a smile. "But I'm here to share some good news," he said. "Just this afternoon, agents of the Atlantic Pacific rail line entered Medicine Rock." There was some murmur at that, but Sharp waved the room to silence. "It seems that the western end of the line has come along faster than the eastern end. Instead of joining up at the edge of Deseret as they had originally planned, the two lines will be joined two days from now." He paused and his smile grew wider. "Right here in Medicine Rock!"

The church was filled with such an uproar that Goldy thought her ears might pop. Behind her people were talking of all the wonders the railroad would bring. They wanted to see the trains and the telegraph. They wanted to order fancy clothes from New York City and see them delivered to Medicine Rock just as if it were Chicago or St. Louis.

Tom Sharp began to field questions. The rail crew would begin arriving within the day. With crews coming from both east and west, there would be a crowd in the town. Stores and boardinghouses could expect a spanking business. More than that, there would be important people coming to see the two lines joined. Mr. Gould, the head of the railroad, would be there, of course. But there would also be the president of the Bear state and of the Union States. Leaders were coming from Deseret, from the Confederacy and from Texas. Even a dozen Indian tribes were sending representatives to the event in recognition of their approval of this intrusion on their land.

It was all too much for the shop owners and farmers of Medicine Rock to take in. They had never expected to meet such high people, or to witness such an event as the completion of a transcontinental railroad. The room grew almost silent as the people ran improbable stacks of money and chances for fame through their heads.

Goldy felt like she'd been crushed down by a heavy weight. Sharp hadn't even mentioned Orpah. She had hoped for news of investigation, of searching houses, of talking to new people in town. Instead there was only the railroad.

Bred Smith leaned in close to her ear. "Don't you fret," he said. "We'll find out who done it."

Goldy nodded. She could count on Bred. She could count on Josie, too, and when Jake returned, she knew he would do whatever it took to root out the culprit. The newcomers to Medicine Rock might forget how things had been, but those who had been there in the lean times were still the heart of the town.

Emboldened by these thoughts, Goldy suddenly stood. "What about Orpah?" she demanded. "What are you going to do about finding the killer?"

There was a shout from the back of the church that Goldy should sit down. A few other voices rose in support. But Goldy did not budge.

Tom Sharp hooked his thumbs into his gun belt. "I'm not forgetting, but there's not much I can do. I've already talked to everybody that was there. You don't know who did it, and neither do I."

"Well then," Goldy said, "if you can't do anything, there's something I can do."

Sharp frowned. "Like what?"

Instead of answering him, Goldy stepped out of her pew and walked up to the raised platform at the front of the church. There was some rumbling at this from the back pews, and Reverend Hardesty's face went red as a hot poker, but Goldy did not care. She marched across the platform and went straight to the pulpit.

She leaned against the wooden stand and glared out at the citizens of Medicine Rock. "You all know me," she said loudly. "You know what I do. You know what I've done. But you also know I've got a talent."

There was no protest from the back rows now. Those prim women might be ready to snicker at Goldy the old bartender, but they were not so quick to laugh when they were reminded that she had talent.

"The deputy here says he can't find out who done for Orpah," Goldy continued. "That might be. But I can find out. I'm marching back to the Kettle Black right now. By morning I'll have a name to give the whole town."

Goldy turned and stepped over to stand almost nose-to-nose with Sharp. It pleased her that she was the taller of the two. "If it's your name I see with my talent," she whispered to him, "then God help you."

With that she stepped off the platform and swept out of the church. Bred Smith and Josie caught up to her before she made it back to the Kettle Black.

" 'Scuse me, Miss Goldy," Bred said. "But can you do that? Can you see who killed poor Miss Orpah?"

"Lord no," Goldy said. "If I could do that, don't you think I would have done it already?"

"Then why?" Josie asked. "Why say you will do something that you cannot do?"

Goldy reached the swinging doors of the Kettle Black and turned to face her friends. "I want to smoke out the snake who's done this. If they think I can find out who it is, then maybe they'll try and stop me from looking."

Bred whistled. He lifted his hat and rubbed a hand over his woolly gray hair. "Hope you'll excuse me from saying so, but that's a damn dangerous game to play."

Goldy fixed him with her sharpest glare. "What do you want me to do, Bred? Let him go?"

"You think it is Tom," Josie said.

"Yes," Goldy said with a nod. "I do."

The Mexican woman shook her head. "I am the one who told Tom to stay in Medicine Rock. I fed him at our table. I even told Jake to take him for a deputy."

There was a babble of voices from up the street. Goldy looked around to see that people were beginning to spill from the doors of the church.

"Come on inside," she said. "We'd best not talk about this in the street." She pushed open the doors but was careful to leave the sign reading "Closed."

Sienna was sweeping up in the saloon when they entered. "Alice is sleeping," the girl said. "I thought I would get things ready for tonight."

Goldy nodded. "That's good. But put the broom down and come over here for a minute. I got something to say and it's better I don't say it twice." She fetched a bottle and a glass from behind the bar and brought it over to the nearest table. "Anyone else wants some whiskey, just get yourself a glass." Both Josie and Bred availed themselves of glasses. Sienna took a seat at the table and waited quietly.

It was heartening for Goldy to look around the table and see the familiar faces. With Jake gone off to New York, this was all that remained of those who had ridden Medicine Rock through the times of Quantrill and Custer. She poured herself a full glass of what Ogallala called whiskey and passed the bottle around the table.

"There'll be other folks in here before we know it," Goldy said. "So I'm going to jump in with two feet." She took a swallow of her whiskey. "I think Tom Sharp is the one that killed Orpah."

"Yeah, but why?" Bred said. "What reason'd he have to go hurting Orpah?"

"I think he killed her to scare me."

Bred laughed so suddenly that he almost choked on a gulp of whiskey. "He sure as God judged that one wrong, didn't he?"

Josie held a glass of whiskey in her hand but she didn't drink. "Did I judge him just as wrongly?" she said softly. "Did I put a killer over our town just because I was worried about my baby?"

"You weren't the only one he fooled," Bred said. "The boy pulled the wool on Jake."

"Jake is always trusting," Josie said. "It is my job to keep him from trusting the wrong people. I may have cost us the town. If he has done what you say, then who is to stop him from killing everyone here?"

"No." It was Sienna who answered, and her soft voice was as full of confidence as Goldy had ever heard it. "Medicine Rock will survive."

"Maybe so," said a voice from the door. "But you won't." Tom Sharp leaned against the wall, a bright smile on his dark face and a gleaming pistol in his hand.

Goldy picked up what was left of her whiskey and threw it at the man. The glass shattered on the wall beside his head, but Sharp did not so much as flinch.

Bred stood up slowly and pushed his chair away. "You going to use that pistol, boy? I thought you had talent."

Sharp gave a slight nod. "I've got more talent than you've ever seen, old man. But I don't think I'll be wasting it on you." He flipped the pistol around expertly in his hand and sent it smoothly into its holster. "I don't aim to kill you now. Not as long as you do what I say."

"And if we don't?"

"You know the law."

"What law?" Goldy asked. "You think the people in this town will let you shoot us down?"

"I think the people in this town will let me do what I want," Sharp replied. "After all, I am the sheriff. It's me that the railroad people will be meeting with, me that's bringing a bounty to this town." He held out a finger and moved it slowly around the room. "I think you better learn to listen to your sheriff."

"You are nothing!" Josie shouted. "Jake is sheriff here."

Sharp heaved a sigh. "That's right," he said. "You left the church before my final announcement."

"What announcement?" Goldy said, but there was a coldness in her gut—a promise of the words about to come.

"Jake Bird is dead," Sharp said. He tipped his hat, turned, and walked out of the Kettle Black.

☆ **20** ☆

Prairie Pete picked up a fork and jabbed it against Jake's foot.

Jake screamed. "Hey, I thought you decided not to eat my legs."

The man who was sometimes a prairie dog let out a laugh. "I'd not eat you even if I was in a people-eating mood," he said. "Too stringy."

Jake pushed himself up on his elbows and looked down at his bare legs. "How does it look?"

"I've seen better." Pete tossed his fork onto the table beside the bed. "But it looks like it's going to stay on there. Considering how it looked two days ago, I'd say that's quite an improvement."

Jake agreed with the changer's assessment. Bad as he felt, it was still miles better than it had been only a couple of days before.

Jake's talent for chattering had saved his leg. With Pete to guide him, Jake had learned to channel his talent against the decay that swarmed in his blood. At a time when Jake had thought he knew his limits well, Pete had shown him that there was a whole new world of tasks within his reach. Shattered bones had been knit. Torn skin was mended. All in all, it was a miracle of the first rank. But it still hurt.

"You'd think if I could chatter enough to knock down a building," Jake said, "I could do a better job on my own leg."

Pete chuckled. "It ain't so easy as all that. Think of shooting." The changer held out his hand like a child imitating a pistol. "It's a lot easier to hit a barn than it is a barn owl.

Even if you've got a cannon, it don't particularly make it better. Sometimes it makes it worse."

A new thought came to Jake. "What about other people? Can I use my talent to doctor up other folks?"

"I ain't going to say it can't be done," Pete said, "but I don't know how to do it. Never met anyone who could."

Jake frowned. It seemed that the need for a doctor in Medicine Rock was not going to be solved through talent.

He picked up his torn pants and slid into them. Unfortunately, no twisting of his talent appeared capable to stitching up ripped trousers. "I guess there's nothing left for me to do but stick my boots on and get home."

"That'd probably be for the best," Pete said. "It's all fine to have company, but after a day or so I get to needing a little quiet. Besides, you're disturbing the boys."

Jake had seen little of the prairie dogs during his stay underground. Occasionally one of the little beasts would stick his head in the burrow and issue some series of squeaks and barks, to which Pete would reply in kind. Twice, one of these visits had been followed by Pete changing into his furrier form and venturing off into the tunnels. What he did on these trips was something he didn't share with Jake, and the dark tunnels were not inviting enough to lure Jake on any investigation of his own.

Jake finished getting ready and stood in the middle of the room. The pale roots of grasses and shrubs hung down into the cavern like thin icicles. Jake had to hunch over to keep his face out of their damp grasp. He looked at Pete and frowned.

"I'm not sure what I ought to say to you besides thank you."

"Thank you sounds right," Pete said.

Jake shook his head. "Thank you's not enough," he said. "If you hadn't helped me, the coyotes would be gnawing my bones right now."

Pete shrugged. "Coyotes are no friends of mine. Now, if you don't mind, I've got things I need to be doing. I'll have some of the boys show you out." He held out his hand.

"That would be fine," Jake said. He gave Pete's hand a solid shake. He wondered for a moment just what chores would

the prairie dog town. Now, near the rail line again, the pain was back.

Jake squinted his eyes against the pain and pushed himself across the twin lines of metal. Once he was a dozen steps on the other side, the pain began to lessen. At twenty paces it was back to a dull thumping. At thirty the pain was gone. He stood there in the shoulder-high grass looking back toward the rail.

He could not figure how strips of metal could cause a man such pain. The other folks on the train hadn't seemed to be hurt by them, but he sure enough was.

Jake stared toward the western horizon. The round form of the Black Hills was sketched across the pale sky. They were probably fifty miles away yet, and even when he made it, he would be facing thirty miles of hills and a hundred miles of plains to get back to Medicine Rock. But Rapid City was up ahead just this side of the hills. He might find help there, some supper, and maybe even someone who would lend him a horse. Jake set off at the best pace he could manage in hopes of reaching the town by nightfall.

Throughout the morning he stayed within sight of the rail line. He was a little concerned about being spotted by Cullen or Kastle should they come along on a train, but considering the abundant tall grass and the noise the engine had made, Jake expected to have plenty of warning to hide. With no more than a few seconds warning, the whole Sioux Nation could hide in grass like this. He was more concerned about finding something to eat than he was about discovery.

Along about noon something broke the smooth rolling hills ahead. At first Jake thought he might have been closer to Rapid City than he thought. Whatever it was up there appeared to be the top of some large building. Maybe a water tower or a grain silo. A little bit after, he saw that there were two of the buildings, but no town to go with them.

The buildings, if they were buildings, were round on the sides and flat on top. Each of them was a good fifty feet across and at least as high. They were metal—more than one metal, it seemed, with some stripes that shined like a mirror and others red as a new penny. Jake had never seen anything like these buildings in his life.

He could see that they stood on either side of the rail line, and figured they had something to do with the trains. Jake made several attempts to get close to the structures, but the pain he had felt in crossing the tracks was even stronger here. By the time he was fifty feet away his head hurt so bad that his only choice was to move away. He walked on, leaving the strange buildings behind.

Jake wondered about the pain caused by the tracks and everything that went along with them. Again it occurred to him that the others on the train hadn't seemed to be hurt by being so close to the rails. It was hard to imagine how anyone ever took to riding on railroads if they hurt so much. Maybe there was something in Kastle's little pocket watch things that kept the others from feeling the hurt.

He kept away from the tracks after that, but then his leg began to bother him. He stopped by a small stream and sat for what must have been an hour. He even called on his chattering and tried to use his talent as Pete had taught him. None of it helped. There was no cure for it but to walk to Rapid City. Maybe he could find a doctor there who would be able to help. He limped on.

Thinking about the doctor brought Jake around to thinking about Medicine Rock and the railroad. His mission to bring a medical man to the town was a failure. Worse than that, he knew now that the railroad men were his enemies. But he still didn't know their reasons for acting the way they had. A man rich enough to build a railroad across the country was rich enough to give one doctor to one little prairie town. And if Gould hadn't wanted to make the deal, all he had to do was run his line somewhere else. Any way Jake turned it, there seemed little reason for the behavior of the rail men.

He could only hope that things would hold up in Medicine Rock until he got back. Tom Sharp might not be tough enough to face down the railroad on his own, but Bred was there, and Josie. Between the three of them, they ought to keep things stirred. Jake increased his pace, pushing his aching leg faster. He wanted to be home.

With the sun hanging on the line of the mountains, Jake at last spotted a line of buildings ahead. He stopped for a minute and dusted himself as best he could. What with his torn and bloody pants, cleaning was a futile effort. Besides, he was hatless and afoot—conditions that ranked a man as low as he could be. But Rapid City was a good size town. Jake wanted to look his best before he marched in to meet the sheriff.

Satisfied that he had as much dust off as was going to come off, Jake straightened himself and walked the last quarter mile to town with as much dignity as he could muster. He was a mite disappointed when no one appeared from the first few buildings to look at him. It was surprisingly quiet in Rapid City. He tried to remember what day it was. If it was Sunday, then the town might be gathered at the church—that is, if churchgoing was more popular in these parts.

The sun slipped down behind the hills and darkness gathered over the town. Jake reached the end of the main street and stood looking at the rows of businesses and houses at the heart of Rapid City. His heart sank. There was not a light anywhere in the town, not one. Rapid City seemed to have emptied.

Jake sat down at the edge of a horse trough and rested his aching leg. It had only been a week or two since some travelers had come to Medicine Rock from Rapid City. Towns had died in much less time, but still it was surprising. The sheriff in Rapid City had a reputation as a hard man, a man who was especially hard on those who crossed him. There were few around with the gumption to raise a challenge against such a man.

More surprising still was that the challenger had not settled in as the new sheriff. Such odd departures happened—it had happened in Medicine Rock, in fact—but generally the only reason anyone would risk challenging a sheriff was because he wanted the position for himself. Now Rapid City had joined the long list of towns like Deadwood, Calio, and Wright, which had not survived when war and talent turned back the tide of people in the West. Jake's greatest fear was that Medicine Rock might join that list.

He was about to move on when he noticed the dark form wedged between the horse trough and the hitching rail. It was a body.

Jake stood up quick, his heart beating. He'd seen plenty of men killed, even killed more than his share, but he did not like associating with the dead any more than most folks.

It took a good minute for his heart to settle and his nerve to gather. Then he went over to the dead man and rolled him up onto the sidewalk. It was a boy. A boy no more than twelve or thirteen, with carrot-orange hair and eyes a deep blue. His eyes were so clear and his body so supple that Jake thought he could not have been dead an hour. But the way the dust covered the boy's clothes suggested he'd been laying there far longer. There was not a wound on his body, or a single spot of blood on his gray wool shirt. But he was most surely dead.

Jake felt for his heavy Colt and was relieved to find it still snug in his holster. He'd cleaned the Colt as best he could back in Pete's tunnels, though the changer had insisted there be no test firing. Jake hoped the weapon had survived the fall from the train and his rude trip to the prairie dog town. Just in case, he tugged at his chattering. The feel of the talent came quickly, giving him a good boost of confidence.

The dark main street of Rapid City seemed to have taken on new character. Before, it had only been deserted, now it was menacing. Jake ran his finger over the dead boy's eyes, closing them as much for his own sake as for any propriety. Then he walked carefully down the center of the street, taking the time to look for anyone who might have caused the boy's death.

What he found was another body. This time it was an older man. He was slumped in a wooden chair outside a barbershop. From the look of the stubble on his chin, he might have been waiting his turn in the chair when death took him. Like the boy, he had no wounds.

Inside the barbershop there were two more bodies. The

barber himself lay on the floor in a mass of hair clippings. His last customer was still in the chair, a towel over his dead face.

That was how it was at the next building, and the next: a dead woman facedown on a table; a bartender amid broken bottles and a fallen tray; two children dead beside a circle in the dust, marbles still clutched in their hands.

It was not only the people that had died. Two horses lay on their sides out front of the smithy. A mongrel dog was in the dust beside the dead children. Even the chickens in the back yards lay in still, feathered heaps.

At the center of the town Jake found the sheriff's office. And inside the office was the sheriff. Whatever his reputation, or his talent, the sheriff of Rapid City had fared no better than its citizens. He was on the floor of his office with a gun in one hand and a line of tobacco juice trailing from his open lips. Unlike the other bodies, the cause of the sheriff's death was clear enough from the two bullet holes in his vest and the dark pool of blood under his body. Toward the back of the office Jake found a second man, also shot.

He walked back onto the sidewalk outside and stared up the street. There was an incredible, impossible quiet. The wind had died. There was no sound of birds or even insects.

Rapid City had not just emptied, it had been slaughtered.

☆ **21** ☆

The brandy burned like fire on Bill Cody's lips, but that did not stop him from downing half the bottle before he passed it back to the Rainmaker. "Much obliged," he said. "I believe that was just what I needed."

The Rainmaker frowned at his vanishing supply of eastern liquor and shoved the bottle back into its hiding hole. "Where do we go now?" he asked.

"To tell you the truth, Mr. Spencer," Bill said, "that is something I do not know."

A look of disapproval settled on the Rainmaker's pale face. It was, Bill noted, the man's most common expression. "You're not like the man in the books."

Bill smiled. "You don't know how many times I've heard that. No, I don't ride two horses at the same time nor shoot sparrows at a thousand yards. I don't eat lead or shit bullets. If these things are disappointing to you, there's damn little I can do about it."

"I'm not a fool," the Rainmaker said. "I know they made up most of the stuff in those books. It's just that—" He stopped and looked down at the floor.

"It's just what?"

The Rainmaker raised his blue eyes. "I just thought you'd be different," he said. "That's all."

Bill had heard such sentiments several times in the past. The same books that had provided some fine dinners had also brought on a good deal of disappointment. It never failed to sting, though—especially this time.

"Truth is," Bill said, "I'm disappointed in myself."

The Rainmaker looked puzzled. "On account of what?"

"On account of Rapid City," Bill said.

"They're all dead, aren't they?" The Rainmaker raised a hand to his bruised face. "That's why they were hitting us."

Bill nodded. "Yes. At least, I think so."

"Did you do it?"

"No!" Bill shook his head violently. "I told you already it was that bald bastard Kastle that done the deed."

"But you never told us why," the Rainmaker said. "And how was such a thing managed?"

Before Bill could answer, there was a sharp squeal of brakes. The rumbling, bouncing passage of the sailing wagon slowed to a stop.

The Rainmaker reached past Bill to open the panel at the front. "Why are we stopping?" he called.

Muley leaned down and pressed his face to the opening. "We're stopping because it's damn near midnight," he said. "There's shelter here, and I'm in the mood for some sleep. You two may want to sit up and drink all night, but I'm the one that has to steer."

Bill found it hard to get his legs moving. People had been telling him for years that he was getting older, but he'd never believed it so much as when he tried to rise from his seat and get down from the wagon. Outside he found a waxing moon shining down on a bubbling stream. It was colder than it had been over the last days, cold enough to turn Bill's breath into a moonlit cloud. In the pale light he could just make out dark hills close at hand and the weathered, worn remains of a farm.

"I know this place," Bill said. "It's the old Schmidt place along the Belle Fourche."

Muley shrugged. "I wouldn't know." He ducked his head into the wagon and came out with a pair of bedrolls. "All I know is there ain't enough room for three people to get comfortable inside the wagon. And there sure ain't no place for a campfire."

Within a few seconds clouds began to obscure the moon and raindrops started to fret the surface of the river. The Rainmaker's storm had caught up to them.

The old farmhouse turned out to be no shelter at all. Somewhere over the last winter or two, snow had brought down its rotten roof, leaving the whole place open to the rain. The barn had fared better. Though the doors had snapped their hinges, the roof was intact, and a dark circle of ash in the center of the floor showed that other travelers had taken shelter in this place. Over thin piles of moldering straw, Muley laid out the bedrolls.

"We're lucky," Bill said. "Late as it is, this place ought to be knee deep in snow."

Muley grunted. "If our luck holds on the way it's been going, there'll be a blizzard by morning." He sat down and rubbed at his foot, which was covered only by a damp, dirty sock. "Then I'll be lucky just to keep my toes."

Bill leaned up against the wall of the barn and held the front of his coat closed with his hands. With no blankets to his name, the coat would have to do for a bedroll. Water already dripped from a dozen places on the roof and splashed on the floor. If the temperature came down a notch or two, it might be snow by morning. Snow or rain, it had all the makings of a cold, miserable night.

The Rainmaker came out of the dark shadows at the back of the barn with a piece of broken lumber in both hands. "There's more wood back there," he said. "Looks like someone stocked it up."

"Another piece of luck," Bill said. He went to the back and returned with a sizable stack of broken lumber that was not too rotten to burn. Some of the wood was so dry it felt like paper, but once it was laid to the flame, it put off good heat.

"We got some salt pork," Muley said. "There's some biscuits, too, though I can't vouch for them. Both of them go all the way back to Medicine Rock." He fished through a leather satchel and held out a handful of each.

Bill took the food gratefully. The salt pork made him thirsty, and he suspected that sometime during the night he was going to have to brave the cold to draw water from the river, but for now he was content to chew on the hard meat and sit close to the fire. Soon enough his eyes began to close.

"You were going to tell us about Rapid City," the Rain-maker said suddenly. "Tell us everything."

Bill straightened with a start. "Yes," he said. "I was." He glanced over at Muley. He was not anxious to talk about what had happened, but the sailor had also taken a beating for what Bill had been accused of doing. He deserved to know what the charges were. Bill put his last bit of pork in his mouth, chewed it, then started in.

"We came to Rapid City early in the morning," he began. "It was a busy place, with lots of folks walking the street. There was several people there what knew me, and I chatted with them for a bit. Then Kastle got impatient and pushed me to see Sheriff Davis."

Bill paused for a second. The story had barely begun and he was already out of breath. "I've known Jim Davis—knew Jim Davis—for better than twenty years. Knew him even before he got the talent, back when he was a quartermaster for the army. He was a good quartermaster, and a hell of a tough sheriff.

"It was me that did most of the talking. That was the way they had planned it. I start the talking, they finish it. I was telling him about the railroad and all the things the railroad men were promising." Bill ran his fingers through his beard, brushing biscuit crumbs onto his lap. "It was going as well as you could want. If it weren't for Cullen, Jim and the rest of them would still be alive."

"What happened?" the Rainmaker asked.

"A girl happened," Bill said. "Jim had a man locked up for robbery. There was a girl there bringing food to the prisoners." The memory was clear enough that Bill put his hands to his temple, remembering the pain that was to come. "She couldn't have been no more than twelve or thirteen, but that didn't stop Cullen. Jim and Cullen got to arguing, and the girl got loose and ran to the back room. After that, Jim didn't want to talk no more."

"They gave up the railroad because Cullen pawed some girl?" the Rainmaker asked.

Bill shrugged. "Jim Davis can be . . . could be an ornery

cuss. Once he took it in his mind not to like you, he was prone to stick to that opinion. He didn't like Cullen, or Kastle, and he wasn't interested in their rail. When he tried to run them off, Cullen shot him down. Shot the thief they was holding in the jail, too. Even shot the girl, God help me."

"Hold on," Muley said. "If this Davis was such a tough sheriff, how could he let himself get shot? I've seen folks with hardly no talent at all that could still set the brakes on a bullet."

Bill nodded. "Jim could have done that, too, only Cullen had some kind of special gun. Damned if I know how it worked, but it put holes through Jim as fast as a Colt would put them through you or me."

Muley picked up an old board and pushed around the wood in the fire. "Was the shooting what had those rail men so riled? Seemed to me it had to be something worse than that. Even if it was a sheriff and a girl both."

"No," Bill said. "After Jim was dead, Kastle and Cullen argued about what was to be done. They decided there was no point in talking to anyone else." He turned away from the fire and stared through the barn door at the rain falling on the weeds outside. "But before we left, Kastle set something down on Jim's desk."

"What kind of thing?" the Rainmaker asked. In the firelight his pale eyes glowed orange, like the eyes of a wildcat.

Bill held out one hand. "A little thing, no bigger than my palm. Something like a pocket watch, only plumper, and with different colors on it. Anywise, after he dropped this thing, we saddled up and rode out of there before anybody else showed up to see what they'd done."

The Rainmaker stood up and walked away from the fire. Standing back in the shadows, there was little that could be seen of him but his white face and hands. "And you rode with them," he said in a cold voice.

"Yes," Bill said.

"Even though they killed the sheriff and a little girl."

"Yes."

"But why?" The Rainmaker's voice was twisted by frustration. "Why ride with outlaws?"

"Wait," Bill said. "You ain't heard it all." He sat for a moment, kicking the toe of his boot against the end of a burning beam. "You ain't even heard the worst. When we were a mile or so outside of town, Kastle orders us to stop and wait and look toward Rapid City. I figured the man for crazy. After all, the only thing we were likely to get if we waited was a bullet from a posse. But we hadn't been sitting there a minute when there was . . ."

Bill stopped, opened his mouth to say more, then closed it again. "I don't know what to call it," he said at last. "It was like a fire, but redder, and colder. Colder than January in the mountains. It came up over all of Rapid City for no more than a second. Rising up like the sun. Then quick as it came, it was gone."

"What was it?" Muley asked. The board in his hand had begun to flame at the far end, but the seaman was yet to notice.

"I don't know," Bill said.

"You know enough," the Rainmaker said from the shadows. "You know what it did."

Bill shook his head. "I can't even swear to that," he said. "We never went back into the town, and I never asked."

"But you know," the Rainmaker insisted.

"Yes," Bill said softly, "I reckon I do know. I figure all those folks in Rapid City are dead."

The Rainmaker came toward the fire, the red light glowing on his skin as well as his eyes. "And even then you rode with them."

Bill hung his head, but he nodded.

"Why? That's the question I still want answered."

"The God's honest truth is that I was scared, sir," Bill said. "They told me in no uncertain terms that if I didn't show them how to reach Medicine Rock and Laramie, they would use one of their little pocket things on me. I was scared."

"Hell, I'd have done the same," Muley said. He looked around at the Rainmaker. "You going to get uppity just because a man was trying to save his own life?"

Bill spat into the fire. "If being scared was all I had to admit to, I'd be glad to do it. But that's not the only reason I hung around."

"The money," the Rainmaker said.

"Yes," Bill said. "They told me I'd not be paid if I didn't finish the job."

"You rode with killers because they offered you money." The Rainmaker sounded as solemn as a judge passing sentence.

"I did," Bill agreed. "And no matter what happened after that, no matter that I got myself banged up for trying to save Laramie, just showing them the way to Medicine Rock is enough to deserve hanging."

Those words put an end to the conversation for the next few minutes. Muley crouched next to the fire, feeding it scraps of old lumber. The Rainmaker paced in the darkness. And the rain continued to fall.

At last Muley tossed his burning plank in with the others and pushed himself back from the flames. "At least you broke off when they went for Laramie," he said.

"I did," Bill said. "By the time we left Medicine Rock, I understood they meant to do the same thing in Laramie that they did in Rapid City. I suppose I got to where I was more scared of staying than I was of running." He ran a finger over the scabs on his forehead. "Wish I had've run a little faster. That damn Irishman's a center shot."

"Did they go on to Laramie without you?"

"I don't know."

"Wonder what happened in Rapid City," Muley said. "It's hard to think something the size of a pocket watch could do for a whole town."

"It did, though," said a new voice.

Bill kicked himself back from the fire and reached for his gun, only to find his holster empty. In the door of the barn stood a broad-shouldered man with wild wet hair and ragged clothes. "Who are you?" Bill asked.

"It's the sheriff," Muley said. "Sheriff Bird."

Bill squinted. "Jake Bird?"

The man in the door nodded. "You mind if I come in to the fire? It's getting awfully cold out here."

"Come ahead," Muley said.

Jake Bird limped across the dirt floor, moving like a man three times his age. The right leg of his trousers was nothing but bloodstained shreds, and the leg inside it was glossy with scars. There were more rips in his shirt and vest, and scratches on his face. He had the slack expression of someone who had reached the edge of exhaustion and gone on beyond.

"You look like you've been a rough trail," Bill said.

The sheriff nodded. "I got here courtesy of the railroad. All of you look like you've been traveling the same course."

"I suppose we are a mess," Bill agreed.

The Rainmaker emerged from the shadows. "Have you been in Rapid City?"

"Yes," Jake said. "And you have the right of it. They're all dead there."

The pale man leaned in close. "What should we do now?" he asked.

"Now?" Jake held out his hands to the flames. "I'd like to say there was something easy, but I've had some experience dealing with folks like this. The only thing we can do now is catch them. We find Cullen, and Kastle, and their boss, Gould." Blue fire licked out from the sheriff's fingers and mingled with the orange flames of the wood. "And once we've caught them," he said, "we kill them all."

☆ PART IV ☆

End of the Line

It was the busiest time Goldy could remember since back before Quantrill had wrecked the town. The Kettle Black had seen more customers in two hours than it generally received in a week. Panny Wadkins had been forced from his stool to help out behind the bar. Sienna was waiting ten tables at a go. Even Black Alice, who was still likely to break into tears without notice, had been pressed into duty carrying whiskey to the tables and bringing back trays of silver coins. Ever since the rail crews had arrived in town, the Kettle Black had been making a mint.

None of which came close to making Goldy see past her own melancholy.

It didn't seem possible that Jake Bird could be dead. Jake had been blessed by more talent than anyone Goldy had ever known. His chattering alone was strength enough to best any two sheriffs she'd ever seen. And there was more than just the talent. There was a solidness to Jake, a feeling of rightness. It was no wonder that Medicine Rock had done so well while he was in office.

If there was only Tom Sharp's word to go on, Goldy would have put no stake in it. But the rail boss agreed with the tale. Something with a boiler on an engine, they said. Terrible accident.

With the railroad folks coming down on the town, there had been no time to mourn Jake's passing—or to figure what was to be done with Tom Sharp.

Now that Jake was gone, the town was left to Sharp. The runt deputy wasted no time declaring himself sheriff, even though he hadn't shown the kind of talent it took to withstand a serious challenge. There had been a few arguments with the railroad workers that required Sharp to draw his pistol. Nothing had yet demanded him to show more than iron. Even so, with word of Jake's death less than a day old, Sharp was already meeting with store owners, negotiating his rate of pay.

Goldy's concern was less with her pocketbook than it was with Josie. The Mexican woman had not shed a tear at Sharp's news. Instead she left the Kettle Black at a run and locked herself in her house. Since then, Goldy, Bred Smith, and a flock of women from the church had all been turned away from her door.

Josie had taken some hard knocks in her life—knocks that should have left her wrecked. Her family had been killed by the blood-talent Quantrill when Josie was small, forcing her into hard jobs and hungry years. Then Quantrill had caught up to her in Medicine Rock, ruining her life again and taking Josie off to work a whorehouse in Laramie. But Josie had the last word in the affair when she planted the eight-gauge under Quantrill's chin and sprayed his head across the ground.

But Goldy didn't know how Josie would take to this loss: Jake dead and a baby on the way. The second would be a blessing, if not for the first.

A new burst of customers came through the door of the Kettle Black, and Goldy went back to serving up busthead. She set her mind on making another attempt at seeing Josie. Even if she couldn't get in, she needed to talk to Bred and Sienna about what they were going to do about Tom. It surprised Goldy that Tom hadn't moved to stop her from using her talent. Either he knew she wasn't up to casting the killer, or he figured it didn't matter. Could be he was right. Goldy knew she had to move quick, or the snake would have the support of half the town. But whatever she was going to do, it would have to wait till the pace slowed down a bit.

She was bringing up more bottles from the back when she saw Bred come through the door. Close behind him was a barrel-chested man who walked with small shuffling steps.

"Look who I brung you," Bred called.

Goldy came to the front, squinting to make out the visitor

more clearly. It was an Indian, she could see that much, even if he did have a city haircut and fancy suit. He was hunched over and he had the thickest glasses Goldy had ever seen. "I don't know as I recall this fellow."

The Indian held out a hand. "Johnson Stone," he said.

"Glad to meet you, I suppose." Goldy put down the bottles of whiskey and shook the man's hand. She looked over at Bred. "What's set you to grinning at a time like this?"

Bred took a bottle from the bar and popped the cork. "Ask the man how he makes his living," he said.

Goldy turned back to the Indian. "Well, Mr. Stone?"

"I'm a doctor."

"Doctor? Looks to me more like you need a doctor."

Stone laughed. "I've seen enough of them, thanks. But I am a doctor."

Goldy put her hands to her hips. "I don't think I've ever heard of an Indian doctor. Medicine man, maybe, but not a proper doctor."

"I've had my things taken over to the Lohman's for boarding," Stone said. "I've a diploma in there says I can practice medicine. I'll be happy to bring it by if you want to see it. Or you can wait till it's up on the wall at my office." If the man was put off by Goldy's skepticism, it didn't show.

"Office?" Goldy frowned. "You mean to stay around here?"

"Yep. I understand there's a need for a doctor in these parts." Stone looked around the bar. "You suppose I can get a drink?"

"I suppose," Goldy said. There were many saloons that had a policy against selling whiskey to Indians. Goldy had herself refused a drink for the old Shoshone man who came into Medicine Rock to trade. But this Johnson Stone didn't look like the kind to cause trouble. The way he was crippled over, Goldy doubted he could find a man's chin to throw a punch. She took out a glass and filled it for him.

"How did you know we were needing a doctor?" she asked.

"Your sheriff. He was the one that was looking for a doctor," Stone said. He took up his whiskey, sipped it, and made a sour face. "What's in this?"

"God knows," Goldy said quickly. "You talked to Sheriff Bird?"

The doctor shook his head. "No. I only know what was passed on to me."

Bred Smith slapped the man on his hunched back. "How about that, though?" he said. "Jake still got what he was going off to get. He's still taking care of Medicine Rock."

"I guess he is," Goldy said softly. The doctor would be a big help to the town, but having Jake back would be far better. She refilled Stone's glass. "You'll pardon me for being blunt, Mr. Stone, but I don't know if folks around here will come to any Indian doctor."

Stone shrugged and pushed his heavy glasses up his nose. "It's Dr. Stone. As for who comes to me, I suppose I'll leave that to them. Next time someone breaks a leg or comes down with a fever, we'll see if they don't get color-blind."

Goldy's lips twitched up at the end. "I believe you'll do, Dr. Stone. Though you've come at a sad time."

"That's something I don't understand," the doctor said. "Bred told me that your sheriff was dead, but I thought—"

He was interrupted by Sienna, who came over at a run. She nodded quickly to Bred then turned toward Goldy. "Excuse me, but there's a fellow in the corner that won't pay," she said. "He says he's a friend of Tom Sharp."

"Does he now?" Goldy straightened and looked over Sienna's head, but she couldn't make out anything special in the direction from which the girl had come. "You stay away from this friend of Sharp. I'll take care of him directly."

Sienna nodded, turned and hurried away.

The doctor watched her. "That's a fine girl you have there," he said.

Goldy scowled. "Don't go getting no thoughts about Sienna. She's not to be bought."

Stone's eyes went wide behind his glasses. "No, no," he said. "I wasn't thinking of anything like that."

The swinging doors of the Kettle Black were suddenly thrown open so hard they smacked against the walls. Goldy looked up and saw a figure that was at once reassuring and worrisome.

Josie Bird stood in the open door. She had on her dungarees and her worn flannel shirt. Her head was topped with the wide-brimmed black vaquero's hat. In her hands was the huge dark weight of the eight-gauge shotgun. On her hip was a soft bag that might have held a dozen of the big shells.

Half the saloon turned to see her. Among the railroad men, there were some words exchanged, and a breath of soft laughter. Goldy suspected they might have been considerably more rowdy were it not for the massive gun.

Josie caught sight of Bred and Goldy and marched toward them. "I am going to kill Tom Sharp," she said. "Who will come with me?" Her voice was loud enough to carry the room.

Goldy felt her heart jump. "But honey, Tom's got talent," she said. "Probably a lot more talent than he's been showing. We don't even know what he can do. Look what he did to Orpah."

"You look what he did to Orpah," Josie said. "You think he murdered her just to frighten us. I think that if he did not kill Jake himself, then he helped to do it. What will he do now?"

Bred Smith frowned, then nodded. "I reckon you're right there. I'll help you if I can."

"No," Goldy said sharply. She pressed her hands against her temples, fighting back a sudden headache. "I already lost two friends this week. Are you going to cost me the rest?"

"If we do not stop Tom Sharp," Josie said, "then the cost will be even higher."

"She may be right there, Miss Goldy," Bred agreed. "We've done let this Sharp fellow buffalo us without showing a lick of tough. We're acting like Jake took all our starch with him when he left."

Goldy looked at the two people in front of her: a young Mexican woman in men's clothes, and a tall black man whose best years were two decades gone. They were an unlikely pair. "Oh, hell's bells," she said. "I'm with you, though I don't know what good I can do."

"Goldy!" Sienna called from across the room. "He's coming!"

There was a sudden grinding and scraping as chairs were pushed out of the way. From across the room a big man was approaching. More than big, huge. He was as tall as Bred, and broader than the old changer had been in his prime. He had legs as big as cottonwood trunks, and arms that looked to weigh a hundred pounds each. At the top of his body sat a small head with small features and a surplus of bristly black hair.

He stopped no more than a stride from Josie and looked at her with a sneer. "You the little whore that says she's going to kill Tommy?"

"I am the woman who will kill him," Josie said. She looked the giant up and down. "I know you. You are the one who tore up the store on the day Tom Sharp came into town. Cap Hardin, the one who became a monkey."

A flush came over what skin of the man's face could be seen between his beard and his hair. "I ain't no damn monkey," he said.

Bred Smith pushed past Josie. "You are Sharp's friend, though, ain't you?"

Hardin looked at Bred, then spat right in the black man's face. "I wasn't talking to you, tar boy."

Bred made no move to wipe away the glob of phlegm that slid slowly down his cheek. "Now, you're wrong there," he said. "Miss Josie's my friend. When you go threatening her, you may as well come for me."

"You don't know what you're messing in," Hardin said. He held up one mountainous fist. The skin of his hand began to ripple, growing larger and darker. "You don't even know what I am, do you, old man?"

There was a click of metal. What with all the talking in the saloon and the clank of glasses, it was a small sound, yet somehow it carried the length of the room. Voices quieted. Glasses stopped on their way to mouths.

Cap Hardin looked down and saw the end of the shotgun shoved up against the bulge of his stomach. "Hell," he said. "That won't kill me."

Josie lowered the barrel of the gun and pushed it forward, driving an inch of dark steel barrel into the softness of the big man's crotch. "When I shot you the first time, I saw how much it hurt. I think if I shoot you like this, it will hurt again. I think it will hurt a lot."

There was a moment when the Kettle Black seemed quiet as a church at midnight. Then Cap Hardin took a step back from the gun.

"You're going to be sorry about this," the big man said. He pointed a thick finger and waved it from Josie to Bred to Goldy. "Not one of you's going to live to see sundown."

Josie raised the shotgun and sighted down the barrels. "What do you think, Goldy? If I shoot his head off, will he heal from that?"

Goldy laughed. "I wouldn't waste the shot. He wouldn't miss that head one bit."

Hardin's face twisted in rage. "You old bitch, I'm—"

Bred moved up to the man with a speed that no one without talent could have matched. He grabbed Hardin by the front of the shirt and lifted him clean off the floor. "You're not going to do nothing."

The expression on Hardin's face turned to surprise. "You're a changer."

"Yep," Bred said with a nod.

"Sheriff Sharp's going to hear about this."

"Sharp is sheriff of nothing," Josie said. "You go to him and tell him that I am challenging him."

Bred dropped the big man, giving him a shove that sent him stumbling back. "You do like the lady says."

"She ain't no lady. She's just some little Mexican bitch." Hardin's face had gone white with anger and shock. His breath came so fast he had trouble getting his words out. "She can't challenge nobody. She ain't even got a talent."

Josie ran a hand along the big shotgun. "I have a gun," she said. "And I will use it on him."

"Run on home to mama," Bred said. "Tell your sheriff we'll be along directly."

The seams along the sleeves of Hardin's shirt split with a sound loud as a pistol shot. The tattered cloth opened to reveal arms that were knotted with muscle and covered with a thick mat of hair. The arms were long enough to dangle below Hardin's knees. His head changed, growing wider, flatter. His eyes moved back under a ridge of bone.

In one swift motion Hardin turned, snatched a table from in front of two startled railroad workers, and held it up above his head. "You come," he snarled in a voice that was little more than the growl of an animal. "You come. I'll be waiting."

With that he smashed the table between his hands. A shower of planks and splinters flew across the room, bringing curses and yelps from all sides. Hardin gave them one last glare, then left the bar traveling on both his feet and the knuckles of his hairy hands. He had to turn sideways to get out the door.

There was a delay of perhaps ten seconds, then the voices and noise of drinking returned.

Bred slumped back on his stool. "Well, it seems we got ourselves a challenge."

"Good," Josie said. "But you do not have to do this. It is my fault that Tom Sharp is wearing a sheriff's badge. I should be the one that takes it from his body."

Goldy thanked her stars that Josie was not after her. "You know, we're going against the sheriff. That makes us all outlaws."

"I been called worse," Bred said. He tipped his hat. "Excuse me, ladies, I think I'll go fix myself a meal before we tangle any more. Changing comes hard on an empty stomach."

"You come with me," Josie said. "I have food at our house." She reached out and touched Goldy's hand for a moment. "We will be back soon." Then she and Bred were gone.

Goldy turned her head and saw Dr. Stone at the end of the bar. His face bore a look of shock and his whiskey glass was bone dry. She picked up the bottle and refilled his glass. "Starting to regret coming to Medicine Rock, Doctor?"

Stone picked up his glass and downed the whiskey in a single gulp. "On the contrary," he said. "It looks to me like I've come to the right place."

"How's that?"

"There should be plenty of work for a doctor here."

☆ **23** ☆

"I don't see any reason why I ought to get near those railroad folks again," the Rainmaker said.

Muley snorted. "Seems to me you were complaining about Mr. Cody here not helping them folks in Rapid City."

The Rainmaker shook his head. "Don't get off track. We're not talking about Rapid City. No one here is riding off with killers."

"But we could be leaving some people to die," Muley said. He hefted his bedroll onto his shoulder and marched out into the rain.

The Rainmaker ran to the door and hollered after him. "You don't know that! We might be risking our necks for nothing!"

The argument had started not long after dawn, and with noon getting near, the positions hadn't changed. Jake closed his eyes and leaned back against the wall of the barn. He was tired enough to spend the day sleeping. God knew, after walking all the previous day and half the night, he needed the rest. The trouble was, he couldn't afford to sleep.

Medicine Rock was still better than a hundred miles away. If he had to walk there, it might take more than a week. With what he'd seen in Rapid City and what he had learned from Cody, Jake was not willing to wait out a week.

He opened his eyes and looked around the barn. The fire had burned out, and all that was left of the supplies had been stowed in the boot of the wagon. Bill Cody stood at the back of the barn, watching the rain through a gap in the boards. Cody had not spoken much since waking. Jake suspected that the man's guilt over what he'd done was gnawing at him.

225

Muley came back in out of the rain. "That's everything," he said. "If we're going to go, we better get going. We've burned up half the day already."

"We're going," the Rainmaker said. "But we're going east. Once we reach Sioux Falls, we can tell the authorities there what's been done."

Jake stretched and stood up. "No," he said. "We're going to Medicine Rock."

The pale man frowned so, lines creased his face from forehead to chin. "Sheriff, I know you're worried, but it's my wagon and I'm going to Sioux City."

"No," Jake said, "you're not." He reached to his holster and drew out his pistol. He didn't aim it at the Rainmaker, but somewhere awfully near.

"You can't mean this," the Rainmaker said. "You're supposed to be a lawman."

"I'm supposed to protect Medicine Rock," Jake said. "I can't very well do that if I'm not in Medicine Rock."

Muley moved closer to the Rainmaker. "Sheriff, I'm pretty much on your side on this thing, but I can't say as I like having a gun pointed at me."

"I can understand that." Jake shoved the Colt back into the holster. "I don't want to have to force you. All I'm saying is that I will force you if I have to."

The Rainmaker stood stiff as a board. "You're no more than a criminal. yourself," he said. "What you're doing is pure robbery."

Jake shrugged. "It's probably kidnapping, but I'm not going to argue." He sighed and held out a hand. "We don't have to do it like this. You heard what happened to Rapid City. You want to let these folks get away with it?"

"It wasn't me that let them get away," the Rainmaker said.

Muley shook his head. "A-yup, you was in a real hurry to kick on Cody. But that don't stop you from doing the same thing, does it?"

The Rainmaker looked down at the ground. "I didn't make myself out to be some kind of hero," he said.

Bill Cody came walking slowly from the back of the barn.

"Neither did I," he said. "It was just somebody's damn cheap novels. I was just a scout and a buffalo runner. I never did anything to make me a hero."

"Well," Jake said, "here's a chance for both of you to be real heroes." He put one hand on the Rainmaker's shoulder and the other on Cody's and shoved both men toward the front of the barn. "Now get in that wagon before I have to pull the pistol again."

The four of them went out into the rain. Bill Cody opened the door of the wagon and climbed in without another word. The Rainmaker stopped in the doorway and gave Jake a hard look.

"You know," he said, "you'd never get this wagon to go without me."

Jake looked up at the rigging of the sails over his head. "That may be," he replied. "But if I was you, I wouldn't bet my life on it. Now, you think you can manage a wind out of the northeast? I want to cut back down toward Rapid City, then follow the rail line west from there."

The Rainmaker nodded. "I can get you a breeze. Though I wish that just once someone would want to go the same way the wind's already blowing." He shut the door of the wagon with a slam.

"Looks like I'm riding with you," Jake said to Muley.

"You sure you don't want to ride with them?" Muley replied. "It can get awful wet up topside."

"I've been wet before. I've never been known to melt."

"Suit yourself."

Jake followed Muley up to the driver's box. "Quite a view."

"A-yup." Muley put his hands to the ropes, then looked over at Jake. "You ain't got much to do up here. Don't touch the ropes. Duck when I say duck. And watch you don't fall off when we hit the bumps. You hear?"

Jake nodded. He watched as the seaman loosed the ropes and began to tug on the lines. Yards of heavy cloth unrolled as the lines pulled them up the single mast. The sailcloth was wet and heavy. At first the changing breeze didn't so much as bring a wrinkle. Then the wind cut around to the east, bringing with it a blast of cold rain. The tall sails bellied out with the force of the wind, snapping out stiff and sending a cold spray over Jake. Muley swung the boom around to the side and leaned on the steering shaft. Slowly at first, then with increasing speed, the wagon began to move.

Jake hung onto the side of the wagon. "You weren't kidding about the bumps."

Muley nodded. "Old Mr. Concord put in lots of springs for the passengers, but he must have expected the driver to have padding on his arse."

There was a well-trod road between the old farm and the city to the south. Following that track, Muley was able to get the wagon to the speed of a sprinting horse. In a few minutes they had the Rainmaker's clouds at their back and the wagon was charging on through sunshine.

"I believe I could get to where I liked this," Jake said. "How come there's so little wind?"

"We're running with the air, not against it like you do on a horse." Muley lifted his eyes to the sun, and Jake saw a smile split the man's weathered face. "I have to say I favor it when it's like this. It's even better than running in a glass sea." He turned and looked at Jake. "But don't you go letting the Rainmaker know I say that, you hear?"

"I don't suppose I'll be saying much of anything to the Rainmaker," Jake said. He thought about the way the pale man had fought going to Medicine Rock and frowned. "I can't say I think much of your friend."

"Hell," Muley said with a shrug. "He ain't so bad as he seems. He don't know anything but the rain and what he reads in his little books. Gives him some funny ideas now and then."

The wind lost steam and Muley started to grumble, but then the breeze gathered again. Muley adjusted his lines and moved the boom around to keep the wagon clipping along.

They were almost to Rapid City when Muley raised a finger and pointed ahead. "Look there."

Jake squinted at the horizon. There was a thin streamer of white smoke above the next rise. At first Jake took it for the sign of a chimney, but the smoke was moving, leaving behind a line that broke up to puffs of white in the distance. "What is that?" he asked.

"A train," Muley said. "We ought to be able to see it once we clear this hill."

Muley's judgment was good. From the top of the rise they could see an engine and five cars steaming hard for the west. It was a much shorter train than the one Jake had seen before, and it was moving at a pace he would have thought impossible.

"It moves like a bullet," Jake said in wonder.

"I'd put him at better than forty knots. Some of them can hit eighty, they say." Muley shook his head. "I rode one once, up in Providence. Can't say that I thought much of it."

The train passed on out of sight among the dark hills. Jake stared after it, watching the steam trail break up and drift away. Unless the plans had changed, that train could be on its way to Medicine Rock. If the track had raced ahead the way it had been moving, the line might run all the way to town by now. Jake wondered if the train might be delivering Kastle or Cullen back to the west. If it was, there was little doubt the easterners would reach the town long before him.

"You don't suppose they intend on doing to Medicine Rock what they already did to Rapid City, do you?" Jake asked.

Muley shook his head. "Naw. If they was going to kill off Medicine Rock, I reckon they'd have done it by now."

Jake was still looking toward the west when a headache struck so sharply that he almost tumbled from the bench. He pitched forward, pushing his head between his hands. The pain was still sharp as a knife when the wagon suddenly slowed to a crawl.

"Damnation," Muley said. He reached for the panel beside his feet and slid it open. "Where's our wind?"

It was Cody's voice that replied. "Your man's sick," he called. "From the way he's acting, it seems serious."

"I better come see." Muley started to rise from his seat, but Jake caught him by the arm.

"Wait," Jake said. "Get the wagon away from the tracks."

"I need to see to the Rainmaker. He's ill."

"So am I," Jake said. "But I think we'll both be better if we can get away from the rails."

Muley looked puzzled at Jake's statement, but he tugged his cords and swung the boom around. Propelled by its own momentum and the flagging wind, the wagon was slow to turn and even slower to move away, but every foot of distance between the tracks and the wagon brought relief to Jake's pain.

Finally the sail wagon had moved off a good hundred feet and the pain in Jake's head was nothing but a memory. He drew in a deep breath. "Thanks. I'm better now. It's only when I'm close to the rail line that I start to feel sickly."

"How can a rail line have anything to do with you getting sick?" Muley asked.

Jake shook his head. "I don't know, but it does. Far as I can see, it only bothers those that have a talent."

Muley opened the panel again and hollered inside. "What's the word in there?"

"I'm better," the Rainmaker replied. "What did you do?"

Jake leaned down to speak into the opening. "I'll tell you when we stop." He pushed the panel closed. "Push on west as best you can," he said to Muley, "but try and stay at least this far from the rails."

The seaman nodded. "I'll play her the best I can," he said. "Don't expect to get far this way. There's trees up ahead, and some rough country. This wagon don't go tough ground any too well, and it don't turn so fast. I reckon we'll be forced back along or over the tracks before too long."

Jake winced, thinking about how much it had hurt him to cross the lines. "You do what you can."

They soon struck a westward track, but it was an old, worn path, cut by gullies and overgrown with sage and knots of grass. The wagon bumped so hard going over the rugged course that Jake had to hold onto the side board, the springs under the cabin giving a chorus of squeals.

Saying he feared damage to the wheels or frame of the wagon, Muley was forced to let the sails slump a few feet to slow their passage. He pointed to a dark spot on the rolling slopes ahead. "If we make it as far as those trees, we'll have to turn there. Those cottonwood branches will make our sails into quilting squares if we don't stay clear."

"All right," Jake said. "Maybe we'll find a better road once we're across." He leaned back in his seat and braced himself for the pain to come. Instead he heard the thump of sailcloth piling against the top of the coach. The wagon began to slow.

"What is it?" Jake asked.

Muley nodded toward the tangle of trees. "Look there."

Jake looked. What he saw at first was a spot of white and a patch of blue. Then he saw that it was a woman, an old woman with a tight cap of braided white hair under a strange blue hat. She was sitting on the stump of a fallen tree and looking their way. It was quite some distance, but Jake thought the woman was smiling.

Muley let the sails fall slack, and the wagon soon slowed to a stop on the bumpy path. "Hello on the ground!" Muley shouted.

The woman stood and waved one thin hand. "Hello, Muley Owens. By God don't you look young!"

"You know this woman?" Jake asked.

Muley shook his head for a moment, then stopped. "A-yup. I think I might," he said quietly. He raised his head and called to the woman. "Why are you here?"

"To help you, of course." The old woman sat down on the log. "Come on over here. I don't want to shout all day."

The door at the side of the wagon opened and Cody stuck his head out. "Why've we stopped?"

"William Cody!" the woman called. "I've not seen you in a coon's age. Come over and talk."

Cody stepped down from the wagon and stood rubbing his beard. "Do I know you, ma'am?"

"You do," the woman said. "Get over here, all of you, and bring that rain fellow with you. I don't remember a thing about him from the first time we met."

Jake stared at the woman a long moment, then climbed down from the driver's box. As he started to cross the stony ground between the wagon and the trees raindrops began to fall.

"You're her," Jake said as he drew up to the woman. "You're the one who took me to the prairie dogs." The woman who had pulled him across the prairie had been no more than in her thirties, and this woman had to be more than two times that. Maybe three. But Jake had no doubt it was the same woman.

The woman nodded. "Long time ago." She smiled brightly, nesting her eyes in laugh lines. "At least it was a long time for me."

The others began to walk up, gathering near Jake and looking at the woman. "Well, sit down, all of you," she said. "Let's have a parley."

The rain began to fall more thickly, reminding Jake that his hat was long missing. "We're going to get wet if we talk out here," he said. "Maybe we can all squeeze into the wagon."

The woman laughed. "I'm too old to squeeze. Anywise, what I've got to say won't take long."

"What did you need to say?" Muley asked.

The woman looked at him with a tender expression. "I'm here to say what you told me to say, Muley. What you taught me fifty years ago."

"I wasn't even born fifty years ago," Muley said.

The woman laughed. "Now that I think of it," she said, "neither was I!"

☆ **24** ☆

For five years Goldy had watched Jake Bird fight his challenges. Before that it had been Sheriff Pridy. Pridy had been fat, but he'd been a good sheriff. Before that, greedy Sheriff Solomon. Now it was Tom Sharp that sat in the whitewashed office and wore a star on his vest.

Goldy had never expected to see the day. Jake had been young, and he'd had talent to spare. With Josie to help him, Goldy had expected Jake to last long enough to see her dead. She'd never expected to see another man in his place. She had surely never expected to be standing in the street challenging the sheriff of Medicine Rock.

"I've not fired a pistol in better than five years," Goldy whispered to Bred. "Ten if you mean firing it at people."

Bred gave a slight nod. "I expect that Colt still works the same as it used to."

Goldy nodded, but she could not stop her hands from shaking. There was little doubt in her mind that she was about to get killed. Bred and Josie might fight their way out of the scrape, they had both survived such tumbles in the past, but she had no experience with such work. Still, she was damned if she was going to let her friends stand alone on this day. Besides, getting killed now might be cleaner than living with what Tom Sharp would do with no one left to challenge him.

"Tom Sharp!" Josie shouted. "Come out and face a challenge!"

Of the three challengers, it was Josie who looked dangerous. Josie stood in front of Bred and Goldy. She had her hat tipped back on her head and the shotgun in her hands. Her eyes as she looked up at the office door were as black as a midnight sky.

Tom Sharp came out of the office with the confidence of a gambler who had already pocketed his winnings. He strolled up to the railing at the side of the walk, looked down and smiled.

"I never thought you'd actually go through with a challenge," he said. "If it wasn't so stupid, it might be funny."

Josie leveled the shotgun at Sharp's pretty face. "Will you come down to the street, or do I shoot you where you stand?"

Sharp raised up his hands. "Don't get in a hurry," he said. "I want to enjoy this for as long as I can."

Cap Hardin came out of the office with an apple. The fruit looked like a cherry in his huge hand. "I thought I told you I was coming to kill you at sundown," he said.

"You said before sundown," Bred said. "Anyhow, we thought we'd save you the trouble of looking for us."

Hardin looked baffled, but Sharp laughed. "You three have more guts than I gave you credit," said the man who called himself sheriff. "Why don't you go on home. I might let you live a day or two longer."

Josie's answer was a blast from the eight gauge.

The sound of the big shotgun letting go was so loud that Goldy let out a yelp. She took a jigger-step back, fumbling her pistol and almost dropping it to the ground.

When she looked up again, Tom Sharp was no longer smiling. He held out his hand and let his fingers open. Buckshot dribbled to the ground. "You'll have to do better than—"

Before he could finish his sentence, Josie fired again. This time Sharp was knocked back. There was a dazed look in his eyes. Blood began to well against his white shirt.

Working unhurriedly and deliberately, Josie broke open the big shotgun and reached in her bag for new shells.

Tom Sharp raised one hand and made a chopping gesture. Fire sprang from his fingertips, arcing toward Josie like water from a burst pipe.

Bred Smith stepped in front of Josie, taking the fire right in his chest. The black man opened his mouth and let go a deep moan, but he did not seem to be burned.

Goldy felt like she was stuck in mud. Everything was going fast, too fast for her to do anything. Even too fast to run away. She raised the pistol in a trembling hand, trying to sight it on Sharp.

Then the ape came crashing through the railing and into the street.

Hardin must have started changing when Josie fired. Goldy hadn't seen it, but she was watching Sharp then. Now, Hardin was finished changing. Goldy had not been around to see the ape the first time Hardin was in town. Descriptions hadn't done it credit.

What Hardin had turned himself into was a hairy, long-armed beast with curving yellow fangs and a chest as broad as an ox. The creature struck Bred like a hammer, sending the black man sprawling in the dust. A hairy hand grabbed the end of Josie's gun and lifted her clean off the ground. Then Hardin shook the woman like a dog wagging its tail until Josie was flung clean across the street to smash against the walls of the Kettle Black. The ape dropped the shotgun into the dust and turned toward Goldy with its yellow fangs bared.

Goldy held up the Colt in both hands. "Get back."

The ape came forward, its hands held out to take her.

Goldy fired. And fired again. And again.

Three red blooms appeared on the bare black chest of the ape. For a moment the beast seemed startled. Then it straightened its bowed legs, raising itself until its small head was twice as high as a tall man. A monstrous hand lashed out and struck the gun away from Goldy. The force of the blow was enough to spin Goldy around and send bolts of electric pain up her arms.

The ape held its long arms up to the sky and roared with such force that the wind of its voice tore through Goldy's hair. She fell in the street, looked up at the monster, and waited to be crushed.

Then an answering roar came from Goldy's right. From the shredded ruins of Bred Smith's clothes a great bear rose to its feet. It was a grizzly almost as tall as the ape, twelve feet high and more. It shuffled forward on its short legs, forepaws raised and claws at the ready.

The ape snarled and dropped onto its knuckles. It took a step back, then another.

The bear dropped down, too, voicing another roar as it came forward on all fours.

Forgotten as the two giant beasts faced off, Goldy grabbed her gun, got to her feet, and moved over to Josie. The Mexican woman was awake and sitting on the dusty boardwalk. Up on the walk in front of the sheriff's office there was no sign of Tom Sharp. Sienna had come out from the Kettle Black and was running a damp cloth over Josie's face.

"Is she all right?" Goldy asked as she bent over them.

Sienna nodded. "The breath has been knocked out of her, but she will be fine."

Another roar made Goldy turn her head. In the street the two giants were circling each other. The bear shuffled forward. The ape raised a fist. The bear moved back. The ape moved in, only to meet with slashing claws that came within inches of its furry hide.

As it circled around to the front of the sheriff's office, the ape suddenly reached down and came up with a piece of the broken railing. It brandished the six-foot length of heavy wood like a man swinging a sapper.

The bear made a low growl. Again it rose on its hind legs, holding its claws high as it moved toward the ape.

With a whistle of wind, the ape swung the wooden beam and brought it crashing against the bear's ribs. The bear dropped down, wheezing, and at once the ape was on it, pounding the bear with blows hard enough to smash timbers.

"We need to do something," Josie said. She pushed away Sienna's hand and stood swaying on her feet.

"No," Goldy said. "You're hurt. Besides, what are you going to do? Bred's not done for, not by a long shot."

The bear rolled to the side, twisting away from the ape's pounding fist. The ape moved to follow, but the bear was faster. There was a bellow of surprise and pain, and the ape backed away. Blood dripped from a line of wounds in the ape's hairy arms.

The bear got on its feet and charged. Before the ape could get away, the long muzzle had closed on its left leg. With a savage shake of its head, the bear tore through flesh and sent blood showering into the dusty street.

Head thrown back in pain, the ape screamed. Its fists came down, pounding on the bear's head with the speed of a smith pounding a horseshoe. The bear released its grip on the savaged leg and backed away.

Blood poured from the bear's mouth, but whether it was its own or that of the ape, Goldy couldn't tell.

Though changers could heal far faster than any normal person, the damage done to the ape's leg was too severe. It was forced to lean on one wide palm, holding the other hand up as a weapon. Through the bloody wound in its leg Goldy could see shredded muscle and gnawed bone.

Moving slowly, the bear began to circle again, forcing its crippled opponent to turn and turn again. The bear darted in, moving like a dog after a cornered cougar, closing to snap its jaws and backing away before the ape could deliver a blow.

The strategy seemed to be working. With each turn, the ape was slower. Its fist hung lower. Even the snarl on its face was fading to a dull stupor.

"Bred has him now," Goldy said.

Sienna glanced toward the street. "No," she said. "Not yet." Then she pushed past the railway workers crowding the door for the Kettle Black and disappeared inside.

Out in the street the bear rose up and moved in for the final blow. Claws raised and teeth bared, it moved in on the exhausted ape.

Only the ape wasn't as exhausted as it seemed. Just as the bear shuffled into arm's reach, the ape suddenly lowered its head and charged.

The impact threw the bear over onto its back. Before it could rise, the ape had moved to stand astride the fallen form, hammering its fists against the bear's head and abdomen. Each blow drew a deep grunt of effort from the ape and sent a spray of blood from the bear's mouth and nostrils. It tried to reach up with its forelegs, but the ape had the advantage of reach. It pushed the bear's claws aside and continued its relentless pounding attack. The bear's eyes rolled back in its head. The spray of blood from its mouth became a gusher.

"Bred!" Goldy cried. She raised her pistol and fired three more shots. The ape seemed too big a target to miss, but if any of the slugs struck home, the creature didn't so much as turn toward their source.

The bear's head fell to the side. Its forearms dropped limp on the dust. The ape pounded its fists a moment longer. Then it raised its arms and roared in triumph.

Behind the ape the bear's hind legs slowly came up.

The ape turned to the people at the Kettle Black, baring its fangs. Its small eyes glowed with a red light. It swung its bloody fists through the air and howled.

The bear's hind claws touched against its stomach.

At that first touch, the ape seemed to realize what was going to come. It made a bleating sound. A sound far too small and too frightened to have come from such a throat.

Then the bear's claws tore its stomach wide open. Coils of yellow-gray intestine spilled onto the ground in a shower of blood and fluids that Goldy couldn't name. The bear surged up from the ground, driving its foreclaws deep into the ape's sides, burying its muzzle in the ape's throat.

The two giant forms fell to the ground, rolling in mud and gore. The ape was still moving at first, pushing against the bear, trying to free itself from the slashing claws and tearing teeth. The bear held on. After a few minutes the ape stopped moving, but the bear wasn't done. Gobbets of flesh flew from the ape's savaged throat. The bear pushed the body of its opponent to the side, turned, and delivered one slashing blow after another with its long curving foreclaws. Finally, the ape's head rolled free on the muddy ground.

Only then did the bear release its hold. It reared again onto its hind legs, took a few unsteady steps, and fell to the ground.

Goldy was running before the creature even hit the ground.

Josie was right behind. Goldy reached the great creature and lay a hand on its long muzzle. "Bred?"

The shaggy form began to shiver and change. The massive shoulders grew smaller, the coat of hair faded away. In a matter of no more than five seconds the giant bear had been replaced by the shape of Bred Smith, a Bred Smith that was bruised and bleeding.

Bred opened his brown eyes and blinked up at the sky. "Damn monkey," he groaned.

"Lay still," Josie said. "We will get help."

"Help is already here," said the voice of Johnson Stone. The hunchbacked doctor bent down over Bred. "You look like hell."

Bred laughed, but the laugh turned into a cough that brought dark blood spilling from Bred's lips.

"Don't do that," Johnson said.

Goldy wiped tears away from her eyes. "Is he going to be all right?"

Stone ran his hand along Bred's side. "From what I can tell, he's got some broken bones. Undoubtedly there's internal damage as well."

Bred spat out another mouthful of blood. "What's broken?" he asked.

"It would be easier to say what isn't," the doctor replied. "I'd say you've got eight or more broken ribs. Cracked sternum. Skull fracture. From the blood you're coughing, you've punctured a lung, probably both. I've no doubt you've ruptured your liver, your kidney. All of those things are fatal. God knows what else you've busted."

Josie dropped to the ground, her black hair falling across Bred's naked chest as she put her face against his cheek. "I have asked too much from you," she said. "You should not have to die like this."

"It's all right," Bred said. He raised one arm and patted Josie on the back, leaving behind bloody handprints on her shirt. "Ever since Jake brought me back up by Calio, I've known I was living on borrowed time."

Dr. Stone chuckled. "My guess is you better go get yourself another loan."

Goldy stared at the Indian doctor. "What does that mean?"

"It means I expect him to live."

"But you said his wounds were fatal," Goldy said.

Stone nodded. "For anyone else they would be. But changers are tough as old cobs. I expect this fellow will be ready to do it all again in a day or so."

Bred groaned. "Don't bet on it, Doc."

Goldy went back to the Kettle Black and tapped the four biggest men she could find. None of them argued as she brought them back to the middle of the street and ordered them to carry Bred inside. With Dr. Stone following, they took the surviving changer off the street.

"Where is Sharp?" Josie asked.

Goldy looked over at the sheriff's office. She hadn't thought about the small man since the fight between ape and bear had started. "He must have run."

"Then we have to run after him," Josie said. She walked across the street and retrieved her shotgun from where Hardin had flung it. Josie looked in the barrel, broke open the chamber, then closed it again. She nodded and looked over at Goldy. "Go reload your weapon," Josie told her. "We must still find Sharp and kill him."

Goldy looked at the torn body of the ape in its lake of gore. She looked down at her own bloodstained dress and at the red that colored Josie's pants and shirt. "Do we have to go now?" she asked. "Maybe we ought to catch our breath first."

Josie nodded. "When I shot him before, he was wounded. We know he can be killed."

"But if we can just—"

"Go and reload your pistol," Josie said firmly. "We must kill him now." She looked up and down the street. "Tom Sharp is no more than an animal. And like any animal, his wounds will make him dangerous."

<h1 style="text-align:center">☆ 25 ☆</h1>

The old woman sat on a stump in the rain and smiled at them with teeth that were so even they had to be store bought.

Her hair was all white, braided around her head and pinned down by a hat the size of a cake tin. Time had faded her skin to a lined ivory and brought out her sharp cheekbones to press against her thin, lined skin. Some disorder of the aged caused her head to tick back and forth, back and forth, like the pendulum of a clock. The clothing that she wore was strange, not like anything Muley had ever seen. The cloth was a shiny blue, more glossy even than silk, but stiffer. The skirt was cut up to the woman's knees, far higher than was decent, showing legs that seemed too tan and too smooth to go with the rest of her.

"I almost forgot this turn was coming," the woman said. "Oh, I was told, of course, but it's been so long since there was a turn . . ." Her voice trailed away and her face turned to the hills around them. "It's so beautiful here. I plumb forgot what things used to be like."

Muley saw little beauty in the rising hills with their clusters of pine. They were obstacles to the wagon and hiding places for men of bad intent. But he saw something in the face of the woman, something he should have seen before.

"You're the same woman, ain't you?" he said. "First I thought you might be her ma, but you're her."

"Of course," the woman said.

"What woman?" the Rainmaker asked.

"The one that talked to me when we were fixing the wagon back at that sodbuster's."

"I didn't see any woman," the Rainmaker said.

Jake Bird wiped the rain off his face. "You're the one that took me to the prairie dogs, right? Only you were younger."

The woman laughed. "You know, I'd forgotten that, too." She rocked back on her stump. "Prairie dogs!"

"Prairie dogs?" the Rainmaker said.

"You're the woman in St. Louis," Bill Cody said. "You're the one that told me about the job with the railway."

The smile on the woman's face froze. "Oh, Bill, I'm sorry for that." She reached out and touched him lightly on the arm. "But we did all need you here."

The Rainmaker pushed his way to the front. "I don't understand any of this," he said. He put out a long white finger and wagged it at the woman. "Who are you and where did you come from?"

The woman pursed her lips and looked him up and down. "I come from walking back and forth in the world," she said. "Going here and there."

"That's no answer," the Rainmaker said.

"No." The woman smiled again. "It's a joke. Muley warned me you never took well to jokes."

Muley shook his head. "I never said that."

"Not yet, but you will. Just like you told me about how we'd meet today and what I ought to tell you." The woman let out a long breath.

"Here's the whole thing in a bread basket," she said. She held her hands together in front of her with her palms turned up, as if holding some small mass. "My life don't run straight, like the rest of you. It's all tangled up like twine that's come loose from the spool." She was silent for a moment, her head keeping up its slow swing from side to side. "Sometimes it gets twisted 'round like a snake on hot coals," she said at last. "Sometimes it even crosses over itself so as I can talk to myself and let myself know where the next turn might take me. It's a talent, they say, but it's come close to making me teched."

Muley reached out and took the old woman's hand. "It was you at the rail camp," he said. "You were the girl."

She nodded. "I don't remember much about that night, but I remember you."

The Rainmaker cleared his throat. "You mean to say that you were that young girl?" He shook his head. "That's not possible."

"That's bold talk for a man with a cloud what follows him around," Muley said. "How do you know what's possible?"

A flush crept over the Rainmaker's face. "I know it's not possible for a person to move around between past and future. She says you told her things that you haven't told her yet, how can that be?"

"Haven't you been listening?"

"I've been listening, but I don't believe it." The Rainmaker turned back to the woman. "Muley told you that we'd meet you today?"

She nodded. "Yes."

"And he told you what to tell us?"

"Everything."

The Rainmaker again leveled his finger at her face. "But you're telling him right now. So who thought it up to begin with?"

The old woman batted the Rainmaker's hand away. "By God, he's worse than you told me." She looked over at Muley. "You better let me get it out before it's too late. You said you'd be in a hurry."

"Where are we hurrying to?" Jake asked.

The woman took a deep breath. "You need to get home, Sheriff. This railroad they're building, it don't have nothing to do with running folks across the country. It has to do with talent."

"The rails make me sick when I get close," Jake said quickly.

"And me," the Rainmaker added.

The woman nodded. "That metal sucks the talent out of you like a tick on a dog. And that ain't the half of it. Right now it only gets you when you're nearly on top of it. If you let this rail line get finished, it'll pull the talent out of everyone for a thousand miles north or south."

The Rainmaker folded his arms across his chest. "That doesn't make any more sense than the rest of it. Talent's not something you can keep in a bucket like a horse's oats. Even if they could do it, what good would talent do anyone but the person it came from?"

"I've already seen what they can do with it," Bill Cody said, "and unless I miss my guess, so has Sheriff Bird."

"Rapid City," Jake said.

Bill nodded. "I saw them working back East, making doohickeys that could stop talent. The thing that Kastle used in Rapid City was probably full of talent from some signers or scribblers better than a thousand miles away."

"So what do we do?" Muley asked. "What'll happen if this railroad gets finished?"

"Don't know for sure," the woman said. "Maybe this Gould will kill everybody. Most likely he'll just kill those what don't kneel down to him. You seen them big drums he's got along-side the rail every few miles?"

"I've seen them," Jake said.

"He can store talent in them to use later. With all these machines that people are making for him, there's nobody to say what he couldn't do. All I know for sure is what you told me." She pointed downslope to the tracks. "When the train comes along, you need to stop it before it gets to Medicine Rock."

Muley started. "But the train's already gone by," he said. "It steamed through here close to an hour ago."

The old woman looked shocked. "Well, I swooney," she said. "I don't think you ever told me that part. It ain't going to do to let that train get there first. You boys really better hurry."

There was a soft pop, like the sound of coffee that was just starting to boil. For a moment Muley thought he saw a room—a room with chairs and tables, and a strange box full of light. Then the room was gone, and so was the old woman.

Muley stepped forward and put his hands on the stump. There was only a dry spot on the damp wood to show that anyone had been there.

"Where did she go?" Bill Cody asked.

"I guess her string took another turn," Muley said.

Jake Bird turned and started walking for the wagon. "Come on," he said. "We've got a train to catch."

Muley nodded and headed for the driver's box. "Going to be quite a trip," he said.

The Rainmaker stomped through the damp weeds to Jake's side. "Sheriff, you're short a hat size if you think we can catch that train. It must be twenty miles gone by now. Thirty. Besides, we couldn't keep up with it even if it was right here."

"You get inside and make the biggest wind you ever made," Jake said. "I'll see if I can't help."

"How?"

"Get inside," Jake repeated. "And you better make a blow like there's no tomorrow. God knows, if we don't stop Gould, there may be no tomorrow."

"Well," the Rainmaker said, "I think that's quite an exaggeration." He opened the door of the wagon and climbed inside.

Cody walked past, stroking his beard and looking at the ground. He started to follow the Rainmaker into the wagon, but Jake stopped him.

"I want you up on top," Jake said. "You've been through this country before, and we need to find the smoothest path we can."

Muley leaned down. "It's going to be tight up here," he said. "This box wasn't made for three."

"Then it'll be tight," Jake said. "Come on."

Muley moved aside so the other men could sit. It was a snug situation, but he could still get a grip on the lines. "Which way do we head?"

Cody waved his hand toward the rails. "You need to cut over the tracks. There's an old coach path south of Deeder's Mountain. We need to be on that path."

The wind whipped up as the Rainmaker gathered his storm. "Hold on," Muley said. "I'm raising the sheets."

He pulled the jib up quickly and let it fill with a snap. The wagon pulled loose of the muddy ground and started its turn. Generally, Muley would have slowed for such a maneuver, but now he raised the mainsail, too. He expected the Rainmaker to falter as they approached the tracks. They would have to muster as much speed as they could while the winds held.

A moment later Jake began to groan. He put his elbows on his knees and clamped his hands to the sides of his head.

"Is it bad?" Cody asked.

"Just keep it going," Jake said.

The winds started dying a moment later. Muley turned back a little to the east, using more slope to compensate for the lost breeze. A second later the wagon went bouncing across the rail tracks. Jake slumped in his seat and might have fallen if Cody hadn't grabbed the back of his shirt. From inside the wagon Muley heard the Rainmaker howl in pain. Then the wagon was south of the rails and moving away.

"You want to head for that notched hill," Cody said. "The track runs that way."

Muley nodded. As they put some distance between themselves and the rails, the winds began to grow stronger and steadier again. Muley was forced to steer the wagon around a series of steep-sided gullies, then around a group of twisted juniper trees. Finally they struck Cody's wagon track.

It was an old path, overgrown by sage and cut by water, but it was far smoother than the land around it. Muley pulled the sails up full and took in all the wind there was to take.

"We're moving about ten, fifteen knots now," he said, "but we'll lose speed when the slopes get steeper. 'Course, we can run a lot faster on the downslopes if the road stays good."

"It's not fast enough," Jake said. "I'm going to see if I can't speed things along."

Muley watched as Jake turned himself around on the bench until he was facing back toward the clouds. A strange, slack expression fell across the sheriff's face. His eyes grew wide and glassy. Then a noise began to emerge from Jake's mouth.

The sound raised the hairs at the back of Muley's neck. It was like fighting cats and sizzling bacon. As it grew louder, notes of steamboat whistles and tearing metal joined in the shriek.

"What are you doing?" Muley shouted.

"He's chattering," Cody said. "It's a wild talent, but a strong one."

Behind the sail wagon the sky grew darker. Clouds began to heave up and down, to roll and buck like wild horses. Gusts of stronger winds emerged, whistling through the rigging of the wagon. A moment later the gusts joined together into a continuous shrieking gale.

The wind hit the wagon like a charging bull. At once their speed was doubled, and it didn't stop there. The sails stood out to their limits. The segmented mast creaked and made an ominous groan.

Muley looked up at the rigging and shook his head. "I don't know if we can take this," he said. "This is a stiffer wind than we've taken with the new mast."

"God damn but we are moving, though," Cody said.

Muley was willing to concede that much. From the way the trees whipped past, they had to be doing better than thirty knots, probably more than forty. The wagon lurched and shook as they carried across a small gully. They topped a hill and Muley hauled hard on the steering cords as they curved off south of the larger hills at the center of the range.

Every bump they hit brought on a new range of pops, cracks, and creaks. The taut rigging hummed in the breeze. The sails stood hard as steel.

They were at the edge, sailing as fast as the vehicle could take and maybe more. It was something Muley had never experienced at sea, where ships were too costly and captains too fearful to press themselves.

Muley pulled himself up on the seat, feeling the cords tremble in his hands and the screaming of the steel-rimmed wheels over stone and earth. It was grand. It was the grandest thing he had ever done.

A blue light began to shine through the gloom of the storm. When Muley looked to the right, he saw blue fire dancing over Jake Bird. More of the strange cold flames danced along the boom, up the mast, and even over the sails.

Cody shied away, pushing himself so far to the side that he was hanging over the edge of the wagon. "What is it?"

"Don't worry," Muley said. "It's St. Elmo's fire. I've never known it to hurt anyone." A ball of blue flames dropped from the sheets and bounced against Muley's chest. Ignoring the wind, it wandered around the front of the wagon, darted back toward Cody, then vanished in a flash of light.

"You sure they won't hurt you?" Cody asked.

"No," Muley said. "I'm only saying they never have. 'Course, I never saw this happen on land, either."

The wagon finished its path around the core of the hills and turned out on more level ground. The St. Elmo's fire came and went several times, and in shades of blue, red, and green. So far Muley's experience had held. The transparent flames did no damage.

"You reckon we're catching up to that train?" Muley asked. Already the storm had carried them as far in an hour as they might have normally gone in a day.

Cody shrugged. "I expect they went straight through the hills. They may have had crews build a trestle over some valleys, or even dug themselves a tunnel. Those boys can do things you wouldn't believe."

Muley squinted ahead. The wagon track ran on dead to the west. If the railroad went to Medicine Rock, it would have to turn south at some point, crossing their path. But for the moment there was no sign of the train or its tracks.

A new note entered the voice of the wind. Muley turned to see that the agitation of the clouds had grown. They were not only moving up and down, but churning about in a circle as well. "I think you'd best ease off, Sheriff, it's looking plumb nasty back there."

Instead of calming, the weather grew still more fierce. The circling clouds moved faster. Lightning struck from the heart of the storm, playing over trees not thirty feet behind the wagon.

"Sheriff?" Muley glanced up. Jake Bird was kneeling on the driver's box with his back bent and his face turned up to the sky. His lips still moved, though if he was still chattering, the noise was not one that Muley could make out. "Sheriff Bird! You need to calm things down!" he shouted over the increasing roar of the storm.

Behind them a dark mass dropped from the clouds.

"Twister!" Cody cried.

The funnel roared along the ground, uprooting trees and flinging boulders into the air. More lightning came down, ringing the tornado in sheets of flickering fire.

The wind from the storm increased. There was a splintering crack from somewhere deep inside the wagon as the mast tipped forward.

"Stop him!" Muley shouted. "It's going to rip us apart!"

"I don't think I can stop him," Cody replied.

Between them Jake Bird threw out his arms and screamed to the storm. There was nothing in his eyes but blue fire.

☆ 26 ☆

Goldy looked along the street. The doors and windows of Medicine Rock had been closed tight. But for the few souls incautious enough to peek between shutters, you might have thought the town was deserted.

When a sheriff was taking on a weaker challenger, it could attract considerable spectators. Folks seemed to enjoy seeing the loser taken apart with talent—so long as it presented no risk to themselves or their businesses. When the challenge was more serious, folks were apt to keep themselves out of harm's way. Apparently, the citizens of Medicine Rock had determined that this was a serious challenge.

Josie stood at the door of the sheriff's office with the shotgun held waist high. "Are you ready?"

"Oh, hell no," Goldy said. She tightened her grip on the pistol as best she could. The blow the ape had given her had left her fingers numb and swollen. It was all she could do to hold the gun. "What if he's in there?" Goldy asked.

"Then I will shoot him."

"He can stop your shot," Goldy said. "You've seen him do that much."

Josie shrugged. "He stopped one shot, but the second one got through. Enough shots will kill him."

Goldy snorted. "One shot will kill you. Me, too, far as that goes. My talent don't include stopping lead." She waved the pistol toward the office. "What if Sharp's waiting on the other side of this door? He might plug us before you can even pull the trigger."

Josie frowned for a moment, then nodded. "You have a

point." She pulled the trigger on the eight-gauge, blowing a hole in the door big enough to swing a pig through. The scrap of wood that remained above the hole swung for a second on its hinge, then fell to the floor with a thump. The front room of the office was full of splinters, buckshot, and blue smoke. There was no sign of Tom Sharp.

"Hell!" Goldy shouted. "I wish you'd tell me when you're going to do that. You've scairt me out of ten years today, and I ain't got ten years to spare."

Josie nodded. "Next time I will tell you." She kicked open what remained of the lower door and stepped into the office.

Goldy followed, blinking against the acrid smoke. The table in the front room held a few scattered papers and a short stack of Union bills. Another handful of cash had been blown onto the floor by the blast.

"Looks like Sharp's done started collecting his fees," Goldy said. She bent and picked up a bill. "Fifty dollars. Lands, I didn't know anyone around these parts had a bill like this."

Josie raised the shotgun to her shoulder and poked around the corner into the back room. "He is not here," she said. "There is no blood. Maybe he did not come here after I shot him."

"Sounds right," Goldy said, but her thoughts for the moment were on the money. The second bill she picked up was also a fifty. So was the next. And the next. What she'd taken for a small amount of money was actually several hundred dollars. Maybe several thousand. She moved to the table and looked at the stack there. It wasn't fifties—it was hundreds.

Josie turned and started for the door. "We need to find Sharp."

"Hold up there," Goldy said. She pointed to the stack of bills. "There's more money on this table than anyone in town has to pay. I don't think Sharp got this from any sort of fees."

Josie glanced over at the stack of cash. "You think he robbed someone?"

Goldy gave a nervous laugh. "He could have robbed us all and not got this much." She shook her head. "I don't think this money came from anywhere in Medicine Rock."

"But Tom Sharp was poor when he came to town," Josie said. "He was almost a beggar."

"At least that's what he wanted us to think." Goldy picked up the wad of bills and handed it to Josie. "You take this. I don't have any pockets."

Josie folded the money and shoved it into her trousers. "You really think he brought all this money to town with him?"

"No," Goldy said. "I think someone's been paying him."

"For what?"

"For getting Jake out of town. For making sure that Medicine Rock didn't cause any trouble."

Josie stared at Goldy for a moment. There was no expression on her face, but her dark eyes were filled with murder. "They paid Tom Sharp to get Jake killed."

"Yes. I think so," Goldy said.

"The railroad paid him."

"They're the only ones I can think of."

Josie stood still a moment longer. "We'll go kill Sharp. Then we'll kill the rail boss. When the leader of this railroad gets to Medicine Rock, we will kill him, too."

Despite herself, Goldy felt shock. "Josie, we can't kill them all."

The Mexican woman nodded. "Probably not, but we can try."

A shadow fell across the boardwalk outside. Goldy needed no instruction as she scrambled around the table and crouched behind its slim cover. Josie stepped back against the wall, her shotgun raised. Goldy held her pistol out with both hands.

There was a step on the boards. Then another. The end of a rifle barrel appeared, followed by hands, arms, and a face with a huge drooping mustache.

There was a click as Josie set the hammer on her scattergun.

"It's Gravy!" Goldy shouted. "Don't shoot him."

The carpenter's eyes went wide and he jumped back away from the door. "Miss Goldy?" he called from outside. "Mrs. Bird? That you in there?"

"It is us," Josie said. "Why are you here?"

Gravy stuck his head back through the door. "It's Tom Sharp."

"You know where he is?" Goldy asked.

The carpenter nodded. "He'd done gone and killed Bill Hare. I think Reverend Hardesty is dead, too, but I ain't sure."

"I don't understand," Goldy said. "Why was Sharp shooting at you?"

Gravy stepped completely into the office. "He told all the store owners to go over to the church this morning. Said he had something to talk to us about."

"He didn't say anything to me," Goldy said.

"That's right." Gravy nodded, making the end of his mustache bob. "But Sheriff Sharp said we shouldn't bother you, on account of how you were Sheriff Bird's best friend and you was too upset."

Josie made a noise. If Goldy didn't know better, she would have said the woman was growling. "What has this to do with Sharp shooting the others?"

"I was coming to that," Gravy said. "See, Sharp was supposed to be there a couple of hours ago. We thought about leaving, but he is the sheriff."

"He is not sheriff," Josie said.

Gravy nodded. "Anyway, we heard all the noise and shooting outside. So me, Bill, and the reverend all came out to see what it was. Only, first thing we see is Sheriff Sharp." He paused there staring off into space.

"And?" Goldy prompted.

"And Bill tried to stop him, and Sharp started shooting." Gravy's face went pale and his voice dropped to a whisper. "He shot Bill right through the face. Right through the face."

Josie moved past Gravy and looked through the door. "Did you see where Sharp went after that?"

"He went up to the barn," Gravy said. "I seen him in there the other day, but he told me he was just looking around."

"The old Absalom house is back of the stables," Goldy said. "Could be that Sharp is holed up there."

Josie nodded. "If he is, then we will find him." She went out the door, stepped down from the boardwalk, and waded through the bloody street.

Goldy looked over at the frightened carpenter. "What caused you to haul out your rifle, Gravy? I've never known you to be a shooter."

Gravy looked at her and blinked his watery eyes. "He was shooting people. I thought maybe we ought to start a posse or something."

"Even though he has talent?"

"Don't make it right for him to kill people," Gravy said.

Goldy grinned at him. "Come on, Gravy. I want you watching our backs." She hurried out of the sheriff's office and followed Josie up the street to the lumber barn.

The door at the front of the building was closed. Goldy waited for Josie to put a load of buckshot through the wood, but instead she grabbed the handle and jerked it open. The wide door—a leftover from the time when the building had been a stable—swung open smoothly, revealing a dim interior full of stacked wood.

"He could be hiding right in there," Goldy said.

Josie nodded. "We cannot know until we look." She moved to the side, pressing herself against the wall.

Goldy held her breath as Josie slowly walked the length of the barn, pointing her gun between stacks of lumber, then moving on.

"He is not here," Josie said at last.

"It must be the house," Goldy said. She walked quickly between a stack of rough pine trunks and a heap of weathered boards salvaged from a fallen ranch house.

At the back of the barn three stone stairs led up to a door. It was the place where Willard Absalom and his daughter Sela had lived back when this place had been a stables. Sela had been tied up with Jake in a way that Goldy did not fully understand. Goldy knew that the girl had died along with Custer up at Calio. There was something about the way she died that had bothered both Jake and Josie; Goldy could hear it in their voices when they talked about that day. But exactly what it was that bothered them was something neither had ever let slip.

Gravy joined the women at the back of the barn. "I don't go in there much," he said, using his rifle to point at the door. "The window glass has been gone five years or more, and the boards are getting soft. I wouldn't go upstairs if I was you."

"Not unless we have to," Josie said. "You stay outside, Gravy. Stop Sharp if he tries to come out this way." She went to the steps and climbed up to the door. Slowly she pulled the door open.

The room beyond the door was not at all what Goldy had expected. She climbed up beside Josie to get a better look. Far from being in ruins, it was filled with plush furniture and thick rugs.

"It looks like someone's been living in here," Goldy said softly.

"Someone has," called the voice of Tom Sharp from somewhere farther inside the house. "Someone still is. I'm coming out now. I'd appreciate it if you don't shoot."

"Are you armed?" Josie asked.

In response, a nickel-plated revolver came spinning into the room. It landed with a thump on one of the plush rugs. "That's the only firearm I have," Sharp said. "Now, can I have your word that you won't shoot me?"

"No," Josie said. "I will not give my word to that. But if you come out now, I will not kill you before we have finished our talk."

Tom Sharp appeared from a hallway on the other side of the room. The blood from Josie's shotgun blast had turned his shirt a soggy crimson, but his face was smooth and calm. "I'm afraid I'm not up to standing for very long," Sharp said. "Why don't we sit down for our talk?" He gestured at a round table in the corner of the room.

"Where did you get all the fancy fixings?" Goldy asked.

Sharp smiled. "The railroad. I thought for sure you'd have figured that much out by now."

"The railroad was paying you to kill Jake?" Josie asked.

"Depends," Sharp said with a shrug. "If he hadn't been so

willing to get out of town, I would have had to go at him myself. But he went along east as easy as a horse after a carrot and got himself killed without my help."

Josie mumbled something in Spanish. Goldy didn't understand the words. She wasn't sure she wanted to.

"Now," Sharp continued, "I'm going to sit. Being shot doesn't agree with me." He turned his back on Josie and Goldy, walked over to the table and dropped into a chair.

Goldy moved around Josie and edged off to the right, keeping her pistol aimed as well as she could on Sharp. She wanted to have a clear shot at him when Josie let loose.

"Then is Jake really dead?" Josie asked.

"Deader than President Washington," Sharp said. He waved his hand at some of the boxes and tins on the table. "Would you care for something to eat? The railroad was good enough to bring me some nice cakes all the way from New York."

Josie shook her head. "No," she said. She brought the shotgun up to her shoulder. "Now we are done talking."

"I don't think so," Sharp said. He clapped his hands together, sending out light like the burst from a photographer's flash pan.

Goldy didn't wait. She pointed the trigger as close to the middle of Sharp's chest as she could and pulled the trigger. The Colt barked. For a moment green light surrounded Sharp, but his smile didn't slip.

Less than a second later Josie fired her shotgun. The big eight-gauge was deafening in the small room and the smoke it produced was like a heavy fog. Once again a green glow burned around Sharp, so bright this time that it seemed the man was on fire. Josie didn't hesitate a moment before she fired the second barrel of the scattergun. More green light shone in the room, but now Sharp was so obscured by smoke that Goldy could barely see the glow.

When the gun smoke cleared, Sharp was sitting calmly at the table. Still smiling, he reached out and dropped a heap of lead onto the table.

"You caught me unprepared before," Sharp said. "But as you can see, I've no reason to be scared of you or your guns."

"If you ain't scairt of us," Goldy said, "then why did you kill Orpah?"

"Because I wanted to," Sharp said. "Oh, I admit I was a little concerned that one of you might be hiding more talent than you had shown. I thought a little blood might draw you out in the open, so I sent a nice little conjuration up to see your old girl. Did a fine job on her, I understand." Sharp gave a quick chuckle. "Funny thing was, there was nothing to draw out. You didn't have enough talent to fill a matchbox."

"Talent's not everything," Goldy said.

"No," Sharp said. "Sometimes it's not. Your shooting at me's caused me to make some decisions I didn't want to make."

Goldy coughed; the bitter powder smoke in the air burned at her eyes and her throat. "What kind of decisions?"

Sharp picked up something from the table. It was a small round object with bands of dull copper and mirror-bright steel. Goldy took it first for a candy tin, but as Sharp turned it over in his hands she saw that the top was hinged like the cover of a pocket watch.

"I was looking forward to remaining here as your sheriff for some time," Sharp said.

"You are no sheriff," Josie said. Her voice was hoarse and low. "You are only a killer and a thief."

Sharp went on as if he hadn't heard her. "It's not a job that pays real well, but there's something about being in charge of folks that I've always liked. But now you two have gone and ruined things."

Sharp opened the lid of the small device. Goldy had a brief glimpse of gears and odd green wires before Sharp placed the object on the table with the raised lid blocking Goldy's view.

"If you're not going to be sheriff," Goldy said, "does that mean you're leaving?"

"Yes," Sharp said. "I'm leaving." He looked up, and the smile on his pretty face seemed full of good cheer. "Only thing is, before I leave, I'm going to have to kill the whole town."

☆ 27 ☆

"What in God's name is going on out there?" the Rainmaker shouted.

Bill leaned down to speak through the small slot. "It's hard to say. Can you stop your wind?"

"Stop it?" the Rainmaker said in an exasperated tone. "Stop it? I stopped it five minutes ago. Why are we moving so fast? Is Sheriff Bird doing it?"

Bill looked around at the young sheriff. "I guess he's doing it. There's no one else here that can."

"Well, stop him!" the Rainmaker shouted. "Can't you people up there tell that this thing is coming apart?"

"You're not telling us anything we don't know," Bill said. "If you think you can stop him, then you crawl up here and do it."

Jake Bird had his knees up on the driver's box. He sat facing backward, kneeling like a man saying a prayer to the god of tornadoes. His arms were stretched out to the sides and his face turned up to the surging clouds. Tears of electric fire rolled from his eyes and streamed away down his cheek. He was motionless except for his lips, which opened and closed as if he were carrying on a conversation with the storm.

No effort from either Muley or Bill had succeeded in waking Jake from his talent.

"How can I come up there when the wagon is moving?" the Rainmaker asked.

"Don't know," Bill said. "Guess you better sit down and hold on." He shoved the slot closed and looked over at Muley. "You have any ideas?"

Muley nodded. "We could reef the sails, but then the storm would have us. We can try to get off to the side, but I expect that the storm will follow the sheriff just like it always follows the Rainmaker. Still, if it comes on slow, we might be able to get out of the way before it catches up. Or we might let it have him and take to our feet."

"You mean leave him up here by himself?" Bill asked.

"A-yup." Muley shrugged. " 'Course there is an easier answer."

"What's that?"

"We pitch the sheriff over the side and keep on going till the wind tuckers out."

Bill looked up at Jake's frozen face. Muley was probably right. Dropping the sheriff was the best chance to save the sail wagon and spare the necks of the other men on it. But it also seemed to Bill that it was a cowardly thing to do.

In his heart Bill knew that he was not the man written up in the novels. He had not saved women and children from an Indian attack, or led men to victory during the war. He had never fought a gunfight. Not one. He had scouted and shot several thousand buffalo—a task that demanded only the determination to keep shooting and the ammunition to carry it out. Still, he regarded himself as a decent man.

Since he'd returned to the West, what he had shown in the main was a cowardly streak. The Rainmaker had dressed him down for it, but it couldn't begin to match the lashing Bill gave himself where no one could hear. He was tired of being ashamed, and he was damned if he would provide more ammunition for either the Rainmaker or his own guilty conscience.

"We ain't dropping the sheriff," Bill said firmly.

"Fine enough," Muley said. "Then what are we going to do?"

At that moment the sun slipped below the western edge of the storm and flooded the plain ahead with brilliant orange light. No more than three hundred yards to their right the railroad tracks gleamed in the light.

"Look ahead!" Muley shouted.

Bill squinted against the sunshine and saw a puff of white cloud low on the horizon. He was about to ask Muley what he was supposed to be looking for when he realized it was no cloud at all, but the plume from a train.

"How far off, do you reckon?" Bill asked.

"Four miles, maybe closer to five."

"Are we closing?"

"A-yup. And closing fast. Looks to me like they're stopped."

Within a space of minutes they were close enough to see the train under the trail of steam. It appeared that Muley was right, the train was halted beside a tower, filling the boilers with a fresh load of water. But even as they got close enough to see this, the train began to move again. The steam shot up in a tall column that was blackened at the base with wood smoke and ash.

"They're pouring on the heat," Bill said. "Do you think they see us?"

"I doubt they're running from us," Muley replied. He jerked a thumb over his shoulder. "I expect they're running from our friend back there."

Bill turned to watch the twister dance over the plains. It seemed to him that the funnel was growing wider, or it could be it was closer. The twister had grown yellow as it sucked up the dry soil. Even the clouds above had taken on colors of tan and brown. It was almost as if the ground had boxed them in from top and bottom. Dark flecks spun 'round the twisting, bending trunk of the storm, to mark trees, shrubs, and even stones ripped up in its fury.

"Who's faster?" Bill asked. "Will we catch them?"

Muley nodded. "We're still pulling up by a darn sight. They may outrun us once they've got her head up, but we'll be on them by then."

"How long?"

"Damn soon," Muley said. "Two minutes. Less."

Cody glanced over at Jake. They had done what was needed to catch the train, but Jake was so locked into driving the storm that he couldn't be broken loose.

The glimmer of the train tracks caught Bill's eye. He looked around and saw that the train was close now, close enough to see the railing at the back of the last car and the bold red letters spelling out "Atlantic Pacific" along the side. Just as clearly, Bill saw what had to be done.

"Drive across the tracks!" he shouted.

"What?"

"Drive across the tracks," Bill said. "You saw how the rails hurt the sheriff the first time, and how they made the Rain-maker falter." He pointed at the glistening lines running to their side. "Swing across to the north side of the line and see if that doesn't knock him loose."

Muley nodded. "It sounds right to me." He jerked in the line, winding the spare rope around cleats as he swung the boom toward the north. The wagon started to turn, clos-ing the distance on both the train and the rails.

Bill began to wonder if there was room to make the cut. They were gaining on the train at such a pace that it seemed they would run into the cars before they reached the rails.

"I'm going to drop the jib down a couple of feet," Muley warned. "Keep an eye on that twister."

Bill nodded. When he looked behind them he saw that the tornado was closer, its dust-colored trunk dancing less than a quarter mile behind, pulling up sage and sand. There was a stutter in the progress of the wagon. Bill looked around and saw that the train had gained a step, moving ahead by a hun-dred feet or so. The rails were close. Fifty feet. Twenty.

Jake's lips stopped their silent movement. The blue sparks died from his eyes. A low moan escaped his mouth.

"It's working!" Bill shouted. "Take us on across the rails."

Muley nodded and increased the northward angle of the wagon. The rails were ten feet away. Then five. Wooden ties began to roll beneath the right-hand wheels, passing so fast they made a high-pitched hum under the steel rims. With a screech of metal the wagon crossed the tracks.

Jake Bird screamed.

Bill watched in shock as the sheriff flew up from his seat, rising into the air until his feet dangled an arm's length above the driver's box. Lightning cracked down from the sky, hammering at Jake over and over. More lightning flowed from Jake, moving back into the clouds. It came out his fingertips, from his eyes, from his open mouth.

There was an explosion, a concussion of sound so loud that it was no longer a sound but a sheer force.

Bill was hurled from his seat. He spun through the air, grabbing desperately at the side of the wagon. Deafened by the blast and half blind, he hung from the side of the wagon, bouncing against the wood with enough force to drive the air from his lungs. He raised his boots and kicked at the side of the wagon, but the whole thing was damnably smooth. Bill could find no footing to get back to the driver's box.

He glanced down and saw the ground going past so quickly that it was only a blur. If he let go now, he might not live, but he was damned if he knew what else to do. Bill gathered what breath he could find and prepared himself for the fall.

A hand reached down from above and grabbed him by the wrist. Another hand followed, and Bill found himself pulled up and over the side.

Jake Bird stood there, his wild hair singed and smoking. The sheriff's shirt had been ripped and burned to black strips. His already tattered trousers were no more than rags.

Jake's lips moved, but Bill heard nothing but the ringing in his head.

"I don't understand," Bill said. Even his own voice was flat and faint inside his skull.

Jake leaned in close. ". . . you . . . right?"

Bill nodded. "What about Muley?" He looked past Jake and saw that the wagon driver was still on his seat, held there by a tangle of ropes. Muley's head was slumped to the side and his mouth hung open.

"Is he dead?" Bill asked.

". . . out," Jake said.

There was a jarring bump as the wagon swept across a gully. Bill looked to his left and saw that they were a dozen yards clear of the track and still moving away. They were also still outdistancing the train. They were running even with the engine now, close enough to see the sparks coming out of the stacks and the churning of the wheels and rods.

"We can . . . the train," Jake said. His voice was coming clearer as the roar in Bill's head began to fade.

"What?"

"We can still catch the train," Jake said. "You steer the wagon up close, and I'll jump across."

"I can't drive the wagon," Bill said. "I don't know how."

A stricken look came over the sheriff's face. "Neither do I."

There was a pounding from the back of the wagon. The panel slid back to show the Rainmaker's eyes. "What happened?"

Jake leaned down close. "Can you run this wagon?"

"Why?" The Rainmaker twisted around, looking back and forth through the slot. "Where's Muley?"

"He's hurt," Jake said.

"How bad?"

"I don't know."

The Rainmaker was silent only for a moment. "Hold on. I'm coming up."

A second later the door at the side of the wagon snapped open and pale hands appeared at the top, struggling for a grip on the smooth wood. Both Bill and Jake moved back to give the Rainmaker a hand, helping the lanky man up onto the box. There was little enough room for three people on the bench, and no room for four. Bill eased back onto the roof of the wagon, balancing himself carefully with one hand on the mast.

The Rainmaker went straight to Muley and leaned down to put one pale hand against the seaman's throat. "He's alive," the Rainmaker said. "I can't tell much more than that till we stop."

"Can you run this thing?" Jake asked. "We need to get over to that train."

"Well, after listening to Muley talk all these years, I'd guess I know which line to jerk." The Rainmaker took a seat at the center of the bench and pried some of the cords from Muley's fingers. He gave one line a tug and looked around. "We've got damage," he said. "The boom's not acting like it should, and the mainsail won't drop."

"Can you get us to the train?" Jake asked.

"Yes," the Rainmaker said. "I can get you to the damn train." He leaned hard into one of the cords. The wagon shuddered, groaned, and turned back to the left. A loose rope swung past Bill's head, forcing him to duck. The train drew closer. It was moving faster than the wagon now, pulling ahead at a slow walk.

"Cody," Jake called. "How do we get on the train?"

Bill watched a passenger car move past. "Between the cars," he said. "Or at the end of the train."

Jake climbed up to stand on the roof next to Bill. "I'm not going to ask that you try this. I'm betting that Gould is on that train, probably a lot of gunmen with him." He nodded to the storm. "The wind should start to die now that I'm not pushing it. You could stay on the wagon and ride it out."

Another train car slid past. Through the windows Bill saw a hallway paneled in wood and trimmed with brass.

"I'm coming," Bill said. "Kastle might be on that train. I haven't finished with him yet."

Jake nodded. "It's going to start to hurt when we get near the rails. I can feel it already. Once we're on the train, I may not be much good for anything."

"Then why don't you stay?" Bill asked.

The sheriff grinned. "I don't think I can." He leaned down to the Rainmaker. "Do it now. I want to get close while there are still two or three cars to go. If we go for the end and miss, we might never catch up again."

The Rainmaker nodded and pulled again on the lines. The boom swung another foot, making Bill and Jake crowd onto a corner of the roof.

They were close to the train now, but the Rainmaker was having difficulty. The pain of being so close to the rails was making his movements clumsy, and he fought the damaged rigging to control the wagon. Another train car slid slowly past. There were only two more to go.

Bill saw the curving steps of a ladder peeking over the back of the next car. "There," he said. "We can jump for that."

Jake nodded. Sweat dripped down his face. "I'll try," he said, his voice soaked in pain.

The Rainmaker's head rolled on his shoulders and he gave out a moan. "Please hurry," he cried.

The wagon drew closer, so close that it almost touched the side of the racing train. Again there was the hum of the ties passing under the steel-rimmed wheels.

The Rainmaker was sobbing, his arms trembling with strain. The gap between the cars was coming, coming faster than before. The difference in speed between the wagon and the train was increasing.

Jake leaped.

It was not a graceful leap. His toe struck the side of the wagon as he jumped, spinning him around. He struck the platform at the back of the train car, banging his head against the back of the car and catching his arm in the ladder. He lay there on the platform, not moving, as the train carried him on past.

There was a loud crack, like the firing of a gun.

Bill looked up and saw the top section of the mast go flying free. It took with it part of the mainsail, ripping away the heavy cloth like newspaper. Instantly the wagon began to slow.

The rear of the train was approaching. The last chance.

Bill reached his hand down to the Rainmaker. "Come on! Jump with me."

"No!" the Rainmaker shouted. "I can't leave Muley."

"But the storm!" Bill cried. "You'll never outrun the storm with the wagon like this."

The Rainmaker shook his head. His pale face was stretched as taut as any rope in the rigging. Blood dripped from his nose. "Muley never left me behind. I can't leave him."

Bill climbed onto the corner of the wagon. He reached down a last time and clasped the pale man on the shoulder. "Good luck!" he said. Then he jumped.

His fingers closed around the railing at the back of the train. The heels of Bill's boots hit the ground for a moment, sending a shock of pain up his legs. Then he scrambled and fought his way up onto the platform.

Trembling, he turned around.

The wagon was a hundred feet back now, its torn sail flapping in the wind. The Rainmaker was trying hard to turn to the north, but the crippled wagon was moving slowly—too slowly.

As Bill watched, the sail wagon was swallowed in the storm.

☆ 28 ☆

Goldy shot at Tom Sharp twice more, then added a third bullet for good measure. Each of the bullets only conjured another flash of green, leaving Sharp unharmed, but the effort made Goldy feel better.

Josie broke open the back of her shotgun and calmly loaded new shells. "You have more talent than you showed us," she said, "but you do not have enough to kill the whole town."

"You're right," Tom Sharp said. He reached out a single finger and touched something inside the device on the table. A faint hum entered the air. "Thing is, I don't have to."

Goldy took a step forward, peering over the lid at the small device. "It's that metal dealie, isn't it? That's how you mean to kill us."

Sharp looked up and smiled. "You know," he said, "I really enjoyed Orpah."

"Why'd you kill her?"

"For you," he said. Then he laughed. "And for me. I wanted to let you know to stay out of my way. Didn't work, but so what? I had a hell of a good time with her."

Anger ate away at Goldy's fear. "You're a runty little bastard, Tom Sharp. I've seen turds bigger than you."

The smile on Sharp's face went flat. "It's not the size," he said. "It's the quality."

Goldy advanced on him another step. "I've seen turds with more quality, too."

"You watch your mouth, old whore." The expression on Sharp's face no longer resembled any kind of smile.

The anger on his face gave Goldy a new thought. It was a

267

risky thought, but just standing in the same room with the man was risky.

"What are you doing in Medicine Rock, anyway?" Goldy said. "Ain't they got no circus back in New York City? Ain't there no call for dwarfs?"

Tom Sharp hissed like a scalded cat. He raised one hand up and brought it down in a sharp chop.

Raw power lifted Goldy and shoved her back against the wall. The force of Sharp's talent held her there, pushing her into the boards.

With some difficulty she drew a deep breath. "Is this it?" she said. "This is your talent? It ain't no bigger than your teeny little carrot."

"Shut up, whore!" Sharp screamed.

He brought his hand down again, and the force pushing against Goldy doubled. It felt as if a freight wagon were trying to run her down. There was no question of drawing more air now. Already her vision was starting to darken. Dancing lights gathered at the corners of her eyes as her hands and feet began to lose tingle from lack of blood. She opened her mouth and coughed out her last gasp of air.

"Shit-ugly runt."

Tom Sharp brought up both hands and shoved them forward. The pain would have drawn a scream from Goldy, but she had no air to scream with.

"Die, you old bitch," Sharp said. He balled his hands into fists and the pressure went higher. Goldy felt something pop in her chest. She hoped it was only a rib. The bones in her skull creaked like dry wood under a heavy foot.

And right then was when Josie let loose both barrels of her gun.

The light that flared from Tom Sharp was bright enough to leave Goldy blinking and to burn the image of the room into her eyes. The pressure that had been crushing her to the wall disappeared. Goldy dropped to her knees on the floor and lay gasping for air against the sharp pain in her chest. She felt wrung out as a worn rag.

Josie's attack had shredded Sharp's already bloody shirt,

and there was more fresh blood welling from his chest and arms. It was clear that his talent had deflected most of the shot—at such short range, a double load from the eight-gauge would have sawed a normal man in half—but some of the shot had gotten past his talent.

Now Sharp was waving his hands again, drawing streamers of energy from the air, which he flung toward Josie. "You little—" he started.

But whatever he was going to call Josie was cut off when Gravy Hodges came charging through the door.

Gravy was no gunman, but he worked his Winchester for all he was worth, getting off four shots in not many more seconds and striking Sharp with three of those shots. One of the bullets tore through the small man's shirt, slicing at his skin. The second hit an inch farther in, ripping through his side and passing on out his back. The third bullet struck lower, taking Sharp in the hip.

There was no series of green flashes this time, no show of talent. What there was instead was blood and cries of pain.

Tom Sharp staggered backward. He swept his hand across his blood-soaked chest, clawing power from the smoky air.

Gravy pulled the trigger again. There was a click, but no sound of a shot. Whether his rifle was empty or had misfired, Goldy couldn't tell. Either way, it was the last chance Gravy had to fire on Sharp.

A ball of white light gathered in Sharp's hand. He flung it against Gravy, and the light swarmed over the carpenter, covering him in a crackling, pulsing sheet. Gravy's rifle fell from his hands. Gravy took a step away, staggered, and fell back through the door of the house.

There was a solid click as Josie shut the breach of her scattergun. Goldy had not even noticed Josie loading the weapon, but she was leveling it now, bringing it to bear on the wounded man.

Sharp dropped to the floor just as Josie pulled the trigger. The tight cluster of shot passed over the little man and punched clean through the wall at his back.

Josie thumbed back the hammer on the second barrel, but

the miss had given Sharp the time he needed. Another ball of light flew out and wrapped itself around Josie. She managed to pull the trigger before the shotgun fell from her hands, but the shot was wild, blowing out another section of wall ten feet to Sharp's left.

Josie fell to the floor with snakes of light chasing themselves over her form. Her arms and legs jerked and twitched. Wisps of foul-smelling smoke rose from her singed hair.

"Damn," Tom Sharp said. "Damn it all." He stumbled across the room to the table and dropped heavily into his chair. He held one hand against the wound in his side, but the hand didn't come close to stopping the flow of blood. A thick red stream came over his fingers in surges, running down his leg and dripping onto the floor. "God damn, I'm shot to pieces," he mumbled.

"Give yourself up," Goldy said.

Sharp jerked at the sound of her voice. He seemed to have forgotten that Goldy was there. "Give myself up for what?" he said.

It was a fair question. There was no way Goldy was going to let the man live. "Give yourself up and I'll end it quick," she said.

Though his own blood was falling like a spring rain, Tom Sharp still laughed at the offer. He reached across the table and snatched up the small metal tin. "This town is dead. I can still get away from here. They'll fix me up on the train."

Goldy walked to the table with the Colt held out in front of her. By her own count she had one shot. Considering the damage that Gravy and Josie had done to Sharp, that one shot might be all it took to finish the man. But she had other plans for the bullet.

With bloody fingers Sharp opened the lid of the little device. His hands were trembling as he reached inside the thing. The object began to whine. The noise was soft at first, but it rose quickly to a painful shriek.

Tom Sharp lifted the round box in his hands. He was smiling again, but this smile had nothing to do with being happy. It had everything to do with being flat crazy mean.

"Say good-bye to life," he said.

"Maybe," Goldy said. She put the nose of her revolver right against the small metal device. "Maybe not."

The gunshot flung Sharp's hand back and sent fragments of metal flying across the room. But his fingers hung onto the box as if glued.

Red light began to drip from the ruined device. It was light that didn't act like light, but more like blood. It fell in fiery drops, splashing against the table and pooling on the dark wood. The flow increased, becoming a stream of crimson that poured off the sides of the table. A scarlet glow filled the room.

"No!" Sharp cried. He shook his hand wildly. He clawed at the device. But the thing would not let go. The red light began to spread up his arm.

Goldy dropped her empty pistol and ran across the room to Josie. The Mexican woman was out cold, maybe dead. Goldy didn't stop to check. She grabbed the collar of Josie's wool shirt and pulled her back across the floor.

At the top of the stairs Goldy turned to look at Sharp. The red light was all over him now, covering everything but his face. It seemed to Goldy that the man was shriveling. His arms and legs looked no bigger around than broomsticks, and his chest was stove in like a hornet's nest that had taken a hard kick. But his eyes were still open, and his mouth was still working. Whatever was left of Tom Sharp, it was sure he could still feel pain.

Goldy dragged Josie down the three steps from the house into the lumber barn. Gravy Hodges was lying there, still as Josie had been. It was all Goldy could do to drag one person at a time. She was not about to start in on two. She pulled Josie on between the rows of stacked timber and outside the door of the barn.

From the street, she looked back into the barn. Red light was shining from the open door of the house. Rivulets of red fire spilled over the edge of the first step and started a cascade to the next.

There was no way of knowing whether Josie was far

enough from the device to be safe. But it was sure that Gravy was not. Goldy dropped her hold on Josie's shirt and hurried back across the barn to Gravy. She grabbed him in the same way she'd taken Josie and began to pull him across the dirt floor.

Gravy was heavy. At each tug Goldy could move him only a few inches.

"Wake up, Gravy," she said. "Come on, you damn tree butcher. Get on your feet." Gravy was limp as a sack of stones.

Goldy was feeling every one of her sixty years now, feeling it in her aching back and her throbbing shoulders. Whatever had broken in her chest was letting itself be known, stabbing at her like an ice pick on each breath.

The red light surged. With it came a breath of wind that was biting cold. Goldy could see her breath as she pulled Gravy another foot. Then another.

The walls of the house began to crack open, letting in shafts of crimson. The liquid light poured out the door in a torrent, washing into the barn. It lifted boards and raw lumber from the ground and carried it along at the front of a scarlet flood.

Goldy cleared the door of the barn not five feet ahead of the wash of fiery light. She dropped Gravy next to Josie, pushed the door at the front of the barn closed and prayed that it would hold. She leaned back against the door and bent over, resting her hands on her knees. If the light began to come under the door, Goldy wasn't sure it would be worth running. From the way her heart was racing, she expected to drop where she stood anyway.

With a moan, Josie began to stir. She opened her eyes, sat up quickly and looked around. "Where is my shotgun?"

"Inside," Goldy said. "I couldn't carry it and you both."

"Where is Tom Sharp?"

"He's inside, too. I wouldn't recommend going in for a visit."

Josie got to her feet and brushed at the dirt on her clothes. "What has happened?"

"I blasted that little doohickey Sharp was carrying," Goldy said. "It let loose and I ran for it."

Josie's dark eyes fixed on Goldy in wonder. "But you got us out of there," she said. "Both me and Gravy."

Goldy shrugged. "Believe you me, honey, you didn't want to stay inside."

A tremendous crash came from somewhere at the back of the barn. Goldy moved away from the door, and together with Josie she stepped out into the street, where they could look across the low roof of the old stables to the house beyond.

The house was gone. In its place was a boiling mass of light and smoke. The smoke twisted and humped, forming itself into shapes that suggested twisted hands, malformed claws, and other things—things not so clear but that made Goldy's stomach do a flutter. One shape was clear enough. At the center of the writhing mass was a face. It was not such a pretty face as it had been, and from the expression, Tom Sharp's pain was not yet over.

With a final burst of cold flame, the whole mess collapsed, leaving nothing in the air but dust. There was a brief rumble and the sound of boards tumbling together. Then silence.

A few folks began to creep out onto the street, staring toward the cloud of dust. Gravy Hodges stirred, turned over in the dusty street, and began to snore.

Josie put an arm around Goldy. "You saved us," she said. "You are the hero today."

"I don't know about that," Goldy said. "Come on. Let's go see if that new doctor can do better fixing other folks than he can himself."

As they walked along the street Goldy realized she was not only hurt but tired. Given a chance, she thought she might sleep for a week. After that she might be up to breakfast.

"I'll tell you one thing," she said to Josie. "If that husband of yours ain't dead, I'm raising his pay. Sheriffing is hard work."

☆ 29 ☆

It seemed to Jake that there ought to come a time when pain got tired. Legs and arms wore out. The muscles that it took to swing a hammer or pull a saw needed to take a rest. But whatever muscle it was that caused you to hurt, it didn't seem to require any breaks.

Jake pulled himself up against the back of the train car and hung from the metal rungs of the ladder. His head and stomach swam with the nearness of the talent-absorbing rails. "Cody?" he said in a whisper. There was no sign of the old hunter.

If Cody had not made it onto the train at this point, then he either missed the train or grabbed on at the back. Jake knew he would have to go through the trailing car to search for him.

The rolling motion of the train did nothing to steady Jake's feet as he released the ladder. The platform at the back of the car was shallow, no more than a foot from front to back. The platform at the front of the rear car was no wider. In between was more than two feet of space with nothing but some kind of metal buckle and plenty of air, through which Jake could see the ground speeding past.

Moving with the smoothness of a man who had downed a tub of busthead whiskey, Jake stepped across the gap and fell against the front of the train car. The door was of an unfamiliar sort, with a latch that did not swing out or in. His head ringing, it took Jake some time to figure that the darned thing slid to the side. What he found inside the car was a dimly lit space full of crates, bags, and boxes.

At the back of the car something moved in the shadows.

Jake reached for his pistol and directed it at the dark form. "Hold there," he said. "I'm armed."

"So am I," Bill Cody said. The scout stepped from behind a stack of boxes and walked toward the front of the car. As he drew near, Jake could see a Colt Single Action in his hand.

"How'd you come by that?" Jake asked.

Cody tipped his head toward the rear of the car. "There was a nice feller back there to provide it for me."

Jake peered into the shadows. If there was another man still in the car, it was a sure bet he wasn't standing. "I'm certain he just handed it over."

"He did," Cody insisted. "Leastwise, he did soon as I combed his hair with a biscuit tin."

As his eyes adjusted to the gloom, Jake saw that there was a wagonload of wonders in the train car. There were barrels of wheat flour and kegs of genuine coffee. White sugar. Black powder. Enough pepper and salt to dress a herd of buffalo. There was more spice in this car than in all the houses in Medicine Rock.

"What do you think they mean to do with all this chicken fixings?" Jake asked.

"Don't know," Cody said. "Strikes me that they could be trading it to the west end of the line, but San Francisco is not a poor place; they already get plenty of stock by sea. If I had to guess, I'd guess this was meant for Medicine Rock and the other towns on the line."

The thought of that made Jake pause a moment. No more than two weeks back he had looked on the promise of the railroad as a blessing. Folks in Medicine Rock were hungry for these things, and for news of the East. He himself would have paid ten dollars just to sit down at a cup of real Arbuckle's coffee. If the goods were meant to go to Medicine Rock, then it was clear everyone wasn't going to be killed right off the bat.

But, of course, the train had to be stopped. If the line was finished, all the talent from one coast to the other would be in the hands of Jay Gould and his helpers. Rapid City was reason enough to see that they couldn't be trusted to put their hands around a gun so large.

"Let's get up to the front," Jake said. "The way things have been moving, we can't have much longer."

Jake was feeling a bit steadier as he crossed the gap back to the fourth car. The pain didn't seem to have decreased, but he'd adjusted to it. Once inside the doorway, the rail car seemed much like the one where he'd been flung from the window. There was a simple hallway down one side, with a runner of blue carpet on the floor and brass trim on the wood-paneled wall.

Two doors led off the hallway. Jake waited until Cody had joined him, then jerked open the first door. Inside was a big closet with sheets, pillows, and some contraptions of metal and spring.

"Folding beds," Cody said. "They can pitch these things in the car at night to make it like a bedroom."

"Let's see what's behind the next one." Jake went to the second door, braced himself, and slung it open.

Inside was a room not too different from the one where he had fought Gould, Kastle, and Cullen. This one had two circular tables, each surrounded by a trio of padded high-back chairs. There were red velvet couches at each end of the room, fronted by tables of brass and some very dark wood. There was a newspaper sprawled across one of the round tables, and a cigar smoking in a marble ashtray, but all of the chairs and couches were empty.

Cody stepped past Jake and took the cigar from the tray. "Somebody was here not too long ago."

Jake stepped into the room and looked at the corners. There was no place to hide. As he turned around he was confronted by an apparition that sent him stumbling back—a man wearing smoking, soot-stained rags, with hair that stood out wildly from his head, scars in a half-dozen places, and holding a pistol in his hand. A heartbeat later he realized he was looking into a mirror.

"There ain't nobody here," Cody said. "Maybe we ought to move on."

"Right." Jake led the way out of the room and down the hallway to the end of the car. From the look of the country passing by, Medicine Rock could be no more than spitting distance away.

"I hope we find someone in the next car," Jake said. "There's not much time left." He reached for the handle.

A gunshot ripped through the door, missing Jake by no more than a finger's width. Close on its heels came a second. Then a third. By then Jake was falling, throwing himself to the hard metal grating of the platform floor. As he fell, more shots cut the door over his back. They came so close on each other that Jake could not tell where one explosion stopped and the next one began. Then all the gunshots stopped and there was only the noise of the train and the more distant roar of the storm.

Jake lay with his face against the cold metal, breathing hard. Someone inside had jumped the gun. If they had waited until he got the door open, there was no way they would have missed. Jake took a deep breath and thanked God for nervous fingers.

"I reckon there's someone in there," Cody said from the door of the car behind.

"Seems so," Jake said. "How many you figure?"

"Five, six." Cody shrugged. "Maybe more."

"So how do we get in?"

"I'm not the one to ask," Cody said. "Scouting's my business, not gunfighting. I thought pitching lead was more your line of work."

It was true as far as it went, though Jake rarely had to depend on his proficiency with firearms. His talent generally took care of the problem, and for the moment his talent was out of reach. He edged carefully away from the door and stood.

"I don't suppose there's any way we can stop the train from back here?" Jake asked.

Cody shrugged again. "Trains ain't exactly my business, either. We get up to the front, we can make the engineer turn it around. From back here, I don't know what I can do."

Jake looked at the shot-up door. Stepping in front of that sort of concentrated firepower looked like a sure way to die.

He tried to stir his talent. Against the pull of the rails, he felt something stir, but he doubted it was enough to stop such a storm of lead.

"I don't guess we've got much choice," Jake said. "This is a train. It's not like we can go around. We either go through that door or we—" A sudden thought stopped him. He looked to his right and saw the rungs of the ladder leading to the top of the train. "We either go through, or we go over!" he said.

Cody looked at the ladder and winced. "It's better than being shot," he said. "At least I hope it is."

Jake set his foot on the first rung of the ladder and climbed to the top of the train. The rush of air that struck his face was tremendous. Pushing the rest of the way up without toppling backward was like forcing his way into a hard-running stream.

"Come on," he called to Cody.

The scout's head appeared at the top of the car, his blond hair and beard streaming back from the wind. "Lord it's brisk up here. You think we can walk it?"

"It's not far," Jake said.

"Then lead the way," Cody replied.

The smoke that had looked so white at a distance was a perfect hell of soot and ash at close hand. Driven by the force of the wind, particles of ash struck Jake like birdshot. He turned his shoulder to the front of the train and trudged forward like a man breasting a heavy hailstorm.

By the time he reached the front of the car, Jake's skin was so crusted with the soot that he was far darker than Bred Smith had ever been. Half blind, he fumbled to find the ladder leading down into the space between the second and third cars. If there had been any gunmen waiting for him, Jake knew he would not have stood a chance, but he made it to the platform without a single shot being fired.

Cody was close behind. The scout's hair and beard were matted with ash. His eyes were white circles in a coal-black face. He dropped to the platform and scraped at the muck around his eyes. "I hope there's no guns in the next car," he said. "If there is, I might just as well get shot."

Jake wiped the dirt away from his own gritty eyes. "No way to know but to try." He started for the door.

"Wait," Cody said.

"I thought you didn't want to go over again?"

"I don't, but look here." Cody pointed into the gap between cars. "That pin's all that holds this car to the next."

"That's good to know," Jake said. "How does it help us?"

Cody pointed at the third car. "We've got five or six shooters in that car that want to punch holes in us. If we're lucky, they're all looking the wrong way." He bent down and stuck the barrel of his revolver through the eye of the heavy pin. "I pull this, and that's five or six guns we don't have to worry about."

Jake smiled. "A fine idea. But what if Gould and the others are in that car? We need to do more than put them afoot."

"We'll stand a better chance of airing Gould if he's walking across the plains than we will in that train car," Cody said. "Hell, you bring me a Sharps 50, and I'll plug him from half a mile away."

"All right," Jake said. "Let her loose."

Cody pushed against the gun. For a moment the pin resisted, then it slipped free with a loud clang. Quickly, the scout joined Jake on the platform of the second car, and the two looked back at the car behind them.

At first, removing the pin seemed to have made no difference. The two cars remained together for a hundred yards or more. Then there was a squeal of metal slipping over metal. The platforms moved apart by half a foot. Then by a whole foot. Then the rear half of the train was rolling smoothly away, dropping back from the racing steam engine and the single passenger car that was left.

With the other cars gone, Jake got his first good view of the storm since leaving the sail wagon. The funnel was still there. It was possible the storm had lost some strength, but if so, that loss was not apparent. The funnel danced back and forth over the rails, pulling up lengths of track as easy as a child twisting taffy.

The door at the front of the third car opened and a trio of

men spilled out onto the small platform. They raised their fists and shouted. A fourth man appeared, pushing the others out of the way. The man was so wrapped in bandages that he seemed more like a conjuration than a man. Even from a distance the bandaged man's bright, mad eyes were familiar to Jake.

"Cullen."

Cody jumped. "Where?"

Jake nodded to the forms on the platform. "The one with the bandages."

"What happened to him?"

"We had something of a tussle."

The bandaged man began to fire his pistol, emptying six chambers toward the forward section of the train. So far as Jake could tell, not one of the bullets came near.

"God help us," Cody said. "Look there!"

The snaky brown trunk of the tornado had reached the last car of the train. Though the car had to weigh several tons, the twister pulled it clean into the air, dragging up the back of the next car. The rear car exploded in a shower of wood and steel. Dark fragments swirled around the storm, moving up the trunk to vanish in the heaving clouds above. The next car followed, breaking in half, then smashing into a flurry of broken brass and wood.

As the twister lifted the back of the third car, Jake saw one man after another jump from the platform. Whether any of them lived, he couldn't say. A curtain of dust and sand covered the men long before they had come to rest. Only Cullen stood his ground, clinging to the railing along the side of the platform and still shaking his fist toward Jake and Cody. A second later the third car was airborne. Unlike the other cars, it held together, staying in one piece as it went round and round the twister, moving up on each circuit until it was lost in the clouds.

"By God," Cody said, "I've never seen anything like that."

"Me neither," Jake said. "Let's get this thing stopped before we end up the same way."

Jake grabbed the door handle and tugged. It was locked.

"Now what?" Cody asked.

"Now we find out who's inside." Jake reached up and rapped his fingers against the door.

There was a fumbling from behind the panel door, then it rolled to the side. "Are they dead?" Edward Kastle said. Then he saw who it was and his eyes went wide.

"I think they're dead, Mr. Kastle," Cody said. He raised his pistol and pointed it to the man's head. "Though I doubt we're talking about the same folks you were hoping to see planted."

The German swallowed once, then shoved the panel closed again.

"Damn," Cody said. He grabbed the edge of the sliding door and pushed it open. Inside was a hallway set with four doors. There was no sign of Kastle. "I should have shot the man while I had the chance."

"Come on," Jake said. "I expect you'll get another chance." He raised his Colt and stepped into the car.

At his first step down the hallway a new wave of sickness and pain swept over Jake. The color ran out of everything, as did the depth. What was left was like looking at an old tintype—flat and gray. Jake's legs went soft. He swayed against the wall, hung there for a moment, then lost his footing altogether and fell to the carpeted floor.

Trembling head to toe, Jake got his hands under him and lifted his head from the carpet. No sooner had he brought his face up than the toe of a dark boot cracked against his chin.

Jake fell over on his side, raising his arms weakly, trying to defend his face.

Another kick came, thumping hard against Jake's ribs. Then his head again. Then his side.

Jake reached for his chattering.

Nothing happened. The last time he was on the train, it had been hard to call his talent and harder still to control it. But now there was nothing at all, not even a stir. It was as if he had no talent.

"Feeling poorly, Sheriff?" Kastle asked.

Jake peeked through his fingers and saw the bald scientist standing just inside an open doorway at the side of the hall. In Kastle's hand there was a small round box, the same device that had frozen Jake's arms and legs before. From the description Cody had given, a device just like it had served to kill everyone in Rapid City.

"You're under arrest," Jake croaked. He put down his hands again and started to sit up.

"I don't think so," Kastle said. He raised up a boot and brought it down hard on Jake's fingers.

Jake jerked his hand back, overbalanced, and fell flat on his face.

"I think you'll give me no trouble this time," Kastle said. There was an edge of satisfaction in his voice. "After we had difficulties last time, I added new features to this car, just to ensure such events would not happen again."

"It works," Jake said.

"That's good to know," Kastle said. He held out the metal box. "Now it's time you saw the other half of my accomplishments."

Bill Cody stepped into the hallway. Though Jake could not look up to see Cody's face, he could hear the click as Cody brought back the hammer on his pistol. "Put it down, Kastle. I've seen all I want of your toys."

Kastle backed away, a sneer on his face, but he did not drop the device.

Jake put his left hand against the wall and got to his knees. "Where's Gould?" he asked.

"Mr. Gould is busy," Kastle said. "Too busy to talk to you." He looked from Cody to Jake and back. "Two dead men. Maybe next time you'll stay dead."

A bolt of red light lanced out from Kastle's weapon. Cody fired. Only one of them hit.

The beam from Kastle's weapon was no wider than a broomstick, but as the light swept across Cody the old scout gave a gasp and fell to the carpet. His soot-stained face fell against Jake's boot.

The slug from Cody's gun went wide, punching into the ceiling of the car.

"Now it's your turn," Kastle said. The light traced over the carpet, moving toward Jake.

Jake reached out, picked up Cody's pistol, and shot Kastle straight through the left eye.

The slug tore the back off Kastle's skull, spraying the hallway with the contents. The scientist crumpled to the floor. The round box slipped from his fingers and rolled away toward the front of the car, still spilling its deadly light as it rolled. From somewhere up ahead there was a thump followed by a crash.

Jay Gould emerged from a door at the center of the hall. He looked at Kastle and the mess of brains and blood that stained the hall. Then he looked at the two men lying on the hallway floor. Despite the situation, Gould's calm expression never faltered. To Jake, he said, "It seems I've badly underestimated both you and Mr. Cody."

Jake tried to get to his feet, but his legs were still not cooperating. He pulled himself back, dragging his legs behind him. "Why did you try to kill me?" he asked.

Gould rubbed his hands lightly together. "You represented a possible threat. The simplest solution was to put a more reliable man in your place."

The first part of the answer was what Jake had expected, but the second half caught him by surprise. "More reliable man?" Jake moved back another foot, toward the rear of the car, hooked his fingers into the metal grate of the platform and began to drag himself back out through the car door.

"Yes," Gould said with a nod. "Now that you've shown me wrong, I think it's high time I revise my offer. What would it take to make you and your compatriot happy?"

Jake pulled himself out onto the platform at the back of the car. Immediately he felt a hundred times better than he had in the hallway. He still felt like someone was hitting his head with an eight-pound hammer, but at least he could make his legs work. Shaky as a newborn colt, he got to his feet. "I don't think there's anything you can do," Jake said. "It's too late to go changing horses now."

"You're missing a great opportunity here," Gould said. "You stand a chance of being one of the most powerful men in this nation."

Jake shook his head. "What would I be as soon as you finish the line and take all the talent to yourself?"

"Come, come, Sheriff. I take care of those who have helped me. Surely there is something that would prove my sincerity."

Bill Cody rolled over and coughed. "You being dead would help," he said.

Gould gave a flat smile. "I don't think I want to oblige you in that respect, Mr. Cody. I was counting on you to see my point in this matter. Surely you don't regard the current tyranny of those with talent as fair."

"No," Cody said. He sat up and wiped a bead of blood from below his nose. "No, I don't appreciate being backed down by folks with talent. But hard as that is, it's better than letting a bastard like you get his hands on more power."

For the first time, Gould's impassive expression slipped to reveal a flash of anger. "I'm sorry to hear you feel that way. We will reach the junction of the two rails in a matter of a few minutes. Perhaps we can discuss this more fully once we've stopped."

Cody reached back toward Jake. "Give me that pistol." Jake handed it over. Cody broke open the gun, looking into the cylinders, and snapped it closed. He smiled. "I don't guess I care to talk to you anymore, Mr. Gould," he said. He snapped off a shot. The bullet knocked the hat from Gould's head and brought sparks from the wall at his side.

The most important man in America did not hesitate further. He turned and ran away.

"This damn gun shoots high," Cody said. He stood and looked down the hallway. "Come on. We need to go get him."

Jake shook his head. "I don't think I can. They've got this car fixed up some way to hurt me."

Cody nodded. "This shouldn't take long." He walked off down the hall with the pistol held waist high.

Jake heard the slap of a pistol shot. Then another. Ten seconds later Cody came running back. Beneath the soot and grime the scout's face had gone white.

"Did you find Gould?" Jake asked.

Cody nodded. "He's holed up in the engine. I can see him around the end of the coal car."

"Did you shoot him?"

"No. That was him doing the shooting," Cody said. "He found a pistol from somewhere. Every time I try to get past the back of the coal car, he was letting fly. It doesn't matter anyway. I found something worse. I found the engineer."

"What?"

"He's laying up there at the side of the coal car with Kastle's pocket watch thing next to him. He must have come back to see what was happening, and that thing rolled up to him. Far as I can tell, he's dead."

Jake looked up the side of the train. There was a slight curve in the track ahead. Around the curve he could see the buildings of Medicine Rock. He could also see the place where the gleaming rails stopped.

"What do we do?" Cody asked.

"I don't suppose you know how to stop a train, do you?"

Cody shook his head. "My association with railroads is strictly on the building end. I've ridden on a train, but I don't know how to run one."

"Then I guess we had better jump," Jake said. "It's that or see what happens when a train runs out of tracks."

"How long do we have to decide?"

Jake looked again. "Not long."

He reached out, grabbed Cody by the vest, and started to jump. But then a cool feeling came over him, a feeling that had not come for years.

"Wait," he said. "Can you get to the pin between this car and the next?"

Cody nodded. "I expect so."

"Pull it."

The scout's eyes went wide. "But the tornado, you think it'll miss us?"

Jake looked around at the brown tempest following along behind. It was weaker now, there was no doubt of that, though it still had enough force to carry off a barn. "It'll miss us," Jake said. "Go on and get that pin."

Cody hurried back down the hall, and Jake leaned up against the side of the door. Though they were crossing the plains faster than any horse ever ran, Jake could see every detail of the sage and every crevice in the rocky ground. For three years the talent for seeing had not come near, but now it was back, bringing with it a certainty that was so firm it almost brought Jake to tears. They were going to be fine. He could see it.

Then Cody came running back. "There's a problem," he said. "I can't get us loose."

Doubt returned to Jake's gut like a swift kick to the stomach. The clarity that surrounded him disappeared in a blink.

"What do we do?" Cody asked. "We're not much more than a mile from the end."

For a moment Jake considered jumping. The seeing had come and gone so fast that he wondered if it had been real. But the talent had never been wrong before, and this seemed like the wrong time to start doubting. "Help me up," Jake said. "We'll do it together."

Cody got an arm around Jake and helped him into the hall. As soon as Jake's feet came down on the carpet, the terrible pain was back. Before they were halfway up the hall his legs had turned soft and his boots scuffed along the floor as Cody dragged him along. Finally they reached the end of the hall and moved out onto the platform at the front of the car. As soon as they were out on the bare metal of the platform, Jake felt the pain ease up a notch. He blinked tears away from his eyes and looked along the side of the coal car at the engine beyond. Just as Cody had said, the slumped form of a man in some sort of dark uniform was visible ahead. The man lay on the thin plank that ran along the side of the coal car with one arm dangling down toward the rails.

"I take it that's the engineer," Jake said.

"That's him," Cody said. "I don't see Gould."

Jake pulled free from Cody and bent down to the join between the rail cars. "I doubt he's gone far. Let's get at that stubborn pin."

Cody knelt at Jake's side. I've tried to wedge it free every way I know how, but it's not moving."

"Maybe we need to try a different sort of pull." Jake placed his hand against the curved metal rod. He didn't bother to tug on it. Bad as he felt, he was sure that Cody had given it a better go than he could manage. Instead he reached again for his talent.

The chattering was distant, and calling it felt about as pleasant as taking a bullet between the eyes. But the talent did come. It was thin, not a shadow of what Jake could draw when he was away from the train, but it was there.

He rested one finger lightly against the top of the pin. "Come out," he said. The chattering emerged from his lips as a yowling whistle, barely audible over the noise of the train and the more distant roar of the storm. The pin jerked under Jake's finger, twisting up and around. It wasn't enough to free the two parts of the train, but it was a start.

"Hurry," Cody said. "We're getting damn close."

Jake nodded. "Come on," he said to the pin. "Come on out of there." The pin jumped, stopped, then jerked again. With a squeal of metal, it fell free from the catch and clattered to the metal platform.

Jake let go of his flagging talent and picked up the bent piece of metal. "Got it."

A bullet rang off the metal next to Jake's hand. He dropped the pin and rolled to the side, forgetting for the moment just how small the platform was. For a moment he was hanging over the side, watching the wooden ties sweep past in a blur. Then Cody's fingers grabbed at Jake's tattered shirt and hauled him back onto the platform.

Another bullet slapped against the front of the train car, and Jake felt hot fragments of the shattered slug rain down on the back of his neck. He raised his head and saw Jay Gould standing at the corner of the coal car. The railroad owner came closer, moving carefully along the narrow plank, a dark pistol in his hand.

"Get back, gentleman," Gould said.

"Back from where?" Cody asked.

"Back into that car." Gould waved the pistol. "Do it quick. I'm coming over." He edged closer along the plank.

Cody got to his feet. Jake felt too tired even to try. The effort of using his talent against the pull of the rails had left him exhausted. He watched Gould edge closer.

"I can see what you two are up to," Gould said, "but this is not finished. I still have a crew of men ahead. We can still finish this rail line. When we reach the junction, everything will change."

There was a thump, a groan, and a shiver that ran through the train car. The connection between the engine and the single passenger car let go.

"No!" Gould shouted. He dropped his pistol and scrambled toward the passenger car, stepping on the dead engineer in his hurry. By the time he reached the back of the coal car, the gap between the two halves of the train had grown to four feet. Gould bent his legs as if he were going to jump, but he hesitated for a moment. In that time, the gap grew to six feet. Then to ten.

"No!" Gould cried again. He stared back at Jake and Cody for a second longer, then spun around and scrambled back toward the engine.

"Maybe he knows how to stop it," Jake said. "He does own the railroad."

Cody shook his head. "Man like Gould, he had other folks do that for him."

The distance expanded to the length of a train car. Gould made it around the edge of the coal car and disappeared into the cab of the train. The engine plunged on, pulling gradually away from the slowing passenger car.

When it was a hundred yards distant, there was a scream from the train whistle and steam poured into the air. The sound was still going on when the engine reached the end of the rails.

For a few seconds it looked like the engine would travel on, rolling across the hard-baked ground. Then the massive machine slewed around, tipped, and rolled over on its side. The boiler burst open in a great explosion of steam. Bolts flew from the seams with such force that they rang against the pas-

senger car like bullets. A whirlwind of fire roared from the
heart of the shattered engine.

"Hang on!" Cody shouted.

There was little choice. Though the passenger car had lost
some of its speed, it had by no means lost it all. Jake and Cody
traveled off the end of the track at a pace that would have
made any horse proud. There was a tremendous thump as the
passenger car slipped from the rails. Then a long series of
bone-jarring jolts as the car plowed through the ruined
remains of the engine.

Jake closed his eyes against a cloud of searing steam and
smoky flame. The car plunged into the heart of the inferno.
The popping of hot metal was all around. The heat rose up till
Jake thought he was going to be boiled.

A moment later they were through into cool air. There was
a final thud, a crunching grind, and the passenger car came to
a stop.

Jake opened his eyes in time to see the tornado dancing
itself to death in the low hills north of Medicine Rock. He
turned his head and saw that the buildings of town were no
more than a stone's throw away.

A small crowd had gathered and more were running from
the town. They stared at the wrecked train with their mouths
open and their eyes wide.

Jake struggled to his feet and stepped down from the platform. "Looks like the end of the line," he said.

Cody came down to stand beside him. "Best part of any
railroad," he said. "Come on. How about we go see if there's
any whiskey left in the saloon?"

Among the burly railway workers running toward the
wreck, Jake spotted a figure that was smaller and far more
familiar. "You go on," he said. "I'll be there directly."

Josie Bird pushed her way between the gathered men, flung
her heavy shotgun to the ground and hurried toward the train
to wrap her arms around her husband.

"They told us you were dead," she said, her voice tight with
pent-up sobs.

"Well," Jake said, "sometimes I thought I was myself." He

put his tired arms around his wife's waist and pulled her against him. "I'm home," Jake whispered into her hair.

For long minutes they stood there. Josie sobbed against his chest, kissed him, then went back to sobbing. Finally, she pushed him away and looked at him with a strange expression. "I am glad you are home," she said. "But . . ."

"But what?" Jake asked.

"But even for a dead man, you are filthy."

Jake gave a tired laugh. "You show me to the bathtub," he said. "I might never get out."

He took his wife's hand and together they walked into Medicine Rock.

☆ **30** ☆

At medical school Johnson Stone had been warned about the perils of setting up practice in a small town. Experienced doctors had warned him of patients without the money to pay and long periods of inactivity. Neither of these things had so far been a problem. The real problem in Medicine Rock was that far too many people needed his attention at the same time.

Stone leaned away from Berdita Hare and pushed his glasses up his nose. "Mrs. Hare, I want you to take a spoonful of this every evening. You understand?"

The woman nodded, but did not speak. Berdita Hare wasn't physically hurt in any way the doctor could find. Stone was concerned about the woman for other reasons. There had been a funeral for her husband two days before, and Berdita had not uttered either a word or shed a tear. Neither had she been to the church, or admitted any of her friends to the house.

Stone feared that Mrs. Hare was sinking into some form of shock. If she did not come around within the next few days, he would have to take stronger measures, but for now he had hopes that a little time and a medicine bottle full of brandy might do the trick.

The doctor packed his instruments into his bag. Across the room, Sienna Truth gathered up the rest of the supplies. Stone said his farewells, reminded Mrs. Hare to get some rest, and left the sad house. Sienna was right behind.

Sienna's presence had been handy at first. With the number of broken limbs to be set and wounds to be bandaged, Stone had found himself needing someone to carry his extra plaster and cloth. Sienna had volunteered for the job. Soon enough,

Stone took her quiet presence for granted. It was pleasant to have her around, even if she rarely spoke, and she was handy for fetching things and toting heavier loads—both chores that Stone found difficult. Already there were some in town that were airing their tonsils about the pairing of the young Indian girl and the older Indian doctor. Stone didn't bother to speak to such rumors.

As they walked down the street, they passed Gravy Hodges and Muley Owens laying long boards to the side of a harness shop. Neither of the men had been seriously hurt by their exposure to bursts of talent, and it was a good thing they weren't. Both had been pressed to use their carpentry skills without pause, boarding windows and repairing roofs damaged by storm and stray bullets.

The next stop for Stone was a bed at the Restful Vista Hotel, where Reverend Hardesty lay coughing out his days. Of those who had been shot during Tom Sharp's run through town, only Hardesty survived. Sharp's bullet had taken the preacher in the chest, punching a hole in one lung and scratching the sack around his heart. The reverend had rallied from his wound several times, sitting up in bed and even asking to be carried to his church so he could address the congregation. But it was Dr. Stone's sad opinion that Hardesty would not live out the week.

There was little he could do for Hardesty but prescribe some laudanum for the pain. Stone was grateful the man made no protest against the alcohol or opium in the painkiller.

Their last stop for the day took them back to Sienna's home at the Kettle Black. Of the four men who had ridden the sail wagon back to Medicine Rock, only one had taken serious injury. The Rainmaker had been flat-out unlucky. After driving the sail wagon around the worst of the storm, he'd been caught in the head by debris when the train and tornado met. The blow did not appear to be serious. Left to his own skills, Stone would have said the man should be fine. But this was a case where he knew better. The Rainmaker would never recover from his wound.

Stone left Sienna tending to the pale man and stepped out into the hallway. There he found Boots waiting for him.

"Well, this is a surprise," the doctor said. "I wasn't expecting you for another month."

Boots nodded and gave him a gentle smile. She was in her thirties, vigorous and beautiful, just the way Stone had seen her when he was first able to see anything at all. "That's when I'll arrive for my long stay," she said. "This is only a small turn. A minute or two."

Stone returned her smile. "I'm glad to see you would spend some of it with me."

"Is Sienna here?" Boots looked up and down the hall. "I was hoping to see her, too."

"She's tending the Rainmaker," Stone said. "I can barely stand to be in the room with him." He clenched his teeth. "It's too frustrating."

"I'm sorry," Boots said. "If I was going anywhere I thought he could get better help, I would take him with me. But when this bend is over, I'm moving backward, not forward. After that, I'll only be back here again."

Stone sighed. "I know you would help if you could. You always do."

"I'm no saint," Boots said. "I've as little control over my talent as the Rainmaker, and it brings me misery as often as it brings me joy."

"Well, it was certainly helpful to me," Stone said. He looked toward the door to the Rainmaker's room. "Do you think Sienna knows me?"

"Of course she does," Boots said.

"But she hasn't said anything."

"You should know by now that she doesn't like to get ahead of herself." Boots reached out and put a hand lightly on the doctor's shoulder. "Just wait. I'll be here soon. The others will be around. We'll have plenty of time to talk."

With that, she was gone.

Stone stood in the hallway long after she had vanished. He could still feel the memory of her touch at his shoulder. He wished that Boots would return, or that Sienna would break her silence.

Knowing the future and not being able to talk about it was its own kind of pain.

Downstairs someone laughed. The doctor straightened himself as best he could and went down to have a drink of what passed for whiskey in Medicine Rock.

OPERATION
SHATTERHAND
by Jake Page

**An alternate-history novel of
Nazi invasion in the
American Southwest.**

OPERATION
SHATTERHAND
by Jake Page

**Published by Del Rey® Books.
Available in your local bookstore.**

DEL REY ONLINE!

The Del Rey Internet Newsletter...

A monthly electronic publication, posted on the Internet, GEnie, CompuServe, BIX, various BBSs, and the Panix gopher (gopher.panix.com). It features hype-free descriptions of books that are new in the stores, a list of our upcoming books, special announcements, a signing/reading/convention-attendance schedule for Del Rey authors, "In Depth" essays in which professionals in the field (authors, artists, designers, sales people, etc.) talk about their jobs in science fiction, a question-and-answer section, behind-the-scenes looks at sf publishing, and more!

Online editorial presence: Many of the Del Rey editors are online, on the Internet, GEnie, CompuServe, America Online, and Delphi. There is a Del Rey topic on GEnie and a Del Rey folder on America Online.

Our official e-mail address for Del Rey Books is delrey@randomhouse.com

Internet information source!

A lot of Del Rey material is available to the Internet on a gopher server: all back issues and the current issue of the Del Rey Internet Newsletter, a description of the DRIN and summaries of all the issues' contents, sample chapters of upcoming or current books (readable or downloadable for free), submission requirements, mail-order information, and much more. We will be adding more items of all sorts (mostly new DRINs and sample chapters) regularly. The address of the gopher is gopher.panix.com

Why? We at Del Rey realize that the networks are the medium of the future. That's where you'll find us promoting our books, socializing with others in the sf field, and—most importantly—making contact and sharing information with sf readers.

For more information, e-mail delrey@randomhouse.com